Death on the Ladies Mile

Death on the Ladies Mile

A "Gaslight and Shadows" Mystery

Diana Haviland

Five Star • Waterville, Maine

This novel is a work of fiction. Names, characters, places and incidents are either the product of the author's imagination, or, if real, used fictitiously.

First Edition
First Printing: March 2006

Published in 2006 in conjunction with Tekno Books and Ed Gorman.

Set in 11 pt. Plantin by Minnie B. Raven.

Printed in the United States on permanent paper.

Library of Congress Cataloging-in-Publication Data

Haviland, Diana.
    Death on the Ladies Mile : a gaslight and shadows mystery / by Diana Haviland.
      p. cm.
    ISBN 1-59414-351-X (hc : alk. paper)
    1. Women journalists—Fiction. 2. Manhattan (New York, N.Y.)—Fiction. I. Title.
    PS3558.A784D43 2006
    813'.54—dc22   2005029766

Death on the Ladies Mile

PROLOGUE

September 1882

The small, dark-haired girl moved quickly through the streets of the Ladies Mile, where silver-grey tendrils of autumn fog obscured the display windows and dimmed the glare of the new electric street lamps. Only a few hours ago, Broadway had been ablaze with dazzling lights. Well-dressed ladies and their escorts rode in hansom cabs or carriages; strolled into Wallack's Theater and dined at the Fifth Avenue Hotel or Delmonico's.

Tina rarely ventured into this part of the city, but in the pre-dawn hours, she knew she would not draw attention, for Broadway was deserted. Even the last of the street-walkers, who had trailed their finery along the damp pavement earlier that evening, had disappeared.

Although the walk from Mulberry Street had tired her, she forced herself to go on. She searched the gutter and peered into the shadows of the alleys, seeking discarded clothes. At twelve, she was already experienced in her trade.

She slowed down when she reached Eighteenth Street. Peering through the plate glass windows of Arnold Constable's massive white marble department store, she caught a glimpse of the splendidly-dressed mannequins inside. She stared in awe at the graceful sweep of a velvet gown, the bodice trimmed with jet beading; at a small, plumed hat set at a fashionable angle atop a carefully arranged wig, the glitter of a jeweled fan, held in a wooden hand.

How real those figures looked, with their elaborate coiffures, their painted eyes. Too real.

Tina shivered slightly, then turned away. She hadn't come this far to waste her time gawking at the store windows. The sky already was growing lighter and she had work to do. In a couple of hours, when the sun rose over the East River, the fog would disappear. The Ladies Mile, from Eighth Street to Twenty-third, soon would be bustling with activity. First the shopgirls and seamstresses would appear, hurrying to work in their dark, serviceable skirts and starched, high-necked blouses. Later a procession of shiny broughams, victorias, and barouches would arrive, carrying wealthy young ladies and their tightly-corseted mothers. Liveried coachmen would halt their high-stepping teams before large department stores and elegant little specialty shops.

Tina tried to imagine what it would feel like: riding in a carriage, spending money on velvet dresses, on opera cloaks, parasols, and kid gloves. To linger over frosted cakes and sherbets in one of the fashionable ice cream saloons. Her mouth watered and she felt the pangs of hunger gnawing at her lean belly.

She would have to work fast now. She drew her faded shawl tighter around her bony shoulders and started moving again, dragging her half-empty burlap sack along the pavement. Papa had provided the shawl and the rest of her garments, down to her cracked shoes with their flapping soles, from the stock of cast-offs that crowded their foul-smelling den in Ragpicker's Row. In the two small rooms, worn-out shoes, threadbare dresses, shawls, and battered hats lay in heaps on the dirty floor. Rags hung from the walls, from the ropes stretched across the cracked ceiling. More rags flapped on the rusty fire escape outside.

She had come a long way from Ragpicker's Row to the

Ladies Mile because she knew she had a chance of finding a choice bit of loot here: a jagged piece of torn silk or brocade from one of the dressmakers' shops, or a lace trimmed handkerchief dropped by one of those rich, uptown ladies, descending from her carriage.

If Tina could bring home even one such piece of finery, Papa would grunt with satisfaction. He would hand her a chunk of bread, a cup of sour wine, maybe even a spicy sausage. After she had eaten, she would crawl into the verminous bed she shared with her two younger sisters and her baby brother. But if tonight's pickings didn't satisfy Papa, he would curse her. His belt would lash her skinny bare legs, searing her skin like a ribbon of fire.

Although the fog made her search more difficult, she could not give up. She stopped at the mouth of an alley that ran beside a tall, narrow brick house with shuttered windows. A flutter of white had caught her eye. It was too big for a handkerchief, or even a shawl. A gust of wind lifted the fabric. Fine and delicate it was, like an enormous cobweb. Moving closer, she crouched down to get a better look. She stared at the lace veil, then reached out to touch it.

She drew in her breath sharply. The veil was fastened to a mass of yellow hair. She stared at the girl in the white gown, who lay on her back on the wet cobblestones. A whore who had collapsed in a drunken stupor? Or who had been beaten senseless by one of her customers?

The wind tossed the veil away from the girl's face. The skin was tinged with purple, the tongue thrust out. The wide-open eyes bulged in their sockets. A wreath of white flowers made of satin and seed pearls had been twisted around the girl's neck. The wire that held the flowers cut deep into her flesh.

Tina's scream echoed down the alley.

"What's goin' on?" She lifted her head and stared down the long, narrow alley. A policeman in a heavy woolen coat blocked the opposite end. He gripped his nightstick in one hand, his bull's-eye lantern in the other. "You there! What're you up to?"

Already on her feet, she fled back to Broadway. From somewhere far behind her, she heard the rap of the nightstick on the pavement, the shriek of a police whistle. Grateful for the concealing fog, she ran past the marble buildings, the darkened show windows. Her torn soles skidding on the damp pavement, she headed to Mulberry Street and the haven of Ragpicker's Row.

CHAPTER ONE

Amanda Whitney leaned forward on the leather seat of the hired hansom and peered through the small window. She felt a flicker of amusement as she caught sight of the turrets, spires, and cupolas of the Spencer mansion at the corner of Fifty-seventh Street. The imposing structure of Wisconsin granite and Ohio sandstone reflected a curious mixture of architectural styles. One newspaper had described it as early English, another as castellated Gothic, while a visiting French nobleman had called it "sumptuous and abominable."

Privately Amanda agreed with him, although she would not have expressed her opinion in her articles for the *Ladies Gazette*. Not if she wanted to keep her new position as society editor.

A few weeks ago, when Mrs. Lavinia Fairlie had summoned Amanda to her office on the top floor of the building on Pearl Street, she had wondered if she was about to be reprimanded for some mistake. Instead, Mrs. Fairlie's words sent her spirits soaring.

"As you may have heard, Carrie Dorset is leaving the *Gazette* to get married. You will take over Miss Dorset's position. You're young to handle such responsibilities; but you're bright and ambitious."

The handsome, red-haired woman only paused long enough to accept Amanda's thanks. "If you avoid outside distractions and concentrate all your energy on your work, I trust I'll have no cause to regret my decision."

Mrs. Fairlie needn't have been concerned, for Amanda was free to devote herself to her work completely. Since Mama had left for Europe early that summer as a paid companion to Mrs. Elvira Dennison, a wealthy widow, she had spent her evenings fixing up her newly-rented flat with Leander, her big black and white tomcat, her only male companion, looking on.

Now, after two months, she had gained a measure of self-assurance. Mrs. Fairlie had read her weekly articles, made a few swift changes, and nodded her approval. She had explained this new assignment with her usual precision. "You will cover the wedding of Miss Jessamyn Spencer and Mr. Howard Thornton. Our readers will want all the details—the bride's gown, her trousseau, the bridesmaids' costumes, the wedding gifts, and the reception." She had smiled wryly. "The Spencers are having a Grace Church wedding. Of course, old Isaac Brown is only giving his permission because Miss Spencer is marrying into the Thornton family."

Isaac Brown, the sexton of Grace Church, also was the arbiter of New York society. The Spencers, who longed to take their place in the city's highest social circle, needed his approval to pass through its gilded portals.

So far, Mrs. Everard Spencer had been most cooperative, for she knew the *Gazette* was read by ladies from the best New York families. On her visits to the mansion, Amanda had accompanied Mrs. Spencer and Jessamyn through the white and gold splendor of the huge ballroom, its ceiling painted with cherubs floating on rosy clouds.

"This room is most suitable for the reception, don't you agree?" Mrs. Spencer had asked.

It would be suitable for the first act of "Aida," with the triumphal march, elephants and all. But Amanda had kept such observations to herself, and had tried to look properly impressed.

Later, her hostess had pointed out the musicians' gallery with its ornately carved railing. "Mr. Spencer bought it from the owner of a seventeenth century English country house." Amanda smiled and kept taking notes, using her newly-acquired Pitman shorthand.

She thought it odd that the bride-to-be had shown no interest in these elaborate preparations, but had stood quietly, her light blue eyes downcast, her thin fingers plucking at a lace handkerchief, as her mother spoke about the arrangements for the wedding. Then she reminded herself that was no concern of hers.

She had satisfied her readers' avid interest with every article. She had described the menu for the wedding buffet, from the cassolettes de foie-gras to the spun-sugar violets on the cake. Her pencil had raced across the page as Ottilie Spencer had described the floral decorations: masses of fragrant white lilies to be banked against the walls; gilded baskets holding four varieties of roses.

She had followed Mrs. Spencer upstairs to Jessamyn's bedroom to look at the bridal gown, a magnificent creation of white brocade and satin-de-Lyon with panniers of crystal and pearl fringe. The Valenciennes lace veil was framed by a wreath of white satin flowers and seed pearls, with long sprays falling over the back.

As usual, Jessamyn had trailed along behind them in silence, without the slightest trace of interest in her expression.

But during last week's visit, Amanda had discovered the terror that lay beneath Jessamyn's facade of indifference. After Mrs. Spencer had shown her Jessamyn's elaborate trousseau, and gone back upstairs, she realized with dismay that she had lost one of her kid gloves. They were her only good pair, and her tight budget would not allow for the purchase of new ones.

A buck-toothed young footman had gone to search for the missing glove in the drawing room. Left alone in the pillared entrance hall, she set about her own search. It was no easy task, what with the clutter of marble statues, suits of armor, and small, inlaid tables. When at last she caught sight of the missing glove near the base of a tall jardinière; she hurried to retrieve it, then stopped, when she heard raised voices through the open library doors.

"Please, Papa, you've got to speak to Howard. It's not too late."

"The hell it's not!" Everard Spencer's deep voice boomed. "Have you lost your wits, girl?"

"Papa! You know I can't marry anyone, ever!"

"That's enough, dammit! I'll have no more of your ridiculous carryings-on! You'll go through with the wedding if I have to drag you to the church."

Moving closer, Amanda caught a glimpse of Mr. Spencer and his daughter. The distraught girl was clutching at her father's sleeve. "What if Howard discovers the truth on our wedding night? What if he finds out I'm not a . . ."

He jerked his arm away. "Once you're married, it won't matter. Thornton's marrying you for the settlement. The fool's up to his neck in debt. Or are you silly enough to imagine he's in love with you?"

Jessamyn flinched. "Don't you care anything about my feelings?"

"Your feelings be damned!" he shouted. "It's lucky for you that I can afford to buy you a husband." He looked her up and down, then spoke with contempt. "You're no better than a common whore."

14

"You can't force me to marry him!" Her voice took on an edge of hysteria. "I'll tell him the truth. I'll go to him today and tell him everything."

"The hell you will!" Spencer drew back his powerful arm and slapped her across the face with such force that she almost lost her balance. She clutched the back of a chair to steady herself.

Amanda, shocked and outraged by his brutality, took a few quick steps toward the library, then stopped abruptly. If she were to confront him now and upbraid him for his treatment of his daughter, she could not hope to enter his home again.

I've got to finish this assignment and hand it in on time. Otherwise, I could lose my promotion.

Without waiting for the young footman to return, she turned and hurried across the entrance hall and out the front door.

In the week that followed, she had not forgotten the appalling quarrel between Mr. Spencer and his daughter, although she had not spoken to any of her co-workers about it. She had not even been able to bring herself to confide in Maude Hamilton, the fashion editor, who had always been generous with her advice and encouragement.

"Here we are, Miss." The hansom stopped in front of the imposing mansion. Although not quite as large as the Cornelius Vanderbilt chateau, it was no less impressive.

She got out, then lingered on the sidewalk, reluctant to enter. She still felt guilty because she had not even tried to defend Jessamyn against her father. How could any man have treated his daughter that way?

Keep your mind on your own business.

Mrs. Spencer had promised to show her the wedding presents today. She had never missed a deadline yet, and she wasn't about to do so now.

In three weeks, she consoled herself, the wedding would be over, and the newlyweds would have departed for their honeymoon tour of Europe. And she would have moved on to her next assignment. She smoothed the skirt of her russet serge dress, adjusted the angle of her matching hat, then walked quickly through the tall wrought-iron gates and up the broad steps.

The buck-toothed young footman who had gone looking for her missing glove only last week now opened the door, but made no move to let her inside. "Mrs. Spencer is not at home," he said. Of course, this did not mean that the lady of the house was not on the premises, only that she did not choose to receive a particular visitor.

But Amanda would not be dismissed so easily. She had a job to do. "Please give Mrs. Spencer my card."

He shifted from one foot to the other. A pretty, young parlor maid in her starched, lace-trimmed apron and cap paused and watched them with scarcely-concealed curiosity. The footman took the white cardboard square, but still he did not step aside. He exchanged glances with the parlor maid, as if hoping she might get him out of his predicament. He looked distinctly relieved when the butler approached.

"I've told Miss Whitney that Mrs. Spencer's not at home, sir," the young man said hastily. The butler, a tall, horse-faced man with thinning grey hair, took charge at once. He dismissed both the footman and the maid with a movement of his hand.

Amanda drew a deep breath, squared her shoulders and advanced on the butler, her eyes fixed on his. He would have to let her pass, or deliberately bar her way. Her gaze did not waver, and, at the last minute, he stepped aside.

She walked into the entrance hall and, glancing in the direction of the library, she saw that the tall oak doors were shut.

"If Mrs. Spencer's occupied, I'll wait," she began.

"Mrs. Spencer is not at home."

"She said she would show me the wedding gifts today."

"Mrs. Spencer is not receiving visitors."

She caught the slight hesitation before the word "visitors." Obviously, he did not think a reporter, even one who worked for the *Ladies Gazette*, was the social equal of the mistress of the house. But Amanda was not concerned with such trivial distinctions.

"I need to see the gifts to complete my article in time for next week's edition," she told him, her tone pleasant, yet business-like. "Perhaps Miss Spencer would show them to me."

"Miss Spencer cannot be disturbed." Although his face remained expressionless, she caught the uneasiness in his voice.

"Harland!" Ottilie Spencer stood at the top of the stairs, her eyes narrowed, her voice shrill. Her hair once might have been blond, like Jessamyn's, but it had faded to a light brown. Her elaborate coiffure was fastened by gold combs. "Why have you disregarded my instructions?" she demanded. She descended swiftly, then paused, resting her hand on the newel post.

Before Harland could reply, Amanda spoke quickly. "Your butler told me you weren't receiving, but I thought perhaps you'd forgotten our appointment."

With an effort, she concealed her urgency. The *Gazette* went to press tomorrow, and she had to fill two columns with detailed descriptions of the wedding presents.

Ottilie Spencer's lips clamped shut.

"With so many preparations for the wedding, I can well

17

understand that your time is fully occupied," Amanda hurried on. "But my readers are so eager to read about the gifts. This is the most important wedding of the season, after all."

Even such shameless flattery met with no response. Mrs. Spencer gripped the newel post, as if for support. Her tightly-corseted body was rigid under her grey taffeta gown.

Amanda made another attempt. "If Miss Spencer can spare me an hour, I'll be able to get all the information I need."

Ottilie Spencer caught her breath and her heavy jaw twitched slightly. "My daughter is unable to see you."

"I hope Miss Spencer hasn't been taken ill."

"She's perfectly well." There was no mistaking the tension in the older woman's voice.

With a persistence Mama would have deplored, she tried again. "Perhaps tomorrow, then." It would be a tight squeeze, but if she worked quickly, she would make her deadline somehow.

Before Ottilie Spencer could reply, the massive library doors parted and Mr. Spencer stood on the threshold, glowering at his wife. His face was brick red, with deep lines bracketing the corners of his mouth. "What the devil is that reporter woman doing here?"

"She's come to see the wedding gifts."

"Get rid of her, and get yourself in here. Be quick about it." He might have been giving orders to a housemaid. His thin veneer of good breeding was starting to crack.

Amanda was not entirely surprised. Maude Hamilton had told her that Everard Spencer had started out as a lumberjack in Wisconsin, and had moved up quickly: lumberjack, timberland contractor, mill foreman. He'd been tough, shrewd, and none too scrupulous in his business dealings. "He bought one mill, then a dozen, and later, a railroad line to carry the lumber east," Maude had said.

After he'd amassed his fortune, he had brought his family to New York, and built himself this mansion. Now ready to take his place among the city's elite, he had moved toward his goal with his usual determination. Although his money could not buy him a box at the Academy of Music, Jessamyn had entered those hallowed precincts on the arm of her fiancé and had taken her place in the Thornton family box. Meanwhile, Spencer had made an enormous donation toward the construction of the Metropolitan Opera House that was rising farther uptown to accommodate the newly rich. In three weeks he would escort his daughter down the aisle at Grace Church, while New York's "Old Knickerbocker" society looked on.

But Amanda doubted he would ever fit in to that society. No man with the slightest pretense of good breeding would have treated his daughter as he had treated Jessamyn; nor would he have spoken to his wife as he had a moment ago.

Ottilie threw her husband a frightened glance. "You must leave at once," she told Amanda.

She scurried into the library. Amanda stared after her, and caught sight of another man, tall and wide-shouldered, standing beside the fireplace in the high-ceilinged, book-lined room. A moment later Everard slammed the library doors shut.

"This way, Miss Whitney," said the butler.

What on earth was going on here? Was Jessamyn pretending to be ill so that the wedding would have to be put off? Or had Everard Spencer locked her in her room to force her to his will?

"Miss Whitney, if you please." He held the door open.

With her chin high, her back straight, she crossed the entrance hall and left the house; then paused on the sidewalk, trying to decide what to do next. How could she hand in this week's assignment unless she could see the wedding gifts? And if she failed to meet her deadline, Mrs. Fairlie would not be moved by her excuses.

She had been lucky to find a position that gave her the independence she valued so much. She relished the privacy of her own flat in one of the fine old houses on West Nineteenth Street; the freedom to come and go as she pleased. Of course, she'd never been able to make her mother understand why she had refused to take a more conventional path, by seeking work as a governess or companion. Mama had not even been impressed by the news of her recent promotion.

Her gloved hand gripped her velvet purse. It held her mother's most recent letter, which had arrived today as she was leaving her apartment. She had read it on the drive uptown. In spite of her duties as paid companion to Mrs. Dennison, Mama found time to write regularly, and this letter was no different from any of her others.

"Since you must earn your own living, you should have followed my example. You have always been headstrong, a most unfortunate trait in a young lady. But it is not too late for you to reconsider. Mrs. Dennison has a dear friend who is seeking a companion to accompany her on a tour of the Lake District."

She knew only too well what such a job would mean. Mrs. Dennison's "dear friend" might not treat her as a servant; but neither would the lady consider her an equal. Her imagination conjured up a thoroughly distasteful picture of the day-to-day life of a paid companion. Yes, she would get an opportunity to travel; to stay at the best hotels and the finest country houses; but only at the cost of her independence.

"I've forgotten my shawl, Amanda. Run and see if I left it in my room."

"No, Amanda, it will not be convenient to give you the day off. I'm expecting guests."

"Really, my dear, you mustn't be over-familiar with Mrs. So-and-so's son. Please remember your position."

It would be useless to write again, and try to explain her decision to her mother; she'd failed often enough in the past. Even now, in 1882, Mama considered it highly improper for a young lady to live alone. Nevertheless, Amanda knew several others who had ignored such outmoded conventions. She had been more fortunate than most, for she'd found a comfortable unfurnished flat that rented for eighteen dollars a month. She'd salvaged a few good pieces from the family home on Stuyvesant Square: her father's handsome black walnut desk, a leather-covered sofa, a pair of rattan chairs and a small table from their summer cottage in the Adirondacks.

But on her only visit to the flat, Mama had not been favorably impressed, and she had expressed her disapproval in every letter. "Your present living arrangements are most unsuitable . . . a rented flat . . . no chaperone. When I think of my daughter, racing around the city in public conveyances . . ."

Amanda sighed ruefully. Maybe Mama wouldn't have cause for complaint much longer. Unless she carried out her assignment, she might lose her position on the *Gazette*. But she was not about to give up—not yet. Right now, she'd find a hansom and ride downtown to Pearl Street, where she'd talk over her problem with Maude Hamilton. Maude, who had worked on the *Gazette* for eight years, must have dealt successfully with many difficult situations.

She looked up and down Fifth Avenue, seeking an empty cab, but in this exclusive neighborhood the residents owned their own carriages. Wealthy ladies in broughams and barouches, phaetons and landaus, drawn by high-stepping thoroughbreds, went driving along the tree-shaded paths in Central Park, or downtown to shop on the Ladies Mile.

Only three years ago, just before she had left for her fall semester at Vassar, she had gone driving with Mama in their family barouche. They had spent a pleasant afternoon at A. T. Stewart's department store shopping for a new wardrobe, then had lingered over hot chocolate and cookies at one of the fashionable new ice cream saloons. Her throat tightened as she remembered how her father had spared no expense to provide her and Mama with every luxury. He had not only been generous, but warm and affectionate, too. She still had not recovered from the shock of his untimely death.

"Miss Whitney."

She turned quickly to see the front door of the Spencer mansion swing open. Her spirits shot up. Maybe Everard Spencer had changed his mind, and decided to allow her to see the wedding gifts after all. If so, she'd be able to hand in her assignment on time.

But it wasn't the butler who stood in the doorway, calling her name. It was the tall, wide-shouldered man she'd glimpsed in the library with Mr. Spencer. He strode over, and stood looking down at her.

"Are you trying to think of an excuse to get back inside the house?" She caught a glint of amusement in his eyes.

She was about to tell him it was none of his business, but she stopped herself. Maybe he would know why the Spencers had turned her away.

"I'm trying to find a hansom, but I haven't had any luck so far." She looked up at him from under the tilted brim of her hat, aware that its russet velvet lining emphasized her amber eyes.

"Wait here." He crossed Fifth Avenue and stood at the entrance to the park. A gust of wind bent the tops of the trees, sending a shower of leaves swirling to the ground. It tugged at her skirt and tossed the plumes atop her hat. She reached up and thrust the jet-tipped hatpin deeper into her thick, chestnut hair.

A hansom cab, just coming out of the park, drew to a stop. Too impatient to wait, she hurried across the avenue, then smiled gratefully as the man helped her inside. "Where are you going?" he asked.

"Back to my office at Twenty-two Pearl Street." She hesitated only a moment, then said, "If you're going in that direction, maybe you'd care to accompany me."

His straight black brows shot up. A respectable lady did not invite a gentleman to share her cab. But she would have to ignore the proprieties, to find out why the Spencers had behaved so peculiarly today.

"Most thoughtful of you, Miss Whitney." He smiled as he seated himself beside her. The driver cracked his whip and the horse trotted down the avenue. "We've not been properly introduced. I'm Ross Buchanan."

"And I am—"

" 'That reporter woman,' " he interrupted, with a grin.

She stiffened. "My name's Amanda Whitney, and I'm the society editor for the *Ladies Gazette*."

"You like your work?"

23

"I find it most rewarding."

"Even when you're turned away as you were just now, without an explanation or apology?"

She forced herself to ignore his sarcasm. "The Spencers have been cooperative on my previous visits. Perhaps there's been a problem with the wedding preparations." She looked up at him inquiringly, but he did not respond. "Mrs. Spencer has a great many details to attend to," she went on.

"Ottilie Spencer has a regiment of servants to carry out her orders."

"Even the best-trained staff makes mistakes," she said. "There may be some confusion about the floral arrangements or the reception menu. No doubt Mrs. Spencer's under considerable stress."

"And you're not?"

"Not at all." She tried to sound self-assured. "I'll get my article in on time, one way or another."

"No doubt you're a most resourceful young lady, but you can't describe gifts you haven't seen. Maybe I can help. Two dozen silver fish forks. A crystal and gold epergne. A Waterford decanter with matching goblets."

"You've already seen the gifts?"

He shook his head. "I was only offering a few likely suggestions. You'll have to fill in the rest for yourself."

She tensed at the implication. "The *Gazette* doesn't give out false information. Mrs. Fairlie insists on accurate reporting."

"Then I suppose you'll have to tell her you were ordered out of the house before you could see the gifts. No doubt she'll be most sympathetic."

He was deliberately baiting her. Perhaps he knew of Lavinia Fairlie's reputation; maybe he'd heard she was a hard-driving perfectionist who demanded total efficiency

24

from her staff. If Amanda could not carry out her assignments, she would be replaced.

But she wasn't about to give up so easily. She'd find a way to get back inside the Spencer mansion and see those wedding gifts; and Ross Buchanan would help her. Since she hadn't gotten any useful information from him so far, she'd use a more direct approach. "Are you related to the Spencers?"

"No, I'm not."

"A close family friend, perhaps?"

"Perhaps."

Drat the man! Couldn't he give her a straight answer? She wanted to order him out of the cab, but she restrained herself. "I wish I might have spoken with Jessamyn today," she said. "No doubt she'd have let me look at her gifts."

"When did you last see Miss Spencer?"

"On Thursday afternoon, when she showed me her trousseau."

But it had been Ottilie who had led the way upstairs to her daughter's suite, and had shown Amanda the lavish traveling costumes of silk and taffeta; the sable-lined cloak, the bonnets decorated with ostrich plumes and velvet roses. There were linen chemises trimmed with Brussels lace; embroidered corset covers and nightgowns. All the while, Jessamyn had stood by the window, her thin fingers plucking at her handkerchief, her pale blue eyes curiously vacant.

"You haven't seen Jessamyn Spencer since then?" His question caught her off-guard.

"No, I haven't, Mr. Buchanan."

But she had thought about Jessamyn often, for she hadn't been able to forget the quarrel between the frail young woman and her domineering father. Everard's brutal words had returned to trouble her, and she'd flinched inwardly every time she'd remembered how he'd slapped his daughter's face. If only she'd made her presence known at once, he might have restrained himself. Or even if he hadn't, she could have offered consolation to Jessamyn. Instead, she'd observed the scene in silence and then had slipped out of the house.

"Have you had any word from Miss Spencer since you last saw her? A note, perhaps?"

Something in his voice turned her cold inside. "What's happened to her? Has she run away?"

"Why would she go running off right before her wedding?" Although he spoke casually, his dark eyes were alert.

Because Jessamyn didn't want to marry Howard Thornton. She hesitated, not sure if she should confide in a man she scarcely knew. "Maybe she realized she didn't love Mr. Thornton enough to marry him."

"Did she tell you so?"

"She would hardly have discussed such an intimate matter with me."

"I suppose she'd have been more likely to share her feelings with one of her bridesmaids. No doubt they've been visiting her often."

"It was Mrs. Spencer who chose the bridesmaids," she said. "I don't believe Jessamyn has any close female friends."

He leaned toward her, his eyes alert. "Then maybe she did confide in you. By the way, just how long have you known her?"

This wasn't going the way she'd planned. She had offered him a ride to get information from him; instead he was cross-examining her.

"I met her only six weeks ago."

26

"Did you ever see her outside her home?"

She eyed him with growing uneasiness.

"Did you ever go out with her?" he persisted. There was no mistaking the urgency in his tone.

"Only once, when we drove down to the Ladies Mile together. Jessamyn wanted to choose the gifts for her bridesmaids and she asked me along."

"She could have left that to her mother."

"I think she just needed to get out of the house for a few hours."

"Where, exactly, did you go?"

"Really, Mr. Buchanan, I don't see why that's any concern of yours." Under his level gaze, she stifled the rest of her rebuke. "We went to Lord & Taylor's and Tiffany's."

"Anywhere else?"

"We stopped at Talley's Ice Cream Saloon." Now he'd probably want to know exactly what refreshments she and Jessamyn had ordered.

Instead, he asked: "Do you like Jessamyn Spencer?"

The question took her by surprise: "I feel sorry for her."

"You're sorry for a wealthy young lady who is about to marry into one of New York's finest families? I should think you'd envy her."

How could she possibly envy Jessamyn, knowing that the girl was being forced into marriage against her will? Once again she felt a surge of revulsion, as she remembered Everard's outrageous behavior toward his daughter.

"My feelings about Jessamyn can be of no possible interest to you."

"You're mistaken," he cut in. "I'm very much concerned with your impressions of Miss Spencer's emotional state."

"Then you're a particular friend of hers. Maybe more than a friend?"

He laughed. "You think I'm a disappointed suitor?"

"Are you?" Her seething impatience overcame her usual tact.

"I have no romantic attachment to her. And if I had, I wouldn't confide in a journalist, who'd use the information to titillate her lady readers."

"If you've ever read the *Gazette*, you'd know Mrs. Fairlie doesn't publish the sort of trash that appears in penny papers like the *Sun* and the *Transcript*." But her irritation quickly gave way to anxiety. "Why are you questioning me about Jessamyn?"

"If I knew about her state of mind, it might make it easier for me to find her."

"I was right, then!" She caught at his sleeve. "She's run away."

"I haven't said that."

"But she is missing."

"She hasn't been seen since yesterday evening," he said.

"You don't suspect she's been kidnapped?"

"Everard Spencer's a very wealthy man."

Amanda's gloved hand tightened on his sleeve. "But if her parents think so too, surely they've already notified the police. Are you a police officer?" That would explain his probing questions.

"I'm a private investigator."

"A detective?"

"If you prefer."

"But I thought private detectives watched for shoplifters in department stores."

"Some do. Others are hired to guard against jewel thieves at important social events. I used to take on such jobs, but that was awhile ago."

At another time, she might have been interested in Ross

Buchanan's profession, but now her only concern was for Jessamyn's safety. "Has Everard Spencer reported his daughter's disappearance to the police?"

"Not yet. He wants her back, but he also wants to avoid an open scandal."

"I can understand that. But you're only one man, Mr. Buchanan. By the time you find her, if you do—" She folded her hands around her purse and drew a steadying breath. "It may be too late."

"Don't jump to conclusions, Miss Whitney. Everard Spencer doesn't believe his daughter was taken from the house against her will," he said. "The servants deny hearing any unusual noises last night. No one admits to having seen a stranger in the house, and I found no signs of forced entry."

"Then she did run away after all." Not a comforting thought, but surely less frightening than the possibility that Jessamyn had been kidnapped.

"Ottilie Spencer says her daughter's flighty and unpredictable, emotionally unstable," he said. "What do you think?"

She remembered Jessamyn's thin, restless fingers plucking at the lace-edged handkerchief, her blank gaze. And then her hysterical outburst in the library. *You can't force me to marry him! I'll tell him the truth. I'll tell everyone . . .*

"I know Jessamyn Spencer was unhappy and frightened," she said.

"Exactly what do you think she was she afraid of?"

Amanda chose her words carefully. "Of marriage, perhaps. She doesn't love Howard Thornton, you see. Her parents arranged the match."

"That's hardly unusual when there's a great fortune involved."

"Jessamyn's shy and sensitive." She looked away, unable to meet his dark grey eyes. "Maybe she's afraid of the responsibilities of the married state." Her cheeks burned. A lady did not discuss such intimate matters with a gentleman. But if Jessamyn had run away, surely she should forget her scruples and do all she could to help Mr. Buchanan find her. "Perhaps she couldn't bring herself to accept the—duties of a wife." She faltered, then fell silent.

"You've made yourself quite clear," he said, with a wry smile. "But Howard Thornton's a gentleman. Surely he'd have shown consideration for his bride's sensitive nature. Look at me, Miss Whitney." His grey eyes probed hers. "There's something you're not telling me."

"Jessamyn and her father don't get along well."

"She told you so?"

"No, but I've sensed a certain tension between them."

"You're not an experienced liar, Miss Whitney."

How dare he! "I'm not lying! Jessamyn's never told me she doesn't get along with her father."

"But you know more about their relationship than you're willing to admit."

She should tell him what she had seen in the Spencers' library last week, even if it meant admitting that she had been eavesdropping on a family quarrel. But how could she repeat the shocking details to this cold-eyed stranger?

"Will you make a bargain with me?"

"What kind of a bargain?" she asked warily.

"I'll get you back inside the Spencer place to look over the gifts."

She stared at him, startled by his unexpected offer. Certainly, if he could carry it out, her immediate problem would be solved. "I'd have to see them tomorrow morning, if I'm to get my article to the printer by four o'clock in the afternoon."

"What a businesslike female you are, Miss Whitney."

She ignored his gibe. "Can you really persuade Mr. Spencer to let me see the gifts?"

"Leave it to me," he said. His jaw tightened. "But if I don't find Jessamyn by tomorrow night, I'll come calling on you, Miss Whitney. And you'll give me some straight answers."

Before she could protest, he called to the driver to stop. He got out, paid the fare, then stood looking up at her for a moment. "Don't worry. Even if Jessamyn Spencer turns up within the hour, I'll still keep my part of the bargain."

He tipped his hat and moved off into the jostling crowd. The hansom rattled on down Broadway, where drivers of delivery wagons, carts, and carriages shouted at one another to yield the right of way. They cursed flower sellers, crossing sweepers, and beggars who dodged through the heavy traffic, barely avoiding the horses' hooves. But, lost in thought, she ignored the tumult around her.

Maybe if she had told Ross Buchanan all she knew, it would have made his task easier. But if he was an experienced detective, she consoled herself, he'd probably find Jessamyn without her help. And he must be experienced, for Everard Spencer could afford to hire the best, when his family's reputation was at stake.

31

CHAPTER TWO

The gas lamps suspended from the high drawing room ceiling shed their soft glow over the long, damask-covered table. Amanda moved quickly, jotting down a brief description of the wedding gifts spread out on display. The light shimmered over the surfaces of the white porcelain; it struck sparks from the glittering crystal and gleamed on the heavily-engraved silver.

A ruby-threaded crystal epergne . . . a set of fern patterned decanters . . . a Spode dinner service for seventy-two . . . another, of Minton with a carefully-executed painting of a different fish on each plate. Amanda's pencil moved quickly. *Set of silver napkin rings . . . mustard pots . . . menu holders . . .* She was aware of the butler's watchful gaze, but she forced herself to keep her attention on her notes; she would have to work quickly, if she was to turn in her article to the printer by four o'clock.

Ross Buchanan had kept his word. She had just seated herself at her office desk that morning, when a messenger had delivered Mrs. Spencer's note. "Since I will be out of the house today, I have instructed Mr. Harland to accompany you to the morning room, where the gifts are on display." No apology, no explanation for the icy dismissal the day before.

"Excuse me, Mr. Harland." The parlor maid spoke from the doorway. "Cook says you're wanted downstairs right away. The delivery van from Potter & Weekes is here, and she needs you to let the footmen into the wine cellar."

In any well-run household, only the butler was entrusted with the responsibility for keeping the key to the wine cellar. Harland crossed the room, then paused in the doorway. "I trust you won't be much longer, Miss Whitney," he said. "As you can see, I have other duties to attend to." His cold glance and clipped tone made it plain that her presence only added to his many important chores.

"I'm almost finished," she assured him.

"Nellie, you will remain with Miss Whitney."

The parlor maid curtsied, then moved to Amanda's side with a quick, light step. "Such handsome presents," said the maid, with a sigh of admiration. "This one arrived a few hours ago. Isn't it lovely?"

Amanda glanced at a pair of smirking porcelain cherubs, their plump, dimpled arms supporting a gilded basket meant for holding sweetmeats and nuts. "Charming," she agreed. This was her chance to learn if Ross Buchanan had already found Jessamyn and brought her home. But she would have to be circumspect about it, for she wasn't even supposed to know the girl was missing.

"I'm sure Miss Spencer was pleased with the gift."

"Miss Spencer isn't—she hasn't seen it yet."

"Indeed?"

"She's gone away to some little town up the Hudson to visit her old governess." Nellie spoke carefully, as if by rote.

"How very thoughtful," said Amanda. She smiled at the parlor maid, inviting further confidences.

"Yes, indeed, Miss. And she took along her wedding gown for the old lady to see." Nellie hesitated. "Leastwise, that's what Sophia Tuttle told Cook."

"Sophia Tuttle?"

"She's Miss Jessamyn's personal maid."

"I suppose Miss Tuttle accompanied Miss Spencer," Amanda persisted.

"No, she didn't. Miss Jessamyn went by herself."

Amanda raised her eyebrows slightly. "I'd have thought . . ." She said no more but her meaning was plain. An unmarried young lady did not go on an overnight trip without a chaperone.

The parlor maid smoothed her starched white apron, then moved on quickly, keeping a little ahead of Amanda as if to hurry her along. "This ivory trinket box is a gift from Mr. and Mrs. Aspinwall."

"Such intricate carving," Amanda said. She made another note, then turned and glanced at the heavy drops spattering against the leaded panes. "This autumn weather's so uncertain." Nellie looked a little surprised at the abrupt shift in the conversation. "Only yesterday it was warm and sunny," Amanda went on. "I do hope Miss Tuttle packed a warm cloak for Miss Spencer."

"I wouldn't know, Miss." The parlor maid lowered her voice. "Sophia Tuttle thinks she's better than the rest of us. She don't say a friendly word to me or any of the other maids."

That didn't surprise Amanda. During the years in her home on Stuyvesant Square, she had learned all about the complicated social hierarchy of the servants' hall.

"Even so, a bright girl like you would surely notice what's going on around her."

"I'm not one to pry into what doesn't concern me," Nellie said. "But I couldn't help hearing Cook and Miss Tuttle gossiping away over their tea."

"I suppose they were talking about the wedding plans."

"Not last night they weren't." Nellie moved closer, and spoke more softly. "Miss Tuttle told Cook that Miss

Jessamyn hadn't gone on any visit to her old governess. But she did go off someplace—and she took her wedding gown with her."

"You're sure about the wedding gown?"

"Becky—she's one of the upstairs maids—told me the dress had disappeared. Along with Miss Jessamyn."

Disappeared. The word sent a chill through her. Although Ross Buchanan had mentioned the possibility of a kidnapping, he hadn't thought it likely, and he was probably right. Why would a kidnapper force his victim to take along a wedding gown?

"Something's wrong in this house," Nellie said. "And there's others below stairs who say so, too. They'd like to know what's been going on here. Why did the master send that Mr. Buchanan to ask us all them peculiar questions yesterday?"

"Mr. Buchanan?" Amanda asked, with an innocent stare. "Who is he?"

"That's what we'd like to know, Miss. You wouldn't believe the questions he asked me! What time did I go to bed, night before last? Did I leave my room during the night? Did I hear any peculiar noises? And Mrs. Spencer gave him permission to search Miss Jessamyn's suite. Her sitting room, bedroom, all the closets. Miss Tuttle was real put out about that, I can tell you."

"I imagine she was," said Amanda.

"And then he went over the whole house, like a tomcat tracking a mouse. Becky saw him trying the locks and bolts on the doors and windows—"

Nellie drew in her breath and whirled about so quickly that her well-rounded hip struck the side of the long table. Amanda put out her hand to save the china cherubs from crashing to the floor. The maid was looking at a young man

35

who stood in the doorway. She dropped a curtsey. "Good morning, Mr. Clifford."

As he approached her, Amanda tried not to stare. Mrs. Spencer had often spoken of her only son with glowing pride, but Amanda had put down such extravagant praise to a mother's natural affection, until now. She had attended the theater with good-looking young men, had flirted with them at charity bazaars and gone ice-skating with them in Central Park. She had waltzed with them at her friends' coming-out balls. And had even imagined herself to be in love with a few of them—for a week or two.

But her lips parted and her breath quickened as she looked at Clifford Spencer; he was the most handsome young man she had ever seen.

Jessamyn's curls were pale yellow, but her brother's smooth blond hair shone like a burnished golden helmet. His eyes were a vivid sapphire blue. Although he might be an inch or two under six feet, he carried himself with an easy assurance that made him appear taller.

He swept off his bowler hat, smiled at Nellie, then turned to Amanda with a look of frank admiration. Earlier this morning, she had ignored the threat of rain and had put on her favorite outfit, a walking suit of golden-brown that emphasized her chestnut hair and amber eyes. Although it was two years old, it had been expertly altered to conform to this autumn's fashion. The bustle had been made smaller, but the back drapery was ample. Her matching bonnet was trimmed with small curling ostrich plumes.

If she shopped carefully, her raise in salary might cover a few extras, but for now she'd have to make do with what she had salvaged from the years on Stuyvesant Square, when she had taken it for granted that her father would provide her with fashionable new clothing for every occasion.

She realized that Clifford still was looking at her closely; his glance flicking from her face to the leather-bound notebook in her hand. "You must be Miss Whitney, from the *Gazette*." His lips curved in a warm smile. "I hope I'm not interrupting your work."

Only yesterday, his father had called her "that reporter woman." Clifford's description was a definite improvement. But she was sure that, under the circumstances, he must be anxious for her to leave the house. A journalist was the last visitor the Spencers needed right now.

"I hadn't planned on staying this long," she said. "But I mustn't neglect to mention any of these gifts in my article."

He inclined his head, and his smile deepened. "A most formidable task," he said. He glanced over the display on the long table, then his gaze met hers. "I'm sure my sister is looking forward to reading your latest article, when she returns from her trip."

So Clifford was going along with the family's official explanation of Jessamyn's absence. "I've just finished," she said quickly. She snapped her notebook shut and put it away in her purse. "I'll be leaving now."

"Please wait, Miss Whitney," he said. "Let me offer you some refreshments. A pot of tea with hot scones, perhaps. Just right for this inclement weather, wouldn't you agree?"

The warmth in his eyes, the eagerness in his voice, assured her that he wasn't going through the ordinary formalities. For a moment she wavered, then shook her head. "Most thoughtful, Mr. Spencer, but I'm afraid I'll have to refuse. I must keep to my schedule."

She drew on her gloves, then glanced anxiously at the rain pelting against the tall windows. Those heavy drops would spot her dress and leave the plumes on her bonnet looking like wet chicken feathers. "If you'd be so kind as to send a footman to find me a hansom—" she began.

"I wouldn't think of it. Our coachman will drive you downtown in the brougham." He pulled at the bell cord. "I'll have him bring it around to the front door at once."

Amanda leaned back against the soft leather seat with a sigh of pure pleasure. A few years ago she would have taken such luxury for granted; although, even at the height of their prosperity, her family's carriage had not been as ornate as this one. She relaxed and watched the raindrops send silver tracks down the window. In the park across the avenue, the trees swayed in the wind, and wet leaves lay thick upon the ground.

Clifford, holding a large umbrella over both of them, had escorted her to the brougham, where a liveried coachman waited on the high seat; and the footman stood on his perch in back. As Clifford had helped her inside, she had caught a glimpse of the Spencers' crest on the door: a black and yellow shield emblazoned with a griffin and a hawk. She had seen a Latin motto, too, but she hadn't had time to try to decipher it.

Now, as the brougham rolled down Fifth Avenue, raindrops drumming on the roof, she smiled at the notion of Everard Spencer, who'd made his start in life as a lumberjack, laying claim to a coat of arms. But she wasn't surprised by his pretensions, for she guessed that he, like so many other newly-rich New Yorkers, had hired a genealogist to establish a tenuous connection between his family and the British nobility. The same crest had been carved on the newel post at the foot of the wide staircase. It was probably engraved on the silver tea service as well. If she had accepted Clifford's invitation to tea, she would have had the chance to find out for herself. She'd also have spent another hour in his company. She gave a rueful sigh as she remembered those vivid blue eyes and winning smile.

All right, so Clifford Spencer's a good-looking man, with more than his fair share of charm. Considerate, too—he sent for the brougham so that you could return to your office in comfort. Forget about him for now. Keep your mind on your work.

She started to plan the opening sentences of this week's article. As the brougham rolled past Madison Square, she tried to shut out the rumble of iron-shod wheels on the pavement; the shouting of a red-faced teamster who'd been cut off by the driver of a horse-car jammed with passengers. A skinny boy held up his rain-spattered newspapers and called out in a loud, shrill voice: *HORRIBLE MURDER OF CHILD IN THE FIVE POINTS . . . SHOCKING SUICIDE OF SEAMSTRESS, BETRAYED BY HER LOVER . . .*

No such scandalous headlines appeared in the *Gazette*. Mrs. Lavinia Fairlie's paper was meant to be read by the ladies in New York's most respectable homes—with the complete approval of their male relatives. Amanda's articles on the preparations for the Thornton-Spencer wedding had been up to the paper's high standards. Mrs. Fairlie had nodded approval as she'd read them, and had made only a few changes. But today, it wasn't easy for Amanda to concentrate on the work before her.

It was most unlikely that the charade about the trip up the Hudson could go on much longer. The Spencers' servants were already suspicious. Did any of them really think it was true that the bride-to-be had gone off unchaperoned to visit her retired governess? From what Nellie had told her, it certainly didn't sound likely. What if Nellie stopped to pass the time of day with a parlor maid from a nearby Fifth Avenue mansion? Or one of the Spencers' footmen, walking out with some other family's nursery maid, wanted to impress her with a choice bit of gossip? Unless Jessamyn were found quickly, there'd be no way to prevent a scandal.

After Amanda had finished her article, she brought it to Mrs. Fairlie's office, and watched anxiously as the publisher picked up one of the black quill pens from the onyx holder, struck out a line or two, added a few words.

"You're improving." Coming from Mrs. Fairlie, that was a compliment. But before Amanda could relax, her employer went on, "But this should have been completed and handed in yesterday afternoon."

"Mrs. Spencer couldn't take time to show me the gifts yesterday. She was too busy with other wedding preparations."

"You are no longer a student at Vassar, Miss Whitney." There was a hard edge to her employer's voice. "You are a working woman now, with professional standards to uphold."

It was no wonder Lavinia Fairlie, widowed three years ago and left to manage her late husband's shaky publishing empire, had already paid off all his creditors. She had rescued the faltering *Ladies Gazette*, along with several other publications, and had sent their sales soaring. And she had done it without exploiting the latest society scandals, or selling advertising space to the makers of dubious, sometimes lethal patent medicines. Last year, when President Garfield had been assassinated, she had brought out three illustrated papers in one week. She, herself, had written the editorial about the national tragedy for the *Gazette*.

She still wore mourning in memory of her late husband, but her red hair lent a vivid touch of color to her appearance. On her yearly visits to Paris, she bought her expensive black grosgrains and fine silks at the House of Worth. Her black kid shoes, with their silver tips, had set a new fashion the first time she wore them. Although Amanda had often flinched under her employer's criticism, she admired and respected the older woman.

"You may go now, Miss Whitney."

She managed to hold back a sigh of relief until she was outside the door of Mrs. Fairlie's office.

The rain had turned to a silvery drizzle by the time Amanda returned to her flat on West Nineteenth Street. After a light dinner, prepared in her small kitchen, she hung away her walking costume, then bathed and changed to a high-necked linen nightgown and a comfortable blue flannel robe, slightly frayed at the cuffs. She brushed her chestnut hair one hundred strokes, then plaited it into a thick, waist-length braid. Now, curled up in a cushioned wicker chair near the fireplace, she was absorbed in Mrs. Helen Hunt Jackson's popular novel, *Ramona*. Leander, her black and white cat, who had been sleeping close by, abruptly raised his head, his ears pointing forward, the tip of his tail switching. His green eyes were fixed on the door. A moment later, she heard a brisk knock, and the voice of the concierge. "You have a visitor, Miss Whitney." She set aside the book and went to open the door to Mrs. Morton, a stout, middle-aged woman. "There's a gentleman downstairs. A Mr. Buchanan, who says he's got to see you right away."

Amanda glanced at the ormolu clock on the mantel shelf—ten minutes after nine. Surely, he should have known it was improper to call upon a lady at such an hour.

"Shall I send him about his business?"

Before Amanda could answer, she caught sight of Ross Buchanan in the narrow hall.

The concierge turned on him with an outraged stare. "See here, sir! You were told to wait downstairs."

He ignored the woman. "May I come in, Miss Whitney?" She saw the harsh lines bracketing his mouth, the bleak expression in his eyes.

"It's all right," she told the concierge.

But the woman did not move, and her stout body was rigid with disapproval. Her eyes raked over Amanda, taking in the high lace collar of her nightgown, the robe and slippers, the long braid that lay over her shoulder. "You didn't say you were expecting a caller."

As commerce had moved uptown, this was one of many fine old houses that had been abandoned by its original owners, and converted into apartments, "French flats" as they were called, to give them a continental touch. They were rented to single ladies. Some shared their quarters with female roommates, while others, like Amanda, chose to live alone. In either case, their references and their conduct were irreproachable.

"Thank you, Mrs. Morton," Amanda said firmly. "Good-night." The concierge stood her ground a moment longer, then turned and stalked down the gas-lit hall.

"Please come in, Mr. Buchanan." He shut the door behind him and removed his hat. She hung it on the rack, then led the way into the parlor. "Have you found Jessamyn?"

He didn't answer, and she felt a rising tension.

"I talked to Nellie this morning—she's the Spencers' parlor maid. She told me that Jessamyn was visiting her retired governess. But I don't think she really believes it, and neither do the other servants. A girl like Jessamyn doesn't go off on an overnight trip without her personal maid." She went on, speaking quickly. "Nellie said that Jessamyn's wedding gown was missing."

He took a step closer and stood looking down at her. "She was wearing the gown and the veil when they found her."

His words sent a chill through Amanda. "Found her?"

"In the Ladies Mile," he said grimly. "Her body was lying in an alley next to Isobel Hewitt's place."

"Isobel Hewitt?" She did not recognize the name. "Is that a dress shop?"

"It's a whorehouse." She drew in her breath sharply and her cheeks burned. "Sorry, Miss Whitney. A house of ill-repute, if you prefer. One of the most exclusive in the city."

"You're sure it was Jessamyn?"

"I was in the Bellevue morgue with Everard Spencer an hour ago. He identified her."

She caught her breath, her knees unsteady. Buchanan took her arm in a firm grip, and led her to the wicker chair. She sank down, and pulled her robe more tightly around her. She remembered the quarrel between Jessamyn and her father. "Mr. Spencer must have been overcome with guilt," she began.

"What makes you say that?"

Even now, she hesitated to tell him how Everard had abused his daughter. "I think that when we lose a loved one, we always have regrets."

He leaned over her, his eyes hard. "I kept my part of our bargain. You went to the Spencers' house today, and this time, you weren't turned away. You did your job. Now I've got to get on with mine. You're going to tell me whatever you were holding back yesterday."

"You're still working for Mr. Spencer?"

"That's right. He hopes I'll find his daughter's killer before the police do. I'm being paid handsomely, to report directly to him. Whatever I discover will be kept strictly confidential."

"But if the police find the killer first—what then?"

He smiled mirthlessly. "In that case Mr. Spenser uses his influence to offer the police commissioner enough money to forget what his department knows. Money will buy silence as well as buying a private investigator."

She started to speak, but he silenced her with an impatient gesture. "All right, so the *Gazette* won't give its readers any of the sordid details. But other papers will. The *Sun* has informants in the police department. So do the *Telegram*, and the *Graphic*."

His cynical tone flicked at her over-strained nerves. "I suppose a private investigator is above such sordid dealings," she said.

"I don't sell information about my clients to the newspapers, but that's only because I find it more profitable not to. A reputation for absolute discretion is a marketable commodity when dealing with a client like Everard Spencer. It's part of my job to act as an intermediary between the police department and the Spencer family."

"You're able to do that?"

"I used to be on the force, and I still have connections there. So far, only the police and the morgue attendants know all the bizarre details of the murder."

"I don't understand."

"When the patrolman found her body in the alley, she was wearing her wedding gown and veil. The killer had strangled her with her own bridal wreath."

She drew in her breath as she remembered the elaborate brocade gown, the lace veil Ottilie had shown her. And the wreath of white blossoms, each petal perfectly formed. The wreath was long enough to touch the hem of the gown, as was the fashion this season; it was made to be held in place with pearl-tipped pins. Orange blossoms, symbol of virginal purity.

"But that's not possible. What would she have been doing down on the Ladies Mile, dressed that way?"

"That's what I'm trying to find out." He spoke brusquely. "When I saw her in the morgue, she was lying on a slab, under a sheet. Her clothes hung on a hook behind the slab. Her dress and veil were muddy and torn. The bridal wreath was made of white blossoms fastened to a wire covered with green silk. The wire had been twisted around her throat so tightly that when it was cut off, bits of her skin were torn away."

"No!" Revulsion gripped her. "Please—I don't want to hear any more!"

But he ignored her protest and went on. "I saw the dried blood on her throat. There were a few streaks of blood on her shoulders, too."

His face was starting to swim before her eyes. His voice came to her through a thin humming inside her head.

"Her skin was the color of a ripe plum. Her eyes were rolled back in her head, so only the whites were visible. Her features were distorted, her tongue thrust out."

Under her warm nightgown and flannel robe, her body was damp with cold perspiration. Nausea welled up inside her. She gripped the arms of the chair, and pulled herself to her feet. He reached out his hand to steady her, but she pushed it away and fled from the parlor.

CHAPTER THREE

"Miss Whitney—wait!" But already she was gone.

He had come to her flat directly from the morgue, and had told her of the murder in graphic detail because he'd hoped to shock her into letting down her guard. When he'd been a detective on the Metropolitan Police Force, such methods had often been successful. But in dealing with Amanda, he'd obviously made a mistake. He should have realized how vulnerable she was, under her veneer of quiet self-assurance.

What did he know about Amanda Whitney? Damn little. Only that she came of a fine old New York family; that her father's trust in a dishonest partner had cost him his business and his fortune; that Amanda had not let herself be broken by the catastrophe. She had clung to her independence, determined to make her own way in the world, even if it meant flouting the strict conventions by which she'd been raised. The poised young lady he'd met yesterday had ignored propriety when she'd invited him to share her cab, and she'd been cool and businesslike when she'd bargained with him to get her back into the Spencer mansion to complete her latest assignment.

He looked about the parlor, and decided that, although there was not much furniture, what there was had been chosen with excellent taste. He gave an approving glance at the heavy walnut desk, the green-cushioned wicker chair, the wide horsehair sofa, and the tall bookcase with its glass doors. The mantelpiece over the small fireplace held only a pair of bronze candlesticks flanking an ormolu clock. There were no knick-knack shelves crowded with small china animals; no dried flowers in gilded frames; no shell-covered boxes; no stuffed birds or squirrels under glass domes. A small Adirondack table, its base made from the twisted roots of a tree, supplied the only touch of whimsy. She chose to live here alone, and had arranged the place to suit herself.

She was unconventional and strong-willed, but now he's seen another side to her character. The girl in the flannel robe, her hair hanging in a thick plait over her shoulder, looked more vulnerable than the fashionably-dressed journalist with whom he'd shared the cab yesterday. Younger, too.

He felt a twinge of uneasiness as he peered into the shadows beyond the half-open parlor door. Although he heard no sound of weeping from wherever she'd taken refuge, she might be the kind who cried in silence. If she'd fled to her bedroom, he couldn't bring himself to go barging in after her. He waited impatiently, as long as he could, then headed for the parlor door. He swore as he tripped over her black and white tomcat. It hissed at him; leaped up on the sofa, its tail switching, and watched him warily.

Then he smelled the aroma of freshly-brewed coffee, and heard the clinking of china from somewhere beyond the parlor. A few moments later, Amanda came in, carrying a tray with two delicate porcelain cups, a silver sugar bowl and cream pitcher, and a steaming coffee pot.

"Please sit down," she said, gesturing in the direction of the big, horsehair sofa. The cat sidled away, as far from him as possible.

"Leander doesn't take to strangers right away." Her

voice was steady, her face pale but composed. She set the tray down on a small table, drew the wicker chair closer and seated herself opposite him. He watched her small, square hands moving deftly as she made a small ceremony of serving the coffee. Probably she'd acquired such ladylike skills in one of New York's most exclusive finishing schools.

"I'm sorry," he began. "I was thoughtless to speak to you that way."

"I don't believe you're a man who often speaks without thinking," she told him, her amber gaze unwavering. "We made a bargain yesterday, didn't we? You said you thought I was holding something back. Some important piece of information. You got me into the Spencer mansion to look at the gifts, and now you've come here to make sure I tell you all I know."

"You said Jessamyn was afraid, that she might have run away to get out of the marriage with Thornton. But you also told me that she'd never spoken to you about such intimate matters."

"She scarcely spoke to me at all. Whenever I came to the house, it was her mother who went on and on about the preparations for the wedding."

"But she asked you to go with her to choose the gifts for the bridesmaids," he reminded her. "When you went down to the Ladies Mile together, what did she talk about?"

Amanda gave him a self-deprecating smile. "As I recall, I did most of the talking."

He made an effort to restrain his impatience. "She must have said something. About the bridesmaids, perhaps, or about the gifts she was buying for them. Didn't she speak about your articles for the *Gazette*? Not even about the weather? Think, Amanda." Although he hadn't called her by her first name before, and should not have done so now, on such short acquaintance, she did not reproach him. But neither did she answer his questions.

"You stopped at Talley's Ice Cream Saloon," he persisted. "Do you expect me to believe that Jessamyn sat there across the table and just stared at you all through lunch, without saying a word?"

"We didn't stay for lunch."

"Why not?"

She spoke slowly, as if she was trying to recall all the details. "The waitress brought us the menus, but before I had time to order, Jessamyn got up and left. She moved so quickly she bumped into a lady with an armload of packages, and didn't even stop to apologize. Of course, I followed her back to the brougham."

"Didn't she make some excuse for running off that way?"

"She only said she was feeling faint. I suppose it was possible. The afternoon was unusually warm and Talley's was crowded, but even so—"

"You think she might have had another reason. What was it?"

"I'm not sure. Unless, perhaps . . ."

"Go on."

"Until that day, she'd left all the wedding preparations to her mother. It was almost as if she couldn't deal with the fact that she really was going to be married. But after she'd bought the bridesmaids' gifts—" She paused. "Maybe that made it suddenly too real for her."

An unlikely notion—but not impossible. After all, Amanda understood the convolutions of the female mind better than he did. "You believe she didn't want to marry Thornton," he prompted her.

"I know it!"

"You've said she'd never confided in you," he reminded her. "So how can you be so sure?"

The words came with a rush. "Because I heard her talking with her father, telling him she couldn't marry anyone, ever. She pleaded with him to call off the wedding. She said that otherwise, she'd tell Mr. Thornton every-thing—"

Her hand flew to her lips and she broke off abruptly.

"And just when did she say all that?" he demanded.

She set her jaw and looked away. He put down the fragile coffee cup with exaggerated care, then got to his feet, circled the small table, and stood over her.

His patience was wearing dangerously thin, and it was all he could do to restrain his impulse to take her by the shoulders, jerk her out of the chair, and shake the truth from her. But such tactics wouldn't do any good—not with Amanda Whitney.

"Nothing you tell me about Jessamyn can harm her now," he reminded her.

She spoke with obvious reluctance. "Her father said she was lucky any man would want to marry her."

"That's ridiculous! Plenty of men would have been at-tracted by the Spencer fortune. What else did he say?"

"He called her—an immoral woman. A—" She sounded as if she might choke before she got the word out. "—a whore."

He stared at her in disbelief. "Everard Spencer said that in front of you?"

"He thought I'd left the house. He didn't know I over-heard him."

"You were eavesdropping, that's what you mean, isn't it?"

"No! It wasn't like that at all." Her voice shook with indignation. "I was searching for a lost glove when I heard them quarreling in the library. The doors were partly open." She stopped short.

He didn't want to break down her hard-won control again, but she left him no choice. "Listen to me, Amanda. Death by strangulation isn't easy. Can you imagine the pain, the terror Jessamyn must have felt during those last moments of her life?"

He reached out and took hold of her. She tried to free herself but he tightened his grip. This time she wasn't going to get away. "Do you want her murderer to go free? Perhaps to kill another innocent young woman?"

"How can you ask me such a question?"

He pressed his advantage. "Then tell me the rest of it. All you can remember."

He felt her body go rigid. "He slapped her hard. I heard her cry out." She raised her eyes to his. "How could he have treated his own daughter that way?"

Obviously, she'd led a sheltered life. He could have told her he'd come across far worse cases of physical abuse; not only in the squalor of Bowery tenements, or the shacks of the Five Points, but in the most elegant mansions on Fifth Avenue.

"When Jessamyn threatened to tell Thornton everything, what do you think she meant?"

"I wondered about that." She hesitated for a moment. "Maybe some time in the past she'd been attracted to an unsuitable young man."

His hands dropped away from her shoulders. "Unsuitable in what way?"

"How can I possibly know that? The young man—if there really was one—might have had no money, no social position. A poor young foreigner, perhaps."

51

"What a romantic notion! Have you been reading the novels of Mrs. Southworth?"

She ignored his sarcasm. "Such things do happen, and not only in novels. When I attended Miss Blakemore's school on Gramercy Square, there was a young Frenchman on the staff who taught sketching and water-color. Many of the girls found him fascinating."

He wondered if she had been one of them. Seeing her in her robe and slippers, with the firelight glinting on her long, chestnut braid, it wasn't hard to imagine her as an impressionable schoolgirl.

"Miss Blakemore discovered a highly improper note he'd written to one of the girls," she went on. "And a locket he'd given her—he said it had belonged to his mother."

"An improper note and a locket. That was all?"

"It was enough to get him dismissed without a reference."

"I don't doubt it. But when Everard called his daughter a whore, I doubt he was speaking of some girlish infatuation in her past."

"No—I suppose not."

"Whatever she'd done, it must have been a lot more serious than that. You overheard a violent quarrel between Jessamyn and her father. Then she disappeared, without a word to anyone. Her body was found in the alley next to Isobel Hewitt's parlor house. I have to know how and where she spent the last hours of her life."

She looked up at him, her amber eyes wide with shock. "You can't suppose there's any connection between Jessamyn and this Hewitt woman?"

"It's unlikely, I'll admit. But you've already said you knew little about Jessamyn."

"I knew her well enough to be sure that if she ever was in

such a dreadful establishment, she must have been taken there against her will." Her voice shook with indignation. "Maybe her kidnappers drugged her, and took her to that awful place."

"What makes you think she was kidnapped? I found no signs of a break-in."

"She might have been taken while she was out of the house."

"You can't really think she walked out of the Spencer mansion and strolled down Fifth Avenue to the Ladies Mile, wearing a wedding gown and veil, without attracting attention."

"Maybe she took them with her in a carpet bag. Or a small traveling case—" She shook her head. "No, that's not possible. She'd have needed a large trunk. The dress was heavy white brocade and satin-de-Lyon, with a full skirt. And there were the white satin slippers. The veil. And the—wreath. When her mother showed me the wedding costume, I thought it was too elaborate for a fragile girl like Jessamyn to wear."

"Never mind the dress," he interrupted. "If Jessamyn ran away, where do you think she might have been going?"

"I don't know."

"The Spencers have no family here in the city. Did she have any close friend—one of her bridesmaids perhaps—who would have helped her to get away before the wedding?"

"I doubt it," she said slowly. "But I can try to find out."

"And how do you propose to do that?"

"I'll talk to Nellie again. And to some of the other servants. There's Miss Tuttle, her personal maid. And the upstairs maid—Becky. I'll question them, too."

"You'll do no such thing. You'll go right back to the *Ga-*

zette tomorrow, and get started on your next assignment. And you'll tell no one at your office that Jessamyn's dead." His eyes hardened. "It will make the headlines soon enough."

"I won't say a word, I promise. But if I go back to the Spencer mansion and talk to the servants, who knows what I may be able to find out?"

He gave her a swift, appraising look, while he weighed the possibilities. She had gotten Nellie to confide in her, and she might do the same with some of the other female servants. Briefly, he considered allowing her to carry out her plan, then dismissed the idea. She was far too impulsive and inexperienced. She'd never be able to carry it off.

"Don't go back to that house, not even to pay the Spencers a condolence call. And don't question the servants." He reached into his pocket and handed her his card. "But if you should remember anything more you think might be important, come to my office and tell me."

Amanda shifted restlessly in her bed, and stared into the darkness. Jessamyn dead—in that horrible way. She turned over, buried her face in the pillow and tried to shut out the sickening images that Ross had conjured up in her mind. He'd been so determined to get her to tell him whatever she could recall, that he hadn't cared how he forced the truth out of her. Had he used the same ruthless tactics when he'd served with the Metropolitan Police?

The only time she'd had any contact with a police officer had been on an evening a few years ago when Ming Toy, Mama's little Pekinese dog, had slipped out of the house on Stuyvesant Square. The burly, uniformed patrolman who had found the dog and brought him back, had spoken politely to her. He had refused her offer of a reward and gone

54

on his way. She had accepted his help as a matter of course. Any policeman assigned to the Square was expected to serve the residents willingly, and to treat them with respect.

Her thoughts turned again to Ross Buchanan. Had he been an ordinary patrolman, or had he held a higher rank on the force? She turned over on her other side and pulled the comforter up around her shoulders, then closed her eyes, but sleep would not come. No one had ever spoken to her as he had, or treated her with such total disregard for her feelings. Resentment stirred in her when she remembered how he had spared her none of the details of Jessamyn's murder; how tightly he had gripped her shoulders, as he'd tried to force her to tell him what he wanted to know.

What he needed to know. Maybe his behavior was understandable, in view of the circumstances. He was faced with a difficult, probably dangerous job and he would have to act quickly, if he were to find the murderer before the police did.

It was nearly dawn when she fell into a restless sleep, troubled by disjointed, frightening dreams.

She arrived at the office promptly at nine the next day, and tried to occupy her thoughts by making a list of upcoming social events she would be covering during the next few months; but she was unable to concentrate. She was relieved when Maude Hamilton paused in the doorway of her office.

The fashion editor, a tall, slender woman in her late thirties, was not pretty in a conventional way; her face was too angular, her mouth too wide. But she had an air of self-assurance Amanda envied. Today she wore a fashionable walking suit in the latest shade—a blue-grey called *nuit de*

55

France, chosen to emphasize the color of her eyes.

Amanda set her pen in its brass holder, pushed aside her notes. "Please, come in."

Maude took a chair, then smoothed the folds of her faille skirt. "I hear you were late handing in this week's article. I suppose the Grand Duchess had something to say about that." Only Maude would have dared to refer to Mrs. Fairlie that way.

Amanda gave her a rueful smile. "She reminded me that I was no longer a student at Vassar, and that I had to uphold the *Gazette*'s professional standards."

"So long as you've described all Jessamyn Spencer's wedding gifts in detail, she'll be satisfied. As for your readers, they will be enthralled—and green with envy."

Amanda's throat tightened. There was no reason for her readers to envy Jessamyn now—and perhaps there never had been. If only she could say as much to Maude. She needed to confide in someone, but she had promised Ross Buchanan she wouldn't speak of the murder, not to anyone.

"Did you go to Victoria Woodhull's seance last night?" she asked.

"I wouldn't have missed her performance for anything," said Maude. "It's remarkable how she can convince her audience that she's able to contact the 'other side,' as she calls it."

"You don't believe she really has—psychic powers?"

"Psychic powers, my foot! Amanda, you should have seen all those foolish women—and a few men, too—sitting around a table in the dark, trying to get in touch with their relations in the great beyond. Victoria and her sister—Tennessee Clafin—are quite a pair. Too bad we can't expose all their chicanery in the *Gazette*. Do you know, they even managed to convince wily old Commodore Vanderbilt of their extraordinary powers? In return, he gave them tips on the stock market, and set them up in business as 'lady brokers.' No wonder his family paid them off to leave the country."

"But now they're back here in New York," Amanda said.

"I doubt they'll stay here long—they seldom do."

"You're sure they're frauds?"

"I'm sure." Maude nodded briskly. "Even if they had any such powers, why would I—or any sensible person—pay good money to speak with the dear departed? Take my late Aunt Hortense, for instance—she was a nattering old bore all her life. I've no desire to listen to her foolish chatter from the 'other side,' not when I still have a couple of aunts still living, and every bit as boring as Hortense. They descend on me from Nyack for regular visits." She gave Amanda a teasing smile. "But if you want to get in touch with someone who's passed on, I'll be happy to take you along to her next seance."

Remembering Jessamyn, a shudder went through her. "No, Maude—no, I don't!"

"For goodness sake, my dear, I wasn't serious. You're far too level-headed to believe in such nonsense."

The following morning, on her ride downtown, Amanda thought of yesterday's talk with Maude; she'd have to be careful to hide her emotions from her co-workers. Thank heaven it was Friday. Tomorrow she might try to distract herself with a brisk walk through Central Park.

The hansom was turning into Pearl Street, when she heard a newsboy shouting above the din of the traffic. *HEIRESS MURDERED—BRIDE-TO-BE FOUND STRANGLED—FIEND AT LARGE—LADIES MILE—*

It hadn't taken long for someone on the police force to

give the story to a reporter on one of the popular scandal sheets. She rapped on the roof of the hansom with her parasol, and the driver reined to a halt. She beckoned to the newsboy, who darted between the wagons and carriages, to hand her a copy of the *Sun*.

Quickly she skimmed the article. Although it said that the body had been discovered on the Ladies Mile, it did not mention Isobel Hewitt's parlor house. There was nothing about the wedding gown and veil worn by the victim, or the bridal wreath that had been used to strangle her. As the hansom jolted along the crowded street, she went on reading. *Miss Spencer was murdered by a fiendish brute, a monster . . . she was returning from a visit up the Hudson . . . police on the trail of the killer. . . .*

Amanda's gloved hands started to shake, as she folded the paper. Everard Spencer had used his influence to prevent the publisher of the *Sun* from revealing all the scandalous details. But would the other newspapers handle the story with the same discretion—and if so, for how long? Even now, reporters would be descending on the Spencer mansion, and milling about in front of the tall, iron gates, clamoring for more facts. Ordinary citizens, possessed by morbid curiosity, would be there, too. Would the servants be able to keep the mob at bay, or would Everard have to send for mounted police?

She felt a swift stab of pity for Clifford, who had treated her with such consideration on her last visit. He must have spent a sleepless night, grieving for his sister, and offering what comfort he could to his mother.

"Here we are, Miss." The hansom had stopped in front of the building that housed the offices of Fairlie Publications. She got down, paid the driver, then hurried inside, still clutching the folded copy of the *Sun*. But she had not yet had time to take off her hat, before Denny, the copyboy, came barging into her office without knocking, to tell her that Mrs. Fairlie wanted to see her at once.

"I'll write the feature article for the *Daily Messenger*," said Mrs. Fairlie. She wore a handsome black grosgrain gown, and her red hair was carefully arranged in a fashionable coiffure with a coiled chignon. Her own copy of the *Sun* was spread out on the desk. "You will do a short piece for the *Gazette*. You must choose your words carefully, of course. Nothing that might give offence to our readers. 'Jessamyn Spencer, the beautiful young heiress, the bride-to-be. A delicate flower, blighted by an untimely frost.' Something of that sort."

Amanda stiffened with indignation. "Jessamyn was strangled—"

"Say only that she met a tragic end. That will be quite sufficient."

"But Mrs. Fairlie—"

"Family in deepest mourning. Mr. Howard Thornton, shattered by grief. I trust I can rely on your good taste and discretion." She pushed the *Sun* away with a gesture of contempt. "I'm sure you know better than to use such expressions as 'fiendish brute,' or to dwell on the way the poor girl was murdered. We must uphold our standard of discretion at all times."

She paused, her green eyes narrowing. "Did Mrs. Spencer mention that her daughter had gone on a trip?"

Amanda looked away. "I didn't see Mrs. Spencer." Amanda chose her words carefully. "The parlor maid who showed me the gifts mentioned that Jessamyn was away on a visit to an elderly lady who used to be her governess."

"And did this parlor maid tell you where the governess

lived? Or when Jessamyn was expected back?"

Before she could answer, Amanda heard a knock at the office door, and turned to see Mr. Elliot, who was in charge of the layout department. "You sent for me, ma'am."

He glanced at the newspaper on Mrs. Fairlie's desk, and shook his head. "Terrible tragedy, isn't it?"

"Shocking, indeed," Mrs. Fairlie agreed. "Naturally, we'll have to kill the article on the *Gazette*'s society page, the one about the wedding gifts. We'll put another of the same length in its place. Miss Whitney will have it ready for you by early afternoon."

Relieved at having escaped any further interrogation, at least for the moment, Amanda left the office and headed downstairs.

CHAPTER FOUR

Back at her desk, Amanda tried to concentrate on her assignment. She jotted down a few random notes, then paused, pen in hand. She would try to use discretion as Mrs. Fairlie had ordered. Even the *Sun*'s reporter had omitted the most scandalous details. He had praised the Metropolitan Police, and had assured his readers that those courageous public servants would soon track down the murderer and bring him to justice. She wasn't surprised that the article made no mention of Everard Spencer's private arrangement with Ross Buchanan.

But she was still shaken by Mrs. Fairlie's matter-of-fact response to the news of Jessamyn's death. Did it mean no more to her than an article that would have to be dropped from the society page, and another put in its place?

A delicate flower, blighted by frost. Did Mrs. Fairlie really expect her to describe Jessamyn that way, in deference to the sensibilities of the readers? The girl had been strangled. Had she tried to fight off her assailant? Had she cried out before the wire had cut off her breathing? How long had it taken for her to die?

"Amanda, my dear—are you all right?"

She gave a start, for she had not heard Maude's light tap at her office door. The fashion editor was carrying a small tray, with a tea pot and two cups. She set it down on a corner of the desk. "I thought perhaps you might want to take a break, about now."

"That was thoughtful of you," said Amanda.

61

"So you won't be covering the Spencer-Thornton wedding after all. And now you have to write another article, in place of the one about the gifts." Maude gave her a sympathetic smile. "This can't be easy for you," she said. "After all, you knew Jessamyn Spencer."

But she hadn't—not really. All she remembered were those thin fingers plucking at a lace handkerchief, and the distant expression in her eyes every time Ottilie had talked about the wedding. Was it possible Jessamyn had known, somehow, that it would never take place—?

She went cold at the thought. Maude came quickly to her side and touched her shoulder lightly. "You'd better get on with your article. Just keep it short and simple. And discreet."

"Yes, I know," Amanda said, with an edge to her voice. "Mrs. Fairlie told me what to say." She stiffened with outrage. "But how can I? Jessamyn wasn't a delicate flower. She was a frightened, helpless girl. And somebody got hold of her and choked the life out of her. And left her body—" She stopped herself in time.

"Amanda, for heaven sake. Get hold of yourself." Maude glanced down at the nearly-empty sheet of paper on the desk. "Do you want me to do the article for you?"

She drew a breath, then shook her head. "This is my job. I'll do it."

"Very well. But first, let's have our tea, shall we?"

Amanda welcomed the steaming brew, for she still felt cold inside. She was also grateful for Maude's frivolous chatter, which was obviously meant to distract her. "You'll be having plenty of new assignments from now right on through the holidays. Everyone's back from Newport and Saratoga and Bar Harbor. By next week, you'll be dashing about to balls and luncheons and charity bazaars. The opera and the theater—I've heard that Lillie Langtry will be coming over shortly. She's going to perform in a melodrama, written by a member of her company. And then she's going to play Rosalind, in *As You Like It.*" She raised her delicately arched brows. "I doubt the Jersey Lily's talents will do justice to Shakespeare, but everyone will go to gape at her because she's the mistress of the Prince of Wales. I expect to see all those women wearing their hair in the Langtry coiffure, and copying those gorgeous hats of hers."

Amanda made an effort to appear interested. "I suppose you'll be going to see one of Mrs. Langtry's performances."

"I'll be there on opening night. It's part of my job, telling our readers what gown Mrs. Astor was wearing, and giving them a description of Mrs. William K. Vanderbilt's bustle. Of course, the bustle's come back. But it's going to be much smaller than it was last season. Feather fans with shaded tips will be all the rage this winter. And as for the hats—have you seen the new millinery display in Lord & Taylor's window? Small bonnets with upright crowns and close brims. Kid bonnets embossed with gold thread. Round plush hats with Tyrolean crowns—although I doubt that those will be at all flattering to most women. And by the way, if you're going to the Ladies Mile this weekend, do tell me what you think of them. Or have you already seen them?"

"Seen them?"

"The new autumn hats, in Lord & Taylor's window." Maude sighed and shook her head. "My dear, I don't believe you've heard a word I've been saying. You really must get hold of yourself. You have a job to do."

They finished their tea, and Maude went out with the tray. Amanda picked up her pen and wrote a couple of sentences, then crossed them out.

She thought again of her visit to the Ladies Mile with Jessamyn. She remembered the procession of expensively-dressed ladies who had paused to look at the lavish window displays, and had strolled in and out of shops. And then she and Jessamyn had stopped at Talley's. Once again, she went over every detail of their brief visit to the fashionable ice cream saloon. The hostess had led them to a small round table near the window. The waitress had brought their menus. Then Jessamyn had looked up at the woman in her starched uniform and her blue eyes had widened. Her face, always pale, had turned a greenish-white. She'd stood up so quickly she'd almost knocked over the chair. Then she hurried out with Amanda close behind her.

Jessamyn had panicked when she'd looked up at the waitress.

But what on earth could have caused her to react that way? It made no sense. She couldn't have known the woman, could she? What possible connection could there have been between the Spencer heiress and a waitress in an ice cream saloon?

She closed her eyes, her fingertips against her forehead, and tried to remember if there had been anything unusual in the waitress's appearance; but she had only a vague recollection of the woman's face, and her light brown hair, pulled back under a starched white cap. She'd worn a long, lace-trimmed apron over a neat black dress.

Although Ross had forbidden her to pursue the investigation on her own, he had told her to contact him if she thought of anything that might possibly be of use to him. Amanda opened her desk drawer, took out her purse and found his business card. She resisted her first impulse, to leave the office right now. She couldn't come and go as she pleased. First she had to write her article and hand it in. She sighed and picked up her pen.

It was late afternoon when Amanda stopped in front of a narrow, four-story building on West Fourteenth Street. The last rays of sunlight slanted across the brick facade. She hurried up the two flights of stairs and found Ross's office at the far end of the hall. She knocked and waited until the door opened and he stood looking down at her.

"I came as quickly as I could," she began. "You said that if I remembered anything about Jessamyn—"

He took her arm and drew her inside. "Sit down and catch your breath." He led her to a horsehair sofa.

"I'd have come at once, but I had to hand in an article, to take the place of the one about the wedding gifts."

He seated himself beside her. "You remembered something about Jessamyn that you thought I should know?"

"I'm not sure it will be of any help, but—that day she and I went shopping for bridesmaids' gifts in the Ladies Mile and stopped at Talley's for lunch—"

His dark grey eyes were alert now. "You think you know why she left so suddenly?"

"I'm not sure. But I do recall that her behavior was perfectly natural. Until she looked up and saw the waitress who brought our menus."

"The waitress? Did she speak to Jessamyn?"

"She only said 'good-afternoon, ladies.' That was all."

"Was there something unusual about her appearance? Was she deformed, or badly pock-marked, perhaps?"

"Certainly not. A place like Talley's wouldn't have hired a woman who was disfigured to wait on the customers."

"What did she look like?"

"There was nothing remarkable about her. She was just

a rather plain-looking woman, with a squarish face. I think she may have been a little taller than average."

"Did Jessamyn appear to recognize her?"

"I don't know. It all happened so quickly. I've been trying to figure out what possible connection there might have been between the two of them, but I can't."

"Maybe I can," Ross said. "It's my job, remember?"

"But I can go back to Talley's. If that waitress is on duty, I can talk to her. I can find out her name, if nothing else."

He shook his head. "You've helped me enough by coming here and telling me this much. Now you can leave the rest to me."

"Gentlemen don't go to Talley's," she said. "You'd be far too conspicuous. And it's not likely that you'd recognize the woman from my description, is it?"

"I know my business, Amanda. I'll find that waitress and question her."

"Then at least let me go back to the Spencer mansion and talk to Nellie again. She likes to gossip. I know I can get her to tell me more about Jessamyn."

"You'll do nothing of the sort."

"But you want to solve the case before the police do. That's what you're being paid for. And I can help you."

His face darkened. "What makes you think you'd be of any use to me? You've had no experience."

"I've already managed to win Nellie's confidence, haven't I? She told me that she and the other servants didn't believe Jessamyn had gone off alone to visit her governess. She also told me that the wedding gown was missing from Jessamyn's closet. I'm sure I could find out much more."

"The last time you went to the Spencer mansion, you

had a reason to be there. Your article about the wedding gifts. What excuse would you use for going back there now?"

"I could pay a condolence call on Mrs. Spencer. That would be perfectly natural, under the circumstances."

"And after you'd offered your condolences, the butler would show you out. Or do you suppose Mrs. Spencer would allow you to go down to the servants' hall to question the staff?"

"I know I could think of some excuse to speak with Nellie, if only for a moment."

"You think that's all the time it would take you to find out anything useful?"

"Not then and there. But I could ask her to meet me on her day off. I believe she's Irish."

"And what has that to do with it?"

"My mother always gave our Irish servants Sunday mornings off to attend mass, of course. It's a customary arrangement. Nellie and I could meet for an hour or so in some secluded spot in Central Park, perhaps. I don't think I'll have any difficulty getting her to confide in me because—"

"She likes to gossip," he finished for her. "About trivial matters, maybe. But I doubt you'll get her to tell you anything important about the family. She has her job to consider. If Everard Spencer had the least suspicion she'd been gossiping about his personal affairs, he'd get rid of her fast. Do you know what happens to a pretty young servant girl who's been dismissed without a reference?"

Before she could answer, he went on quickly, his face hardening. "If she's lucky, she might get into an exclusive parlor house like Isobel Hewitt's. Otherwise, she'll find herself entertaining the customers in a concert saloon like

Harry Hill's. And when she loses her looks, she'll be out on the streets, where she'll sell herself to any man who can pay for her services."

"A girl like Nellie would never—"

"She would if she had no other choice except slow starvation."

She got to her feet and turned on him, her voice shaking with anger. "I came here to try to help you. And you've refused my help—you've insulted me with your indecent talk—you're the most arrogant, ill-bred man I've ever met!"

"Your experience with men is probably limited," he said calmly. "Amanda, hasn't it occurred to you that whoever killed Jessamyn is still out there? If you go prying into her murder you could end up like she did." His eyes searched hers. "Tell me, why do you want to find out who killed her?"

"I'm not sure you'd understand."

"Try me."

"That day I overheard the quarrel between Jessamyn and her father, I did nothing. Even when he struck her—"

"What could you have done?"

"If I'd stayed, and spoken to her, she might have confided in me."

"So you want to make amends by helping find her killer. Forget it. Have you ever been to Hell's Kitchen or the Five Points? Because that's where he's likely to be hiding."

"I'm not so foolhardy," she told him. "But as society editor for the *Gazette*, I'll be talking to people who moved in the same social circles as the Spencers. None of them will suspect I'm looking for information about Jessamyn."

He considered her words thoughtfully. "It's possible, I suppose," he conceded.

"Then you will let me help."

"I haven't said that."

"You certainly can't object if I try to find out what I can about that waitress. And I'll be safe enough in Talley's Ice Cream Saloon."

CHAPTER FIVE

The autumn sunlight glinted on the windows of Lord & Taylor's department store, where a group of well-dressed ladies were gathered to see the enticing collection of autumn hats. Amanda, in her bottle-green faille walking suit and matching bonnet, edged forward for a closer look. On Monday, she would give the fashion editor her opinion of these latest Parisian imports. But she did not linger, for she was anxious to get on to Talley's.

When she walked in a few minutes later, the ice cream saloon already was doing a brisk business. She glanced around the spacious dining room, with its high, vaulted ceiling and the ornate gold-leaf design on its white walls. Some of the customers were milling about the polished walnut counter, with its lavish display of candied fruit and chocolate bonbons, while others were already seated at the round, marble-topped tables, where they studied the glossy, gold-tasseled menus and chatted with their friends.

She watched the waitresses who trotted back and forth, balancing trays laden with dainty sandwiches, ice cream, and fancy pastries. Yesterday, she'd assured Ross Buchanan that she would find the waitress who had frightened Jessamyn, but now she wasn't quite so sure of herself. From a distance, they all looked alike in their starched black uniforms, with lace-trimmed aprons and caps.

"Good afternoon, Miss Whitney." The manageress, a lean, sharp-featured woman in her late forties, greeted her with a smile. She wore a grey faille dress set off with an embroidered collar and a small jet brooch. "This way, please."

When Amanda did not follow, she asked: "Is there a particular table you would prefer? That one by the window, perhaps?"

"I'm looking for a certain waitress," Amanda said. The manageress gave her a curious glance. "She's most efficient."

"All our waitresses are efficient and courteous." She led the way to a small table near the window. "Will this do?"

Amanda nodded and took a seat. "The waitress I'm looking for brought the menus to our table a few weeks ago, when I was with Miss Jessamyn Spencer—"

"Poor Miss Spencer—such a shocking tragedy. A young lady with everything to live for. On the threshold of matrimonial bliss, as one might say." Her voice hardened. "I'm sure the police soon will apprehend the fiend who committed the dreadful crime."

"No doubt they will," she agreed. The manageress started to turn away, but Amanda said: "Just a moment. The waitress who served Miss Spencer and me—I need to speak to her. She's a tall woman with a squarish face and light brown hair."

The manageress's smile looked a little forced now. Although she was making an effort to be polite, she had other duties to attend to. "I'm afraid I don't know which of our waitresses you're speaking of," she said. She beckoned to a young girl with a round, ruddy face, who hurried over with a menu.

Amanda scarcely glanced at the long list of delicacies before she ordered. "Jellied chicken salad and coffee, please."

She ate slowly, pausing from time to time to look around the crowded room. From the nearby tables she caught the chatter of other diners, well-to-do ladies with ample wardrobe allowances from husbands or fathers, and too much time on their hands.

"—and can you imagine—she wore black stockings with a pink tulle gown—such shockingly poor taste—"

"No doubt she wished to draw attention to her ankles—shameless, I call it—"

"—the Gainsborough hat she was wearing—all those yellow plumes—"

"—Yellow is so trying to the complexion—"

And from another table: "—Mama is planning a winter white dessert party—quite the rage this year. Decorations and refreshments, all in white. A white damask cloth—or perhaps lace. A centerpiece of white and cream roses—"

The conversations swirled around her, but she shut them out when her waitress returned. "Will there be anything else, ma'am? A glazed fruit tart with brandy sauce, perhaps? Or a lime sorbet?"

Amanda reached into her purse and set down a silver dollar, a tip so unusually generous that the girl's eyes widened. "Perhaps you can help me," she said. "I'm looking for a particular waitress, who served me at lunch three weeks ago, when I was dining with another young lady." She repeated the description she'd given the manageress.

The girl hesitated. "I'm not sure, ma'am. Tall, you say? With light brown hair?"

"That's right," Amanda said. "Her complexion was fair. Or perhaps she used a dusting of rice powder."

"Not while she was working here, she didn't. We're not allowed to wear powder or lip rouge, ma'am." She sounded scandalized at the notion. "It could be Gertrude Marek you're looking for. I do hope she hasn't got into more trouble."

Gertrude Marek. Now at least she had a name to go on, she thought with satisfaction. "What sort of trouble?"

"I really shouldn't talk about it," the waitress said with an uneasy frown. "Gertrude wasn't to blame—she always was a hard worker. It was that husband of hers who made that awful ruckus."

She broke off abruptly, as she caught the disapproving stare of the manageress. Were the waitresses forbidden to carry on any personal conversation with customers? Amanda wondered. She picked up the menu. "I believe I will have dessert, after all. The glazed fruit tart. And another pot of coffee."

"Yes, ma'am." The waitress hurried off, her starched skirt swaying. When she returned, Amanda spoke quickly. "You said Mrs. Marek's husband caused a—ruckus. What was it he did?"

"He came barging in here—week before last, it was. He'd had too much to drink, and he made an awful scene. He pushed one of our customers out of his way, and nearly knocked her down. And then he started cursing a blue streak—calling poor Gertrude the most shocking names— begging your pardon, ma'am. Of course, nothing like that ever happened here at Talley's before. The manageress called for a policeman to take him away."

"And what about Mrs. Marek?" Amanda prompted.

"Why, she was fired on the spot."

Amanda stiffened with outrage at the thought of such injustice. "But it wasn't her fault."

"That makes no difference, ma'am," the waitress said, with a look of resignation. "The manageress couldn't take a chance on Mr. Marek coming in and making such a scene here again, could she?"

"I suppose not," Amanda said reluctantly. "I wonder if Mrs. Marek's found another place yet."

"Not likely."

"But she wasn't to blame for her husband's behavior."

"Lot of good that'll do her. No decent place will hire her, because the manageress wouldn't give her a reference."

It was bad enough that Gertrude Marek was married to an evil-tempered drunkard, Amanda thought. Now she was without a job, too. Then she reminded herself of her own problem. How was she going to find Mrs. Marek? The waitress was already turning away, but Amanda stopped her. "You did say she's a hard worker."

"Yes, indeed, ma'am. Neat and quick, she is, too."

Amanda improvised quickly. "I might have work for her," she said. "Only for one evening, serving at a large party."

"That is kind of you. I'm sure she'd be grateful for the work."

"Can you give me her address?"

"She lives down on the Bowery, near Chatham Square."

"What's the house number?"

The girl's face fell. "I don't know—she never said."

"You're quite sure?"

The waitress nodded. "But wait—I do remember her saying the house was right across the street from a German beer garden."

"What was the name of the place?" There might be dozens of beer gardens on the Bowery for all she knew.

The girl's brow furrowed as she searched her memory. "Havemeyer's, that's the one. She used to say it wasn't easy for her to sleep, what with that oompah band blaring away half the night and all those shooting galleries. And the El trains rattling by."

Amanda felt a glow of satisfaction as she rode uptown in a hansom to Ross Buchanan's office. She had done her part.

He could take the search for Gertrude Marek from here. He knew his way around the city, and he'd have no trouble finding Havemeyer's Beer Garden. With his experience, she had no doubt he'd find out what connection—if any—there had been between Jessamyn and Mrs. Marek.

A charwoman was scrubbing the wooden steps, and Amanda lifted her skirt of her bottle-green walking suit to keep the hem from getting splashed. She stopped before his office door, knocked and waited, but she heard no sound from inside. She knocked again, harder this time, then turned the knob. The door was locked.

"If it's Mr. Buchanan yer lookin' for, he ain't here," the charwoman called out to her.

"You're sure?"

"He won't be back 'til Monday, miss—I heard him tell the janitor so."

Her spirits plummeted. She'd have to wait the rest of the weekend, and then get through her day's work at the *Gazette* before she could tell him what she'd discovered.

Outside in the street again, she stood in the autumn sunlight, and tried to decide what to do in the meantime. She could go home and tidy up her flat, and on the way, she might stop at the butcher shop and pick up a lamb chop for her dinner, a choice bit of liver for Leander. Or maybe he'd rather have sardines. For a cat she'd found half-starved, crouching in the courtyard of her apartment building, he certainly had developed a fussy appetite.

A self-deprecating smile touched her lips. Dinner with Leander, and then maybe she'd start the new novel by Marie Corelli.

Or . . . she could go down to the Bowery, and look for Gertrude Marek. But even if she succeeded in finding the woman, what excuse could she offer for having tracked her down? She thought for a moment, then decided to use the same reason she'd given the waitress at Talley's. True, she didn't have any need for someone to serve at a party, and it seemed unfair—even cruel—to raise false hopes. But maybe Maude, with her wide circle of acquaintances, might know of such an opportunity. First, she'd find Havemeyer's Beer Garden, and then, with any luck, she'd locate Gertrude Marek's flat.

A hansom rounded the corner, and stopped to let a passenger out. The driver picked up his whip, but before he could start off again, she raised her hand, then hurried over. "I want to go to Havemeyer's Beer Garden. I don't know which street, but it's somewhere on the Bowery—"

The driver peered down at her, his gaze moving from the jaunty ostrich plumes atop her bonnet to the elaborate passementerie trimming on her skirt. His shaggy eyebrows drew together in a puzzled frown. "Just a minute, Miss. Yer sure you want to go down to the Bowery?"

"Yes, I am." Although she spoke with confidence, she felt a small flicker of doubt.

"The Bowery on a Saturday night!" he muttered. Then he shrugged. "As ye please, Miss." He cracked his whip and they started off.

What would Ross say, if he knew what she was up to? True, he hadn't expressly forbidden her to go to the Bowery; but that was probably because it hadn't occurred to him that she might want to. She had heard of its unsavory reputation, and the cabbie's tone, his look of disapproval, confirmed her guess that it was no place for a lady. There was still time to tell him to take her straight home. But if the very sight of Gertrude Marek had thrown Jessamyn into a panic, she was determined to find out the reason why.

★ ★ ★ ★ ★

The hansom stopped in front of a low wooden building with an ornately-lettered sign: Havemeyer's Beer Garden. Amanda got out and paid her fare. The cabbie looked as if he were about to speak, then shook his head and drove off. A train rumbled by on the elevated tracks overhead, showering cinders on the crowd below. A man came down the long flight of metal steps, and a girl younger than Amanda, with lips and cheeks brightly rouged, sauntered up to him, the hem of her sleazy silk dress dragging on the dirty pavement. "Lookin' for a good time, Mister?" Her smile was bold and inviting. "Just you come along with me." They haggled for a moment, then she took his arm and led him down a flight of steps into a windowless basement next-door to the beer garden.

Amanda remembered the cabbie's look of disapproval when she'd mentioned her destination, but she wasn't about to turn back now. She stepped off the curb, then quickly lifted her skirt to keep it from dragging in the heaps of horse manure on the paving stones. Uptown, the streets were kept clean by city trash collectors, and the small boys who swept the crossings.

She reached the other side, where slatternly women lounged on the stoops, talking, drinking beer from tin cans and munching on sausages. One of them, thin and haggard, her hair straggling down around her face, held a wailing infant. She set down her beer can, unbuttoned her dress and shoved her nipple into the baby's mouth. Amanda quickly looked away.

She hurried past a second-hand clothing store, a pawnshop, and a shooting gallery, then paused before a stoop, where two women who'd been sharing a can of beer stopped drinking and stared at her. "Pardon me. I'm looking for a Mrs. Marek," she said. "Do either of you happen to know her address?"

"What d'ye want with her?" one of them asked. Amanda caught the suspicion in her voice. "Are ye one of them snooping settlement house ladies, come to poke yer nose into other peoples' business, wot don't concern ye?"

"Not this one, Lizzie! See them fancy feathers in 'er hat, an' that stylish dress. Got a good shape on 'er, too. Looks like a high-class whore t' me."

Amanda caught her breath, and her face went hot. Such language was no worse than she should have expected, when she'd come down to such a neighborhood. Her mother had often reproached her for acting impulsively. Maybe Mama had been right. After she had found out the name of the waitress who'd frightened Jessamyn, she should have left the rest to Ross Buchanan.

"An' what would a high-class whore be doin' down here, when she could be peddlin' her goods in the Tenderloin?" As Amanda hurried away, their shrill, derisive laughter followed her down the crowded street.

Near the corner she saw a group of noisy half-naked children sitting on the curb, splashing their bare feet in a stream of dirty water, indifferent to the rotting carcass of a horse nearby, swarming with flies. She looked away, her stomach churning, and fought down her impulse to find a cab—to get away from these loathsome surroundings as quickly as she could. But she'd come this far, and she wasn't about to turn back.

She caught sight of a young woman with a tangle of long black hair, sitting alone on a stoop, a cheap, tattered shawl wrapped around her shoulders. If she had washed her face and combed her hair, she might have been pretty.

She hesitated, reluctant to expose herself to further insult. Then she set her jaw and walked to the foot of the stoop. "I'm looking for Gertrude Marek. Do you know where she lives?"

"What d'ye want to know for?"

"I was told she'd lost her position at Talley's," she began.

"An' so she has! With that no-good husband bargin' into that fancy place where she was workin', it ain't surprisin'. The cops locked him up in jail overnight, but then they turned him loose, and he went off on another bender. Came home an' knocked her around somethin' awful. He's a mean-tempered bastard, that one."

Amanda flinched slightly. "I might have work for her." She rattled off the same improvised story about a possible job, waiting on guests at a large party.

"An' what's so special about Gertrude? There's plenty of women waitin' t' be hired cheap, at the slave market over on Grand Street."

"The—slave market?"

The young woman grinned. "Don't know what I'm talkin' about, do ye? That's what they call the corner where them women—Irish, most of 'em, right off the boat—go out early in the mornin' and wait to get a few hours' work."

"But I don't want just anyone," she said. "Mrs. Marek is an experienced waitress—she's neat and hard-working."

"And a fat lot o' good that'll do her, married to that lousy son-of-a—"

Amanda cut in hastily. "If you'll just tell me where she lives—"

"Next door to the pawnshop an' two flights up."

She thanked the woman and hurried on, past the pawnshop; hesitated a moment, before a wooden door, then entered the dark, narrow hall. A rat skittered by. She bit back a cry of revulsion, and started up the sagging stairway.

On the second floor, a skinny, ragged boy sauntered out of a cubbyhole, still buttoning his knickers. She caught a glimpse of the small, filthy toilet, and gagged at the overpowering stench. The boy grinned up at her. "Lookin' fer somebody, lady?"

"Mrs. Marek. Which flat is hers?"

He jerked his thumb to the right. "In there," he said.

She knocked, and after a moment the door swung open. "Good afternoon, Mrs. Marek—may I come in?"

"Who are you?" She spoke with a slight foreign accent Amanda couldn't quite place. Her housedress was faded, but clean. Her light brown hair was pulled back from her square face, and fastened in a bun. She was taller than Amanda, with wide shoulders and ample hips.

"My name's Amanda Whitney." She spoke quickly. "One of the waitresses at Talley's said you might want an evening's work."

"What kind of work?" She eyed Amanda with suspicion.

"A friend of mine needs an extra waitress, to serve at a large dinner party."

The woman hesitated, then stood aside. "Come in."

The room was poorly-furnished, but the floor was well-scoured, and a starched, white curtain covered the window. The large cast-iron sink in the corner had been well-scrubbed, and so had a wooden cupboard that held a mismatched set of clean dishes.

"Plenty of women need work—so why do you come here looking for me?"

She was still wary, but Amanda caught a flicker of hope in her gaze. "You waited on my table at Talley's a few weeks ago."

Mrs. Marek gestured toward a worn plush armchair. "Sit

down, please." Amanda seated herself, and the other woman took a straight-backed wooden chair opposite.

"I don't remember you, Miss—so many customers."

Though she'd found Gertrude Marek, the most difficult part of her task still lay ahead. She took a deep breath and plunged on. "I wasn't alone that day—a friend was lunching with me. I believe she knew you."

Mrs. Marek stiffened slightly. "Those fine ladies who came to Talley's—I served them, that's all."

But Amanda caught the look of fear in her eyes.

"Are you sure you don't remember me? Or the other lady?"

"Like I just told you, I didn't make friends with the customers. I was paid to wait on them, and that's all I did. Now, about this job?" She searched Amanda's face. "Do you really have a job for me? I think maybe you have another reason for coming here—yes?"

Amanda was in over her depth. She should have left this part of the investigation to Ross Buchanan, who would have known how to deal with Gertrude Marek. "I do have work for you, if you want it—"

But Gertrude stood up, and turned to stare anxiously at the door. Amanda caught the sound of heavy footsteps out in the hall. "You better go now, Miss."

"But the job—surely you can use the money."

Someone was fumbling with the knob. The door swung open and slammed into the wall. A piece of loose paint chipped off and fell to the floor. A big, burly man with a heavy mustache lurched into the room. His broad face was flushed, his chin and jowls dark with stubble. He wore no jacket, and his shirt was stained down the front. Even from where she sat, Amanda caught the reek of whiskey. He swayed, steadied himself against the doorframe, then glared at her. "Who's she? What's she doin' here?"

"She came here by mistake, Barney. She got the wrong address—she's just going."

"Don't lie to me, woman! I heard her sayin' somethin' about a job."

Amanda stood up and faced him. "I came to offer your wife an evening's work, waiting on guests at a private party." She hoped she sounded more self-assured than she felt.

"How much ye payin', lady?"

"A dollar—maybe two."

He seized his wife by the shoulder, and shook her. "So much money, for a few hours work, and ye said no?" He shoved her backward. Her body slammed into the cupboard with such force that the dishes rattled. "Rent's past due an' ain't a cent comin' in. Tell her ye'll take the job. Go on and tell her right now!"

"Barney, wait!" She clutched at his arm. "I don't believe she came here about any job—that was only an excuse—"

"What did she come for, then?"

"She's been asking questions about the Spencer girl. She was with her at Talley's that day when I—"

"That's enough! Shut yer mouth, woman." He pushed her away, then turned on Amanda. "We got nothin' to do with the Spencers! Don't know nothin' about them."

"Perhaps you know that Jessamyn Spencer was murdered," she said.

"Saw it in the papers, yesterday, like everybody else."

She kept her voice low, and chose her words with care. "I went to lunch with Miss Spencer at Talley's—your wife brought us the menus."

"So what? That was her job, wasn't it?" Barney advanced on Amanda. "Bringin' menus, carryin' trays. What's it yer business, anyhow?"

She saw the heavy shoulder muscles bunch up under the stained shirt. Fear shot through her, but she stood her ground. "When Miss Spencer saw Mrs. Marek, she ran out of Talley's, and back to her carriage."

"What're you gettin' at?"

"I think she recognized your wife—"

"I told you she wasn't here about any job," Gertrude interrupted.

"Shut up, ye stupid cow! I'll do the talkin' here!"

Now he was so close to Amanda that his whiskey breath enveloped her, and her insides started to churn.

"I don't know who the hell ye are, lady. But if ye think the likes of us ever had anything to do with that Spencer girl or any of her kind, ye must be loony."

It took all her will-power to keep her voice steady. "I only thought perhaps—"

His harsh laugh mocked her. "Ye figure we used to go to tea in that mansion on Fifth Avenue?" Even as he ridiculed her, Amanda glimpsed the suppressed violence in his small, pale eyes, the set of his unshaven jaw. "Or maybe ye think we were invited to that fancy weddin'—is that it?"

Too frightened to speak, she shook her head, then retreated toward the door.

"Ye come here lookin' for trouble, didn't ye?" He advanced on her, his face brick red.

"Barney, no!" his wife cried out. "Don't you lay your hands on her."

But he ignored the warning. He gripped Amanda's arm so tightly that she cried out. He pushed her through the door. "Nosey, high-tone bitch! You want trouble? I'll give you plenty!"

He forced her into the foul-smelling hallway. She struggled to break his hold, but it was useless. He was dragging her to the top of the steep stairs. He was going to throw her down. White-hot pain shot through her arm and into her shoulder. She drew back her foot and kicked him in the shin as hard as she could.

"Bitch!" His grip loosened for an instant, but it was long enough for her to wrench her arm free. She swung her arm, striking him on the side of the face with her fist. He shouted another curse and his hands closed around her shoulders.

He gave her a hard shove, and now she was falling backward down the stairs. She made a grab for the banister, caught it and regained her balance. He started after her.

Then Gertrude was beside him, clutching at his arm. "Let her go, Barney!"

"I'll break her neck!"

"No, Barney! Let her go!"

She ran down the stairs, dizzy with fear, afraid to look back. Somehow she reached the ground floor hall, dashed through the front door and out onto the sidewalk.

The El tracks blocked out the late afternoon sunlight and a few gas lamps already had been lit. As she started across the street, a brewery truck pulled by a team of Clydesdales bore down on her, and she heard the teamster shout a warning. She dodged the flailing hooves, and reached the opposite curb.

Couples decked out in cheap, gaudy finery went strolling into Havemeyer's, where a band was blaring out a polka. She paused to catch her breath, then she stared in dismay at her reflection in the window of the beer garden. Her jacket was ripped at the shoulder, her hat had been pushed to one side, and she'd lost some of her hairpins. She pushed a straggling lock of hair back into place, then straightened her hat.

"All alone on this fine Saturday night?" A man in a red and blue checked jacket and a cheap derby stopped and grinned at her. "What's the matter, did yer fella stand ye up? Come on inside with me and I'll treat ye to a first-class dinner." She turned away and hurried to the corner. There wasn't a cab in sight, and she dared not leave this busy street for fear she would lose her bearings. The green painted iron steps leading to the Elevated line loomed up ahead. Raising her skirt, she started to climb, jostled by the crowd.

At the top of the steps she hesitated, then fumbled in her purse. She had never ridden on the El before, but she watched the other passengers. Then she took out a nickel for her ticket, dropped it in the box, and went out onto the crowded platform.

"Always a mob like this during the five-cent hours," said a stout woman beside her. "But it's the fastest way t' get up town—and the cheapest." The train came rattling into the station and Amanda was pushed on board by the people behind her.

She sat down with a sigh of relief, smoothed her skirt and stared out the window. She caught a glimpse of brightly-lit saloons below, and rows of flats, with the shades pulled up on the second-floor windows. But she paid no attention to the people who were moving about inside; she was still far too shaken by her encounter with the Mareks.

Gertrude had lied to her. The woman had known Jessamyn, and so had Barney.

Her questions had frightened them both, and fear had unleashed Barney's capacity for violence. She shuddered, remembering his grip on her arm, the strength in his powerful hands.

But the ordeal had been worth it, for she had managed to get the information that would surely be useful to Ross Buchanan.

CHAPTER SIX

Ross rang the doorbell of a tall, red brick house with drawn shades, on a side street in the Ladies Mile. The parlor maid who opened the door would have done credit to any Fifth Avenue mansion.

"I wish to speak with Miss Hewitt," he said. He had put on an expensive suit of dark grey cashmere, grey kid gloves, and a black, Windsor silk scarf; only prosperous gentlemen were allowed inside Isobel Hewitt's establishment. He handed the maid his card.

"I'm sorry, sir," she said. "Miss Hewitt does not receive visitors this early in the evening. If you care to return in an hour or so—"

"I think she'll see me now."

She hesitated, looked him over with a quick, appraising glance, then stood aside. "Please wait in here, sir."

He followed her through the entrance hall and into the parlor, a large, high-ceilinged room; its tall windows covered by burgundy velvet drapes, trimmed with gold fringe and tassels. An ornate brass and wrought-iron chandelier cast a soft glow over the wide sofas heaped with brocade pillows. The fronds of giant potted ferns in the corners of the room cast intricate designs on the embossed, wine-colored wallpaper. Bouquets of full-blown roses—peach, dark red, and pink—scented the warm air. A pair of tall, silver candelabra stood on the polished mahogany piano, but the candles had not yet been lit.

Soon, the first of the guests would arrive. A pretty girl,

decked out in the height of fashion, would play the piano while another sang a sentimental ballad: "Only Friends and Nothing More," or "Let Me Dream Again." The others would carry on polite conversation with the gentlemen. Isobel Hewitt was highly selective, choosing her girls for their polished manners as well as their physical charms— nothing but the best would do for her select clientele.

He heard the rustle of taffeta, and turned to face the tall, shapely woman whose jet-black hair was set off with yellow ostrich plumes, fastened to a diamond band. Her pale yellow gown was trimmed with black lace. "Ross!" She smiled up at him. "It's been a long time."

As he bent and touched his lips to her cheek, he caught the delicate scent of her heliotrope perfume. "I need to talk to you, Isobel."

"Come along, then." She took his arm and led him up-stairs to her private drawing room. "Make yourself comfort-able." She gestured at a wide silk-covered sofa, and when he had seated himself, she said, "You're looking prosperous these days. Your services must be in great demand."

As hers always were, he thought. He glanced around the room, which was smaller and not as over-furnished as the downstairs parlor. She rang for the maid, who brought a de-canter of brandy and two bell-shaped glasses, then seated herself beside him, her full skirt billowing out around her. Although in her forties, her breasts still were high and firm, her throat and shoulders smooth and white.

They sipped their brandy in companionable silence for a few moments before she spoke. "I have a couple of new girls. One of them's a redhead—a lovely little thing, from Ireland. The other's a Swedish girl, right off the farm."

"I'm here on business, Isobel."

She eyed him warily.

"I'm working for Everard Spencer." Her lips tightened and he saw the lines of tension around her mouth. "He sent for me when his daughter disappeared last week. He wanted me to find her and bring her back before her wedding day. But now, of course—"

"He wants you to find her murderer." She was making an effort to sound detached, but she couldn't quite carry it off. "Doesn't he have any confidence in Superintendent Walling and his police force?"

"The police are doing their job, and he knows it. But he wants me to get to the killer first, and help him arrange a cover-up."

"Isn't it a little late for that now? Everybody knows the girl was strangled."

"But the newspapers are still holding back the most scandalous stuff," he said.

His eyes locked on hers. "They say the body was found in the Ladies Mile—but they don't mention that alley down there." He jerked his head toward the window. "I'm sure you can imagine how they'd like to handle that juicy bit of information. 'Miss Jessamyn Spencer, bride-to-be, found in the alley next to a bordello.' 'Did she come down here with the killer of her own free will and did you rent them one of your rooms for an assignation?' " He put a hand on her arm. "Just how much do you know about it, Isobel?"

"Are you going to cross-examine me, too?" Her eyes hardened. "Oh, yes—the police have been here. Not during business hours, of course. I paid them well for showing that much discretion. But they went poking around every room, and they questioned me and my girls. I told them the truth—I don't know anything about it."

"And, of course, your girls backed you up."

Her face went taut, and her skin stretched tightly over

her cheekbones. She no longer looked younger than her age. "It's true, Ross! I don't know a damn thing about Jessamyn Spencer's murder!"

"So Jessamyn was never inside your house, and it was only by chance that the killer tossed the body in your alley. You really expect the police to believe that?"

"They can believe whatever they want to," she shot back. "And so can you." She took a swallow of brandy, then spoke more softly. "But you should know better. It's taken me years to get where I am now, and it wasn't easy!"

"I know all about it, Isobel," he said.

"Who told you? Captain Rafferty?"

He nodded. "I worked with Rafferty before I quit the force."

"Then how can you possibly think I'd risk everything I've built up? That I'd get myself involved in the murder of Everard Spencer's daughter?"

"Is it possible that one of your clients sneaked her in here without your knowing about it?"

"Nothing happens in this house I don't know about. I think you're grasping at straws, Ross—because you haven't got any real suspects, yet."

"Anyone who's had any connection with Jessamyn Spencer is a suspect."

"I had no connection with the girl, or her family. We don't exactly move in the same circles."

"But maybe you know some of the same people. What about Howard Thornton? Is he one of your regular clients?"

"My clients are important politicians, bankers, railroad tycoons—the minister of one of New York's most fashionable churches turns up here regularly. Men like that pay well for my discretion."

"Does Thornton come here?"

"Suppose I don't tell you?"

"Don't play games with me, Isobel. I still have connections on the force. If you don't tell me what I need to know, you'll find the police camped on your doorstep during business hours. Along with a dozen reporters. How will your distinguished clients feel about that?"

He saw a glint of fear in her eyes. "Ross, I give you my word. I don't know anything about the murder!"

"Or maybe you're so concerned with protecting your business, you don't care that a frightened young girl had the life choked out of her?"

"That's a rotten thing to say! I hope the bastard gets caught—the sooner the better." He heard the rising tension in her voice. "I hope they hang him."

"Then start cooperating, Isobel. If I get to him before the police do, I'll see that your name's kept out of the papers."

"You're sure you can manage that?"

"Everard Spencer can."

As usual, the Spencer name had its effect. "All right, then. Thornton's not one of my regulars. But he's been here a few times."

"How did he behave?"

She spoke carefully. "He didn't get drunk or cause any trouble. He's a gentleman."

"What else can you tell me about him?"

She shrugged. "He's been living way beyond his means for years now. His racing stable's costing him a king's ransom. His yacht's damn near as expensive as Vanderbilt's *Corsair*. He's lost a fortune, gambling at Daly's place—he can't keep away from the faro tables. And he's in big debt to Canfield. Lost a bundle up there in Saratoga last summer. He was going to marry the Spencer girl for her father's money. But I'm sure you know all that—everybody else does."

"I happen to know something else—Jessamyn didn't want to marry him."

"So what? Her parents wanted them to marry. I guess the connection with the Thornton family would have meant a lot to a man who started out as a lumberjack, and married a laundress."

"The Spencers have come a long way since then," he reminded her. "That mansion on Fifth Avenue. A box at the Metropolitan Opera House, when it opens next fall."

"But they still aren't accepted in the best circles, are they? Jessamyn's marriage would've changed all that. Thornton's mother comes from the old Knickerbocker society. His father's side of the family settled upstate over a century ago."

"Jessamyn didn't want to marry Thornton, or any other man."

Isobel's delicately-arched brows rose slightly. "Did Everard tell you that?"

"I have a few other sources." He found himself thinking of Amanda, who was wracked by guilt, because she hadn't intervened in the quarrel between Everard and his daughter. Had he been wise to agree to let her help in the investigation? She was intelligent enough—and observant. But she was also impulsive and inexperienced.

He realized that Isobel was speaking again. "You can't seriously believe Thornton's a suspect. If he needed to marry the Spencer girl for her dowry, why would he want to kill her?"

"Tell me, Isobel—was there anything unusual about Thornton's behavior when he was with any of your girls?"

She took another sip of brandy, then set down her glass. "How should I know?"

"You just said nothing happened here you didn't know about," he reminded her.

"I didn't mean that every girl gives me a detailed report about the man she spent the night with. There are some who have their own peculiar—needs."

"How peculiar?"

"They want certain little extras—the kind their wives would refuse them."

"But your girls never refuse?"

She shrugged. "It's their business to satisfy the customers."

"Go on."

"There's a man who wants two girls in the room—one to share his bed, the other to watch. He pays double and never touches the second girl. He only wants her to sit there and pretend to be getting hot. She pleads with him to take her, but he refuses. She crawls to the bed on her hands and knees. She weeps with frustration."

"A girl like that could earn her living on the stage," Ross said dryly.

"Too bad these respectable wives aren't accomplished enough to do a little acting in the bedroom, too." She laughed. "If they did, it would be bad for my kind of business." Then she went on, "There's a mill owner who comes down from New England, a few times a year. He only wants twin sisters—beautiful, of course. They're not always easy to find on short notice."

"But you manage to give your customers what they want."

She drew a quick breath. "I don't have my girls chained or whipped or branded." Her eyes were shadowed, her face

93

grim. "You should know that much."

"I believe you," he said.

"I run a decent place. My girls are professionals. They work here because they want to. If they decide to leave, I never force them to stay." Her voice took on a hard edge. "And I don't use little girls—or boys."

He touched her arm lightly. "Let's get back to Thornton."

"Thornton's a little odd, but harmless."

"How odd?"

"Once he wanted a girl to get dressed up in a special outfit. She was supposed to be a virgin bride. Shy, frightened. I had to get her decked out in a bridal gown and veil."

"A bridal gown?" He was careful not to sound surprised; only casually curious.

"What of it? I've had more than one customer who wanted a girl dressed like a nun."

"You must have quite a collection of costumes here."

"Only a few, really—those that are most often in demand," she said. "If I need something special, there are theatrical costumers who can supply me on short notice."

"Never mind about them," he cut in. His eyes locked on hers.

She took a quick, sharp breath. "Ross—no! You can't think I'm mixed up in this!"

"When was Thornton here last?"

"Not for months. It's true, Ross! I give you my word."

"Do any of your patrons bring their own girls here?"

"I don't run that kind of a business—it's more trouble than it's worth. And even if I did, do you really believe I allowed Thornton to bring Everard Spencer's daughter into my house?"

Not Isobel, he thought. She was far too shrewd to take

such risks. But he couldn't give up his only solid lead. "You wouldn't have had to provide the outfit," he persisted. "Jessamyn was wearing her own gown and veil, white silk stockings and satin slippers with diamond buckles, when she was found in the alley."

"I don't want to hear any more about it!" Isobel interrupted. "I pay the police off, that's part of my overhead. And I paid a whole lot more to those officers who came here, asking about the murder. Dammit, Ross! I'll pay you off, too! Just keep me out of it!"

He got to his feet. "You should know I didn't come here for a pay-off," he said coldly.

"Sorry, Ross. I guess all this has shaken me up more than I realized."

"Spencer's paying me twice my usual fee. He wants the case closed before the *Sun* and the rest of those papers tell their readers that his daughter's body was found in an alley next to a parlor house."

The rouge stood out against the pallor of her face, but she put her hand on his arm and forced a smile. "Look, Ross, even you can't work day and night. The girls'll be coming downstairs soon. Choose any one you like, courtesy of the house."

He shook his head. "I'd like to take you up on that. But right now, I need you to answer a few more questions."

"I don't have much time," she began. Then, under his implacable stare, she gave way. "What do you want to know?"

"Have Everard Spencer or his son ever come here?"

"Not Clifford Spencer."

"What about Everard?"

"He used to drop by now and then. But he hasn't been around lately. He keeps a girl in a fancy flat over in the

Tenderloin now, or so I've heard."

"Do you know her name?"

"No, I don't."

"All right. But if you should happen to find out, let me know."

"Just keep me out of this, and I'll help you all I can."

She stood up, led the way to the door and out into the hall. As he followed her downstairs, he heard men's voices from the parlor. He pressed her hand lightly and said goodnight. She smiled and motioned to the maid to show him out. Then she turned away and went to greet her customers.

He went down the front steps, turned and walked into the narrow alley where Jessamyn's body, in her white gown and veil, had lain. The police had already searched the alley thoroughly; he wouldn't find so much as a lace handkerchief here, or a shoe buckle. He stared up at the windows on the second floor. None of the girls who occupied those rooms had admitted to having seen Jessamyn's body, or the man who had placed it there. Isobel's private suite was in the front of the house, overlooking the street. None of her windows looked out on the alley.

How long had the body lain here, before it had been found? Ross already had questioned Doctor Fergusen, the police surgeon; he knew the man from his days on the force. "Jessamyn Spencer was dead at least eight hours—maybe a little longer—before the cop found her," Fergusen had told him.

But it was unlikely Jessamyn had been brought to the alley by her killer before midnight, because there still would have been too many people about. Where had he killed her, and where had he hidden her body before he'd brought it here? And how had he carried the corpse down here to the Ladies Mile? In a closed carriage, perhaps? Or a wagon?

Ross heard the clop of hooves, and turned toward the street, where two men in evening dress, wearing high silk hats, were getting out of a hansom. They climbed the steps to Isobel's door. He waited until they'd gone inside, then hailed the driver.

Seated inside the cab, he looked out at the autumn fog that swirled along the deserted streets, softening the lines of the white marble storefronts and blurring the glow of the electric lamps. At Twenty-third Street the driver turned west, and took a shortcut through a side street, the cab jouncing over the cobblestones. Ross caught a glimpse of a woman in a dark dress and cloak. What was she doing out here at such an hour? The lady shoppers had departed long ago, and the salesgirls, too, had left the Ladies Mile.

The woman wasn't wearing the gaudy finery of a street-walker, and her head was covered by a shawl. Probably she was a seamstress who'd been forced to work late in the backroom of some fashionable dress shop. Seamstresses put in twelve hours of painstaking labor, sometimes more, to finish an order. Although she must have been exhausted from her long stint, she moved quickly on her way. Since the *Sun* had printed the account of the murder, no female would have dared to linger in the Ladies Mile after dark. The woman disappeared around a corner. She wouldn't feel easy until she was safe inside her home, with the door bolted behind her.

Seamstresses worked hard, but the women in the factories toiled even longer hours, and under more wretched conditions. Overwork, a poor diet, and the lint-filled air made them easy prey to consumption. Who could blame a girl for turning her back on the dubious benefits of respectability and going to work in a parlor house, if she was young and pretty enough?

But few parlor houses were as luxurious as Isobel's, and few madams treated their girls as well. During his days on the force, he'd come to know too many crib houses, down on the waterfront, or over in Hell's Kitchen, run by harridans who forced their girls to submit to whatever brutal treatment their customers inflicted on them.

I don't have my girls chained or whipped or branded. He believed what Isobel had said because he'd heard something about her background from Captain Rafferty, who'd long since retired from the force. At fourteen, she had been working in a brothel on Greene Street. When one of the other girls had been beaten to death by a customer, the place had been raided. Rafferty had led the raid. The madam had been sent to Blackwell's Island, and the girls placed in a refuge for fallen women, to be taught a useful trade. But Isobel was shrewd and ambitious—she had other plans. After a few months at the refuge, she'd walked out.

"I don't know where she went from there," Rafferty had told him, "but somewhere along the way, she found herself a wealthy old gent, who left her a legacy: enough so she could set herself up in her own business."

Ross had to give her credit for her determination. She had known what she wanted and she'd gone after it. As Amanda had done. He smiled at the unlikely comparison between Amanda and Isobel.

Amanda had led a sheltered life in her home on Stuyvesant Square. Although her father had lost his fortune, he had managed to pay off all his creditors. Amanda was driven by ambition; set on making her own way in an occupation not often open to women; but her job on the *Gazette* was respectable enough so that she was still accepted in the best society. She had been carefully sheltered from any sort of intimate contact with the opposite sex. He recalled her ingenuous account of the scandal at her school—a secret exchange of notes between a young French teacher and one of his pupils.

No doubt Amanda's own experience with men had been limited to a chaste kiss from a proper young gentleman in a darkened conservatory, or on a sleigh ride through the park. Had she reproached the gentleman with a few well-chosen words? Or had she responded with pleasure? Annoyed by his unlikely train of thought, he reminded himself that such personal matters were no concern of his. Amanda was not his responsibility.

Once again, he remembered how she'd looked, wrapped in her robe, her hair hanging in a braid over her shoulder: younger, and far more vulnerable, than she had at their first meeting.

He'd been right to make her promise to confine her investigation to places like Talley's Ice Cream Saloon. Moodily, he stared out at the dark, fog-shrouded streets. Probably he would have been wiser not to allow her to get mixed up in his investigation at all.

CHAPTER SEVEN

Because she had to attend a tea party at the home of Mrs. Stuyvesant Fish for the *Gazette*, it was nearly four o'clock before Amanda was able to go to Ross's office on Monday afternoon. She lifted the skirt of her burgundy velvet dress, then hurried up the stairs, and down the hall. She rapped on his door and waited with rising impatience until he opened it.

She was scarcely inside his office before she began to speak, her words coming with a rush. "I've found her, Ross, the waitress I told you about—the one who frightened Jessamyn. I went to Talley's for lunch on Saturday—"

"Slow down, Amanda." Ross took her arm and led her to the wide, leather sofa. "You sound as if you'd come running up here all the way from your office."

"I came in a hansom," she said. "Now, about the waitress—Mrs. Marek's her name."

"Are you sure it was seeing her that threw Jessamyn into a panic?"

"Quite sure. She wouldn't even admit she remembered having waited on Jessamyn and me—but I know she was lying!"

"What makes you think so?"

"Because she didn't even stop for a moment and try to remember. She answered right away."

"That proves nothing," he interrupted. "Talley's must have been crowded with shoppers on Saturday. Did you expect her to neglect her other customers and stand there at your table while you cross-examined her?"

"But I didn't speak to Gertrude Marek at Talley's. She isn't working there anymore—she was let go. But it wasn't her fault. Barney was to blame."

His dark brows drew together in a puzzled frown. "Barney?"

"Mr. Marek—her husband. He came to Talley's one afternoon, a few weeks ago. He was quite inebriated, and he made a shocking scene. The police had to be called to take him away. The manageress let Mrs. Marek go, without even a reference."

"And just how did you find out all this?"

"One of the other waitresses told me all about it. She didn't know the Mareks' address, but she did remember Mrs. Marek saying she lived across the street from Havemeyer's. That's a beer garden—"

"I know what it is—and where it is." His voice was tight with anger, and she flinched under his hard gaze.

"I came here first, straight from Talley's, but your office was locked, and the cleaning woman said you wouldn't be back until today."

"And then? Is it possible you were foolish enough to go traipsing down to the Bowery alone?"

"I didn't know how to get in touch with you."

He brushed aside her excuse. "So why didn't you wait until today?"

"Because I was trying to help," she said. "Mr. Spencer wants you to find Jessamyn's killer before the police do. That's what he's paying you for. So I thought the sooner I spoke with Mrs. Marek—"

"No, Amanda, you didn't take time to think. You forgot your promise to me, didn't you? Or maybe you chose to ignore it."

She'd come here expecting him to show some appreciation. How could he be so unfair? "I did find Mrs. Marek," she reminded him. "I thought that was what you wanted."

"Not if it meant your roaming around on the Bowery." With one swift movement, he was on his feet, glaring down at her. "We made an agreement. You'd try to pick up whatever information you could while you were carrying out your assignments for the *Gazette*, and leave the rest to me."

"And I will—from now on." She shivered at the memory of her brief foray into the slums. "I'll never go to the Bowery again, or Hell's Kitchen or—"

"Damn right you won't." He was too angry to choose his words with care, but that didn't seem important to her now.

"Ross, if you'll just calm down and let me finish—"

"I've heard enough. Now you're going back to the *Gazette*, where you belong."

"Not until I've told you what I found out about Gertrude Marek."

"I ought to carry you downstairs, toss you into a cab, and escort you back to your office."

She forced herself to meet his eyes. "But you won't. Because you need to know about Gertrude, and her husband."

"And how did you track him down? I suppose you made a tour of all the Bowery saloons."

She decided to ignore his sarcasm. "I talked to the women who were sitting out on the stoops of the houses across from Havemeyer's. One of them told me where Gertrude lived. Oh, Ross, it's such an awful place. The halls and stairs were littered with filth. A rat ran past me—one privy for all the families on each floor." She shuddered at the memory. "How can people live like that?"

"You think they live that way by choice?" he demanded.

"It's all they can afford. And there are plenty of worse places than the Bowery. Like that shanty-town north of Central Park—windowless shacks crowded with Irish immigrants right off the boat. And the filthy cellars in the Five Points, where men and women—children, too—sleep on damp straw mattresses for a nickel a night. Those cellars are a breeding ground for cholera and typhus, because they get the run-off from the sewers in Paradise Square."

She lapsed into stunned silence, as she tried to take in his description of a side of New York life that had been hidden from her until now. "Such places should be closed down," she said indignantly.

"Should they? On a freezing winter night, even a few feet of space in a Five Points cellar is better than a doorway. When I was on the force, the station houses were crowded with vagrants in winter. The cops let them bed down on wooden planks, and turned them out in the morning, so that the rooms could be hosed down. Believe me, Amanda, if the Mareks can afford to pay rent for a Bowery tenement flat, they're better off than some."

"That may be so," she conceded. "But Ross, I don't think has Gertrude Marek always lived in such squalor."

"What makes you think that?"

"I only saw the front room of her flat. The floor was scarred but it had been well-scrubbed. Her dress and apron were shabby but clean and starched. She wore her hair pulled back in a bun. She offered me a seat on a plush armchair, the only decent chair in the room."

"Wait a minute. Are you saying she let you in without asking why you'd come there?"

"She was suspicious at first," Amanda conceded. "But when I said I could get her an evening's work as a waitress at a private party, she wanted to know more about it. She'd been out of work for more than two weeks, and she needed money badly."

He gave her a look of reluctant approval. "You have a gift for inventing a plausible lie on short notice, I'll say that much for you."

She supposed he meant it as a compliment.

"Didn't she want to know why you'd come all the way down to the Bowery looking for her, when there are so many women who need employment?"

"I told her I'd been to Talley's that day, and I'd heard she'd lost her job. But when I mentioned that she'd waited on Jessamyn and me, a few weeks ago, she backed off. She insisted that she didn't remember anything about it. But surely she would have remembered Jessamyn's odd behavior—how she went running out of Talley's that way. Why do you suppose she was afraid to admit she'd waited on Jessamyn and me?"

"How should I know?" But he no longer sounded angry; she thought she saw a flicker of respect in his eyes. "Did you ask her any more questions?"

"I didn't get the chance, because that was when her husband came staggering in, reeking of whiskey. He'd heard me talking about the job, and at first, he was furious with her for refusing my offer. But as soon as she told him I'd been asking questions about Jessamyn, he forgot all about the money. He ordered me out."

"And you had sense enough to get out of there as fast as you could." When she didn't answer, his face darkened. "You did, didn't you?"

She chose her words carefully. "Not right away."

"Are you telling me you were foolish enough to stay there and tangle with a bad-tempered drunk?"

"I needed to find out if he'd known Jessamyn. I started

questioning him and he—"

"Go on."

"He took hold of me and forced me out into the hall. Gertrude tried to stop him—she kept begging him to take his hands off me. But he wouldn't listen. He dragged me to the stairs. So I kicked him in the ankle, hard. He loosened his hold for a minute, and I struck him in the face, as hard as I could. Then I ran downstairs and out the front door. My dress was ripped at the shoulder, but I wasn't hurt."

"You needn't sound so smug about it. I hope you realize that was pure luck."

"I know," she admitted, then went on quickly. "It was getting dark out and I couldn't find a hansom so I took an elevated train. I'd never ridden on one before. It was crowded and noisy but it was fast." If only he would stop looking at her that accusing way.

"You're pleased with yourself, aren't you? Don't you realize that drunken bum might have shoved you down the stairs?"

"But he didn't, and as you see, I'm quite all right. I admit I acted recklessly—but how was I to know what might happen, when I'd never been down to the Bowery before?"

"Do you honestly expect me to believe you never even heard what kind of a neighborhood it was?"

"I've read that the draft riots started down there, but those happened years ago during the war."

"And of course you don't know what goes on there now?" She shook her head. "You never heard about the concert saloons."

"Are they like Havemeyer's?"

"Havemeyer's is a respectable German beer garden, one of the few decent places down there. A concert saloon's no better than a brothel. There's a dance floor, and music—if you can call it that. But the 'pretty waiter girls' bring in the trade. They wear short skirts and white boots with bells around the ankles. If a waiter girl wants to keep her job, she takes a man upstairs to one of the little booths on the balcony above the dance floor. Once she gets him inside, she closes the curtains. Then she gives him whatever—services—he asks for."

"Ross!" Her cheeks flamed. "I don't want to hear another word!"

But he ignored her protest. "And there are peepholes in the walls, for men who want to watch."

How dare he speak to her of such obscenities? "That's enough!"

But he went on, his voice hard and inexorable. "The Bowery has plenty of cheap parlor houses, too. They get the girls young. Some of them no more than twelve. Of course, with disease and rough handling, they lose their looks fast, but there are always pimps on the prowl, looking for likely new recruits. Fresh and pretty with a good shape to them."

She flinched inwardly as she remembered the women she'd spoken to on one of the stoops. *Looks like a high-class whore t' me.*

"You're deliberately trying to shock me, aren't you?"

"Why would I waste my time doing that?" he demanded. "I'm trying to make you understand the risk you were taking, when you went down to the Bowery alone. I can see you're proud of yourself because you managed to get away with nothing worse than a torn dress. But you're not likely to be so fortunate, next time. So get out and go back to your respectable office, Amanda. Tell your eager readers all about the delights of the social season. Just don't come back here."

She sat motionless, her gloved hands folded in her lap.

"What are you waiting for?"

"I don't have to go back to the *Gazette* today. Mrs. Fairlie said I might have the rest of the day off, and write my article at home. I came here from the home of Mrs. Stuyvesant Fish. She entertained her guests with a 'pink-on-pink' tea party."

He stared down at her. "A what?"

She took advantage of his momentary distraction. "An 'all one color' party, if you prefer. They're the latest craze this season," she went on. "There were pink roses and carnations in little vases. Pink candles, pink linens and napkin rings. Pastries with pink frosting, and Rosy Trifle, topped with pink-tinted whipped cream."

"Enough!" But she saw the corners of his mouth twitch slightly.

"Mrs. Fairlie wants my article for this week's society page, so I'll have to get it done this evening and hand it in tomorrow."

"Then you'd better go home right away, and get started." He spoke more quietly now. "You only got mixed up in this case to salve your conscience. Because you have some farfetched notion that if you'd befriended Jessamyn, she'd have confided in you. And you believe that somehow, you might have prevented her death."

"It's possible, isn't it?"

"I doubt it. All right, Amanda, you've been of some help to me. But I've got no time to waste, keeping you out of danger. So you'll go back to your work, and I'll find out if there was any connection between the Marek woman and Jessamyn Spencer."

"I'm sure there was!"

"You think they might have known each other socially?"

"That's what Barney asked me. And he was even more sarcastic than you're being right now."

He ignored her gibe. "What did he say? Try to remember his exact words, if you can."

"I think so. He asked me if—if I thought his wife used to go to tea at 'that big mansion on Fifth Avenue.' That's what he called it. And then he said maybe I supposed he and his wife had been invited to the wedding. He sounded so resentful, as if he had reason to dislike the Spencers."

"Plenty of poor people are jealous of the wealthy."

"But he knew where the Spencers lived. And about Jessamyn's engagement."

"So does half of New York. Anybody who's been reading the papers would know all that."

"I think Barney Marek had a more personal cause for speaking as he did," she insisted.

"And what would that have been?"

"Maybe his wife used to be a servant in the Spencers' home. And perhaps she was badly treated there—maybe she lost her position, through no fault of her own," she hurried on. "It does happen, you know. Ottilie cannot have been easy to work for."

"Are you saying Barney Marek killed Jessamyn because the Spencers treated his wife unjustly? We don't even know that Gertrude worked for them, let alone that she was fired."

She brushed aside his objection. "Maybe he hadn't intended to kill her—only to kidnap her—"

"And just how do you think he got into the Spencer mansion without attracting the attention of the servants?"

"He might have passed himself off as an ordinary workman. There were so many strangers coming and going at all hours, preparing for the wedding reception. Decorators and florists and caterers. The Spencers' staff couldn't possibly have kept track of all of them."

"So Barney got in and concealed himself until late at night?"

"The house has a great many rooms that are rarely used."

"And then, when everyone was asleep, he slipped into Jessamyn's room—is that what you think?"

"It's possible, isn't it? Maybe Jessamyn put up a struggle. She started to scream and he only meant to silence her—"

"Even if Barney strangled her, he'd have used his bare hands."

"Suppose she was wearing her wedding gown, with the veil and wreath, when he came into her room."

"Why would she have been dressed like that, late at night?"

She ignored his look of disbelief. "The gown was sent over from the House of Worth, in Paris, but it needed alterations. Maybe Madame Duval—she's one of the most fashionable dressmakers in New York—what if she was still working on the gown, the afternoon of the day Jessamyn was killed?"

"Maybe! What if! You have quite an imagination, I'll say that for you. If you ever decide to quit the *Gazette*, you'll surely be able to earn a decent living writing those penny dreadfuls."

Penny dreadfuls, indeed! As if she'd even consider writing those lurid, yellow-covered novels that were devoured by servants and shop girls. But she refused to be side-tracked by his mockery. "Suppose, when Jessamyn saw herself in the mirror, wearing the wedding gown, she had another fit of panic like the one she had at Talley's."

"Because the sight of the gown reminded her that the wedding day was getting closer. And there was no way out?" Ross sounded doubtful, but at least he didn't dismiss her theory outright.

"I'm sure those fittings must have been a dreadful ordeal for Jessamyn."

"If it happened that way—and you're only guessing— wouldn't Madam Duval have helped her off with the outfit and taken it back to the shop?"

"I doubt it. If Ottilie thought that Jessamyn was on the verge of hysterics, she'd have wanted Madam Duval out of the house as fast as possible. Before she could get hold of a choice bit of gossip to share with her other customers."

"All right, so maybe the dressmaker left Jessamyn wearing her gown and veil. But one of the maids would have taken off the outfit and put it away. Or do you have a farfetched explanation as to why Jessamyn would have been in her room late at night, still decked out in her wedding finery?"

"No, I don't," she admitted. "But at least I can find out how Jessamyn behaved that afternoon, and whether or not she was still wearing her wedding gown when Madam Duval left."

"I suppose you're going to stroll into her shop and cross-examine her."

"There are less obvious ways of gathering information," she said. "I have a few dresses that need alterations. I'll visit the shop tomorrow and ask to see the latest fashion plates from Paris. And then—"

"And then, if you can't get her to tell you what you want to know, you'll find one of her seamstresses, who lives in Hell's Kitchen. And go running down there to question her."

"Not after what happened on the Bowery. Ross, I promise!"

"I know just how much your promises are worth. So you'll forget about the dressmaker and the rest of it. You'll go home right now, and write that article about Mrs. Stuyvesant Fish and her pink tea party."

He reached down, took her arm and jerked her to her feet.

She gave a sharp cry of pain and his hand dropped away. "I'm sorry. I didn't mean to hurt you."

"I'm not hurt. You startled me, that's all," she said quickly.

"You're a poor liar, Amanda. When you struggled with Marek in the hall, he only tore your dress. Or so you said." His face went dark with anger. "What else did he do?"

"Really, there no need for you to make such a fuss."

"He hurt you, didn't he? Let me have a look at your shoulder."

She gave him an indignant stare. "I most certainly will not."

"Take off your jacket, and open your shirtwaist." And when she made no move to obey, he took a step closer. "Or must I do it for you?"

She didn't doubt that he meant it.

"You told me to leave." She started to back away, but he was too quick for her.

He stood blocking the door. "Not until I see what that drunken ape did to you."

Her fingers were stiff and clumsy as she opened her jacket, then fumbled with the small bow at the throat of her embroidered cambric shirtwaist. He waited a moment longer, then pushed away her hand, undid the bow and the buttons.

Although the neckline of her linen chemise was far less revealing than the top of any low-cut ballgown, she felt painfully self-conscious under his dark, steady gaze. "Now, show me your shoulder."

She obeyed reluctantly, for she didn't doubt that, if she delayed even for a moment, he would push aside her undergarment, too. She heard the harsh intake of his breath, as he stared at the livid bruises.

Then he nodded brusquely. "All right," he said. "I've seen enough."

"I should hope so." She pulled her chemise back in place, buttoned her shirtwaist and jacket, speaking quickly all the while to cover her embarrassment. "I've had worse bruises from the recoil of a hunting rifle. I don't hunt animals," she went on. "But Papa taught me to shoot at targets, when we spent the summers together at our camp in the Adirondacks. And I've been thrown by a horse, more than once. I'm not a porcelain doll, you know."

"So you can handle a rifle and ride a horse. I'm sure you have many other accomplishments I know nothing about." He took her hands in his, and she found the warmth of his light grip surprisingly comforting. "Now, I want you to go home and soak a flannel cloth in arnica and keep it on those bruises overnight."

"I know how to take care of myself," she said, but she was moved by his concern.

"You haven't done such a good job of it so far." He glanced at her shoulder, now covered by her jacket. "You need a man to take care of you."

"I have no desire to marry."

"Why not? Do you dislike men?"

"Not at all." She gave him a level look. "But so far, I haven't met any man I'd care to marry."

"You'll have plenty of opportunities this season, with all those parties you'll be attending. And the opera, the theater, the charity bazaars. Surely there'll be more than one man who can meet even your exacting requirements." He smiled down at her. "By the way, what qualities would you demand in a prospective suitor?"

She drew her hands from his. "I hardly think that concerns you. I came here to tell you about my progress on the case—that's all."

"Then we probably won't be seeing each other again. This case doesn't concern you any longer, and we're not likely to meet by chance. We don't travel in the same social circles."

"Ross, be reasonable! I brought you some useful information—and I'll find more. As you've just reminded me, the season's in full swing now. Since I'll be mingling with people who are acquainted with the Spencers, I see no reason I shouldn't ask a few tactful questions."

Before he had a chance to protest, she went on. "You needn't look so grim. I've learned my lesson. From now on, I'll stay where I belong."

"I wish I could believe that."

She started for the door. "I'll be back to see you when I have something useful to report."

"Wait." He took out a business card, wrote on the back, then handed it to her. He gestured toward the instrument on the wall. "That's the number for my telephone," he said. "Now you'll have no excuse for taking a Saturday night stroll on the Bowery. Or go rambling around the Five Points. You will call me instead."

"Certainly, Ross." She gave him a quick nod, then left the office.

He stared moodily at the closed door, listening to the

click of her heels on the stairs. Amanda Whitney had a will of her own. He had ordered her off the case, but he couldn't force her to obey. And she knew it. He wasn't paying her a salary—Mrs. Fairlie was. So he couldn't stop her from going about her business for the *Gazette* and if she chose to make discreet inquiries, there wasn't much he could do about it. At least, she had promised to report back to him. That might be for the best, since it would allow him to keep track of her movements.

Why should he care if she got herself into a tight corner again? Just when had he decided he was responsible for her safety? He remembered those livid bruises on her soft white skin. All right, so he disliked the thought of any woman's being manhandled by a drunken ape like Barney Marek.

But Amanda wasn't just any woman. He was startled to realize that somehow, in the course of their brief acquaintance, he'd found himself thinking about her more often than he wanted to.

She wasn't a fragile creature whose pale complexion, small pouting mouth, and blonde curls fulfilled the conventional ideal of feminine beauty. Her cheekbones were strongly-defined, her jawline a bit too square. But, in her own way, she was strikingly attractive, with her wide-set amber eyes; her lustrous chestnut hair. Even without a fortune, she could marry a gentleman of her own class.

She had said she wasn't interested in finding herself a husband. And, as she had pointed out, there was no need for him to be concerned with her personal affairs. In spite of her frightening encounter with Marek down on the Bowery, she still was determined to help him with his investigation. It was just possible that she might be of some use to him.

He couldn't deny that she was observant and quick-witted. She had found Gertrude Marek, had contrived a plausible excuse to get into the flat, and had made a swift but thorough study of the place. And she'd even come up with an explanation—farfetched, perhaps, but not impossible—as to why Jessamyn could have been wearing her wedding outfit when she'd been killed.

Alterations, dressmakers, the House of Worth. He knew nothing of such matters; they were part of the society in which she'd grown up. Her breeding, her family background, still gave her access to that society.

When she'd spoken of her father and their summers together, in their camp in the Adirondacks, she hadn't been talking about a crude log cabin. The camp had been a handsome, well-furnished house with a staff of servants. There had been a stable with thoroughbred horses for Amanda and her father to ride on the secluded mountain trails; a lake for boating and fishing.

Probably her father had been forced to sell the place, along with the townhouse on Stuyvesant Square, in order to help pay off his creditors. And he had paid them off, down to the last dollar. He'd been a man of honor, determined to make up for the depredations of his larcenous partner.

She had inherited her father's sense of honor, his inflexible conscience. She really believed that, because she hadn't intervened between Everard and Jessamyn—much good it would have done—she had an obligation to help find Jessamyn's killer.

All right, he couldn't stop her from trying. But he could see to it she didn't risk her neck again.

CHAPTER EIGHT

Although Amanda was anxious to question Madame Duval as soon as possible, her time was no longer her own; she had to restrain her impatience until she had completed her day's assignments for the *Gazette*. She had selected two of her dresses, and had taken them with her to the office, but it was not until late in the afternoon that she arrived at the dressmaker's shop, carrying the large, pasteboard boxes. Even at this hour, there still were a few other customers ahead of her. She politely refused the services of an assistant, seated herself on a small rosewood and velvet chair, and flipped through the pages of *Madame Demorest's Mirror of Fashions*, the *Gazette*'s closest competitor. "This elegant dress of magnolia satin . . . pointed basques . . . feather fans with shaded tips . . ."

"Mademoiselle Whitney. I have not had the pleasure of seeing you for some time." Madame Duval, a tall, thin woman, with a long, narrow face, had served Amanda and her mother in the past. When Amanda explained the purpose of her visit, the dressmaker led her to one of the fitting rooms. She looked over the cinnamon taffeta ball gown, with swift expertise. "We will add a small bustle and a train of dark brown silk," she said. And for the blue visiting costume, she assured Amanda that a frill of guipure lace, to be inserted at the neck and down the front, would be most suitable.

"Now, do let me show you our new shipment of fine fabrics. We have a golden brown Bengaline that would be most

116

flattering for a walking suit, and an apple green faille for a ball gown. A cloak in jade velvet, perhaps. It is not too soon to start on your new winter wardrobe."

"The two gowns I've brought you, once they've been altered, will be all I'll need," she said firmly.

"For the whole season? Surely not, Mademoiselle!" She gave Amanda a conspiratorial smile. "I should ask only for some small mention of my shop in the *Gazette* now and then."

Of course, Madam Duval knew of her family's changed circumstances. Although she told herself it was nothing to feel ashamed of, her cheeks went hot, and she looked away. "Perhaps we will discuss it another time."

"As you wish," said Madame Duval, then tactfully changed the subject. "I read your article about Mademoiselle Spencer in the *Gazette*. *Pauvre petite*—such a tragic fate for one so young." She sighed. "And to think that I was with her that last afternoon."

"Were you, indeed?"

"Ah, yes. I brought her wedding gown to her home for the final alterations." She shook her head and sighed. "Who would have imagined that she would never wear it?"

So Ross had been right: Everard Spencer commanded enough influence to silence the press, at least for the time being. Although more than one reporter with a connection to an officer on the police force already must have discovered that Jessamyn had been wearing her wedding gown when she had been found in the alley, none of the newspapers had printed a word about it.

"I suppose you completed all the alterations that afternoon?" she asked.

"Not quite all." The dressmaker's dark eyes narrowed slightly, and a crease between her arched brows deepened.

"Mademoiselle Spencer usually was most patient and obliging through all her other fittings. But on that last visit, she appeared to be restless—distressed."

"Perhaps she was fatigued?" Amanda prompted.

"No doubt you are right." The dressmaker shrugged. "At any rate, Madame Spencer asked me to leave before I was able to complete the alterations."

"And so you brought the gown back here to the shop."

"Mais non." The dressmaker shook her head. "Madame Spencer would not even permit that I should help her daughter off with the gown and veil." She sighed. "To think of that exquisite gown, designed by Worth, himself. A gown that was to have been worn to the altar. I wonder what has become of it?"

What would the dressmaker say, if she knew that Jessamyn had been wearing the gown when she had been killed—that her body had been found in the alley next to a brothel, still clad in white satin and lace, with the wreath of orange blossoms wrapped around her throat?

Although Amanda briefly considered telephoning Ross, to tell him what she'd already learned, she decided to wait and to try to gather more information before she saw him again. The following day, she left the office early in the afternoon and went to pay a condolence call on Ottilie Spencer.

"Mrs. Spencer is not at home," Nellie told her.

Of course, Amanda recognized the formal excuse for what it was: a polite refusal to see an unwanted visitor.

"I trust that Mrs. Spencer has begun to recover from the shock of her bereavement," she said.

"She's bearing up, Miss."

"Such a dreadful experience. It must have been difficult

for the staff to carry on with their customary duties."

"Yes, indeed! Miss Tuttle took on something awful. And in all the time I've been working here, I've never seen Cook that upset before."

"How long have you worked here, Nellie?"

"Six years, Miss."

"And you plan to stay on?"

"Of course, Miss. It's as good a place as any other. Mr. Harland is a bit strict sometimes, but he's decent enough."

"And I suppose you get time off to visit with your family."

"I don't have family over here, Miss—they're all back in Ireland. But I get one afternoon a month to visit with friends. And I have my Sunday mornings off, for early Mass."

When Amanda asked Nellie to meet her at the Dairy in Central Park, after church, the girl looked surprised, but she agreed readily enough.

On the following Sunday morning, Amanda waited in front of the Dairy, a small, gothic style structure on the south end of Central Park. She had chosen the place for privacy; mothers and nursemaids, with their small charges in tow, would not start converging on the Dairy for at least an hour. The music had not yet started at the carousel nearby, and its brightly-painted horses stood motionless in the bright autumn sunlight. The only sounds were the occasional rattle of carriage wheels in the distance, the dry rustle of maple and sour gum leaves. From time to time, the breeze sent a shower of crimson, copper, and gold swirling to the ground.

"Good-morning, Miss Whitney." Amanda turned and saw Nellie hurrying toward her, dressed in her Sunday best:

a dark-grey flannel suit trimmed with soutache braid, and a black felt hat with a jaunty feather. "I'm sorry I kept you waiting, Miss," she said. "I got here fast as I could."

"Have you had your breakfast?"

"No, Miss. But Cook always keeps the porridge and tea hot on Sundays, for them that go to early Mass."

"Come along with me." She led the way into the Dairy, chose one of the small tables, then ordered a pot of hot chocolate and a plate of cinnamon buns. Nellie waited until Amanda started to drink, before she picked up her own cup.

Amanda said: "I'm sorry I didn't have an opportunity to speak with Mrs. Spencer the other day, but I quite understand. It must be such a difficult time for the family."

"Yes, Miss."

"And the staff, too, of course. I suppose Miss Tuttle felt the loss most keenly."

"Indeed, she did."

"No doubt she was devoted to Jessamyn."

"Miss Tuttle was afraid she'd be let go." Nellie broke off a piece of her frosted cinnamon bun. "It's not easy to find another position at her age. But Mrs. Spencer said she could stay on to help with mending and ironing the linens and such."

It hadn't occurred to Amanda that, although Miss Tuttle might have mourned Jessamyn's untimely death, she'd had more practical matters to consider. "It was thoughtful of Mrs. Spencer to keep her on," Amanda said. "Although Miss Tuttle's present duties are quite different than what she's been used to."

"It's been a comedown for her, and no mistake. And she's always been uppity, has Miss Tuttle." She finished her chocolate and set down her cup. "Not a bit like Gertrude— she acted civil to the rest of us."

"Gertrude?" It took some effort to keep her tone casual.

"She was Miss Jessamyn's personal maid long before Miss Tuttle took the position. The Spencers found her when they were traveling around Europe. She'd worked for a high-class German lady over there. An—aristocrat, with a fancy foreign title and all."

Amanda guessed that Ottilie Spencer, impressed by such lofty credentials, had spared no expense to get Gertrude to leave her employer and come to New York.

"But even so, Gertrude didn't put on airs. And she was real good at her work," Nellie went on. "She could iron the finest lace edging on one of Miss Jessamyn's gowns, without ever scorching it the least bit. And mend a rip in a silk petticoat or a stocking so you couldn't see the stitches. A willing, sensible girl, she was—at least we all thought so. And then what did she do but go and marry the head coachman!" She set down her empty cup.

"You think she chose unwisely?"

"I do. And Cook thought the same." She cocked her head to one side and smiled. "Still, I'll admit Marek was a fine figure of a man decked out in his black coat with all that gold braid."

So, both Barney and Gertrude had worked for the Spencers. She could hardly wait to see the look on Ross's face when she told him. But with Nellie here, and in a talkative mood, she might be able to gather even more information, if she went about it the right way.

"Another cup of chocolate?" she asked.

"Yes please, Miss." She smiled shyly. "This is a real treat. I never expected to be sittin' here with a lady like yourself."

But Amanda was not about to be side-tracked. "Did the Spencers approve of the match?"

"Gertrude didn't need their approval, because she married him after the Spencers let her go."

"They dismissed her?"

"They did, in a manner of speaking. But Mrs. Spencer wrote her a good reference, and the master gave her a handsome sum of money. Cook told her she ought to put the money into a savings bank and then look for another position. Plenty of ladies would've hired her. But she married Barney Marek instead, and he quit his job, too, and off they went."

"When did all this happen?"

Nellie thought for a moment. "A little while after she brought Miss Jessamyn home from that town up the Hudson."

Amanda wanted to ask her the name of the town—Ross would want to know—but she hesitated to question her outright, for fear the girl might become suspicious of her interest in the Spencer family. "There are so many charming towns along the Hudson." She waited for Nellie to supply the name; when she didn't, Amanda went on. "And such delightful pastimes—dances, picnics, boating on the river, and ice-skating in winter. Nothing so elaborate as we have here in the city, but perhaps Jessamyn felt more at ease in quiet surroundings."

"I think she did," Nellie agreed. "She wasn't much for big parties and such, Mrs. Spencer sent her to dancing classes and hired the best teachers—piano, singing, sketching—and I don't remember what else. And the Spencers gave a fancy birthday party for her every year." She sighed and shook her head. "But it seemed to me the guests enjoyed themselves more than Miss Jessamyn. She'd sit off to one side, with hardly a word to say to any of them."

"Still, she must have had a few close friends of her own age."

"Not that I know of. But she did have her pets, though. Her Persian kitten, and that big hound—a Newfoundland, they call it. And she was most especially fond of horses, so Mr. Spencer hired a riding master to give her lessons. Devin O'Shea, his name was. He had black hair, blue eyes, and a smile that would charm the birds from the trees."

And had he charmed Jessamyn? Amanda forced herself to remain silent.

"They went riding in the park nearly every day," Nellie went on. "It seemed like she might be comin' out of her shell, as you might say. And then that Devin O'Shea, he went off—just like that. He never gave the master a word of notice."

"I suppose Jessamyn must have been surprised?"

"Surprised! It was a lot worse than that, I can tell you, Miss. She took on dreadful, she did."

Amanda finished her chocolate and set down her cup. "How old was she then?"

"Fourteen—no, fifteen. Right after her fifteenth birthday, it was. She went into a—decline. That's what Mrs. Spencer called it. She wouldn't come out of her room, not even to have dinner with the family. Took her meals upstairs. Cook fixed all her favorite dishes, but the trays came back to the kitchen hardly touched. Then, after a month or so, the master sent her away, with Gertrude to look after her."

"I suppose he thought a rest cure might help—a visit to a spa, perhaps?"

"It would've taken more than a rest cure to get her out of that sort of trouble—" Nellie broke off abruptly, and her round cheeks went deep pink. She caught her underlip between her teeth and fixed her eyes on her cup.

Amanda pretended not to notice. "A stay at a well-run

spa, with plenty of fresh air and exercise can be most beneficial."

"Yes, Miss," Nellie agreed dutifully. "I suppose so."

"But didn't Gertrude object to being separated from the coachman?"

Nellie stared at her in surprise. "It isn't a servant's place to question the master's orders."

"And I suppose the separation wasn't a long one."

"Oh, but it was, Miss. They were gone nearly a year. Then, right after they got back, Gertrude was let go."

A stout, well-dressed lady entered the Dairy, accompanied by two small boys in sailor suits. From nearby, Amanda heard the lively music of the merry-go-round. The painted horses were moving up and down now, and the two boys clamored for a ride. "First you will have your milk and gingercakes," the lady said firmly.

Nellie would have to return to the Spencer mansion soon. Amanda spoke quickly. "Did you ever hear from Gertrude after that?"

"She dropped by once, dressed fine as you please in a coat trimmed with passementerie, French-kid boots, and a big hat with ostrich feathers. Came right down to the servants' hall, she did, and told us that Marek had bought himself a business of his own—with her money, I suppose. Wasn't much of a business, to my way of thinking. One of them shooting galleries. With a space for dog fights in the cellar. A nasty kind of sport, dog-fighting, wouldn't you say, Miss?"

"It certainly is," Amanda agreed. "I hope when she went upstairs to visit with Jessamyn, she said nothing about the dog fights. Jessamyn was so fond of animals."

"Why, she never went up to see Miss Jessamyn at all. She took tea with us in the kitchen, then she went straight off. Back to her precious Mr. Marek, I suppose. And that was the last we saw of her."

"Had Mrs. Spencer already hired Miss Tuttle to take her place?"

"Oh, no, Miss! She'd had to hire and fire three others before Miss Tuttle."

"But surely Jessamyn wasn't so hard to please."

"She didn't seem to care about how any of the maids dressed her hair, nor what outfit she wore, if that's what you mean."

"Then why was it so difficult to find her a suitable maid?"

"Because—" Nellie hesitated, her eyes troubled. "She used to take on something awful—mostly at night. We heard her crying—and more than once she screamed like she was having a nightmare, poor thing. Other times she'd get up and roam around the house until dawn. Mrs. Spencer blamed the maids, but it wasn't their fault, was it?"

"I don't see how it could have been."

More customers had come into the Dairy. Nellie stood up quickly. "I'd better be getting back now. I do thank you for the chocolate and buns. It's been a real special treat for me."

"You didn't lose any time making use of my telephone number," Ross said, as he seated himself on the sofa in Amanda's parlor. Leander, who had been curled up asleep on the opposite end, awoke and regarded the visitor with a fixed stare.

"I'd have called even sooner," she said. "My visit to Madame Duval's shop wasn't a waste of time, but I wanted to find out more, before I called. And now I have."

The late afternoon sunlight, slanting through the tall

parlor windows, caught glints of auburn in her dark brown hair. She leaned forward in her wicker chair, her cheeks flushed, her amber eyes aglow, and told him of her talk with Nellie. "As soon as Nellie left the Park, I went to telephone you from the lobby of the Fifth Avenue Hotel."

"Wait a minute," he interrupted. "You met the Spencers' parlor maid in the park, purely by chance?"

"Certainly not. I paid a condolence call on Mrs. Spencer, last week. She didn't receive me, but Nellie agreed to meet me today, after she'd come back from church. We stopped at the Dairy, and I found out more than I'd expected to."

He held up his hand. "Maybe you'd better start with Madame Duval."

"If you wish," she said, with obvious impatience. "I brought two dresses to her shop to be altered. She wanted to provide me with a whole new wardrobe, in return for mention of her shop in the *Gazette*."

"And you refused."

She looked surprised. "How did you know?"

"It was the only ladylike response," he said.

"But I do need more clothes for the season."

"Then by all means, take her up on the offer," he said. "Now, what about Jessamyn's wedding gown?"

She repeated her conversation with the dressmaker. "So you see, I was right. Jessamyn was on the verge of hysterics, that last afternoon. And she was still wearing her wedding gown when Madame Duval left the house."

"But what about the rest of it? How do Gertrude and Barney fit in?"

"Gertrude worked for the Spencers years ago, when Jessamyn was fifteen. She was Jessamyn's personal maid. And Barney was their head coachman. Nellie told me so."

She paused to savor her triumph. "And there's more. When Gertrude left the Spencers, Everard gave her an excellent reference and a handsome sum of money. Enough so that, when she married Barney, she was able to set him up in business."

"I wouldn't have expected Everard to be so generous, unless he had something to gain."

"Maybe he did. I think Everard was trying to make sure Gertrude wouldn't talk about—a family scandal."

"What kind of a scandal?"

"When Jessamyn was fifteen she became infatuated with her riding master, Devin O'Shea. They were together nearly every day. Then he left without giving notice, and Jessamyn was so devastated that she went into a decline. Her parents sent her away to a town up the Hudson."

"What town was it?"

"Nellie didn't say, and I didn't want to ask outright. But when I suggested Jessamyn might have gone to a spa for a rest cure, she said—" She looked away.

"Go on."

"She said it would have taken more than a rest cure to help Jessamyn out of 'that sort of trouble.' "

She heard the quick intake of his breath. "And just how long was Jessamyn gone?"

"Nearly a year. Ross, do you think that she and the riding master—that he seduced her and left her in a—in the—"

A proper young lady like Amanda didn't use the word 'pregnant'—certainly not in speaking with a man. "It's possible Jessamyn was carrying his child, and was sent away to save her reputation. That's what you're trying to say, isn't it?"

"Yes, but—" She gave him a puzzled frown. "Suppose it

happened that way. What could have become of the baby?"

"An abortion?" He ignored her shocked expression. "But why would the Spencers have sent her away when there are plenty of midwives and 'female physicians' here in New York who practice that trade? If Jessamyn was gone all that time, it's because her parents allowed her to go through with her pregnancy."

"But what about the baby?"

"She probably left it at a baby farm." He saw the complete lack of comprehension in her eyes. "A home out somewhere in the country where an unmarried young lady can leave her unwanted offspring."

"But how dreadful for Jessamyn—to give up her child—"

"It would have been a lot worse for the child," he said. "A baby farm's a living hell, run by some harridan who gets as much money as she can up front." The color drained from Amanda's face. "Many of the babies die of disease, starvation, neglect, before the end of their first year." The stricken look in her eyes told him he had already said too much, but anger drove him on. Anger at a system that tolerated such places—anger at Amanda, who had been sheltered from even knowing that they existed.

"Of course, some of them grow up in spite of all the odds. And the creature who runs the place makes a profit off them. A pretty little girl of eight or nine brings a good price."

"She is adopted?"

"She's sold into a brothel."

"No! I don't—I can't believe that!"

Or, more than likely, she didn't want to. "Some men take their pleasure with children."

She swallowed hard and pressed her clenched fist to her lips. For a moment he thought she was going to be sick.

He'd gone too far, and now he searched his mind for some way to distract her.

"There's one thing I don't understand, though. If Jessamyn had been carrying Devin O'Shea's child, how could she have kept her secret from her personal maid?" he said.

"Gertrude knew about it, because she went with Jessamyn on the trip up the Hudson." Although Amanda spoke in an even tone, she still had not regained her color. "Then, after nearly a year, Gertrude accompanied her home. And shortly afterward, the Spencers let her go."

She went on to tell him the rest. "Gertrude married Barney, and set him up in a shooting gallery. She came back to the Spencer mansion only once, to visit with the servants. But she didn't go upstairs to speak with Jessamyn at all."

"Then, as far as we know, Jessamyn never saw Gertrude again until that day at Talley's. That might explain why she panicked and ran."

"But what about the rest of it? Isn't it possible that Gertrude told Barney she'd seen Jessamyn?"

"And he decided to kidnap Jessamyn, but the kidnapping went wrong, and he killed her." He shook his head. "You're only guessing, Amanda."

"Barney would have been capable of murder. He's hot-tempered and brutal."

"So is Everard," Ross observed. "He struck her in a fit of rage, didn't he? I'm not saying he killed her. The day he called me in on the case, he gave me a solid alibi, even before I'd asked him. He told me he hadn't come home to dinner, that he'd been out all that night, and never returned until the following morning. That's when Ottilie told him that Jessamyn was missing."

"Did he say where he'd been all that time?"

"He spent the night with his mistress," he said.

"He admitted it?"

His dark grey eyes glinted with amusement. "Does that shock you?"

She was silent for a moment. The only sounds in the parlor were the ticking of the mantel clock, the crackling of the fire on the hearth.

"I don't suppose I should be surprised that a man like Everard Spencer would consort with—such women. Do you think she would confirm Everard's whereabouts that night?"

"She will, if Everard tells her to."

"Are you saying you don't believe him?"

"I don't believe anyone, until I have every possible proof."

"Then perhaps you should question Clifford, too," she said. There was a sharp edge to her tone.

"You don't believe that a handsome gentleman with elegant manners is capable of committing murder?" He did not wait for her answer. "I've already questioned him, and it would seem there's no reason to suspect him. He had dinner at home that night, with his mother, before they went to Wallack's Theater together. They were seen there, they talked with friends during the intermissions. And after they returned home, one of the maids brought them a light supper. They both retired shortly after midnight."

Leander opened his eyes, stretched, then came and sat beside Ross, who reached down and rubbed his jowls.

"Did you also speak with Clifford's valet and Ottilie's personal maid—just to make sure they went to bed?"

"Clifford told his valet not to wait up. As for Ottilie's maid, maybe you could speak to her. You certainly managed to win Nellie's confidence on short acquaintance. By the way, did she tell you what became of that dashing Irish riding master?"

"She only said he'd left without a word to anyone."

As she spoke, he saw her glance quickly at the mantel clock.

He stopped rubbing the cat's jowls. Leander gave him a reproachful look, then leaped to the floor. "It's time I was leaving," he said. "You've done well, Amanda. Just remember to stay on your own side of town."

"I'm going to the Academy of Music, this evening," she told him, with a slight smile. "I hope that meets with your approval."

When he emerged from the house, the sunlight had faded. Upstairs, Amanda would be starting to get ready for her evening at the opera. Did she have an escort, a gentleman of her own class? Suppose she had? It was no concern of his. Theirs was a working relationship, and she had provided him with several promising leads. She had done well—far better than he'd expected.

So why hadn't he shown some consideration for her sheltered upbringing? Why had he spoken to her with such unnecessary bluntness? Baby farms and child brothels!

But since she had involved herself in this case, there was no way he could hope to shield her from an awareness of the underside of society. Right now, he had more immediate concerns than guarding Amanda's delicate sensibilities.

He'd already questioned the stablehands, along with the rest of the Spencers' staff, but he'd known nothing then about Devin O'Shea. Or Barney Marek. Armed with these new leads, he'd go back tomorrow morning, and see what more he could find out.

CHAPTER NINE

Although Amanda's father had been forced to sell his private box at the Academy of Music, Quentin Van Wyck, a friend of the Whitney family, had offered her the use of his own box, before he and his wife had departed for the more congenial climate of North Carolina. The Van Wyck box was the ideal place from which to observe not only the occupants of the other seventeen red and gold boxes, but the rest of the audience in the orchestra stalls below.

She drew her small, leather-covered notebook from her purse, took down half a page of notes. Her eyes moved quickly over the crowd. Some were still applauding, after the first act of *Lucia di Lammermore*; others were already moving toward the lobby, to enjoy refreshments and gossip. She jotted down a few more lines, then rose, with a rustle of taffeta. Madame Duval had completed her alterations on time, and Amanda was satisfied that the two year old garment was now quite suitable for the new season.

She left the box, and followed the crowd out into the lobby, where bejeweled ladies and their escorts were gathering around the long refreshment table.

"Miss Whitney, this is an unexpected pleasure." She turned to see Clifford Spencer smiling down at her. "Would you care for a glass of champagne?"

"Thank you, Mr. Spencer." It took some effort for her to conceal her surprise. She had not expected that he would attend a public entertainment so soon after Jessamyn's death.

As they stood sipping their champagne, she caught the envious glances of the young ladies, the speculative looks of their mothers. Opening night at the Academy was the start of the match-making season; ladies with marriageable daughters were sizing up the field of eligible young gentlemen.

"I'm sorry my mother wasn't able to take tea with you, when you called on us last week," Clifford said. "She has not been able to receive visitors as yet. She is still prostrate with grief. I'm sure you understand."

"Yes, indeed," said Amanda. Although she had never noticed any particular warmth or affection between mother and daughter, she reminded herself that, as an outsider, she knew little about their deeper feelings.

If Jessamyn had, indeed, borne a baby out of wedlock, and Ottilie had agreed that the child must be given up, she might now feel guilty over her decision. Perhaps, now that she had lost Jessamyn, she wished to claim her only grandchild. Did she even know where the child was, or if it was still living?

Amanda realized that Clifford was speaking to her. "I hope you don't disapprove of my being here tonight." He looked down at her, his eyes filled with concern, as if her opinion was of great importance to him.

"Each of us must deal with bereavement in our own way," she said. "Soon after my father passed away, I went to work for the *Gazette*, and I found that the work absorbed my attention and helped to keep me from brooding." It had also enabled her to support herself, but one did not discuss one's financial situation with acquaintances. "It was fortunate that Mrs. Fairlie hired me, since I'd had no previous experience in such a position—or any other. I hope to justify her confidence in my ability."

Although Clifford appeared to be listening, she saw that his smile had disappeared and he was looking past her. She followed the direction of his gaze, and saw Howard Thornton was coming toward them. He was a stocky man in his early forties, with blunt, heavy features and a florid complexion. She did not know him well. Once, he had been seated across from her at a dinner; and another time, they'd spoken briefly at a charity bazaar.

"Good evening, Miss Whitney," he said. She inclined her head and smiled politely. But when he held out his hand to Clifford, the younger man made no move to take it. His jaw went rigid, and his blue eyes were totally devoid of warmth as he stared at the man who was to have married his sister.

She spoke quickly, to cover the awkward moment. "Are you enjoying the performance, Mr. Thornton?"

"Indeed, I am. Vittori is in fine voice tonight—her coloratura passages were excellent. Although it seemed to me that a silk gown was most unsuitable for a midnight tryst in a Highland glen. In real life, her teeth would have been chattering so hard, she wouldn't have been able to reveal her tender feelings to Edgardo."

"And, if it comes to that, a Scottish maiden would not have been expressing those feelings in Italian," she said. "But we don't expect realism from an opera, do we?" She turned her head and directed her question to Clifford, hoping to draw him into the conversation, but he remained silent, his lips pressed together, his gloved fingers gripping the slender stem of his glass so tightly she feared it might snap.

She was relieved when the bell signaled the end of the first intermission. Although Thornton did not offer Clifford his hand again, he gave the younger man an amiable nod, choosing to ignore his icy manner. Then he bowed to Amanda and went back inside.

With Thornton's departure, she saw the tension leave Clifford's face, and when he had escorted her to the door at the back of her box, he stood for a moment, smiling down at her.

"The Van Wycks were kind enough to offer me the use of their box for the season," she told Clifford. "Perhaps you would care to join me? The view is excellent and—" Then she stopped short, realizing her offer, although well-meant, might not have been entirely tactful. Maude Hamilton had told her that Everard Spencer had offered thirty thousand dollars for a box and had been refused. "But he's made an enormous contribution to the Metropolitan Opera House," Maude had added. "So of course he'll get a private box there, when it opens."

But if he was offended, he certainly did not show it. "I accept with pleasure, Miss Whitney—if you'll allow me to drive you home afterward."

After the performance they stood together in the crowd gathered under the portico, waiting as a line of carriages moved up slowly. It had turned colder, and the stars glittered with icy brilliance. A brisk wind tugged at the hood of her cloak, and tossed back the folds of Clifford's fur-collared opera cape. He drew Amanda's hand into the crook of his arm.

She caught sight of Howard Thornton, who raised his high silk hat and nodded to them, before getting into his landau. Although Clifford pretended not to notice, she felt the muscles of his arm tense beneath her fingers.

She was determined to find out the cause of Clifford's deep dislike for Thornton. If there had been a quarrel between them, at some time in the past, Ross would want to know. A few moments later, when they were seated inside the Spencers' brougham, and the horses set off at a brisk clip, she said: "It's too bad Mr. Thornton was here tonight. No doubt our meeting him so unexpectedly awoke unhappy memories for you."

"Indeed," he said, his tone expressionless.

"Forgive me, but I felt that there might have been something more—a dislike, on your part."

He nodded brusquely. "You're quite right."

She remembered her mother's stern admonition: *Never, directly or indirectly, refer to the affairs of others, which it will give them pain to recall.* But she pushed the memory aside. "Your parents approved of him."

His gaze was remote. "They did—I did not."

"Surely you had some reason for feeling that way."

She heard the harsh intake of his breath. Had she gone too far? Clifford had every right to be offended by such intimate questions. "My parents didn't understand Jessamyn, as I did. Only I knew how fragile she was, how sensitive. A delicate creature, who lived in a world of her own." He spoke with quiet intensity. "I did all I could to convince them that she should not be forced to marry against her will." His eyes were bleak now, his voice unsteady.

Everard had been well aware of Thornton's failings: his debts, his extravagant way of life. But perhaps there was a more serious flaw in the man's character, known only to Clifford.

Although Ross would want to know what it might be, she could not bring herself to question Clifford further. She searched for a more impersonal topic with which to break the charged silence.

"When I get home, I would like to relax before the fire

and relive the pleasure of the performance. But instead, I must organize my notes." She caught his puzzled look. "The opening night of the opera is to be the subject of my article for the *Gazette*'s society page."

"But doesn't that detract from your evening's enjoyment?"

"Not at all. I take notes before the overture. The rest of the time, I'm free to relax and enjoy the performance."

"Tell me, Miss Whitney, do you like your work?"

"Yes, indeed. It's often interesting, sometimes amusing. And it allows me to live independently, and to come and go as I please."

The brougham turned into Nineteenth Street and halted in front of her door. Clifford quickly got out and helped her to descend. When they stood face to face on the sidewalk, his gloved hand still held hers. She felt his warm breath on her cheek and caught the mingled scents of his spicy cologne and the carnation in his buttonhole.

"I'm going to attend a reception at the Metropolitan Museum next Saturday evening," he said. "It would give me great pleasure if you would accompany me." She looked up and saw the boyish eagerness in his smile, the longing in his eyes.

"Please say you'll come," he urged. She hesitated for a moment. "It's being held to raise money for a most worthy cause—Mr. Henry Bergh's Society for the Prevention of Cruelty to Animals."

"You're fond of animals, Mr. Spencer?"

"My sister was."

Once again, she was moved by the sadness in his voice. "And so am I," she said. "I'd be pleased to come to the reception with you."

Long past midnight, she was still seated at her desk, trying to work on her article, but she found her thoughts straying. What could she wear to the museum reception? Clifford had already seen her in her cinnamon taffeta this evening. Surely he knew that, in her present circumstances, she could not afford an expensive new gown for every occasion, but many of the ladies who'd seen her at the opera, would be attending the reception, too. They'd recognize the gown, and tongues would wag.

And how would she get through the rest of the social season, when she would have to wear that same gown, or the blue visiting costume with its new lace trimming? Madame Duval had been right; she could not possibly get through autumn, and then winter, with only those two outfits.

Did she dare ask Lavinia Fairlie for an increase in salary? No, that wouldn't do. She hadn't been working at the *Gazette* nearly long enough to make such a request.

Then she remembered the length of coral taffeta Mama had sent her, a few months ago. *I bought it on impulse, intending to have it made into a gown. But now I realize that such a striking color would not be quite suitable.*

There had been no need for further explanation. A paid companion was neither an ordinary servant, nor a social equal to her employer. Like a governess, she was expected to dress inconspicuously, so as not to call attention to herself.

And to think she might have been trapped in the same situation as her mother, if she hadn't been fortunate enough to have found a position on the *Gazette*. She had told Clifford she enjoyed her work, and she had meant it.

But how long would she feel that way, as one season followed another and she went on turning out her descriptions of the social scene?

Maude Hamilton still took a keen interest in every

change in fashion, and, as far as Amanda knew, she had no other goal. Had she ever thought about marriage? Lavinia Fairlie was driven by ambition now, but she'd been married and widowed, twice. She'd known what it was to share complete intimacy with a man . . .

But what about me?

She found herself thinking of Clifford in a disturbingly intimate way; the scent of him, the warmth of his breath on her cheek, the pressure of his fingers on her gloved hand. Had he asked her to the reception only as a courtesy, in return for her sharing the Van Wyck's box with him tonight? Then, remembering his look, as he waited for her answer, she sensed that his invitation was more than a polite gesture.

When Ross arrived at the stables behind the Spencer mansion, a chill October wind blew the fan-shaped, yellow leaves of a ginkgo tree across the paving stones of the yard. From inside the long brick building, he heard the voices of stablehands, who started work at six in the morning, long before the Spencers were likely to need any of their carriages. The head coachman would report to the house at ten, to receive the orders of the day, confident that he could turn out a team of perfectly-groomed horses and immaculate carriages on command.

Ross had come here before—the day Everard had hired him—but now, thanks in part to all he'd learned from Amanda, he needed to find out more. As he entered the stables, and breathed the mingled smells of fresh hay, leather, and manure, the men paused in their work. He walked over to a tall, rangy young man, who was cleaning the brougham.

"Winfield, isn't it?"

The young man nodded, and went on polishing the crest on the brougham door. "I already told you all I know, Mr. Buchanan, and that's a fact."

Ross peered inside the brougham and saw that the leather upholstery, the carpeted floor, were spotless. "You've done a thorough job. Tell me, were you as careful the morning after the crime?"

"Mr. Spencer pays us good wages, and he gets his money's worth."

"I'm sure he does. When you cleaned out the brougham the morning after Miss Spencer's disappearance, did you find anything unusual on the seats, or on the floor?"

"Nothing special. A program from the theater."

"Did you keep it?"

" 'Course not. What would I want with it?"

"Anything else? A few feathers from Mrs. Spencer's fan? A flower Clifford Spencer wore in his buttonhole?"

"Could've been. I don't look over the sweepings—I just throw them away."

"I believe you said none of these carriages had been taken out of the stables after Mrs. Spencer and her son returned from the theater?"

"That's right." He shot Ross a wary look, then fixed his eyes on the gilded crest again, and went on with the polishing.

Ross started to turn away, then paused and asked: "Would you be able to hitch up the team to the brougham if you needed to?"

"That's Kendall's job," he said, nodding in the direction of the head coachman, who was rubbing down a big grey gelding.

"But you could do it."

"Sure I could—and drive it around town, as good as him."

"Did you leave the stable at any time during the night of the murder?"

He stiffened. "No! I already told you, last time you were here."

"You didn't leave the stables that night, not even for a minute?"

The groom shifted his weight uneasily.

"So if somebody had come out of the house, carrying Miss Spencer, you'd have been here to help him get her inside the brougham. And with the team hitched up, you could have driven him downtown to the Ladies Mile."

Winfield dropped his polishing cloth. The color drained from his face. The other men stopped working, their eyes fixed on Ross and the groom.

"It's a damn lie! I don't know nothin' about what happened that night—"

"Miss Spencer disappeared from the house. She was found in the Ladies Mile. She didn't walk down there in her wedding outfit, or hail a hansom and drive down. How did her killer get her away?"

Winfield stared at him in desperation. "How should I know?"

"You were here in the stables," Ross said.

"No I wasn't—not all night!"

"How long were you gone?"

The groom swallowed hard and looked away. Kendall put down his brush and moved with a purposeful stride. The head coachman was as tall as Ross, lean and wiry, with an angular, weather-beaten face. "Mr. Buchanan asked you a question. Answer him."

The groom threw him a sullen look. "I don't remember! Maybe—a couple of hours."

"And where did you go?" Ross asked.

"Out chasing some tart, like as not," Kendall cut in.

"She ain't no tart. She's a nursery maid, from down the avenue."

"You went calling on her after midnight? And she let you in?"

"She ain't allowed to have followers. We been meeting out back in the garden gazebo."

"When the master hears of this, you'll find yourself out of a job." Kendall looked around the stable, and the other stablehands, who had stopped to listen, took up their chores again.

"You don't have to tell him, do you?"

But Kendall already had turned away. He went back to the grey gelding, and Ross followed him. "A handsome animal," Ross said, stroking the powerful neck.

"You should see him in harness, along with Aries over there." He jerked his head in the direction of one of the nearby stalls. "There's no finer-looking team in the city, or better behaved, either." He picked up his brush and went on grooming the gelding's lustrous coat.

"You told me you drove Mrs. Spencer and her son to the theater and back, on the night of the murder," Ross said. "And you unhitched the team afterward, rubbed them down, and put them in their stalls. Then you went upstairs to your quarters and went to sleep."

The coachman nodded. "I did."

"And Winfield had gone calling. So could somebody have carried Miss Spencer out here, hitched up the team again that night and driven off with her?"

"It's not likely."

"Why not?"

"I know how to handle these two, but they're high-spirited, like all thoroughbreds. They'd have kicked up a hell of a rumpus, if some stranger walked in here and started hitchin' them up. If that good-for-nothin' Winfield had been here, like he was supposed to be—"

Ross interrupted the digression. "So you heard no unusual noises from the stable that night?"

"I did not."

"And the next morning? You saw nothing out of the way, when you came down here?"

"Everything was the same as always."

"What about your coat?" Ross wheeled around. Winfield had crossed the stable and now confronted Kendall. "Big stain on it, wasn't there? And one of the buttons was pulled loose, hangin' by a thread."

Kendall gave him a hard stare. "Get back to your work."

But the groom went on: "I remember 'cause it was me took the coat over to the house."

"You didn't say anything about that, last time I was here," Ross said.

"You didn't ask me."

"I'm asking you now," Ross said.

"I gave the coat to Miss Tuttle so she could take out the stain and sew the button on good and tight. The old crow wasn't happy about that, I can tell you. She don't like doin' such chores. Not after havin' been poor Miss Jessamyn's maid. I guess it's been a real come-down for her."

"What goes on inside the house is no concern of ours," Kendall interrupted. "You'll mind your tongue, if you know what's good for you."

Winfield looked as if he might speak, then obviously thought better of it, and returned to the brougham.

"I didn't think to tell you about the coat," said Kendall. "What with all those other carriages and drays and such splashing muck about, it's not easy to keep my uniform clean. And it's up to me to set a good example for the grooms—spotless livery, brushed hat, polished boots."

"I'm sure you do," Ross said. "You've been working here for—how long?"

"Ten years now."

"It's no easy job, overseeing the stable hands, and driving a carriage and pair in all this heavy traffic."

"That's the truth, Mr. Buchanan—though there's not many who realize it." He had finished brushing the gelding's coat; now he started on its mane. "I've been working around horses since I was a lad of ten. I learned how to drive on these New York streets. But the traffic's getting worse all the time, what with all them horsecars and hansoms and wagons. And the damn elevated trains rattling overhead, showering down soot and sparks. You got to know how to handle a high-steppin' team. I don't use the whip any more than I have to—not like some do. And I can come to a smooth stop at a moment's notice, so my passengers won't get tossed around."

"That must take real skill." Ross spoke with unfeigned admiration.

"Skill and experience. Now these younger fellows." He made a sweeping gesture with his brush. "A feckless lot, most of them. Some go chasing after anything in skirts, like Winfield there. And some get itchy feet, and go off without even giving notice." The coachman gave a short, derisive laugh. "Probably go out west, thinking they'll make their fortune in the gold fields."

"Is that what Devin O'Shea did?"

"O'Shea?" The coachman's heavy brows shot up. "How'd you know about him? He's been gone for years. He never wanted to be a coachman, anyway. A riding master, he was."

"A good one?"

"He was good with horses."

"And with people?"

"He got along well enough with the rest of us. Had a ready smile and an easy-going disposition."

"He had a way with the women, too, so I've heard. And not just housemaids, either."

The coachman set down his brush, and gave Ross a flinty stare. "Some of them servant girls forget their place, gossiping about their betters. But I'm tellin' you there wasn't a word of truth in that foolish talk about O'Shea and Miss Jessamyn." He spoke with absolute conviction. "Why would a rich, well-bred young lady give any thought to an Irish riding master?"

"No doubt she was courted by the most eligible gentlemen. I suppose she was always off to cotillions and dinner parties and carriage rides."

The coachman shook his head. "Not Miss Spencer. She was kind of shy and quiet. She lived in a world of her own, as you might say. She had her pets, of course. And she liked horses, so the master hired O'Shea to give her riding lessons. And that's all there was to it." His steady gaze challenged Ross to question his word.

"But when O'Shea left, she took it hard, didn't she?"

"I guess maybe her feelings were hurt, him leavin' without a word of goodbye."

"Was it only a case of hurt feelings?" Ross asked. "I'm told she went into a nervous decline."

"Miss Jessamyn was kind of—high-strung, as you might say. But there's other young ladies like that. They take on over every little thing. Cry their eyes out over a lost kitten, or a sad song, and go into hysterics, if a party dress don't arrive on time. Just a young girl's nature, I guess."

"I don't suppose any of the young servant girls behave that way."

"Servant girls! I should say not! Any servant girl who took on so, would be turned out into the street." He shrugged. "But they're a different breed entirely, y' see—strong and sensible. They got to be, to work from early morning to late at night. They're not plagued with nerves and such."

"That's fortunate for them." Ross could not keep a touch of irony out of his voice. "But as for Miss Spencer, she was in such a bad state after O'Shea left that her parents sent her to recuperate in a town on the Hudson. Isn't that so?"

"I guess they figured a change of scene would do her good. I drove her up to Rhinebeck myself."

"Did her mother go with her?"

"No, her maid did."

"Her maid. That would have been Gertrude—the one who married Barney Marek. He was head coachman back then."

Kendall looked surprised. "You found out a lot in just these past few weeks, haven't you?"

"That's what I'm paid for," Ross said. "What did you think of Marek?"

"He did his work well enough."

"But he was over-fond of the bottle, wasn't he?"

"He stayed sober during the day—he had to. The master wouldn't have put up with a drunken coachman handling his horses."

"And after working hours?"

"He'd start drinkin' right after he was off duty. Many's the night one of the lads had to help him up to his quarters. And he'd turn nasty when he'd had too much."

146

"Picked fights with the other hands, did he?"

"Sometimes. But more often than not, he'd start ranting about how it wasn't right for him to have to kowtow to the Spencers. Because Mr. Spencer started out as a lumberjack, and wasn't no better than them that worked for him—that was what Marek said. Said somebody ought to blow up the house—with the Spencers in it."

"And nobody ever repeated any of that to Everard Spencer?"

"They didn't want to tangle with him. He was one bad customer when the booze was in him. I guess Mr. Spencer would have found out about it, sooner or later. But it never came to that."

"Why not?"

"Because he married Gertrude and off they went." Kendall shook his head. "You'd have thought a woman like her would've had too much good sense to marry such a man."

"Maybe she hoped she could reform him," said Ross.

"Take more than a woman to straighten him out."

The coachman glanced toward the open stable door, where long, slanting bars of sunlight streamed in. "I've kept you long enough," Ross said. "Time I was going."

Kendall set down his brush, led the gelding back into the stall, then accompanied Ross to the door, pausing briefly to call Ross's attention to the open carriages: the four-in-hand, the landau, the barouche. "They're not practical on a chilly morning," he said. "But they give the ladies a chance to show off their fine outfits."

He gestured at a shiny black sleigh with gilded trimming. "Cost a pretty penny, this one did. You ought to see it all decked out. The horses wear them fancy plumes on their heads—aigrettes, they call 'em—and gilt tassels, and gold bells on the harness. And an ermine rug to keep the ladies warm."

"Must be an impressive sight." He stopped and shook hands with Kendall. "Thanks for your time."

"Pleased to be of help, Mr. Buchanan. I only hope you get the bastard that did poor Miss Jessamyn in, that terrible way. I hope he swings for what he did."

The morning was cool and bathed in autumn sunlight. Ross walked down Fifth Avenue, reviewing the information he'd gathered in the stables. Kendall had said that Jessamyn had shared a mutual fondness for horses with Devin O'Shea, and perhaps she'd been infatuated with the good-looking young Irishman. But while Nellie was sure Jessamyn had been pregnant by her riding master, that she'd been sent away to bear her child in secret, Kendall had denied that there had been anything more than a friendly relationship between the two.

Was the coachman shading the truth to protect the dead girl's reputation?

He hailed a hansom for the long, slow trip through heavy traffic. The cab had barely come to a stop on Twenty-third Street before he got down at Bellevue Hospital, a massive grey stone building. He went through the low door, with a single word, MORGUE, chiseled over it. He walked quickly down a long corridor to a half-open office door. Saul Goldman, a thin, red-haired young resident, looked up from his desk. "Come in," he said. "Sit down." He indicated a chair and Ross seated himself.

"How's the Spencer case going?" Saul asked.

"That's what I'm here about. I need your help."

"The girl was strangled. What else can I tell you?"

"Was she raped?"

Saul shook his head. "Not raped, no. But she—"

"Go on."

"I'm not supposed to give out such information."

Ross gave him a long, steady look, but said nothing. Saul understood. A couple of years ago, when Lena, his beautiful, red-haired sister had gotten involved with a Hungarian fiddle-player twice her age, he'd persuaded Ross to check out the smooth-talking stranger. It hadn't taken long to find out that Lena's suitor already had a wife and five children over in Brooklyn. Ross had convinced the man that it would be most unwise for him to come calling on Lena Goldman again.

"Jessamyn Spencer wasn't a virgin," said Saul.

"Anything else I should know?"

"She'd borne a child a few years ago. It was a difficult birth. The skin of the perineum had been torn and scarred, but there was no lasting injury to the vaginal wall." He drained his coffee cup, and poured himself another.

"Everard Spencer didn't tell you she'd ever been pregnant?"

"Maybe he didn't know. Maybe the girl's mother handled the whole thing herself, because she was afraid her husband would blame her for not watching their daughter more carefully."

"It's possible," Ross agreed. "Spencer's got a hell of a temper. I wouldn't blame her if—"

"Dr. Goldman!" An attendant in a soiled white smock stood in the doorway. "You're wanted in the dead room right away."

"What's the hurry?"

"Better come right now, doctor."

"Sorry, Ross," said the resident. "I'll be back as soon as I can."

Ross nodded, then leaned back in his chair and considered what Saul had told him. Amanda surely would have had a deeper insight into such feminine matters; but right now, it was up to him to try to deal with this new information.

Jessamyn, a shy fifteen-year-old, had fallen in love for the first time. Had she confided in O'Shea out of some foolish romantic notion that he would marry her, and take her away? If so, she'd been disillusioned when he'd disappeared, leaving her to bear the baby in secret.

It had been a difficult birth, Saul had said. Had the memories of fear and pain left scars not only on her body but on her mind as well? Was that why she'd told her father she could not marry Thornton or any other man?

His speculations were interrupted by Saul's return. His face was drawn, his lean body tense. "They've brought in another one—a woman in a wedding gown and veil."

"She was strangled?"

"With her own bridal wreath—those white blossoms fastened to a wire."

"Are the police still here?" Ross asked.

"They just left. But they'll be back. So if you want to see her, you'd better come with me."

Ross was on his feet. They walked swiftly down the long, narrow corridor.

The dead room was twenty feet square, with a floor of brick tile, and four stone tables on iron frames. All the tables were occupied. A steady stream of water from an overhead jet sprayed on each of the faces. The water would retard decay for awhile, to make it easier to identify the corpse.

"She's over here," Saul said, but before Ross could follow him, the attendant stepped in.

"Now just a minute, mister. The coroner ain't shown up yet and nobody except the doctor and the cops get to see the body until the coroner—"

"Mr. Buchanan works for Everard Spencer," Saul interrupted.

The attendant stared at Ross with a new respect. "I guess it's okay, then."

Saul led the way to the table on the end, where a woman's naked body was covered by a sheet. It was impossible now to tell whether she had been pretty or homely; her features were contorted, her face swollen, the skin blue. The wreath had been removed, but a deep scar encircled her throat. The running water had plastered the strands of her light brown hair to her forehead and cheeks. Her left eye was swollen shut and there was a deep cut on the side of her jaw.

Ross asked: "Was she found on the Ladies Mile?"

"Not this one," Saul said. "The police found her in the backyard of a house at Fifty-second and Fifth."

"Do they know who she was?"

"Not yet. They're checking out all the precincts, to find out if anybody's reported a missing relative."

The attendant, unwilling to be ignored, gestured to one of the hooks on the rack behind the tables. "There's her clothes." A soiled white gown and a torn veil hung from the hook. "The wire with them flowers on it is in the canvas bag there, with her underwear. An' her wedding band."

"Any inscription inside the band?" Ross asked him.

"Nope."

Ross studied the bruises on her face. "She put up quite a struggle."

"And that ain't all." The attendant pulled the sheet down to her waist. "Take a look at them black an' blue marks on her arms an' this here cut on her shoulder. Husky female, she was. Big, round tits an' good strong legs." He whipped back the sheet all the way.

She had been taller than average—five feet six, maybe seven. Probably in her early thirties. Even now, as Ross looked at the broad hips, the thatch of pubic hair, the muscular thighs, he was repelled by this final violation of decency.

"All right. Cover her," he said. The attendant drew up the sheet.

"You're sure she wasn't carrying anything that might identify her? A tradesman's bill? A handkerchief with her initials on it? A locket with a picture inside? A shop label sewn inside her dress?"

"Not a damn thing. Look, Mr. Buchanan—we get more than a thousand bodies a year in here. Most of them ain't never claimed. There's whores that're pulled out of the East River. And drunken bums that die in doorways. Newborn babies tossed into tenement airshafts. You think they're claimed by their lovin' family or friends? They get shipped out to Hart Island, an' buried in Potter's Field."

Ross knew all that, and more. "Let's go," he said. He and Saul left the dead room and walked down the hall to the outside door.

"If we find out who she is, I'll get word to you," Saul promised.

By four o'clock that afternoon, the newsboys were out on the streets with the extra editions. Ross, standing at his office window, heard a shrill voice from below: "Horrible Murder—Ladies Mile Maniac Strikes Again!"

The second victim had been found in the yard of a house at Fifty-second and Fifth, but the newspapers seldom were strictly accurate in reporting a scandal like this one. Two murdered brides, both found on the Ladies Mile—that made for more dramatic headlines—and sold more papers.

Fifty-second and Fifth. There was something familiar about that address. He searched his memory.

Madame Restell, that was it. New York's most notorious abortionist. "Madame Killer," they'd called her. Her profits from her trade had bought her a mansion, on Fifty-second and Fifth. She'd been hunted down by the fanatical reformer, Anthony Comstock; then, to escape the consequences of a trial, she'd climbed into her bathtub and slit her throat.

The ringing of the telephone interrupted his thoughts; he picked up the receiver.

"Buchanan!" Everard Spencer spoke brusquely. "Get over to my home, right away."

CHAPTER TEN

Everard Spencer paced the library, his heavy features flushed with anger. "I hired you because I was told you were the best! Maybe I was misinformed. If you'd done your job right, this killer would already have been caught and locked up in the Tombs!"

Ross had been standing before the fireplace for the last five minutes, while Spencer carried on his tirade. "Now those damn reporters are brewing up a juicy scandal about this second murder. And they're rehashing all the details about Jessamyn, too!"

"Not all," Ross said. "They haven't written anything about where the body was found. Or do you think they still don't know?"

"There's nothing they don't know."

"I wouldn't say that. You've kept some information from them. And from me, too." Ross's voice hardened. "You didn't tell me that Jessamyn got pregnant by her riding master when she was fifteen."

"That's not true!"

"Isn't it? Or maybe your wife didn't tell you."

"There's nothing to tell!" He did not look away, but Ross caught the brief flicker of uncertainty in his eyes.

"Why not call her down here, and ask her?"

"There's no need to drag her into it!" Beads of sweat glistened on Everard's forehead. His heavy neck bulged over his starched collar. "That happened five years ago. Why go into it now?"

"Because everything concerning Jessamyn could have a bearing on the case. Because I can work better and faster if you don't hold back any more of these family secrets."

"There are no more—secrets!" Everard pulled out a linen handkerchief and wiped the sweat from his face. "Who'd have thought that fool girl, just out of the schoolroom, would've carried on like a bitch in heat! Chasing after hired help! Letting O'Shea bed her in the stables!"

"Careful," Ross jerked his head in the direction of the doors.

Although they were shut, Everard broke off. He drew a breath, released it audibly, then sank into a wide leather chair. "Horny Irish son-of-a-bitch!" He was no longer shouting, but his voice shook with suppressed rage. "If I'd gotten my hands on him before he went sneaking off, I'd have broken his neck." Under Everard's perfectly-tailored cassimere suit, starched linen shirt and silk cravat were the massive shoulders, bull neck, and powerful arms of a lumberjack. Up north, in the logging camps, a man learned to fight hard and dirty if he wanted to survive. Although Spencer had taken on weight with middle-age and good living, Ross had no doubt that he still could hold his own in a brawl.

"What became of the baby?" he asked.

Spencer looked at him without comprehension.

"Jessamyn's baby. Your grandchild."

"How the hell should I know? That maid of hers—that Gertrude—she got rid it." He might have been speaking of an unwanted cat.

Had he even inquired about the sex of the infant? Ross didn't think it likely.

"I paid Gertrude to find a place for it."

"You mean a baby farm?"

"I suppose so."

155

"And when Gertrude came back to New York, you gave her more money and then dismissed her. She married your coachman and went off with him. He used her money to buy a shooting gallery."

Spencer nodded with grudging approval. "So you haven't been wasting all your time." Then he added, "Too bad you didn't catch this lunatic before he killed again."

"You're sure both murders were committed by the same man?" Ross asked.

"Certainly I am!" He rose, and led Ross to the library door. "Now, get out there and find him."

The crimson sunset had faded over the Hudson, and as Ross turned into West Nineteenth Street, he saw that the gas lamp in front of Amanda's house was already aglow. He climbed the front steps and rang the bell. The concierge opened the door. "If you're here to see Miss Whitney, you're too late. She left a few minutes ago with a gentleman friend. He called for her in a fine, big carriage. She looked real elegant, like she was going to a ball. Decked out in a stylish velvet cape, she was, and carrying a beautiful ostrich feather fan."

It was unlikely that Amanda would return early, she and her "gentleman friend" with his fine carriage. Who was he? A member of an old, established "Knickerbocker family," who had been a welcome visitor in the house on Stuyvesant Square?

"You could wait in the downstairs sitting room, I suppose . . ."

It had been a rough day, so far. All he needed now was to sit for hours with a gaggle of curious females looking him over and speculating on why he was there. "No thank you, ma'am," he said.

"Just as you please." She closed the door, and he waited a moment longer on the top of the steps. He needed to talk to Amanda tonight, no matter how late she got home.

He went back along Nineteenth Street to Broadway, and headed for Charles F. Murphy's saloon on Avenue C. Murphy's all-male clientele included office clerks, ward-heelers from Tammany Hall, and newspapermen. It was a long walk over to the East Side, but he had plenty of time.

He quickened his step, as he strode past brightly-lit theaters, restaurants, and hotels. Outside Wallack's Theater, a newspaper boy was shouting out: "Horrible Murder! Another Bride Strangled! Fiend on the Loose!"

The boy, who looked no more than ten, would stay outside in his torn jacket and cap until all his papers were sold. Then he'd go home to a filthy, overcrowded tenement flat—if he was lucky enough to have a home. Otherwise he'd sleep in an alley or a doorway.

Ross had sold papers when he'd been no older than that kid, and he'd slept on the streets. When he hadn't earned enough to pay for a meal, he stole from the food stands on Rivington or Delancey. He went on to stealing from the warehouses along East River, first on his own, then with a gang of boys like himself. At twelve, tall for his age, and a formidable street fighter, he had become their leader. But he wasn't like the others: the nameless offspring of a street-walker, or a servant girl.

His father, a doctor with strong abolitionist sentiments, and his mother, a schoolmaster's daughter, had married and come to New York, shortly before the war had begun. He'd been eight when his father had joined the Union Army, and been killed by a sniper's bullet at Bull Run. Because no one would hire a governess or housekeeper who was burdened with a young child, his mother had gone to work in a factory, sewing army uniforms. She had come home, white-faced with exhaustion after her twelve hour shift, but somehow she'd managed to teach him to read and write.

"You will be a doctor, like your father," she'd told him.

That had been before she'd taken ill from breathing the stifling, lint-filled air in the workroom. She had died of consumption before his tenth birthday, and had been buried in Potter's Field.

When Ross walked into Murphy's saloon, it was already crowded with customers, who paused between drinks to gaze across the bar at the large, tinted photograph of the enticing Lillian Russell, blonde and voluptuous in her purple tights. Photographs of prize-fighters and race horses decorated the smoke-darkened walls.

Ross looked around the room, and caught sight of Jerry Costello, a reporter on the *New York Graphic*. Costello, a stout, middle-aged man with a round red face, bloodshot blue eyes, and a fringe of greying hair, was seated alone at his usual table. "Come on over," the reporter called. Ross took the chair opposite him, then motioned to the waiter to bring another bottle.

"You boys must be having a field day, down on Printing House Row," Ross said.

"That's a fact. And if you ask me, there'll be more to come. I wouldn't be surprised if that loony's out there looking for another poor female right now. The Ladies Mile Maniac. That has a fine ring to it."

"But this one was found in the back garden of a house on Fifty-second and Fifth," Ross reminded him.

Costello shrugged off the objection. "What do the readers care about such piddling details? All they want is a rip-roaring yarn, with plenty of racy details. And that's what we're giving them. We haven't had a story like this since the 'Terrible Trunk Mystery' back in '71."

"This one's even better," said Ross, dryly. "The Trunk Murderer only killed one woman."

"But he made great headlines all the same." Costello gave a sigh of recollection. "A naked female butchered by an abortionist, stuffed into a trunk and left at the Hudson River Depot. Poor, unlucky bitch."

"Alice Bowlsby was her name," said Ross.

"So it was. But Bowlsby was just a nobody—"

"And you're hoping the maniac's second victim will turn out to be an heiress, like Jessamyn Spencer?"

"It's possible, isn't it? Anyway, we still have plenty of hot stuff about the Spencer girl." He set down his glass, leaned toward Ross, and lowered his voice. "More than the boss'll let us print as yet."

"You're doing all right. This afternoon's *Graphic* threw Spencer into one hell of a temper."

Costello's bloodshot blue eyes went alert. "Still working for him, are you?" Ross nodded. "So maybe you can tell me how a fine young lady like Miss Jessamyn Spencer came to end up in the alley by Isobel Hewitt's whorehouse."

"I don't have the answer to that one. And when I do, I'll have to go straight to the police with the information, like any decent, law-abiding citizen."

"Sure you will," Costello said with a laugh. "Can you at least get me a photograph of Miss Spencer?"

"Not a chance."

"Too bad. We can print good halftones, these days."

"You'll have to make do with the facade of the Spencer mansion," Ross said.

"And the garden on the house on Fifty-second Street."

He shrugged. "That'll have to keep our readers satisfied, for now."

The house on Fifty-second and Fifth. *The Restell house. Why had the second body been dumped there? Perhaps only a coincidence.* But right now, he had more urgent matters to pursue. He had to get back across to the West Side, to talk to Amanda.

It was close to midnight when he returned to her house. He was approaching the front steps when he heard the clop of hooves. A brougham turned into the street. He recognized it at once: he'd got a look at it only that morning, in the Spencers' stables. He stepped into the shadows as the brougham stopped beside the gas lamp. A liveried footman sprang down from the box and opened the door. Clifford Spencer, a slim, elegant figure in evening clothes, swept off his high silk hat and helped Amanda descend.

Ross heard him saying: ". . . a most delightful evening, Miss Whitney . . . I trust I may have the pleasure of your company again—soon—"

Was Clifford going to escort her upstairs? No, he was too well-bred to make such a suggestion. She handed him her key, and he unlocked the front door for her. Then he returned to the brougham and climbed inside.

As the brougham sped away, Ross mounted the steps, and entered the dimly-lit vestibule. "Good-evening," he said.

She cried out and whirled around. "Ross! What are you doing here?"

"Waiting for you to say good-night to your escort," he said. "I need to talk to you."

"It's late."

"I called earlier but you'd already gone."

"And you've been waiting out here all this time?"

"Your concierge said I could wait in the sitting room, but I went over to Murphy's saloon instead."

She looked at him doubtfully. "Don't worry," he said. "I'm cold sober. I figured I might as well make good use of the time. A lot of reporters hang out at Murphy's."

She unlocked the inner door and led the way down the hall and up the stairs to her flat. Once inside, she turned up the lamps. In the parlor, he stopped short when he heard a high-pitched chittering sound. The cat stood at Amanda's feet, green eyes glowing balefully, tail switching.

"Leander doesn't like being left alone all evening," she explained.

She bent and stroked the cat. His ears flicked forward and the eerie chittering subsided.

"I always thought cats were independent beasts," he said.

"Alley cats, maybe." She laughed softly. "Leander's a proper housecat."

As Ross helped her off with her velvet cloak, he caught the delicate scent of her freesia cologne. Her coral gown was cut low, revealing her smooth white shoulders, the rounds of her breasts, the curve of her throat. Her hair was swept up and fastened with a pair of glittering clips. She laid her fan on a small table, unbuttoned her long, satin gloves and stripped them off.

She turned up another lamp and waved him to the sofa, while she took the wicker chair nearby. Leander, having delivered his rebuke, leaped up onto the sofa and stretched out his sinuous body full-length. He closed his eyes, but his tail still twitched from time to time.

"This second victim—who was she? The newspapers didn't give her name."

"Nobody's been able to identify her, not yet," he said. "That's what Costello told me."

"Costello? Is he a police officer?"

"Jerry Costello's a reporter for the *Graphic*. Murphy's saloon's a hangout for reporters and Tammany wardheelers. Costello says the police don't know who she is, either. There was no identification on the body."

"But she was wearing a wedding gown and veil when they found her?"

"That's right."

"But surely her husband would have reported her missing by now."

"He hasn't, though."

"Why not? Think about it, Ross. A bride disappears right after her wedding—"

"We don't know exactly when she disappeared."

"Of course we do," she interrupted impatiently. "She hadn't even had time to change to her traveling clothes."

"That means it must have happened at the reception."

"In full view of the guests—and her bridegroom?"

"Maybe the killer was one of the guests—someone she knew and trusted enough to go off alone with him."

"And she wasn't missed at once? Not by her bridegroom or any of her family?"

"I don't claim to have any of the answers. Maybe I will, when I know who she was."

"But if no one's reported her missing—and there was no identification on the body—"

"You may be able to identify her."

"Ross! What makes you think that I—"

"The woman I saw at the morgue this morning had light brown hair, a squarish face," he went on. "She was taller than average and muscular. She put up a hard fight."

He heard the sharp intake of her breath. "Gertrude Marek?"

"It's possible." He had to force himself to go on. "I have no right to ask you to do this, but—"

"You want me to go down to the morgue to identify her, if I can."

"It won't be pleasant. If you don't think you're up to it, I'll try to find another way."

She stood up, with a soft rustle of taffeta. "It won't take me long to change."

He watched her turn and leave the parlor. In less than twenty minutes, she returned, wearing a plain grey flannel skirt and jacket, and a starched white shirtwaist. "Shall we go now?" she said.

The horse's hooves and the iron-clad wheels shattered the quiet of the deserted streets. Amanda held herself erect and stared straight ahead. She was bracing herself for the coming ordeal. He reached out and took her hand in his.

When they reached Bellevue, he ordered the driver to wait; it wouldn't be easy finding another hansom here, not at this hour. He helped her down, then led the way to the door of the morgue. A cold, damp wind blew in from the East River. She hesitated, then stopped and looked up at him, her face a white oval in the lamplight.

"If you can't go through with this, I'll understand," he said.

But she ignored his offer of reprieve. "Will we be permitted to see the body? Aren't there any rules about that?"

"The law says no one's allowed to view a murder victim, except in the presence of the coroner. But I know the night attendant. He'll forget the rules, if I make it worth his while."

★ ★ ★ ★ ★

The air in the dead room was heavy with the odor of carbolic. The attendant stood at the far end of the room, watching them with indifference.

Amanda looked down at the bruised, distorted face of the dead woman. The skin glistened with water from the overhead jets. She nodded. "This is Gertrude Marek." Her voice was bleak, but steady. "Is it possible for me to see— more of her?"

Although Ross was startled by her request, he motioned to the attendant to join them. "Pull down the sheet."

The attendant shrugged. "Just as you please, Miss." He grasped a corner of the sheet. "You can look her over from head to toe."

"No! I only want to see her hands." At a nod from Ross, the man complied.

"Please, Ross—I need a closer look—"

"Nobody ain't suppose to handle the body," the attendant said. Ross turned and gave him a cold stare.

Ross lifted one of the hands, then the other. Amanda leaned forward and examined the woman's broad, blunt-fingered hands. "All right," she said. "That's enough."

That attendant drew the sheet up again.

"Now, may I see what she was wearing when she was brought in?" she asked. The man took a gown and veil from the hook and handed them to Amanda, who examined them with meticulous care. "An' here's the shoes," he said, handing them to her. She looked them over, first the uppers, then the worn soles.

"And her—undergarments?"

"Right here in this bag, Miss," the attendant said. "Along with the wreath that loony used t' do her in."

Ross stood by, his curiosity mounting steadily, as he

watched her handle the drawers, the camisole, the stockings and garters Gertrude had been wearing when she died. When she saw the wreath, she put out her hand, then drew it back. He held it up for her. The light from the hissing gas jets flickered over the silk blossoms, some of them stained with dried blood.

Every trace of color left her face and her skin took on a greenish cast.

While the attendant was replacing the dress and veil on the hook behind the slab, then shoving the petticoat, the drawers, and camisole back into the coarse canvas bag, she stepped back, and swayed slightly. Ross put his arm around her shoulders. "That'll be all," he told the attendant.

He led her outside, still supporting her. "Take a deep breath," he said. She obeyed.

"Now, let's go," he said, as he led her to the waiting cab. "You'll be all right, once we're away from here."

When they were back inside her parlor, he lit the fire and stirred it to a blaze. She sat down on the sofa. "You need something stronger than coffee," he said. He half-expected her to refuse but instead, she motioned to the sideboard. He found a decanter of brandy inside, and filled two glasses, then came and seated himself beside her.

Leander, who'd been sleeping on one of the broad leather arms, awoke and came to settle on her lap. This time he didn't chitter at her. Maybe he was becoming resigned to the changes in her routine.

She took a sip of brandy, then another. Ross waited until he saw a touch of color return to her cheeks.

"Feeling better?"

She forced a smile. "I'm quite all right now."

He didn't want to question her so soon after her ordeal,

but he had no time to waste. "Can you tell me what you were looking for back there?"

"You said Gertrude had tried to fight off her attacker. But I don't believe that a woman—even a strong one—would have used only her fists to fight off an attacker. She'd have scratched his face with her fingernails, too."

"What makes you think she didn't?"

"I saw no blood or—bits of skin—under her nails. So maybe she didn't get a chance to put up a struggle after all. Maybe he got the wreath around her throat before she could fight back."

"And the bruises on her face?"

"I don't know. Maybe—"

"There were bruises on the rest of her body, too." He could find no tactful way of expressing himself. "I looked the whole body over on my first visit to the morgue."

"Ross—No! Surely you didn't—" She looked away, and he waited for her to recover her composure. "Her husband has a vile temper," she said slowly. "Maybe he came home and beat her—"

"And after he left, the maniac just happened to drop in and strangle her? Not likely, is it?" He didn't wait for her to answer. "The newspapers are saying both murders are the work of a lunatic who kills at random. But now we know there was a connection between the two victims. Gertrude was Jessamyn's maid. She saw Jessamyn through her pregnancy and the baby's birth."

"Nellie was only repeating the servants' gossip. She has no real proof that Jessamyn had a child out of wedlock," she reminded him.

"But I have proof. Everard Spencer admitted it to me this afternoon." He decided not to mention the information provided by Saul Goldman.

"Surely only a madman would have chosen brides as his victims."

"Gertrude was no bride. And why would she have kept her wedding gown all these years? Out of love for that drunken bum, Marek?"

"That wedding gown," Amanda interrupted. "Ross—it wasn't hers."

"How can you possibly know that?"

"That gown was at least two sizes too small for her. And not nearly long enough."

"What are you saying? That her killer stole a wedding gown from a shop, and forced her to put it on before he strangled her? Or maybe afterward?"

She flinched at the thought, but went on. "I only know it wasn't hers. And there's something else. All the seams had been basted, so that they could be easily altered."

"What about the veil?"

"The lace trimming was imitation Brussels—cheap imitation, at that. And the undergarments she'd been wearing—" He saw the color rise in her face. It was the height of impropriety for her to discuss female underwear with a man, and even at a time like this, she could not forget her mother's training.

"Are you saying her drawers and camisole were also too small?"

She fixed her gaze on Leander, and stroked his furry head.

"Were they too small?"

"No, but they—"

"Go on," he said impatiently. This was no time for lady-like scruples.

"They weren't suitable—not with a wedding gown."

"Why not?"

"They were made of thick outing flannel," she said. "There was no embroidery or trimming of any kind. Her stockings were heavy lisle, and her shoes were black. Common-sense black walking boots with water-proof, double-cork soles—and badly-worn."

He looked at her with unwilling respect. Although she'd been badly shaken back in the morgue, she had forced herself to observe and remember all those small details. Amanda Whitney surely was a most remarkable woman. He would have told her so, but she didn't give him the chance.

"You won't tell the police that I identified the body, will you?" she asked anxiously. "You won't give them my name—"

"Don't worry," he said. "I have no intention of taking this information to the police."

"But you must! It's your duty to assist them in any way you can."

"The hell it is! Have you forgotten that Spencer's paying me to find the killer before the police do?"

"That fiend's got to be caught before he kills another woman. It doesn't matter who finds him!"

"It does to me."

"But the police have the men and the resources to pursue the case."

"I have resources of my own."

"Give me your word you'll tell the police that Gertrude's the second victim. Otherwise, I'll go to them myself."

"No you won't. Because if you do, your name will be on the front page of every one of tomorrow morning's papers. You don't want that, do you?"

"Certainly not." There was a hard edge to her voice he hadn't heard before. "But since you're more concerned with the money you're being paid by Everard Spencer than with doing what's right, you leave me no other choice."

"And will you tell the police about your visit to the morgue tonight?"

Her amber eyes did not waver. "I'll tell them the truth—all of it."

"I'm sure the readers of the *Graphic* and the *Tribune* will be interested in what you have to say. And so will Lavinia Fairlie. You think she'll approve of her society editor working on a case of murder, with a private detective? Spending your off-hours roving the Bowery, and making midnight visits to the morgue? Hasn't it occurred to you that this could cost you your job?"

"I'll have to take that risk."

And she would do it, too—he didn't doubt that for a minute. "You win, Amanda. I'll go to the police myself. And I'll keep your name out of it."

She sat back in her chair and gave a small sigh of relief. He saw the tension leave her face. "Thank you, Ross."

He was moved by her belief that he would do as he had promised. He got to his feet. "If you're feeling better, I'll go now. It's time you went to bed."

"I am a little tired," she admitted.

"I'm not surprised. You've had quite a busy evening, haven't you? Clifford didn't bring you home until after midnight. And how long has he been squiring you around town?"

"We met by chance at the opera. As for tonight's reception at the museum—"

"Another chance meeting?"

"He invited me."

"The other young ladies must have envied you. All that Spencer money. And Clifford's fine manners. He's good-looking, too."

"Yes, indeed," she agreed, a little too readily.

"But you only accepted his invitation to gather material for your society page." He didn't bother to hide his disbelief.

"Your career's important to you, isn't it?" she asked. "Why should you doubt that I care as much about mine?"

He looked her up and down, then smiled. "I think that's plain enough."

She stiffened. Then she lifted Leander off her lap, carefully set him down on the floor, and stood up. "You're really a little behind the times, aren't you, Ross?" she said lightly. "I'm not the only woman who's chosen a career over hearth and home."

"You value your independence, the right to live as you please. So you've told me. But is that enough for a woman like you?"

"I suppose you think I need a husband to take care of me. To give me his name, and his protection." He caught the hint of mockery in her tone. "My mother surely would agree with you—but then, she's never understood me, either."

"And how well do you understand yourself?"

She squared her shoulders, her body slender and erect in her starched, high-necked blouse, her plain grey skirt. He took a step toward her, and caught the light scent of her freesia cologne. He remembered how she'd looked earlier that evening, with the enticing curves of her breasts, revealed by the low-cut bodice of her gown.

Probably she'd been kissed before. Maybe she'd even defied convention long enough to permit a respectful embrace from a proper young gentleman in the dimly-lit warmth of a conservatory. He guessed that had been the limit of her experience.

If he were to kiss her now, would she feel obliged to slap his face? Or would he arouse the latent sensuality he'd sensed in her, even at their first meeting? After the first brief resistance, would she respond, her body molding itself to his? He felt a need to hold her, to urge her lips apart, to explore the moist warmth of her mouth. He wanted to feel the softness of her breasts against his chest.

He took a long breath, and forced the thoughts away. Amanda Whitney was the daughter of an excellent family; she'd been brought up to follow the conventions of her class.

She was not for him.

Their meeting had been accidental, and their partnership would be a brief one. She would not give herself to a man without marriage.

"It's nearly dawn," he said. "You'll have to get back to the *Gazette* in a few hours. You'd better get what sleep you can."

CHAPTER ELEVEN

Ross caught a downtown train on the Third Avenue Elevated line and headed to the Bowery. He crossed Chatham Square and went on to the tenement where the Mareks had lived. Although he had not forgotten his promise to Amanda, the visit to the stationhouse could wait, for he had to take care of his own business first. He wasn't surprised to find the front door unlocked. Few slum dwellings had janitors, to see to such details.

He climbed the stairs and let himself into the Mareks' flat. In the grey light of dawn, he saw the unmistakable signs of a violent struggle: a cupboard overturned, with pots and pans scattered across the floor. His shoes crunched on the shards of broken dishes.

He struck a match and lit a kerosene lamp that had somehow escaped destruction, and went on into the windowless bedroom, where a white-enameled iron bed bore further signs of battle: a torn pillow lay on the floor, and the worn sheet was spotted with dark, reddish-brown stains. The closet held three clean, starched housedresses, a straw bonnet, a handsome cashmere shawl that might have been one of Jessamyn's cast-offs. He looked over the remaining garments: a man's blue and brown checked flannel suit, another in olive green, its trousers frayed at the cuffs, a cheap wool cap and a straw boater with a soiled green band. A canvas Gladstone bag stood on the floor. The top drawer of the pine dresser held a woman's flannel underwear and corset covers, neatly folded. The other two were filled with a man's shirts, balbriggans, and socks.

He returned to the front room, put out the lamp, then went back downstairs.

Outside on the stoop, he stopped to fill his lungs with the cold early morning air. How had Amanda forced herself into that reeking hallway and up those narrow, garbage-strewn stairs to confront Gertrude Marek? Where had she found the courage to stand her ground, to cross-examine that drunken ape, Barney, until he'd dragged her outside and tried to push her down the stairs?

She'd been moved by her sense of duty; the same stern conviction that would have driven her to the nearest police station first thing this morning, had he not agreed to go. She'd have told the police of her unauthorized visit to the morgue, and informed them it was Gertrude Marek's body lying on that slab in Bellevue's morgue. She'd have risked her reputation, her job at the *Gazette,* the independence that meant so much to her.

Why hadn't he allowed her to go? He pushed the question aside. He wasn't about to analyze his feelings, or be distracted from the most important case that had come his way since he'd left the force and gone into business for himself.

He stood a moment longer, looking at the deserted street. The garish lights above the entrance to Havemeyer's Beer Garden across the way had been dimmed, and he heard no crack of rifle fire from the shooting galleries. But he knew that the saloons carried on their trade around the clock. In their shuttered back rooms, the streetwalkers, having turned over their night's earnings, now lingered with their pimps, downing a few shots of whisky, or a stein of beer.

If Marek had killed his wife, he should have had sense enough to get away from the Bowery. He should have left the city; the freighters over at the South Street piers were always short of seamen. But his brain had been soaked with booze, and even now he might be lying in one of the "velvet rooms" where a man could buy a night's oblivion for a quarter. Ross decided to take time for a quick search.

He started down the front steps, then paused as he caught sight of a girl approaching the house. Her long, dark hair, loose and disheveled, straggled over her shoulders. No woman with the slightest claim to respectability would be roaming the streets at this hour, and certainly not bareheaded. Even the poorest workman's wife, if she couldn't afford a hat, would cover her head with a shawl. This was a whore, returning from a night on the streets.

She moved in a stupor, her shoulders slumped forward, the hem of her organdy dress dragging on the pavement, then halted at the foot of the stoop, unaware of his presence until he stepped in front of her, blocking her way.

"May I talk with you a minute, Miss?"

She looked up at him warily, and he saw she was younger than he'd supposed. Probably no more than fifteen. Her face was white with rice powder, caked and damp; her lip-rouge was smeared. She gave him a swift, appraising look: her gaze darted from his face to his well-cut brown tweed coat, kid gloves, dark silk cravat. Her mouth curved in a smile that looked almost genuine.

"I always got time t' talk with a gent like you." She took his hand. "Come along, dearie."

"You live here?"

"Yes—but I can't take you upstairs," she said. "Ma's up there, and the kids—" She led him back inside the evil-smelling hall, then drew him into the narrow space under the stairs. "We'll be nice an' private right here. I get fifty cents," she went on quickly. "An' I'm worth it, I promise you."

When he didn't respond she lowered her lids and looked up at him from under her lashes. "But for a good-looking fella like yerself, I'll take a quarter. And an extra dime if ye want something special like."

She rubbed herself against him, and when he made no move to embrace her, she pulled up her skirt. She wore nothing underneath. She pressed his hand to the patch of soft, damp hair between her legs, and he caught her musky odor. He jerked his hand away.

"Now don't tell me you're bashful—a big, handsome fella like you."

"I want to talk," he said. "That's all."

She dropped her skirt and took a step back, her smile gone. "You're a cop, ain't you?" she asked. "I already paid Officer Sullivan, same as always. I can't shell out to the whole force, can I?" Although she tried to sound defiant, she couldn't carry it off.

"I'm not a cop."

Although he meant to reassure her, he saw that his words had the opposite effect. She drew her breath in sharply, her eyes widening with fear. "Then—what do you want?" She took a few steps back, her body taut. "Let me go upstairs— please, mister. Just let me go."

He took out a silver dollar and held it up, so that it caught the wavering light from the gas jet. She stared at the coin, torn between greed and another, more powerful emotion.

A streetwalker had to go with any stranger who wanted her; she had to sell herself in dark alleys or deserted shacks. This girl, young as she was, had already endured plenty of rough handling like all her kind. Sometimes she had the bad luck to find a man who needed to satisfy himself by deliberately inflicting pain. But last night had been different—last night she'd feared for her life, and only desperation had kept her out on the streets.

Maybe she couldn't read the headlines, but she'd surely heard the cries of the newsboys:

HORRIBLE MURDER! MANIAC STRIKES AGAIN!

He spoke quietly. "What's your name?"

"Kathleen."

"A pretty name, that is. And you're a pretty girl."

"Let me go upstairs," she pleaded. "Ma's expectin' me—she'll come down here lookin' for me—"

"Don't be frightened. I won't hurt you. I'm here because I've got a job for that lout, Marek. I looked for him in his flat, but he's not there." He held up the coin. "If you can tell me where he is, it's yours."

"I ain't seen him, mister, not for awhile," she said. "That's the truth."

"But maybe you have some notion of where he'd be right now? A saloon in the neighborhood?"

"Why didn't you ask his wife?"

"She isn't in the flat, either."

"That so?" A look of anger crossed her face. "They were up there the other day, they were. I'd just got to bed when all hell broke loose, with him bellowin' like a Ballinderry bull, an' her beggin' him to stop. Holy saints, what a racket!"

"Marek's a mean drunk and no mistake," he agreed. "When was that brawl?"

"I forget . . ."

"Try to remember." He spun the coin between his fingers.

"A few days ago . . . I guess."

He restrained his impatience. "How many, Kathleen? Two? Three?"

"Friday! Yeah, it happened on Friday, right before daylight."

"How can you be sure it was Friday?"

"Because the landlord's man was comin' on Saturday to collect the rent, same as always. I gave Ma the money to pay him an' she said there'd be hardly anythin' left over for food. But I told her I'd done my best. Worn out, I was, so I laid myself down to sleep. An' didn't that drunken bum wake me up with his carryin' on! Smashin' up the place, by the sound of it. Knockin' his wife about, callin' her dirty names." Her lips tightened. "An' her always puttin' on airs, like she's better than me, cause she's married an' all. What's she's got to be so uppity about, with such as him for a husband, I'd like to know?"

"And you haven't seen Marek since Friday?"

"No, I ain't! An' good riddance, I say. Ain't seen her neither. Maybe she finally got some sense an' walked out on him." She sighed and let her thin shoulders slump with exhaustion. "That's all I know, mister." She looked at him hopefully. He dropped the coin in her hand, and closed her fingers around it.

Now her smile was warm and genuine. "Thanks, mister. I knew right off you was a real fine gent."

As she started to turn away, he put a hand on her arm. "Wait a bit, Kathleen. Can you tell me where he worked last?"

"He used to run his own shooting gallery. After he lost that, he worked as a bouncer at Harry Hill's place, over on West Houston, 'til he got himself kicked out. And then at Ryan's—that's two blocks down from here." She gave a short, derisive laugh. "Now he don't work at all—just takes his wife's money and spends it on drink. I saw him staggerin' out of Donahue's, one time—slipped an' landed flat on his arse, he did."

"Where else does he do his drinking?"

She named a few more Bowery saloons.

"All right, Kathleen. That'll do," he said. He reached into his pocket and handed her another two dollars.

Her lips parted in awed disbelief. "Oh my! It's a good man, you are." He saw the glitter of tears in her blue eyes.

"Upstairs with you now. And stay off the streets these next few nights, Kathleen."

"You think they'll have caught that loony by then?"

"Likely they will." It could do no harm to offer the reassurance she craved.

Police Headquarters at 300 Mulberry Street between Houston and Bleeker was an impressive brick building, trimmed with marble. He exchanged a brief greeting with the desk sergeant, then asked: "Tom Fallon come in yet?"

"He's been here all night," the sergeant said.

Ross wasn't surprised. Since Jessamyn's murder, Fallon and his men would have been under tremendous pressure from Superintendent Walling, and now, with the discovery of a second victim, they'd be driven harder than ever.

He went upstairs to the office of the Detective Squad, where he found Fallon, a broad-faced giant of a man with small, pale eyes, seated behind a wide desk. A brass tray held the heavy locust wood club he'd used with such memorable effect when he'd been a patrolman, that it had earned him his nickname, "Locust Fallon," among the criminals who'd felt its weight.

"Mornin', Buchanan," he said. "Come to offer us your help on the case?"

"Maybe so."

Fallon leaned forward in his big leather chair. "Now why'd you want to do that, when you're workin' for Spencer?"

"Mind if I sit down?"

Fallon shrugged, then jerked his head in the direction of a straight-backed wooden chair.

"The woman your boys found yesterday in the garden back of the Restell house. She been identified yet?"

Fallon didn't answer but his pale eyes were alert.

"I can tell you who she is," Ross said.

"I'm listening."

"Her name's Gertrude Marek. She lived with her husband, down on the Bowery."

"And maybe you'll be obligin' enough to give me her address."

"Number Twenty-two, a tenement across the street from Havemeyer's Beer Garden."

"So tell me more about this Marek woman and her husband."

"That's all I know."

Fallon gave him a tight-lipped grin. "Buchanan, you're a damn liar."

"All I can tell you now," he said.

Fallon stood up. He was taller than Ross and broader in the chest and shoulders. He slid his thick fingers along the locust wood club. He was still smiling. "Been up to the Mareks' place, have you?"

"I have."

"How many times?" Fallon asked.

"Only once. About an hour ago."

"And you came hot-footing it down here right away, to share the information with me. Just for old times' sake."

"I didn't say that."

"So why did you come?"

He thought of Amanda, and smiled faintly. "You wouldn't believe me if I told you."

"Try me."

"Not right now." Ross got to his feet. He tried to ignore the cold, hard knot in the pit of his stomach. He wouldn't make it through the door, if Fallon chose to keep him here. "I've got business of my own to attend to," he said. "Everard Spencer's like all rich men. He expects full value for every dollar he lays out."

The Spencer name had its hoped-for effect. A few minutes later, he was back out on the street again.

Ottilie, wearing a pink satin combing jacket over her camisole, sat before her ebony dressing table, and tried to restrain her impatience while her maid arranged her elaborate coiffure. Her hair had faded from its youthful red-gold to a nondescript ginger, and even frequent applications of chamomile, beaten eggs, and hot olive oil had not restored its luster. An imposing collection of expensive creams and lotions, some imported from Paris, had done little to soften the lines that bracketed her mouth or the deep vertical crease between her eyes. She sighed and her gaze dropped from the gold-framed mirror to the array of cut glass bottles and jars before her.

Yesterday, after she'd seen the papers, she'd gone in search of her husband, but he'd already left the house and had not returned for dinner. Clifford hadn't been at home either; he'd left a message that he'd be escorting Miss

Amanda Whitney to the reception at the Metropolitan Museum.

"Get out, girl!"

Ottilie started at the sound of her husband's voice. He was standing in the doorway of her ebony and gold dressing room, his face flushed, his jaw hard with anger.

The maid set down the brush at once, curtsied and hurried out.

Everard strode to the dressing table and tossed down a pile of newspapers with such force that the jars and bottles clinked against one another. "Take a look," he said.

On the front page of the *Graphic*, she saw a halftone photograph of the facade of their house. "Who gave them permission to use this?" she demanded.

"Never mind the picture. Read this!" He moved his thick finger to the top of the first column, and she skimmed the printed lines.

"Gertrude Marek! She's the one they found murdered? Everard—no! It's a mistake."

"Positive identification by the police, that's what it says right here. And the Marek woman was wearing a wedding gown, and strangled with her own bridal wreath."

Shaken as she was, she forced herself to go on reading and found a slight reassurance in the newspaper's account of the murder. "They don't say Gertrude used to work for us."

"Not yet," he said grimly. "But now they know who she was, how long do you think it'll take them to find out the rest?"

"What about that detective—that Ross Buchanan. You said he was the best in the city. So why hasn't he caught this—this maniac? What's he done to earn his wages?"

Everard did not answer.

Her anger gave way to rising fear. "Do you know what will happen now? Do you?" Her voice was shrill and unsteady. "Everyone will be talking about us. Spreading wicked lies. My friends won't be at home to me when I call—they'll look away when they pass me in the street. All that money you paid for our box at the new opera house— how can we show our faces there? And Clifford—poor boy! What about his reputation—his future? What about—"

"Shut up, Lottie!"

Lottie.

She'd been Lottie Schultz when she'd worked as a laundress back in Cedar Ridge, but after she married Everard, and they left the timber country for Milwaukee, she had changed her given name to Ottilie, because it sounded more genteel.

"I sent for Buchanan yesterday." Everard gave her a tight, humorless smile. "He's been doing his job all right. He found out that Gertrude used to be Jessamyn's maid."

"You never should have let him question the servants. You know how they love to gossip about their betters—"

He brushed aside the interruption. "And that's not all. He knows about Jessamyn and O'Shea, too."

"What if he goes to the police, and tells them about it?" Fear erupted inside her. "Maybe he already has."

"Don't talk like a fool! I'm paying him a small fortune for his services. And it's not just the money. His reputation's at stake, too. If he finds the killer before the police do, he'll have more rich clients than he can handle. He'll be able to build an agency as big as Pinkerton's. Why would he risk all that to go blabbing to the police?"

Although his words seemed to make sense, they did little to calm her. She had never fainted in her life, but now she went weak and light-headed. The walls of the room started to swim before her eyes. She tried to draw a deep breath, but the cruel pressure of her tightly-laced corset made that impossible.

She gripped the edge of the dressing table. "But even if Buchanan doesn't tell them, somebody else might talk. A scandal like that would destroy us." She tried to collect her scattered thoughts. "Who else knows about Devin O'Shea and—"

"And that bastard brat he fathered on Jessamyn? Gertrude did, that's for damn sure. And the midwife upstate—whoever she was. She knows. And the hag who runs the baby farm."

She clutched his sleeve. "Everard! You've got to stop the newspapers from printing one word about Jessamyn and O'Shea. You've got to go straight down to Park Row, first thing tomorrow and forbid James Bennett and Pulitzer and the rest of them to print such filth about us. Tell them if they do, you'll ruin them."

He jerked his arm free. "Even I can't muzzle every reporter in New York."

"Yes you can—and you will! It's your responsibility!"

"Since when have you started giving me orders?" He looked down at her with open contempt. "I know my responsibilities. Too bad I can't say as much for you. If you'd trained Jessamyn right, she wouldn't have gone off to the stables and spread her legs for that Irish bog-trotter. But no—that was too much to expect from you. Like mother, like daughter."

"How can you—"

"It's the truth, isn't it? Didn't you trick me into marrying you?" He ignored her cry of protest. "You waited until I'd gotten my first big promotion. Then you told me that lie about being pregnant. If I hadn't married you, you'd have gone running to that stiff-necked Methodist boss of mine and he'd have fired me."

"It wasn't like that—I swear it. You were the only man who ever touched me. There were plenty of men who wanted me, but I saved myself for you."

"Sure you did! Because you knew I wasn't like those other lumberjacks. You knew I'd make it to the top. You got your hooks into me so I'd take you away from that stinking laundry shed in Cedar Ridge."

"That's not true. I skipped a month and I was sick every morning and one of the girls said that meant I was going to have a baby."

"And you gave birth to Clifford—two years after the wedding."

"Clifford! What will become of him now? This scandal will ruin him. He'll be an outcast."

"I doubt it," he said dryly. "With his looks and my money, he'll still have his pick of those pretty young girls who've been chasing after him."

"You think a Schuyler or a Brevoort will allow his daughter to marry into our family after this?" She jabbed a finger at the newspaper. "He'll have to leave the city— maybe go to live abroad!"

"Stop screeching like a scalded cat. Stop it, I say!" The steel in his tone silenced her. "Once they've caught the killer and put a rope around his neck, some new scandal will push this one off the front page. By next year, Clifford will have married into one of those old Knickerbocker families, see if he doesn't."

"Next year?" The words made her feel vaguely uneasy. Of course, Clifford would marry one day—but not so soon. "He's only a boy."

"When I was his age, I was boss of a lumber gang."

"But Clifford's different. He's fine and sensitive—"

"He's ready to stand on his own, right now. Time to turn him loose, Lottie."

How could she stand aside and let some simpering young girl come between her and her son? "I won't let him be pushed into marriage with a silly little fool—"

"Amanda Whitney's no fool."

She gave him a blank stare. Why was he talking about that Whitney girl?

"She's got a good head on her shoulders," he went on. "Fine-looking female, too. Carries herself like a thorough-bred. Didn't she go to that reception with him last night? She's probably told everyone at the *Gazette* that young Clifford Spencer's been courting her."

"Courting her? Because he spent one evening with her? Oh, I don't doubt she's taken with him—what girl wouldn't be? But what about her family?"

"You needn't worry about them. Her father died a bankrupt. Damn fool worked himself to death to pay back every cent his partner embezzled from their clients. And her mother's over in Europe, as a paid companion to a Mrs. Dennison."

So he'd already checked out the girl's background. "Amanda Whitney wasn't brought up to earn her own living," he went on. "Once the novelty wears off, she'll jump at the chance to marry Clifford."

He turned away and strode to the door. "Invite her to the house."

"We can't possibly have a dinner party here, not so soon after a death in the family. It wouldn't be proper."

"Ask her to tea, then."

"But Everard—"

"Do as I say!"

She searched for an excuse, but under his hard gaze, her thoughts scattered, and she couldn't speak. Or was she afraid to oppose him? Still, she was unwilling to give way, with Clifford's future at stake. She forced a placating smile. "After dinner, we'll go into the library and talk this over."

"I'm dining out tonight. And there's nothing more to talk about. I've told you what to do, so do it." He gave her a brief, cold stare and walked out, slamming the door shut behind him.

She sat motionless, watching the last of the crimson sunset fade to grey outside the tall, arched windows. She reached up an unsteady hand and smoothed the puffs atop her coiffure. No need for her maid to come back and do the finishing touches, or help her on with her dinner gown. Everard wouldn't be there and Clifford had already left the house to dine with a party of friends at Delmonico's. She shrank from the prospect of having her dinner alone, seated at the long, candle-lit table.

Slowly she got to her feet and crossed the ebony and gold bedroom; the architect had assured her it was of Moorish design—whatever that might be. She looked away as she passed the enormous bed—ten feet high and curtained with mauve satin draperies. Not once, since they'd moved into the mansion had Everard shared it with her. He was a man of lusty appetites, and she didn't doubt he was keeping a mistress.

Her legs felt shaky as she went on through one of the three gilded arches leading to her bathroom. She stopped before the oval basin, inlaid with an elaborate mother-of-pearl design. Her cheeks were hot, her temples pounding. She ran the cold water, soaked a washcloth and patted her face. Then she turned, her gaze moving around the magnificently-furnished room, with its tiled floor arranged in a mosaic of sea horses and shells; its swan-shaped marble tub.

Back in Cedar Ridge, she had taken her turn with the other girls every Saturday night, using the tin tub at the public bathhouse. Some of them had been too exhausted or indifferent to bathe—but not Lottie Schultz. She'd washed her long, thick hair in rain water, then let it dry in the sun. No matter how tired she had been after six days of scrubbing the lumbermen's filthy woolen underwear and socks, she kept herself clean, held her head high. And waited for her chance.

She'd have earned more on her back in one of the cribhouses on the hill, but that hadn't been for her. She'd been young and strong, filled with ambition. And when she'd first caught Everard Spencer's eye, she knew she'd found a means of moving up to a better sort of life. Not that she'd ever imagined, even in her most fantastic dreams, anything like this splendid mansion on Fifth Avenue. But she had known instinctively that this shrewd, hard-faced young man would rise to the top, and she had been determined to go with him.

Had she ever really loved him? She'd never stopped to question her feelings too closely. She had set out to catch his eye, and she'd succeeded. He had taken her riding in a rented buggy, given her presents, and from their first night together, he had satisfied the needs of her robust young body.

But she hadn't tricked him into marriage. She'd skipped a month, and she'd believed, she'd hoped, she was carrying his child.

And you gave birth to Clifford. Two years after the wedding.

By the time he'd been born, they had moved to a fine house in Milwaukee, and although Everard spent a great deal of his time traveling on business, laying the foundations of his fortune, he had been there when Clifford was born. He'd been pleased that his first child was a fine, healthy boy, who would be heir to his growing empire.

As for Ottilie, she showered her affections on her firstborn. Even as a toddler, he was blessed with excellent health and an amiable disposition. She was so proud when she took him out walking, dressed up in his kilt and velvet jacket. Even strangers had stopped to praise his winning smile, his dark blue eyes and long, golden ringlets.

Jessamyn had given her no such pleasure. After a long and difficult labor, the infant had come into the world, a scrawny little thing who kept Ottilie awake with her plaintive wailing; until she lost patience and turned the fretful infant over to a wet nurse. As for Ottilie, she continued to devote all her time and attention to her son.

Clifford, her wonderful son. To think that she was the mother of that fine, handsome young gentleman. And such a good son, too. He escorted her to the theater, to musicales, and charity bazaars; he went driving with her in the park. He flattered her almost as if he were her beau. He made her feel young again.

Everard was right when he said that the Whitney girl would jump at an offer to marry the Spencer fortune, and get herself a handsome young husband. She'd be dazzled by her good luck. But Amanda Whitney was no shy young thing, to be controlled by her mother-in-law. Not that one. She had no money but she did have intelligence, and the poise that came from generations of good breeding.

Ottilie tried to convince herself that she ought to go along with her husband's demand, and do what she could to encourage the match, no matter what her private reservations might be. That was her wifely duty. But she had more urgent reason to do his bidding, for she knew and feared the streak of violence in him.

It seemed incredible that Jessamyn, frail and timid, had summoned the courage to oppose him. She'd refused to have an abortion and all his ranting, his threats, had not shaken her. At last he'd been forced to give way and share the dangerous secret of their daughter's pregnancy with Gertrude Marek. Not that it had mattered in the long run, because the infant had been taken from her at birth, and sent to a baby farm, where few survived the first year.

Jessamyn had tried to thwart his wishes again, by insisting she wouldn't marry Howard Thornton. When he'd refused to give way, she'd withdrawn, as if by ignoring the inevitability of the marriage, she could avoid it. Would she have gone through with the wedding in that same trance-like state? A terrible suspicion stirred in Ottilie's mind, and she could not ignore it.

Had Jessamyn somehow found the courage to oppose Everard one last time? Perhaps, after she and Clifford had returned from the theater that night; after they, and all the servants, were asleep, Jessamyn had waited up for her father, and had told him she would avoid the marriage—even if it meant letting everyone know about her disgrace?

And then? Ottilie had a swift, terrifying vision of her husband striking his daughter with more force than he'd intended; hard enough to knock her down. Maybe Jessamyn had struck her head on a piece of furniture, a corner of the fireplace, as she fell, and Everard, kneeling over her, had realized that he'd killed her. What then? He wouldn't have panicked—not Everard. He would have moved with cold determination to protect himself.

But even supposing that were so, why dress her in her wedding gown and veil, why put the wreath around her neck to make it appear she'd been strangled? Why take her body from the house and leave it in that alley in the Ladies Mile?

A shudder ran through her, as she fought her way back to sanity. Only the unremitting stress of these past weeks could have allowed her to abandon her common sense, to even consider such nightmarish fancies. If she didn't get hold of herself, she'd go into a nervous collapse.

She'd heard whispers about women afflicted in that way. A few had recovered under the treatment of Dr. S. Weir Mitchell of Philadelphia, now famous for his "rest cure": complete isolation of the patient in a darkened room, for weeks, even months, with no activities of any sort, and only a trained nurse to carry out the doctor's orders.

But sometimes an unfortunate female proved to be beyond even Dr. Mitchell's formidable skills, and then stronger measures were called for. She remembered what she'd heard about Mrs. Oliver Rhysdael, who had suffered a nervous collapse after her fourth miscarriage in as many years. Her husband had sent her off to the Bloomingdale Asylum and, so far as Ottilie knew, the poor woman was still shut up there.

Everard had made it plain that he no longer had the slightest affection for her. If she posed a threat to him, he wouldn't hesitate to ship her off to an asylum, and leave her there.

The devil he would! Her jaw hardened. Lottie Schultz of Cedar Ridge hadn't been any delicate flower. She'd been tough and determined—she'd had to be, to get this far. Jessamyn's murder and the threat of social ruin had left her badly shaken, but she'd survive. She'd move past it all, and one day she'd walk into Grace Church, splendidly dressed, to see her son make a suitable marriage. If he chose the Whitney girl, she'd find a way of coping with her new daughter-in-law.

She returned to her bedroom. She wasn't hungry but nevertheless, she would have her maid bring up dinner on a tray. And a glass of port wine, or maybe two, to help her relax. A good, nourishing meal and a sound night's sleep would strengthen her, so she could handle whatever lay ahead.

CHAPTER TWELVE

The late afternoon sunlight was slanting through the tall windows of Amanda's office when Maude dropped in for the daily chat that now had become a ritual. She took a seat and asked, "Have you decided what to wear to the Autumn Fete?"

"My cinnamon silk, I suppose. Or the coral taffeta."

"But you can't. Clifford Spencer's already seen both."

Amanda gave a little shrug. "He's not escorting me to the Fete. What made you suppose he would be?"

"He shared your box at the opera, didn't he?"

"The Van Wycks' box," Amanda corrected her. "And we only met by chance."

"But you didn't meet by chance at the Museum reception. You made a grand entrance, when you walked in together."

"Good heavens! Does anything happen in New York society without your hearing about it?"

"Not much," she said. "So you're going to the Fete alone?"

"I am. Mrs. Fairlie wants an article about the Fete for next week's *Gazette*."

"Even so, you must have a new gown. Otherwise there'll be plenty of old cats—and young ones, too—whose tongues will be wagging. 'Poor Amanda—is she going to have to wear those same two dresses all season long?' "

"My mother sent me that length of coral taffeta, and it would have been a pity to let it go to waste." She looked away uneasily. "Madam Duval asked no payment for making the gown—only a mention of her shop on the society page."

"Then you must ask Madame Duval to make another gown for the Fete."

"No—I couldn't do that," she protested.

"You want to be a credit to the *Ladies Gazette*, don't you? Just mention Madame's name in the *Gazette* again, and I will, too."

"That's kind of you, but it doesn't seem—right."

"You can't possibly afford a new outfit for every occasion of the season," Maude said firmly. "Anymore than you can give a large contribution to the Chinese Mission and Rescue Society or whatever they call that charity that will benefit from the Fete." Maude gave her a reassuring smile. "It's all right. Mrs. Fairlie's already sent them a check. Now, as for your new gown, you had better get in touch with Madam Duval right away. She's probably swamped with orders, and it's only three days to the Fete, after all."

"That's not enough time—" Amanda protested.

"Just come down to my office and use my telephone. Say you'll be at her shop late this afternoon."

"It must be a great convenience, having a telephone of your own."

"I don't know how I managed without one. And if you go on as you have, you'll be getting your own before long. Mrs. Fairlie's pleased with your work."

"She hasn't mentioned it to me."

"That's not her way." Maude gave a little laugh. "If she praises you too lavishly, you might ask for a raise in salary."

"Maude, really!" She still wasn't used to her friend speaking so openly about money.

"Of course, if you were to find yourself a wealthy husband, you wouldn't have to concern yourself with such mundane matters. He'd pay your dressmaker's bills and deck you out in diamonds." Her blue-grey eyes sparkled mischievously. "Wouldn't you rather go driving around in the Spencers' brougham, than chasing after a hansom cab?"

"Clifford Spencer has never given me the slightest reason to suppose he feels anything more than friendship for me—" But she remembered the warmth in his eyes, the pressure of his hand on hers, when he'd said good-night after the reception.

"Just give him a little encouragement, and he'll propose before the end of the season."

Amanda stood up quickly. "I'd better call Madame Duval now," she said.

The elegant public reception rooms on the ground floor of the Park Avenue Armory, home of New York's elite Seventh Regiment, were often used for dances, teas, and even polo matches. Tonight they were lavishly decorated with gilded branches thick with red and gold leaves. Bunches of purple velvet grapes hung from lattices. Now, as the music began, all eyes turned to the curtained enclosures that concealed the *tableaux vivants*.

Several attractive young women had volunteered to pose as 'living statues' for a worthy cause. They were to represent the ladies of King Arthur's Court, described in Tennyson's *Idylls of the King*, an epic poem Mrs. August Belmont had pronounced "most uplifting."

"He writes nothing that would offend even the most delicate sensibilities," Mrs. Stuyvesant Fish had agreed. "So much modern poetry is quite unsuitable for ladies. But Mr. Tennyson is above reproach."

"Why, even Queen Victoria thinks most highly of him,"

Mrs. William Astor said. Her pronouncement had settled the matter.

Now, as Amanda took her seat, she knew she'd been right to accept Maude's advice. The new russet gown accented the auburn lights in her chestnut hair, and although her amber necklace, a gift from her father on her eighteenth birthday, could not rival the jewels worn by the women around her, it had a special significance for her.

"It matches your eyes, my dear," her father had said, as he had fastened it around her throat.

She leaned forward in her chair as the first of the velvet curtains parted. A murmur of approval ran through the audience at the sight of Miss Ellen Murray, clad in white satin, a lily clasped in her hand, lying prone in the black-draped barge that carried her down the stream to Camelot. The backdrops had been created by Mr. Frederick Lucas, one of the city's most talented theatrical designers. The painted waves rose and fell in a most realistic way, as the barge slowly moved along.

"How touching," Amanda heard one of the ladies murmur. The audience applauded and the curtains closed.

The next tableau revealed Guinevere, decked out in a splendid robe of apple green and gold, waving a silk scarf and gazing raptly at a painted representation of a tournament, complete with knights, chargers, and brilliantly-colored banners.

But even as Amanda admired the "living portraits," her attention began to stray. The Armory's reception hall, warm and fragrant with the mingled scents of hot-house flowers and expensive perfumes, crowded with bejeweled ladies in silks and velvets, was a world apart from the streets outside. She could not forget her first impressions of the Bowery: its filthy tenements and ragged children, the rattling of the elevated railway. Or her visit to the morgue. She repressed a shudder at the memory of Gertrude Marek's body on a slab, her hair plastered to her bruised face by the stream of water from the overhead jet.

With an effort, she forced her thoughts away and fixed her gaze on last tableau: Mrs. Harry Lehr, as Morgan le Fey, stood at the entrance to a rocky cavern, a crescent-topped wand in her hand, and a circlet of diamonds on her long, flowing black hair.

After a final round of applause, the members of the audience rose and began moving in the direction of the adjoining room, where a buffet supper was to be served. Amanda mingled with the crowd, then paused to greet Mrs. Euphemia Armstead, and her daughter, Phoebe, who was decked out in white tulle and pink ribbons, with a string of pearls around her neck.

The Armstead Woolen Mills had provided the Union soldiers with shoddy blankets and uniforms that had worn out after a few months. Out of his enormous profits, Mr. Armstead had built an imposing brownstone on Fifth Avenue and a twenty-eight room "cottage" in Newport.

But her father's fortune and her mother's unceasing efforts had not yet attracted a prospective suitor. The girl's face was long and bony; her front teeth protruded, so that her face, in repose, had the look of a melancholy horse.

"The *tableaux* were most original, were they not, Miss Whitney?" said the stout matron. Without waiting for Amanda's reply, she chattered on. "And let us not forget that the donations from tonight's entertainment will go to such a worthy cause—a mission school where unfortunate little Chinese girls will be properly cared for. It's shocking that those poor little creatures are abandoned or sold into slavery—by their own parents! But then, what else can one expect from a nation of barbarians?"

"Papa says the government should have passed the Chinese Exclusion Act long ago, instead of waiting until now," said Phoebe. "He says we don't want our country overrun by a horde of yellow-skinned heathens."

"I would not call them heathens," Amanda said quietly. "Their civilization is far older than our own."

"Their civilization!" Mrs. Armstead interrupted. "Surely you can't possibly consider such creatures civilized—not when they treat their own children so shamefully."

Amanda stiffened with indignation. "And what about the children right here in our own city, who are forced to live in Bowery tenements? Or those who have no homes at all, and sleep in our streets and alleys? And the—unwanted—infants sent off to baby farms by mothers who are ashamed to acknowledge their existence?" she went on. "Few of them survive their first year, and those who do—if they're pretty enough—are sold into another sort of slavery."

Phoebe stared at Amanda with avid curiosity. "Slavery? Here in our city? Why whatever do you mean, Miss Whitney?"

Euphemia drew in her breath with a hiss, and two spots of red appeared on her plump cheeks. "I hardly think that's a fit subject for young ladies to discuss."

Amanda's gloved hand tightened around the ivory handle of her fan, as she searched for a suitable reply. She heard a deep masculine laugh, turned quickly and saw Howard Thornton.

He bowed to Mrs. Armstead and her daughter, then offered his arm to Amanda. "Miss Whitney. I have been looking for you. You haven't forgotten you promised to take supper with me?"

She hadn't even known he was here tonight, but now she

gave him a grateful smile as she accompanied him into the adjoining room, where the guests already clustered around candlelit buffet tables spread with damask cloths, and decorated with gilded cornucopias overflowing with a variety of brightly-colored fruit.

She was spared the need for further conversation while she made her selection from among the trays of cold sliced ham, turkey, and venison, and a variety of elaborate desserts. A waiter carried their tray to an alcove at the side of the room, where potted palms and towering ferns offered privacy. Thornton seated himself beside her, his eyes glinting with amusement. "I do believe you shocked Euphemia Armstead out of her wits."

"That wasn't my intention," she said. "But if she and her daughter know nothing about our city's neglected children, it's high time they learned."

His brows rose slightly. "And how do you happen to know about conditions on the baby farms? Or the unhappy fate of those pretty little girls who manage to survive?"

She wasn't about to admit that Ross Buchanan had told her; it would be best if no one knew they were acquainted. "I heard about it at a lecture given by Miss Lucy Larcom—at Cooper Union," she improvised quickly.

"Indeed? And did you go there seeking material for an article about conditions on baby farms for the *Gazette*? I didn't think Mrs. Fairlie approved of such sensationalism. You might try such a piece with Mr. Pulitzer's *Journal*—or maybe the *Graphic*."

"I don't know enough about it. But someone who is better informed than I am should tell the public what is happening to these unfortunate children."

She remembered the anger in Ross's face when he had told her about conditions on the baby farms. He was thoroughly familiar with the sordid side of New York, but he was still capable of outrage at its injustices. He was a complicated man, and his reactions often baffled her, but one thing she had discovered: he lived by his own code of decency. He had kept his word, and spared her the ordeal of going to the police to identify the second victim; the day after their visit to the morgue, she'd seen Gertrude's name in the headlines.

The Spencers must have been dismayed by this new revelation, fearful of what more the newspapers might discover about their family affairs.

"Miss Whitney?" She realized Howard Thornton was speaking to her, and she gave him an apologetic smile. "I thought Clifford Spencer might have escorted you here tonight."

"Why would you have supposed that?"

"I meant no offense," he said quickly. "One should ignore such gossip."

"Yes, indeed. If anyone had noticed Clifford's behavior toward you, that evening at the opera, they might have supposed he disapproved of you."

"And they'd have been right. He was against his sister's engagement to me from the start."

She was pushing the bounds of propriety, and she knew it—but she might not have another opportunity to question Howard Thornton. "Perhaps he had some reason . . ."

"Clifford's reasons didn't concern me," he said with a slight shrug. "Her parents approved of the match."

"And did Jessamyn share her parents' feelings?"

"She was a shy little thing, with no opinions of her own." Amanda could have told him otherwise, but she chose not to. "Even at her coming-out ball, she was a wallflower," he went on. "If I hadn't proposed, she'd have remained a spinster."

"A dreadful fate for any female!" Amanda said, with mock horror.

"There are exceptions, of course," he assured her. "If you don't marry, Miss Whitney, it will be by your own choice. As for Jessamyn, had she married me, she'd have had much to gain. The most exclusive circles would have been open to her. And, of course, I'd have treated her with respect and kindness, always."

"Is that enough to ensure a successful marriage?" she asked.

"I think so," he said. "But perhaps you don't agree. Perhaps, unless you meet your ideal mate, your own Sir Galahad, you'll be content to go on working at the *Gazette*?"

She caught the hint of mockery in his voice. "I find my work most rewarding."

First Clifford, then Ross had asked her that same question. And now Howard Thornton. And always with that same air of amused disbelief. Was it so difficult for them to believe that a woman could find fulfillment in her career?

"And you came here tonight only to gather material for one of your articles?" He gave her a teasing smile. "Tell me, would you allow a gentleman to share your company one evening, purely for your enjoyment?"

"That would depend upon the gentleman—and the occasion."

"I've reserved a box at Wallack's Theater for Mrs. Lillie Langtry's New York debut next week. If you're not otherwise engaged on Saturday evening, will you attend the opening performance with me?"

When she did not answer at once, he went on quickly. "If you must bring along that little notebook of yours, I'm sure your readers will be fascinated by your impressions of the lady."

Of course, he was right about that: even the most carefully-sheltered young ladies in New York knew of the liaison between Mrs. Langtry and Edward VII, Prince of Wales. Should she accept the invitation? It was most unlikely that Thornton had the slightest connection with Jessamyn's murder, since he'd had so much to gain from their marriage. Her dowry would have enabled him to pay off his debts.

Amanda's thoughts went racing ahead. If she spent another evening in Thornton's company, she might be able to learn more about him. Whatever she could find out might be of use to Ross.

"You must not be put off by Clifford's unfavorable opinion of me," he was saying. "No doubt he'd have come to accept me into the family, given time."

"And what about Jessamyn?" she said. "Suppose she had refused to go through with the wedding?" It was a most improper question and, for a moment, she feared she had gone too far.

He laughed softly. "Jessamyn wouldn't have dared to oppose her parents, and cause a scandal." He spoke with complete confidence. "She had reservations about marrying me, I won't deny it. But if her brother hadn't prevented me from seeing her that last time, I could have reassured her."

"That last time?"

"I went to the Spencers' home to speak with her, but Clifford said she'd retired and was not to be disturbed. He was quite vehement about it. I didn't wish to make a scene so I took my leave and went to dine at my club. I was sure I'd find another opportunity to speak to her. How could I have known that I'd never see her again?"

Amanda understood, and a shudder ran through her.

In the strained silence that followed, she heard the orchestra tuning up. He offered her his arm, and they returned the reception room, where a soprano was singing the opening lines of Tosti's ballad, *Good-bye.*

"Falling leaf and fading tree, lines of white on a cloudy sea . . ."

But Amanda paid little attention to the melancholy words, and she scarcely listened to the lady harpist that concluded the evening's entertainment. She was remembering Jessamyn, who had refused to have an abortion, and had insisted on bearing her illegitimate child. Jessamyn, who had quarreled with her father over her arranged marriage. Had Thornton really been so sure she'd go through with the wedding? If so, why had he gone to her home and asked to speak with her?

A round of applause startled Amanda, and she realized that the musicale was over. As a shower of red and gold leaves drifted down from the gallery, the guests rose and started moving toward the exit.

After she'd retrieved her cloak, she found Thornton waiting for her outside the ladies' retiring room. He accompanied her outside, then said, "You must allow me to escort you home."

She smiled and inclined her head.

Because of the frigid weather, he had not taken his open landau tonight; instead, he helped her into his handsome town coach, drawn by a pair of high-stepping horses with silver-plated harness.

During the drive downtown, as she kept up her part of the conversation, she wondered why he was being so attentive to her that evening. With so many wealthy young ladies at tonight's fete, why had he sought her out?

The carriage turned into Nineteenth Street and stopped in front of her house. The light from the gas lamp was blurred by the autumn fog.

"You haven't yet said you'd come to the theater with me," he reminded her, with an ingratiating smile.

"I'm a working woman, remember?" She spoke lightly. "I'll have to go over my assignments with Mrs. Fairlie, before I can give you my answer."

When Amanda telephoned Ross, early the following morning, he heard the barely-suppressed excitement in her voice. He suggested that they should meet at Fleischmann's Vienna Bakery, a continental style shop and café at Broadway and Tenth Street. It was shortly after five that evening when she came hurrying down the street. As she drew near, he saw that her cheeks were flushed and her amber eyes glowed with triumph. He recognized the look: she had come upon some new information, and she could scarcely wait to share it with him.

He led her inside, and chose a small table at the rear, where he ordered thick ham sandwiches on rye bread, a Sacher torte for her, and a pot of steaming coffee. Scarcely waiting to catch her breath, she began: "I happened to meet Howard Thornton at the Autumn Fete last night." Then she went on to tell him the details of their conversation. "After Clifford sent him away, he went on to his club," she finished.

"Which club was that?"

Her face fell. "I didn't think to ask." She paused for a moment, brows drawn together. "But my father mentioned having seen him at the Harvard Club from time to time."

No doubt a man like Thornton belonged to more than one exclusive club here in the city, he thought. But the Harvard Club was as good a place as any with which to start.

Amanda finished her sandwich, then took a sip of coffee. "Mr. Thornton has invited me to attend the theater with him next week. I think I should accept, don't you?"

"I didn't realize you took such pleasure in his company."

"That has nothing whatever to do with it," she said impatiently. "I am hoping to find out more about what happened during his visit to the Spencers' home."

"What more can there be? He didn't get a chance to see Jessamyn, because her brother sent him away."

"But suppose he didn't tell me everything? Suppose he went back later that evening?"

"Why do you think he might have done that?"

"He knew Jessamyn did not love him, any more than he loved her. But he hoped to reassure her that their marriage still could be a successful one. As his wife, she would be welcomed into the best society. He would treat her with respect and consideration. But maybe when he spoke with her that way, his words did not have the effect he'd expected. Maybe she decided, once and for all, that she couldn't possibly go through with the wedding—and she told him so."

He considered her words carefully. "And if she had, how do you think he'd have reacted?"

"He would have been angry, of course."

"Angry enough to have lost control and killed her?"

She stared at him, rigid with outraged disbelief. "No! That's not what I meant. He couldn't have done that!"

"Why not?"

"He's not capable of murder."

"You don't know him all that well, do you?"

"No, but—"

"Then how can you be sure?"

"Why because—he is a Thornton. His family's one of the finest in New York."

His jaw hardened. He was aware, as never before, of the gulf between them. "He comes from a good family, therefore he is incapable of murder. I don't see the connection. Suppose you explain it to me."

"One of his ancestors, Sir Richard Thornton, was knighted by Charles the Second," she went on. "Another was lady-in-waiting to Queen Anne. And Colonel James Thornton distinguished himself at Waterloo."

"That's quite a fancy pedigree," he said. "Go on and tell me the rest of it."

She looked at him closely, as if sensing that she had not yet convinced him. "His mother was a Van Vorst, a direct descendant of a patroon. But perhaps you don't know what that means."

Her barbed words, her arrogant tone, found their mark. For the first time since they had met, she was reminding him of the social distance that separated them.

"I think I do. It means that his great-grandfather, on his mother's side, grabbed himself a big chunk of land on the Hudson, where he lived in luxury on the rents from his tenants and lorded it over them. It means his father's family belonged to the British aristocracy. But all that says nothing about Howard Thornton. Not to me." He went on, without bothering to hide his contempt. "Have you forgotten that he was ready and willing to swallow his pride? To marry Jessamyn for her money, so he could pay off his creditors and go on living in high style?" He didn't give her time to answer. "Nobody who was closely involved with Jessamyn Spencer is above suspicion. That includes Thornton, doesn't it?"

Her cheeks went scarlet and she fixed her gaze on her coffee cup.

"Doesn't it?" he repeated.

"The man who killed Jessamyn was insane," she said. "Who but a maniac could have been capable of such a crime?"

"And of course you don't doubt that Howard Thornton is sound of mind. He's a compulsive gambler, an unprincipled fortune hunter, but nothing worse?"

This was the time to tell her what he'd learned about Thornton's sexual peculiarities and exactly where he'd heard about them. But he was surprised and annoyed with himself when he couldn't bring himself to repeat the facts with the same frankness Isobel Hewitt had used when she had told him.

During these past weeks, Amanda had already seen too much of the dark underside of the city: the violence and ugliness that had been hidden from her until she had become involved with him. He sought for a suitable way to warn her against further contact with Howard Thornton. And found himself at a loss. How much did she know about the ordinary sexual relations between men and women? He understood that a proper young lady of her class went to her marriage bed with only the vaguest ideas of what her husband expected of her.

"A man like Thornton may behave with perfect propriety in polite society, but show a different side of his character in other surroundings." *Like those upstairs rooms in Isobel Hewitt's brothel.*

"I've no idea what you mean."

How could she, when he'd spoken so indirectly?

He pushed away his empty cup and tried again. "There are certain men, perhaps jaded with the commonplace, who can only respond to other, more unusual forms of stimulation."

He saw he was getting nowhere; that she was even more baffled than before.

"I'm telling you, there's no need for you to get mixed up with a man like Howard Thornton. I don't want you to get to know him better. Don't see him again, don't go to the theater with him. Or anywhere else." He was speaking more forcefully than he would have wanted to, but he had no other choice. "Leave him to me. I'll check out what he told you about his visit to the Spencer mansion and his run-in with Clifford. You stay away from him, Amanda."

He heard the sharp intake of her breath. She raised her chin, and her outraged gaze locked with his. "Is that an order, Mr. Buchanan?"

She was challenging his authority; reminding him that he had no right to tell her what she might or might not do.

It took all his self-control to keep his tone level. "I wouldn't think of ordering you about, Miss Whitney. I'm only trying to give you some well-meant advice. You're an independent woman. You're free to do as you please."

CHAPTER THIRTEEN

The day after his meeting with Amanda, Ross went uptown to the Spencer mansion, where he was admitted by Nellie, the parlor maid. "I'll tell the master you're here, sir."

"That won't be necessary. It's you I want to speak with today."

"I've already told you all I know, sir." She sounded uneasy.

"I only need to ask you a few more questions. I won't keep you from your duties long," he said, with a reassuring smile. "It's about Mr. Thornton. I've heard that he came to visit Miss Spencer on the night of the murder."

"Yes, sir—now you mention it, I remember he did." She lapsed into silence.

"And you let him in."

Nellie had gossiped freely, that day in Central Park; she'd shared all those family secrets with Amanda. Why was she so reticent with him today? Had Everard ordered the staff not to answer any more questions unless the butler was there to supervise them?

"And then?" he prompted.

"I was about to go and tell Miss Jessamyn that Mr. Thornton was here to see her. But then Mr. Clifford came out of the library, and sent me away."

"Do you happen to recall what Clifford said to Thornton?"

"No sir." Her fair skin flushed slightly.

"I'm sure you don't eavesdrop, Nellie. But perhaps, as

you were leaving the entrance hall, you might have over-heard them by chance."

"I—don't think so."

"You do want to help, don't you? You want this maniac brought to justice."

"Oh yes, sir! Of course I do! Just to think of such a crea-ture roaming the city—it's enough to scare a girl out of her wits."

"Then tell me whatever you remember about Mr. Thornton's visit that evening."

"Well, now . . ." She smoothed the folds of her starched apron. "Mr. Clifford said that Miss Jessamyn couldn't re-ceive any visitors that evening."

"Not even her future husband?" He feigned surprise.

"He said Miss Jessamyn had retired for the night."

"Retired? At five o'clock?"

"Miss Jessamyn never was strong. She'd got herself worn out, preparing for the wedding. And that afternoon, she'd been on her feet for hours, while the dressmaker did all those alterations on her gown." Nellie sighed wistfully. "Such an elegant gown it was—brocade and satin, and those crystals and pearls—"

Ross steered the conversation back on track. "So Clif-ford sent Thornton away. And he left the house without protest."

"I'm not sure I take your meaning, sir."

"Howard Thornton wasn't an ordinary visitor. He had come to call on his bride-to-be. Didn't he suggest that you should go upstairs and ask her if she wished to see him?"

"Oh no, sir. He did sound disappointed-like. But I guess he knew Mr. Clifford was only thinking of what was best for Miss Jessamyn. She had 'a delicate constitution'—that's what those doctors called it."

"Can you think of any other reason why Clifford might have sent Mr. Thornton away that night?"

"No, sir."

He tried to conceal his impatience. "I've heard that Clifford disapproved of the match."

"I wouldn't know nothing about that, sir."

He was willing to bet there wasn't much that she and the rest of the staff did not know about the Spencers' personal affairs. "So Thornton went away without seeing Jessamyn. Did he return later that evening, perhaps?"

She gave him a reproachful look. "Mr. Thornton certainly wouldn't have intruded again after Mr. Clifford told him that Miss Jessamyn had retired for the night."

But after Clifford and Mrs. Spencer had left for the theater, and Everard had gone off to spend the night with his mistress, maybe Thornton had come back. Maybe he had gone directly to Jessamyn's suite without being seen by any of the servants. Might Jessamyn then have summoned up her last reserves of courage and told him she wouldn't go through with the wedding?

The loss of her dowry would mean his social and financial ruin. Such a prospect might have driven him into a fit of uncontrollable anger. It seemed most unlikely, but Ross wasn't ready to dismiss the possibility.

"Will that be all, sir?"

"It will, for now." She curtseyed and led the way to the front door. Her neatly-fitted uniform drew attention to her narrow waist and rounded hips; she moved with a quick, light step, the bow on her starched lace apron bobbing.

"Just a minute, Buchanan." He stopped short, and turned at the sound of that harsh command. Everard stood at the foot of the staircase, his broad face flushed and truculent. "I want to talk to you. Now!" He might have been rapping out an order to a careless footman.

Ross stiffened.

"Not here," said Everard. "In the library."

With an effort, Ross stifled his anger, and followed him into the dark-paneled, book-lined room. Everard planted himself in front of the fireplace, his thick legs set apart, his hands thrust into his pockets. "You've already questioned the staff. So why the devil were you wasting time, talking to Nellie?"

"My time wasn't wasted. Now I know that Thornton came calling on Jessamyn the night she died. Your son said she'd already retired for the night—at five o'clock—and sent him away. Clifford disliked Thornton. He was opposed to the marriage. You never bothered to tell me that."

"Why should I? It's got nothing to do with her murder!" His thick features darkened. "You think Thornton killed her?"

"It doesn't seem likely. He had too much to gain from marrying your daughter."

"Or maybe Clifford—or my wife? Would you like me to get them in here so you can question them again?"

"Not at the moment," he said evenly. "If I need to talk to them again, I'll let you know."

"Or maybe you'd rather spend more time hanging around that parlor maid, listening to her silly gossip." A thick vein stood out in his forehead. "Get out there on the street, dammit! Find Marek. He killed his wife, exactly the same way he killed Jessamyn. All the papers say so. I can't drive downtown without hearing a newsie on every corner, screeching those damn headlines about—"

"The Ladies Mile Maniac," Ross couldn't restrain himself any longer. "It's good copy. It sells papers. But I'm not sure Marek killed his wife. No one's come up with a plausible reason why he might have killed Jessamyn."

"A maniac doesn't need reasons!"

"But even a maniac needs an opportunity to get to his victim," Ross reminded him. "You think Barney Marek could have walked into a house like this one, and gone upstairs to Jessamyn's suite, without being seen? How did he manage that?"

"You won't know that until you've caught him!" Everard shouted. "Track him down, Buchanan! Find him, and get him to talk, any way you can. You used to be on the force. You're not too squeamish to beat the truth out of him, are you?"

Ross gave him a tight smile. "I'll do what I have to do."

"Then get moving. Go through every slum in the city. Hell's Kitchen. The South Street waterfront. That Irish shantytown north of the park. Until Marek's locked up in the Tombs, those damn reporters'll keep prying into our family's affairs. I hired you to do a job, so get out there and do it."

Ross fought the impulse to tell Everard to find himself another detective. "I'm handling the case my own way," he said evenly.

"And I'm paying you a damn sight more than any client's paid you've worked for," Everard reminded him.

Before Ross could answer, Everard walked to the library doors and pushed them open. "Now, start earning your pay. I want to see results, fast!"

Ross stepped into the entrance hall, and did not turn as the doors slammed shut behind him.

Outside the house, he stood for awhile, his eyes fixed on the bare branches of the trees in the park across the way. He waited for the hard knot in the pit of his stomach to ease, for the tension to go out of his muscles. It had taken all his self-control to keep him from walking off the job, then and there. But if he dropped the assignment now, he'd never get another like it. Everard Spencer would see to that. The bastard didn't care whether or not Marek was Jessamyn's killer. He'd just made that plain enough. What he wanted was a convenient scapegoat to send to the gallows. The sooner the case was closed, the sooner the scandal would be forgotten.

Ross started down Fifth Avenue, walking fast, to work off his anger. Although he'd already searched countless dives on the Bowery—saloons, crib houses, dog fighting rings, even a couple of opium dens, he'd go back and comb the place again.

But he had one stop to make along the way: the Harvard Club, a handsome red brick building on West Forty-fourth Street. Amanda had told him Thornton was a member. As her father had been. He looked up at this bastion of social solidarity, and his mouth tightened with resentment. Thornton was not capable of murder, she was sure of it. Because he was one of her own kind. *One of us*—that's what she might have said.

When he'd been a half-starved street kid, huddled in a warehouse or a waterfront shanty with others like him, he'd decided that there were only two kinds of people. Those who had money and those who didn't. The men who rode in their fine carriages, and the kids who swept up the horse manure. With money, you could buy food, instead of stealing it; boys like him had to steal and lie and fight dirty to survive, and the girls had to sell themselves, as soon as they were old enough.

Now he knew it wasn't quite so simple. Amanda had no money, but she still had her old and respected family name, her good breeding. And her memories of her father, who'd taught her his own inflexible sense of duty.

Her father, who had belonged to the Harvard Club.

The club steward was reluctant to give out information about a member. But when Ross handed him his business card, and said he was employed by Everard Spencer, to try to track down Miss Spencer's murderer, the steward relented slightly. Yes, Mr. Howard Thornton had come to the club around six o'clock on the evening in question. He'd dined here, too.

"Do you happen to recall what time he left?" Ross asked.

"I believe it was close to midnight, sir."

"Did he leave alone?"

The man thought for a moment, before he answered. "No, sir. Now you mention it, he left with a couple of other gentlemen."

"Do you know where they were going?"

The man's stiffened slightly, and his face took on a shuttered look. "I couldn't say, sir."

"Two women have been murdered," Ross said grimly. "Unless this maniac is found, there'll be more victims. Surely it's your duty to cooperate in any way you can."

"I've already told you all I know, sir."

Ross decided there would be no point in pressing him further. He'd have to try elsewhere to find out where Thornton had gone later that night.

He left the Harvard Club, hailed a hansom and directed the driver to take him on to the Bowery. With Everard's money in his pocket, he could afford the luxury of going about his work in a hansom, instead of an omnibus or elevated train.

Although he stared out at the streets, he was scarcely

aware of the noisy traffic all around him. Probably he should have let his questions about Thornton go, for now. But he felt uneasy about the man's interest in Amanda. He'd assured her he'd make the necessary inquiries about Thornton's movements on the night of the murder, that there was no need for her to see the man again. But he couldn't stop her from going to the theater with Thornton, and she'd be safe enough with him, in one of the velvet and gilt boxes at Wallack's Theater. Still, he disliked the idea of Amanda getting involved with Thornton.

It was none of his business what she chose to do with her evenings. But why was Thornton so interested in Amanda, all at once? She was good-looking—some men might think her beautiful—with those amber eyes and dark chestnut hair; she had a fine figure, too. But even if Thornton was infatuated with her, he couldn't afford to court any female, unless she had a substantial dowry.

The cab jerked to a stop, and he put aside all thought of Amanda. The afternoon was unseasonably mild and sunny for late October, a mixed blessing: the stench of garbage and horse manure was even more pungent than usual. The elevated train rattled by overhead, and a shower of cinders drifted down on the passersby.

He shouldered his way across Chatham Square and along the crowded street, past shooting galleries and saloons, then stopped in front of the grimy tenement next to the pawnshop. He climbed the rickety stairs, knocked on doors, questioned tenants; no one admitted to having seen Marek since the night of the drunken brawl with his wife. Outside again, he stopped at the foot of the stoop to speak to a fat, slatternly woman who was drinking beer from a can, only stirring herself from time to time, to aim a slap at one or another of her noisy, bare-footed brood. Most of the buttons were missing from her soiled cotton wrapper, and her pendulous breasts were half-revealed every time she moved.

"You one of them plain clothes cops?" she asked.

"I'm no cop."

"Then you got no right to come around botherin' decent people."

"I'm a newspaper reporter, ma'am," he improvised. "I work for the *Graphic*. My readers want to know what Marek's neighbors thought about the man."

"That no-good bum! He came home with a skinful, and done his wife in, that's what I think. I heard them carryin' on somethin' fierce that night. Him cursin', and her screamin'. They woke the kids with their carryin-on. I had hell's own time gettin' them back t' sleep again."

"What were they fighting about?"

"A drunk don't need no reason—he'll start a fight over nothin'."

"True enough," he agreed. "But with all that uproar, maybe you caught a few words."

She scratched her head and took another swig of beer. "Sounded like he was tryin' to get her to do somethin' an' she kept sayin' she wouldn't."

"What did he want her to do?"

The woman shrugged her heavy shoulders.

"Go out thieving, maybe?" he prompted.

"Didn't sound like it t' me. Unless he wanted her t' rob a bank. 'Do it and we'll be set for life!' That's what he kept sayin'."

"What else? Did you hear anything else?"

"Not that I remember. Only her yowlin' like a banshee. Guess he lit into her with both fists. And then the next day, the poor bitch turns up dead on the Ladies Mile. In a white weddin' gown, an' veil no less! The man was a loony, an' no mistake."

Ross didn't bother to tell her that Gertrude's body had been found in the backyard of the house that had once been owned by Madam Restell.

"Why haven't the cops caught him yet?" the woman demanded. "Are they too busy goin' around to the saloons and whorehouses, collectin' graft money? Why don't ye ask that in yer paper?"

"I'll make a special point of it, ma'am. Now about the white wedding gown and veil Mrs. Marek was wearing when she was murdered. Did she own any such outfit?"

"How should I know? She didn't have much to do with the rest of us. Kept herself to herself." She took another swallow of beer, then wiped her mouth with the back of her hand.

"I don't suppose you happened to see Marek since the night of her murder?"

"Wouldn't be likely to be hangin' around here after he done it, would he?" She drained the can, and grabbed the arm of a little girl with dirty, straggling hair. "Lizzie! Get yerself over t' Ryan's an' bring back another pint. An' be quick about it."

"Thanks for your help, ma'am." He turned away and started down the street.

"Hey, wait mister!" A skinny boy who might have been twelve came sidling up to him. He wore rags and his face was grimy; but his eyes were alert, like those of a prowling cat. "Yer the gent who's been comin' around askin' questions about Barney Marek."

"Have you seen him?"

He gave Ross an ingratiating smile. "No, I ain't. But I know somethin' none of them others know—not even that whore, Kathleen. Somethin' ye can write about in yer paper."

"You live in there?" Ross jerked his head in the direction of the tenement.

"Sure I do—on the second floor with my Pa."

"What's your name?"

"Pete Conners."

"All right, Pete, what can you tell me about Marek, that no one else knows?"

The boy scuffed his torn shoe on the pavement. "Look, mister, I can't remember so good right now, 'cause I ain't had nothin' to eat all day," he said. Ross had no reason to doubt him; his face was thin, his cheeks hollow. His bony wrists protruded from the sleeves of his grimy shirt.

"Come with me," Ross said. "I'll buy you a square meal and we'll have a talk."

But, to his surprise, the boy hung back. "Kathleen's brother told me ye gave her three silver dollars an' ye didn't even fuck her." He shot Ross an uneasy look. "Say, ye ain't one o' them kind wot likes boys, are ye?"

He couldn't blame Pete for being wary. Back in the days when he'd been a street kid, he'd have asked the same question. "Look, Pete, I'll buy you a meal—and no strings attached. And if you can tell me more about Marek, I'll throw in something extra."

The boy hesitated only a moment longer. "Okay, mister."

Ross led the way across the street to Havemeyers, and as they approached the door, the boy's eyes widened. "Say, this is a real high-class place," he said, as if unable to believe his luck. "I ain't never been in here before." He looked down self-consciously at his torn shirt and grubby knickers.

Havemeyer's was one of the few respectable restaurants

in the neighborhood, for it catered to a German family trade. Although the stout head waiter who approached them in the lobby gave Pete a look of distaste, Ross's prosperous appearance seemed to reassure him.

"I want a table out back," Ross said. The man led the way to a small garden, where the dry leaves still clung to the branches of the spindly elm trees. There were only a few other customers, and Ross chose a table a discreet distance away.

He gave a waiter his order, and when the meal—potato and leek soup, sauerbraten, thick black bread, and a pitcher of beer—was set down before them he realized that he had worked up a sharp appetite. As for Pete, he ate as if he was famished. He crammed the food into his mouth, scarcely pausing for breath, like a stray cat that fears its meal might be snatched away by some larger animal. Ross waited until he had finished, before starting to question him.

"So what can you tell me about the Mareks? What were they fighting about that night?"

Pete polished his plate with a crust of bread, took a long swallow of beer, and wiped his mouth with the back of his hand. "I don't know." He gave an indifferent shrug. "He was always yellin' at her, an' knockin' her around."

"Have you seen him anywhere in the neighborhood since then?"

Pete gave him a scornful look. " 'Course not! Even a loony like him wouldn't be hangin' about here with the cops lookin' for him."

"Then what do you have to tell me, that you think is so important?"

The boy leaned forward in his chair. "I seen her—Mrs. Marek. The night she an' her ol' man had that brawl. I was comin' home an' I seen 'er leavin' the house."

Ross felt his muscles tense. "You're sure it was Gertrude Marek you saw?"

"It was her, all right." The boy spoke with absolute assurance.

But Ross was not yet convinced. "What time was that?"

"I don't carry no gold watch an' chain." Pete grinned. "It was just startin' to get light out—that's all I know."

"Five o'clock? Or six?"

"About five I guess."

"What were you doing on the streets at that hour?"

"Been out workin' all night. Got me a shoe shine box—"

"And I suppose you get plenty of customers down here?" Pete looked away. "I do all right."

"Not shining shoes, you don't. I think you make your money rolling drunks in the tenement halls or the alleys back of the saloons." As Ross, himself, had done, when he'd been this kid's age.

"What if I do? Pa don't ask no questions, long as I bring home the cash," the boy said with a defiant stare.

"So you were coming home, and you saw Gertrude Marek." He gave the boy a hard, level look. "You recognized her even though it was barely light out."

"Sure I did. She stopped for a minute under the street lamp."

"How did she look?"

"How do you think she looked, after Marek finished knockin' her around? Had a big black and blue mark on her face, an' she was holdin' a handkerchief to her mouth."

"What was she wearing?"

"A plain kind o' dress—black or maybe brown. An' a hat."

"Not a white wedding gown and veil?"

Pete gave a short, derisive laugh. "I guess that's sup-

220

posed t' be some kind of a joke, mister."

"So she was wearing a plain, dark street dress. Anything else you can remember?"

"She was carryin' a suitcase."

Was it possible that the boy was telling the truth? If so, this trip down to the Bowery hadn't been a waste of time. Marek had come home drunk and beaten his wife. But he hadn't killed her.

Had she finally decided she'd had enough of her husband's abuse and run away, wanting only to get as far from the house as she could, before he came back? Maybe she'd had a friend in the neighborhood, someone she hoped would give her shelter. But she'd never gotten there. Somewhere along the way, she'd come face to face with her killer.

CHAPTER FOURTEEN

Amanda carefully arranged the folds of her green taffeta skirt and smoothed the low-cut neckline of her velvet bodice. Leander, who lay sleeping at the foot of her bed with chin on paws, raised his head, and opened his eyes. He fixed his gaze on her briefly, stretched his furry body to its full length, showed his pink tongue in a wide yawn, then curled up and went back to sleep.

Only a few years ago, she had thought she couldn't possibly dress for an evening at the theater without the help of her maid. Now, although it took considerable patience and a long-handled button-hook, she had learned to manage on her own.

She took one more look at her reflection in the mirror, then, satisfied with her appearance, she went into the parlor to wait for Howard Thornton. She would take her notebook. Her readers would be eager for every detail of Lillie Langtry's opening night performance. She opened her desk drawer, then paused as she caught sight of Mama's latest letter. She had put it aside earlier, when she had returned from the office. Now she opened the heavy, cream-colored envelope, and as she began reading, she felt a rising uneasiness.

Until now, her mother had seemed satisfied with her position, but perhaps it was inevitable that, once the novelty of her new surroundings had worn off, Mama would become discontented.

"*Last week Mrs. Dennison's personal maid had the after-*

noon off, and she asked me to wash and arrange her hair. Naturally I was offended. I would have told her that I do not consider such menial service part of my duties as her companion, but I did not want to provoke an open confrontation."

The letter went on in the same petulant tone. On one occasion, when the hotel accommodations in Venice had not been to her employer's liking, she'd been sent down to confront the hotel manager and demand a better suite. *"The man was positively rude, and when I complained to Mrs. Dennison, she shrugged off the whole incident, as if she did not think it important."*

Poor Mama. Was she remembering her honeymoon tour, when her husband had taken care of all such mundane details? Perhaps it was too much to expect her to adjust to a change in circumstances, after all these years. But there was no way Amanda could hope to provide for her mother on her own modest income.

When the concierge knocked and announced that Mr. Howard Thornton was waiting in the downstairs sitting room, she gave a sigh of relief. She put the letter back in the drawer, slid her notebook into her velvet purse, picked up her cloak, and went down to meet him. Tonight she would have the chance to become better acquainted with him, and perhaps to find out something about him that might be useful to Ross. If not, she would at least take advantage of the opportunity to gather enough material for next week's article.

Stay away from him, Amanda. She hadn't forgotten Ross's warning, but he'd given her no convincing reason why she should heed it.

Wallack's Theater was filled to capacity tonight. Seated beside her escort in one of the boxes, Amanda took out her opera glasses and leaned forward. She recognized Astors, Vanderbilts, Lorillards, and Belmonts; although she left her notebook in her purse, she was already making mental notes for her article while waiting for the first act curtain to rise. All the ladies in the audience were decked out in their most fashionable silks and velvets; their jeweled tiaras, necklaces, and earrings glittered in the light of the chandeliers. They fluttered their fans as they chatted with each other, or with their elegantly-clad escorts.

Howard Thornton cut a fine figure in his perfectly-tailored evening clothes. She wondered if he had paid for his expensive suit, his gold and pearl cufflinks and the matching pin in his black silk cravat. And how had he been able to afford this private box?

"Every ticket was auctioned off at the Turf Club Theatre," Maude had told her that morning. "One of the boxes went for three hundred and twenty-five dollars. Can you imagine that?" She'd grinned and added: "It would seem that Mr. Thornton has no intention of changing his extravagant habits."

Jessamyn's dowry would have covered his debts, and allowed him to go on as before. But how did he expect to keep up his lavish way of life from now on?

Amanda heard the chime of the bell that preceded the rising of the curtain, and shared the sense of anticipation that rippled through the audience. Ever since Lillie Langtry had disembarked in New York, to be greeted by a brass band playing "God Save the Queen," reporters had followed her everywhere. The newspapers had been filled with articles about her. The city was plastered with posters advertising her show; her tinted photographs appeared in shop windows. An enterprising song writer had composed "The Jersey Lily Waltz" in her honor. When she had gone for a carriage ride in Central Park a few weeks ago, traffic had come to a stop all along the avenue. Women copied her hats, her gowns, her coiffures—although few could hope to rival her dazzling beauty.

Tonight, reviewers and reporters from all the New York newspapers were here; others had come from Philadelphia, Boston, and Baltimore. Oscar Wilde had taken time from his lecture tour to put in an appearance, as guest critic for the *World*.

Now, as the overture began, an expectant hush fell over the crowd. The curtain rose and the star made her entrance as a milkmaid, carrying a bucket on her arm. Her copper curls framed her oval face and her wide-set eyes were a deep blue-violet.

At the close of the act, the audience applauded enthusiastically, then went to seek refreshments in the lobby or to visit back and forth between the boxes. Would Howard be offended if she took out her notebook and jotted down a few of her impressions? But then she realized he wasn't looking at her. His gaze was fixed on the occupants of a nearby box: Mrs. Armstead, and her daughter, Phoebe.

"Shall we go over and visit with them?" he asked.

"I don't think Euphemia Armstead would wish to speak with me—not after our run-in at the Armory."

"Surely she's forgotten all about that," he said lightly.

Amanda wasn't so sure. "Perhaps it would be better if I stayed here." She started to take her notebook from her purse, but he reached over, slid it back inside.

"Forget about the *Gazette*. You deserve an evening off."

Phoebe Armstead was looking over at their box now. Howard smiled and nodded in her direction. "Come along," he urged. Amanda repressed a sigh as she rose and took his arm.

Although Mrs. Armstead's greeting was cool and distant, her daughter welcomed Amanda as if she were a close friend, rather than a casual acquaintance. Phoebe's high-pitched laugh and breathless chatter set Amanda's teeth on edge—maybe they'd had a similar effect on prospective suitors. After three seasons of relentless husband-hunting, Phoebe must be getting desperate. And who could blame her, Amanda thought. If she didn't marry soon, she'd face a dreary future as the Armsteads' spinster daughter.

Phoebe fluttered her sparse lashes at Howard, who leaned toward her and listened with seeming interest to her vapid chatter about Mrs. Langtry's appearance, her acting ability, and the play, itself. "Such a delightful play," she said.

"Indeed it is," he agreed, then asked: "Do you plan to attend her next performance in *As You Like It*?"

"Mama and I have not yet decided. You know, Mr. Thornton, I've never been all that fond of Shakespeare's plays," she went on, as if sharing a precious secret, "I can't follow all the twists and turns of his plots. And I find some of the speeches difficult to understand—"

"That may be as well, my dear," her mother interrupted. "So much of Shakespeare's language is unsuitable for the ears of a well-bred young lady. Don't you agree, Miss Whitney?"

While Amanda searched for a tactful reply, Phoebe was already rattling on. "Mrs. Langtry's as beautiful as everyone says. And her first act costume was charming—although it was rather plain, of course. But one doesn't expect a milk-maid to go about in satin and lace, does one?"

"Hardly," Thornton agreed. "And speaking of costumes, may I make so bold as to compliment you on your gown, Miss Armstead," he said softly. "You should always wear that shade of pink. It's most becoming."

Phoebe blushed, then looked up at him coquettishly over her ostrich feather fan. "Indeed, Mr. Thornton, you must not flatter me."

"I assure you, Miss Armstead, I only speak the truth."

A bell tinkled, signaling the start of the next act. He bowed to Euphemia, gave Phoebe a warm smile, then he turned to Amanda. "We must be getting back now." He offered his arm, but as she placed her gloved hand on his sleeve, she felt a surge of distaste. He'd flattered poor Phoebe shamelessly and the foolish girl had taken in his every word with undisguised delight.

They returned to their box and seated themselves for the second act. Mrs. Langtry was doing her best with what dramatic talent she possessed, but it was her dazzling appearance that captivated the spectators. Her gown of cream velvet and ecru lace set off her superb figure to perfection—the humble milkmaid had caught the eye of a nobleman and was already climbing up the social ladder.

But Amanda could not concentrate on the contrived melodrama, for she was remembering her conversation with Ross. He'd made it plain that he disliked and distrusted Howard Thornton. And now, having watched him ingratiating himself with Phoebe, she shared Ross's opinion.

Howard been willing to trade his family name for Jessamyn's dowry. Since that prize was lost to him, he'd wasted no time—he was doing all he could to win Phoebe's affections, with his flowery compliments, his long, meaningful glances. And Phoebe probably would be willing, even eager to accept him as a suitor. But surely Euphemia would refuse to consider such a match. Or would she? Perhaps she and her husband, like the Spencers, would decide that

Thornton's illustrious background outweighed the man's dubious reputation.

Amanda kept her gaze fixed on the stage, but she was relieved when the curtain went down on the last act. Mrs. Langtry took her bows amid enthusiastic applause. An usher hurried down the aisle and presented her with a large bouquet of lilies.

"If you would care to come backstage, I'll introduce you to Mrs. Langtry," Howard offered.

She shook her head. "I won't be able to get the sort of interview I want, not tonight—her dressing room will be crowded with her admirers."

"As you wish," he said.

As they waited outside, she shivered slightly, for the night had turned much colder. She was grateful for the warmth of Howard's luxurious carriage, with its high-stepping bays. But how much had he paid for the handsome team, she wondered? And how could he afford to keep a coachman and footman, in their elegant livery?

He must have noticed her preoccupation. "Still brooding about that article of yours?" His eyes glinted with amusement. "Why not forget it for now, and let yourself enjoy Delmonico's fine cuisine?"

Did he consider her work a trivial feminine pastime, like painting on china or crocheting doilies?

"I'm afraid I must go straight home," she said stiffly. "I have to be at my office by nine o'clock tomorrow."

"Surely Mrs. Fairlie's not such a stern tyrant."

"She's not a tyrant at all. She is a successful business woman, who works as hard as any of her staff. In fact, she often returns to her office after the rest of us have left, and stays late into the night."

"Good heavens!" he said, with mock dismay. "I hope

you won't model yourself after her."

"I can think of worse fates."

"Can you, indeed? Name one."

"A loveless marriage to an opportunist—a shameless fortune hunter." Her words came out before she could stop them. When would she learn to curb her tongue?

She braced herself for his angry retort, but instead, he shrugged and gave a short, self-deprecating laugh. "My dear Amanda, do you really suppose I'd consider marrying Phoebe, if I had any other choice?"

But he did have other choices. It was not too late for him to find some kind of employment. This time, she managed to remain silent; for she suspected such a suggestion would either amuse or repel him. She fixed her eyes on her purse and after a moment, he turned the conversation to the evening's entertainment. "Tomorrow's newspaper reviews will probably have more to say about Mrs. Langtry's appearance than her talent. Except, perhaps, for Oscar Wilde's. But he's a personal friend."

When the carriage turned into Nineteenth Street and drew to a stop in front of Amanda's house, he said nothing about seeing her again. He must have known what her answer would be. He escorted her to her front door, bowed and said good-night. She gave a sigh of relief as she watched his carriage drive off.

Upstairs in her flat, Leander greeted her with a hopeful meow. After she hung away her green gown, he led the way to the kitchen, with his tail held high. She warmed a saucer of milk and set it down for him. She thought of the elaborate dinner she might have been enjoying right now at Delmonico's, sighed, and fixed herself a sandwich.

Later, as she sat before her bedroom mirror brushing her hair, she went over the events of the evening. Although she'd found out nothing important enough to justify a call to Ross, she certainly had formed a more accurate estimate of Howard Thornton's character. Faced with a mountain of unpaid debts, unwilling to give up his extravagant way of life, he'd fixed his sights on Phoebe and, if he married her, no doubt he'd use the Armstead fortune to pay off his creditors, and go on enjoying his extravagant way of life.

But then why he had been so attentive to her when they'd met at the Armory, she wondered? And why had he asked her out tonight? Her lips tightened with distaste, as she thought of the most likely explanation. He'd wanted to be seen with her at the theater, then at Delmonico's, where they'd have drawn enough attention to start a round of gossip. It would have been to his advantage to be seen with her during the season. It would keep Euphemia off guard until he was sure Phoebe was completely infatuated with him. Although he cared no more for Phoebe than he had for Jessamyn, he'd marry her if she'd have him—and if her parents consented to the match.

Yes, Howard Thornton was thoroughly ruthless and unprincipled. But was he capable of murder? She had denied it vehemently, the last time she'd talked to Ross—but now she was no longer sure. Suppose Howard had managed to get back into the Spencer mansion that night, after Clifford had turned him away; and had gone to Jessamyn's room without being seen by any of the servants. And what if she'd told him she would not go through with the wedding? Would he have lost control and strangled her in a fit of rage? Only a lunatic could have done that.

Or someone who wanted his crime to appear to be the act of a lunatic.

Someone who was so calculating that he could have dressed Jessamyn's lifeless body in her wedding gown and veil, and twisted the wreath of orange blossoms around her neck, then smuggled the body out of the house and dumped it the alley in the Ladies Mile.

But even if Thornton had killed Jessamyn, why in heaven's name would he have gone on to kill Gertrude? Would he have taken another life, to bolster the theory that there was a madman on the loose?

She set down her brush and pressed her fingers to her temples, as she tried to collect her racing thoughts. Maybe she should go see Ross tomorrow. But what did she have to tell him? Only that she was sure Howard was courting Phoebe to get his hands on her dowry. And that probably would not come as a surprise to Ross. It would only confirm his opinion of the other man.

She lowered the flame in the lamp on her dressing table, then took off her robe and climbed into bed. Leander leaped up, curled himself at her feet, and began to purr. His presence was comforting, but she was too tense to fall asleep at once.

She hadn't seen Ross since their meeting at Fleischmann's Vienna Bakery. Although she'd hoped he would get in touch with her, she really wasn't surprised that he hadn't. What else could she have expected? How could she have spoken to him that way, telling him that Howard Thornton couldn't be guilty of murder because he came from a fine old family? She wondered what Ross felt about her now. She couldn't blame him if he thought she was a snob, a superficial fool who judged a man only by his background.

She pressed her face into her pillow. She shouldn't care what Ross thought of her. But she did.

In the weeks that followed, the pace of the social season speeded up, Amanda was kept occupied by her work. Mrs.

Fairlie was pleased with her article about Lillie Langtry's opening night performance, and her interview with the actress, shortly after that.

The first week in December, she received a modest raise in salary, a telephone for her office, and an invitation to Mrs. Fairlie's brownstone near Gramercy Park for one of her evening receptions. Lavinia Fairlie defied convention so far as to invite artists, authors, advocates of woman's suffrage, and even an occasional actor. Amanda was introduced to Adelina Patti, who graciously consented to sing for the guests; and Oscar Wilde, resplendent in his velvet suit, embroidered waistcoat, and knee breeches. She enjoyed a stimulating conversation with Jacob Riis, a social reformer and passionate advocate for the tide of immigrants who were crowding into the city.

With the approach of the holiday season, her schedule grew more crowded than ever. But busy as she was, she could not ignore the glaring newspaper headlines, or the impassioned editorials demanding to know why the fiendish Barney Marek, the Ladies Mile Maniac, was still at large. And they berated the police for their lack of progress in the case. How could any woman hope to go about the city safely with such a creature on the loose?

Ottilie, who had just returned from a drive through the park on a crisp, cold afternoon, handed her sable-lined cloak to Nellie, and hurried over to the silver card tray on one of the tables in the entrance hall. Only a single visiting card—and that had been left by Miss Ione Bainbridge, an earnest spinster who was forever taking up collections for good causes.

It was just as she'd feared: she was already being ostracized by society. This very afternoon, she'd smiled and nodded to the occupants of several carriages, only to see them turn away without a smile, or any sign of recognition. She'd made no close female friends since she and Everard had moved to New York, but a constant procession of acquaintances had come to call. Over tea and sandwiches, they'd made polite conversation about the latest fashions, about the opera or the theater. And about the latest titillating scandals.

Her spirits plummeted even lower. Were they gossiping about her now? Were they avoiding her because of the shocking circumstances surrounding Jessamyn's murder?

Thank heaven, Everard had managed to keep the most shocking details out of the papers. No publisher, not even the arrogant James Gordon Bennett Jr., had allowed their reporters to say that Jessamyn's body had been found in the alley next to Isobel Hewitt's parlorhouse. But those same snooping reporters had discovered that Gertrude Marek had worked for the Spencers; that she'd been Jessamyn's personal maid—and the wife of their head coachman. That juicy piece of information had appeared in all the papers.

How long before one of them uncovered the relationship between Jessamyn and Devin O'Shea and made it public?

She was still standing in the hall, staring down at the card tray, when Everard came in and handed his coat and hat to Nellie.

He glanced at his wife, and spoke impatiently. "What's the matter with you?"

She started at the sound of his voice, then turned and said, "How can you ask that? Haven't you been reading the newspapers? Don't you know what they've been saying about us—"

His look silenced her. He dismissed Nellie with a gesture of his hand.

When the parlor maid was gone, he said, "You'd better get used to those newspaper articles. Because you'll be seeing them until Marek's caught and locked up."

"And when will that be? The police are worse than useless. And as for that man, Buchanan, all he's done is to dig up a lot of stuff about us that has nothing to do with Jessamyn's murder. If you'd listened to me when I told you to let him go and hire another investigator—"

"Drop it, Lottie! I had a talk with Buchanan. He knows what's expected of him." Everard gave a harsh laugh. "He's an arrogant bastard, though. When I asked him whether he wanted to question you and Clifford again, he only said, 'not for the time being'."

Her voice shook with indignation. "How dare he? Clifford was with me that night, at the theater. He knows that. I won't have him asking my boy any more questions!"

"Don't upset yourself, Mother."

She turned and saw her son standing at the foot of the stairs. He hurried to her and put his arm around her shoulders. "I doubt Buchanan's going to question either of us again. If he does, I'm quite capable of dealing with him."

Although Clifford had gone out to dine with friends this evening, Everard remained at home for a change. After dinner, Ottilie followed him into the library and confronted him. "It's begun already," she said, "and it's sure to get worse."

He looked up from the latest *Harper's Weekly* and glared at her. "What the devil are you nattering about now?"

"I went driving in the park this afternoon, and it was like I'd been invisible. Not a smile—not even a nod from any of the other ladies. And only a single visitor while I was out—that awful Ione Bainbridge. If I sent out invitations for tea, I just know I'll get back a pile of polite excuses—"

He slapped down the magazine on the table beside him. "What about Amanda Whitney? She hasn't refused your invitation, has she?"

She hesitated, then decided that since Everard was sure to get at the truth, she might as well tell him. "I—haven't asked her yet."

He got to his feet, crossed the room and stood scowling down at her. "Why the hell not?"

"Suppose she refuses? Think how humiliating that would be." She stopped short as he seized her shoulder in a punishing grip. The jet trimming on her black surah gown bit into her flesh.

"Stop your babbling, and do as you're told. The Whitney girl won't refuse. Not if you mention that Clifford will be joining the two of you." He jerked her out of her chair and led her to the desk.

It didn't take her long to pen the few lines, blot the paper, and put the note into an envelope that bore the Spencer crest. He reached out and took it from her. "I'll send one of the servants to deliver it first thing tomorrow morning," he said.

CHAPTER FIFTEEN

The snow had stopped falling early that morning, but its white covering softened the shapes of the turrets and pinnaces against the grey sky. As Amanda went up the steps to the front door of the Spencer mansion, she was still puzzled, as she had been since she had received the invitation to tea. Ottilie had never shown any particular friendliness toward her before. Had Clifford prevailed upon his mother to invite her to their home?

No matter. With any luck, her visit offered an opportunity to speak with some of the other servants. She hadn't seen Ross, or heard from him, since that afternoon at Fleischmann's Vienna Bakery, but if the afternoon went as she planned, she might gather new information for him.

Under her brown velvet cloak, she wore a new gown of golden brown wool, the close-fitting bodice trimmed with narrow lace frills. Back in her flat, she had felt a brief pang of regret, when she'd used her sewing scissors to pick out some of the tiny stitches from the lace at the wrist.

The butler led the way through the entrance hall to the morning room, where Ottilie and Clifford were waiting. Ottilie's face was drawn, and there were dark smudges under her eyes. There was a brief flurry of activity as a maid brought in the elaborate silver tea service, the plates of cucumber and watercress sandwiches, and an elaborate array of pastries—petit fours, fruit tarts, and tiny croissants. Although Ottilie's cordiality was forced, Clifford gave Amanda a warm smile. "I read your article in this week's

Gazette," he said. "Your description of Macy's Christmas show windows made me feel I was seeing it for myself. Did you read it, Mama?"

"No, I haven't."

Seizing the opportunity to draw her hostess into the conversation, Amanda said, "One of Macy's windows was most attractive—Parisian dolls on a skating pond. They were dressed in real furs and velvets and silks. And miniature boots with tiny skates—all in the latest fashions. You really should see the display for yourself, Mrs. Spencer."

"An excellent idea." He turned to Ottilie. "Shall we drive down and have a look? The excursion will do you good."

"Perhaps." But there wasn't the slightest enthusiasm in her voice.

"We'll go tomorrow afternoon," he said. "We'll take the brougham, and tuck a warm laprobe around you, to keep off the chill."

"You'd best start out early," said Amanda. "The Ladies Mile is crowded with shoppers at this time of year."

Ottilie's body went rigid. She no longer looked depressed, but deeply agitated. "I don't want to go anywhere near the Ladies Mile!"

Amanda caught her breath, startled by the vehemence in the older woman's tone. "I'm sorry," she said quickly. "It was thoughtless of me. No doubt the Ladies Mile has unhappy associations for you. Perhaps a drive in the park—?"

"What does it matter where I go?" Ottilie interrupted. "Even here in my own home, I can't pick up a newspaper without reading about our bereavement. Those reporters—snooping and prying! Journalists, they call themselves! They're no better than a flock of vultures, feeding off the misery of their betters—"

"Mama! Surely you have no wish to offend Miss Whitney, by speaking this way of her profession."

Splotches of color stood out against her faded skin. "Miss Whitney only writes those little society pieces for the *Gazette*."

Amanda smiled and inclined her head. "You're quite right," she said, but she felt a brief annoyance at hearing her work dismissed so casually.

"It's those others," Ottilie went on. "Bennett and Whitlaw Reid and the rest—they ought to be fined for allowing their reporters to meddle in the affairs of decent citizens—"

"Please don't distress yourself," Clifford said. "We needn't go downtown tomorrow, if you don't want to. But you can't stay shut up in the house forever. You must make an effort to start going out."

"Not until that creature—that Marek—has been caught and punished," Ottilie sniffed. "What's wrong with our police force? And that useless bungling investigator—that Buchanan fellow. What is he doing to earn his pay? Besides poking around here, ogling the maids while he pretends to be questioning them?"

"Ross is doing all he can. He's working day and night, going into the most dangerous parts of the city—places like the Five Points and Hell's Kitchen. Even the police are afraid to go there, except in pairs and—"

Amanda broke off abruptly when she saw Clifford was staring at her. "You know Ross Buchanan?"

It would be useless to deny it now. "We've met," she said carefully.

"Have you, indeed?"

"It was just a chance meeting. I was leaving your house, and I couldn't find a hansom. Ross—Mr. Buchanan—was thoughtful enough to get one for me."

Surely it could not have escaped his notice that she had called Ross by his first name. A slight smile touched his lips. "And in those few moments he managed to convince you of his skill as an investigator?"

"No, but—since he was going downtown, too, I offered to share the hansom. We talked a little, and—he impressed me as a man who would do his work to the best of his ability."

"I see. Then you are guided by intuition like most ladies."

Realizing that she'd already said too much, she looked away, then picked up an almond croissant from the platter before her. "This is delicious," she said, turning to Ottilie. "You have a most accomplished cook."

"She's been with us for years," she said.

"You are fortunate. My mother often said that although most good cooks could turn out an excellent meal, their skill with pastry was the true test of their skills." Although Amanda had shifted the conversation to domestic matters, she still felt a palpable tension in the air.

She was relieved when a quick glance at the clock told her that a suitable time had passed, and she might leave without offending either Clifford or his mother. She rose and crossed the room, then stumbled against a small table that held a Chinese temple dog, made of bronze. She kept her back to Clifford and Ottilie, as she tugged at the lace frill at her wrist. Then she cried out.

A moment later, Clifford was at her side. "Are you hurt, Miss Whitney?"

"No—but I'm afraid I've torn my dress." She held out her arm and showed him the loose frill.

"That is too bad." He sounded genuinely concerned.

"Such a becoming dress, too. Can you have it mended?"

"Of course. But you see, I'd planned to go straight from here to the St. Thomas's holiday bazaar. Now I'll have to drive back home first, and change."

"That won't be necessary," Ottilie said. "Miss Tuttle's handy with the needle. If you wish to go upstairs, I'll send her to you."

"Come along," Clifford said. "Let me show you the way."

In one of the guestrooms, Miss Sophia Tuttle, a small, thin woman with iron-grey hair, brought her sewing basket, then helped Amanda off with her dress. She sat before the fireplace in her chemise and petticoats, while Miss Tuttle set about repairing the damage.

"This is a handsome gown." She peered through her steel-rimmed spectacles. "And of excellent quality, too. I'm surprised the stitching tore away so easily."

"It was my fault. I caught it on that Chinese statuette, and I was foolish enough to tug at it, trying to get free."

Miss Tuttle nodded briefly, then lapsed into silence as she went on working. Amanda felt a stir of sympathy. It could not have been easy for Jessamyn's personal maid to descend the servants' hierarchy to this inferior position, where she was on call whenever there was a task none of the others had time for. But she looked to be in her fifties, and probably set in her ways. It would not be easy for her to find work as a ladies' maid in another household.

"I wish I were skilled at sewing, as you are," Amanda said. "I know so little about taking care of my wardrobe."

"Why should you?" The thin lips tightened. "Your maid does such chores."

"I have no maid," Amanda confided, with a smile.

Miss Tuttle looked up from her work for a moment, and raised her eyebrows. "Indeed, Miss Whitney?" She went on taking tiny stitches in the delicate lace.

"And I have so much to learn," Amanda said. "Dealing with stains, for instance. A small stain on silk or velvet can ruin a dress."

"Not if it is taken care of promptly." Miss Tuttle spoke with authority.

"Even an ink stain?"

"Why, certainly. To remove ink stains from silk or worsted, take a pint of soft water—rain water's best—and dissolve in it an ounce of oxalic acid. Lay the part with the stain over a bowl of hot water and let the steam evaporate. Then shake up the solution and dip a sponge into it. Rub it well, until the stain disappears."

"I never knew that. Next time, I'll follow your direction exactly." She shook her head ruefully. "I do have such trouble with ink stains."

The older woman's face softened a little. "I suppose that's a hazard of your profession." She went on to explain the virtues of soft soap and orris in removing stains from embroidery, and Amanda listened attentively.

"Mrs. Spencer is lucky to have someone as skillful as you, to take care of her clothes," she said.

"That's not all I'm expected to do." There was an edge to her voice. "Why even Mr. Kendall—he's the head coachman—expects me to clean his uniform."

She probably would not have spoken so freely to any member of the staff, Amanda thought. A ladies' maid, like a governess, was in a class apart from the rest of the staff. It would have been demeaning for her to gossip with Nellie or any of the other maids below stairs. No doubt she'd been holding back her resentment since she'd been demoted.

"Perhaps the coachman thought no one else could handle the task as well as you could," Amanda said.

"But it was a most unpleasant chore. The stain was large and oily—and foul-smelling."

"Were you able to get it out?"

"Certainly. And I fastened on that loose button so it won't come off again soon."

"It sounds as if Mr. Kendall's rather careless."

"But he isn't," Miss Tuttle interrupted. "He's a most efficient driver—and neat about his person. He's been with the family for years." She leaned forward, her eyes narrowing. "If you ask me, it wasn't Mr. Kendall who soiled his uniform that night. It was one of the grooms—probably young Winfield."

"Is this Winfield in the habit of borrowing the coachman's uniforms?" Amanda asked.

"I wouldn't put it past him, to get himself dressed up in style and take one of the carriages out."

Amanda gave her a wide-eyed look of surprise. "But why?"

"To impress some silly young female—a maid from one of the other houses on the avenue, perhaps." She lowered her voice and leaned forward. "There were long strands of hair twisted around the button. Blonde hair."

Amanda tried to look properly outraged. "How shocking!"

"And that's not all," Miss Tuttle went on. "It wouldn't surprise me if that young good-for-nothing was the one who took Miss Jessamyn's jewelry to give to his lady-love."

"Her jewelry?"

"Nothing valuable—Mr. Spencer keeps all the good pieces in his safe. But there was a locket missing, and an amethyst ring. Both were gifts from Mr. Clifford. He was so devoted to her. Poor young man. He keeps up a brave front, but he hasn't recovered from the tragedy—I doubt he ever will."

"But the jewelry." Amanda steered her back. "Was it ever recovered?"

Miss Tuttle shook her head. "Miss Jessamyn never said a thing about it. And she made me promise not to speak of it either."

"Whyever not? If this Winfield person is a thief, surely he deserves to be arrested."

"That's what I said. But poor Miss Jessamyn became quite distraught at the suggestion, and I thought it best to do as she wished. She was so sensitive, you know. It took so little to bring on a nervous spell. And what with the wedding only a few weeks off—"

"I understand. But what about the head coachman? I should think he'd have complained to Mr. Spencer about the damage to his uniform—and mentioned the possibility that Winfield might have borrowed the carriage."

"And so he would have done. But that morning, with the whole house in a turmoil—and that stranger—that Mr. Buchanan—going around asking questions—" A spasm of grief touched her lined face. "It was the morning after Miss Jessamyn—disappeared." She went on, her voice unsteady. "Even now, I can't believe she's gone. I keep remembering the last time I saw her."

"And when was that?" Amanda prompted.

"The afternoon before she died. She was standing before the mirror in her bedroom, wearing her wedding gown. I thought the gown was far too elaborate for Miss Jessamyn, all those pearls and crystals—and the weight of it—Her face was so pale, and she was unsteady on her feet—as if she might faint. But no one seemed to notice.

Certainly not that French woman—"

"You were with Jessamyn, while Madame Duval was making the alterations?"

She shook her head. "I was downstairs, ordering the tea tray. I'd carried up the tea tray myself. But Mrs. Spencer took it from me and ordered me out." Her voice quivered with resentment.

"I suppose one of the other maids helped her to take off her gown—"

"But that was my responsibility."

How pathetic it was, that all Miss Tuttle's self-esteem was bound up in the performance of her duties. Had she ever had a life of her own? "And you didn't see her again, after that?"

Miss Tuttle shook her head. She blinked, forcing back tears, as she took the last few stitches, then snipped off the thread. "There now, your dress is as good as new. I'll help you on with it, Miss Whitney."

Amanda thanked Miss Tuttle, then hurried down the hall and descended the wide staircase. When she'd made the rip in her sleeve, she had hoped for the chance to speak with one of the downstairs maids. But her plan had worked out even better than she'd hoped.

She hadn't forgotten about the bazaar, but first she'd call Ross. She'd set up a meeting, and tell him what she'd found out. She couldn't telephone from the Spencers' home, but she'd find a public telephone somewhere along her way. But when she reached the foot of the stairs, Clifford was waiting for her, holding her cloak over his arm. "May I escort you to the bazaar?" he asked.

She could hardly refuse without offering a reason. "It's only a sale of handiwork, contributed by the ladies of the congregation. And a refreshment booth with hot lemonade and gingerbread, I suppose." Amanda had attended many such affairs in the past. "I'm afraid you'll find it boring."

"I could never be bored in your company, Miss Whitney," he assured her.

They drove directly to the parish house, and Amanda tried to curb her impatience while Clifford escorted her from one booth to the next. If he was bored, he showed no sign of it. He kept up an easy flow of conversation, and made several purchases: a needlecase embroidered with pansies, a patchwork pin cushion, a framed silhouette that might have represented Queen Victoria. "I hope you will make allowances for my mother's lack of tact this afternoon. She has been under a dreadful strain, these past months."

"That's perfectly understandable," Amanda assured him.

"As for her slighting remarks about journalists, she spoke without thinking."

"It must be distressing to see one's private affairs discussed in the newspapers," she said. "Mrs. Fairlie insists on absolute discretion in all her publications." She smiled ruefully. "Even so, my mother disapproves of my choice of a profession. She wanted me to seek a post as a governess or paid companion."

"Perhaps that would have suited most young ladies," he said. "But I believe you would not have been happy unless you had the opportunity to develop your natural talents." They had paused before a booth devoted to shellwork ornaments. "Tell me, Miss Whitney—Amanda, if I may—suppose there was no need for you to work at all. Would you still wish to go on working at the *Gazette*?"

Before she could answer, the lady behind the counter smiled and asked if she could be of help. Clifford looked over the display, then picked up a small trinket box, decorated with a variety of miniature seashells and lined with red velvet. "I believe I'll take this one," he said.

They waited while the lady wrapped the box in green paper and tied it with a ribbon. Then he handed it to Amanda, with a slight bow. "Please take it, as a memento of our afternoon together."

She hesitated briefly. It was not quite proper to accept a gift from a young man, unless they were engaged. She could not resist his smile or the genuine warmth in his dark-blue eyes. She thanked him and tucked it into a pocket inside her cloak.

He drove her home in the brougham, and when they stopped in front of her house, he said: "Would you take luncheon with me tomorrow?"

"I'm afraid I can't. I have several assignments tomorrow."

"Then perhaps you can fit me into your schedule later in the week. Please say you will?"

"Shall we make it Thursday?"

"I'll call for you at your office at noon, and have you back in plenty of time to take care of the rest of your work."

She did not go up to her flat; instead, she headed for the downstairs sitting room, where she stood by the window, watching until his brougham had disappeared into the deepening twilight. Then she went back outside, and pulled her cloak around her against the icy wind. She rounded the corner to Broadway, and stopped before the cigar store, where the painted wooden Indian wore a mantel of snow. Inside, the warmth and the heady odor of fine tobacco enveloped her. She was the only woman in the place, but she ignored the glances of the customers, and walked briskly to the rear to use the public telephone.

She gave the operator Ross's office number, then let the phone ring until it became obvious that there would be no answer. She needed to tell him what she'd learned from her talk with Miss Tuttle, but she'd have to wait until tomorrow. She placed a nickel on the polished counter and left.

She walked quickly back to the house. When she opened the door to her flat, she found an envelope under the door. She picked it up and felt an uneasy pang when she saw the foreign postmark, and her mother's neat handwriting.

It was after six, and the winter twilight had darkened into evening. She set down the little trinket box, still in its wrappings, and lit the desk lamp, then opened the envelope. Leander came padding across the carpet to rub against her ankles; she bent and stroked his head absently, then started reading. Her spirits plummeted.

Her mother had quarreled with Mrs. Dennison and left her employ—Amanda suspected she had been dismissed. She had remained behind in Venice, where she'd found a room in a small hotel, but she was already dissatisfied with her new accommodations. *"The whole place smells of garlic—even the upstairs rooms."* Amanda went on reading. *"I am teaching English to four little girls. Or trying to, for they are dreadfully spoiled, and unwilling to concentrate on their lessons."*

Amanda sighed, as she set down the letter beside the trinket box. She doubted that her mother would keep her new position long. And what was to become of her then?

Even with her raise, Amanda was only making ends meet. Eighteen dollars a month rent, and another eight for fuel, light, and food. But money was not the only problem. In the months she had been living here, she'd come to regard the small flat as her home; after each busy day, she had returned and gratefully allowed the warmth, the quiet, to envelop her. Many of the young ladies who lived in the house shared their quarters for reasons of economy or companionship, but she preferred to have only Leander for company.

She undid the ribbon and removed the paper from Clifford's gift. The tiny, polished shells gleamed in the lamplight.

Clifford seemed genuinely fond of her—perhaps more than fond. Maude had said that, with the proper encouragement, he would ask her to marry him. If she and Clifford were to marry, she would be able to provide generously for her mother. A small house, or perhaps a suite with a maid, in a good residential hotel. There would be no need for Mama to cater to the whims of ladies like Mrs. Dennison, or to work as a teacher; she could return to the leisurely way of life she'd always known.

Amanda stopped herself and smiled wryly. Clifford had said nothing about marriage. But suppose he did. Would she accept his proposal? She wasn't in love with him. But Mama had often said that, for a lady, love should come after marriage. He was well-bred and considerate. And the most handsome man she had ever known.

She supposed Ross might be considered good-looking enough. But his was a hard face, with its aquiline nose, thin lips, and prominent cheekbones. He could be agreeable enough, when he chose to. But she had seen the streak of ruthlessness left from those early years, when he'd fought for survival in a world completely different from her own.

Why was she thinking of Ross?

Why now, of all times, was she remembering that day in his office, when she'd told him about her encounter with Barney Marek? He'd bared her shoulder and examined her bruises. His face dark with anger, he'd reprimanded her for her reckless behavior. Yet, even as she'd bridled at his words, she had responded to his touch, his tone. She'd been frightened but oddly stirred by the unfamiliar sensations he'd awakened in her.

She forced such disturbing thoughts aside, and reminded herself that Ross was only a partner—a temporary one, at that. She had offered her help in finding Jessamyn's killer, and he'd accepted, however reluctantly. Once Marek was caught and locked away, they would have no reason to see each other again.

Leander leaped up on the desk and butted his head against her hand. He wasn't used to being ignored.

"You want your dinner, don't you?"

He stared at her fixedly, then led the way to the kitchen, tail held high, while she tied an apron over her dress, opened the built-in icebox, then filled his dish with chopped chicken livers. Apparently mollified, he devoted himself to his meal, while she fixed herself a pot of coffee and an omelet.

After she'd piled the dishes in the sink, she went back into the parlor and peered out the window. It had started snowing again; white flakes whirled about, glittering in the lamplight.

She took off her apron, put on her cloak and went out again. This time, there were no customers in the cigar store, and the man behind the counter was probably getting ready to close. She hurried past him to the telephone and placed her call again. And again, no one answered. Taut with impatience, she handed the man a nickel for the call, then headed for the door.

"You oughtn't to be out tonight, Miss," the man called to her.

Probably he thought the weather was too harsh for a lady to be abroad. As if a snowfall here in the city could do her any harm! When she and her father had spent a winter vacation in the Adirondacks, they'd put on sturdy boots, gone hiking through the snowy woods, and come back to the lodge, cold but invigorated. Papa had been a firm believer in outdoor exercise for girls, and she shared his views.

Even so, she was relieved to get back into the warmth of the hallway. She was about to climb the stairs when the concierge called to her from the sitting room. "Miss Whitney! Good heavens, I hope you weren't out there alone, at this hour!"

Only common courtesy kept her from saying that it was no one else's concern where she had been—alone or otherwise. "It's not a blizzard, Mrs. Morton." But something in the woman's face silenced her. The concierge's plump face was flushed, her eyes wide with dismay.

"You haven't heard then!"

"Heard what?"

"He's gone and done it again." She motioned Amanda into the sitting room and thrust a damp newspaper into her hands. "That fiend—that Barney Marek—he's killed another woman."

CHAPTER SIXTEEN

Amanda stared down at the front page of the *Graphic*.

Ladies Mile Maniac! Actress Found Strangled!

She gripped the back of the nearest chair to steady herself, her eyes fixed on the paper. "Clad in a wedding gown . . . a bridal wreath twisted around her fair white throat . . . discovered in dressing room of the Savoy Theater by a charwoman who summoned police and . . ."

She sank into the chair, afraid her legs would not support her.

"The man's a monster!" the concierge was saying. "Until they catch him, no woman's safe out on the streets after dark!"

"But this—" She searched this column. "This Violet Yates was found inside the theater."

"That doesn't mean he killed her there. Maybe he caught her outside after the show. He could have dragged her into a dark alley and—done it—and then he could have carried her back into the theater afterward. Of course, I've always said these actresses are no better than they should be. Flaunting themselves in front of all those men. But even so, no female deserves to meet such a horrid end—"

"Do you mind if I keep the paper?" Amanda interrupted.

"If you like," the concierge said with a shrug. "I've already read it through twice."

Amanda thanked her, said good-night and hurried upstairs. Once inside, she bolted the door, then rested against it. "Ross." As her lips shaped his name, she felt a need to have him here with her, right now.

The same night the news of Violet Yates's murder had blazed across the front pages of every newspaper in the city, Ross went to the Bellevue morgue and viewed the body. It was impossible to tell what she had looked like before she had been strangled with the wreath of artificial orange blossoms. Like the other two victims, her face was discolored, her features distorted. There was a single bruise on her right shoulder. Only her hair, long, thick, and black, hinted that she might have been pretty.

He examined the white wedding gown and veil, undergarments, and shoes she had been wearing when she had been brought in. He wondered if Amanda might have noticed some small details that he had missed. He thought of calling on her and bringing her down here, then swiftly dismissed the idea. This was no place for her. She had already done more than was necessary. Let her stay in her own safe little world from now on.

The following evening, the police permitted the Savoy Theater to reopen. Ross arrived at the shabby, second-rate variety theater on Stanton Street at the close of the performance, and waited at the stage door until the audience started leaving, then questioned the elderly doorman. "Did Violet Yates have the dressing room to herself?"

The old man grinned and shook his head. "This ain't Wallack's, mister. All the girls share one dressing room. But most of them have left already—can't say I blame them. They don't want to hang around here, not now." Then he added, "I ain't seen Cora yet—guess she'll be along any minute now."

Ross handed him a tip, then walked down a corridor

where a single overhead gas jet threw a flickering light on the dirty plaster walls. He paused at the half-opened door to the dressing room. A plump blonde sat at the dressing table littered with bottles and jars and soiled rags. She pulled off a tarnished sequin headdress and tossed it aside. She cried out when she saw his reflection in the mirror.

He gave her what he hoped was a reassuring smile, and took off his hat. "Good-evening, Miss—Cora, is it? My name's Ross Buchanan. May I speak with you for a few minutes?"

"No, you can't! My gentleman friend's waiting for me right outside."

"He won't mind waiting a little longer for a lovely young lady like you," he said. He handed her his business card. "I'm trying to find the man who killed Miss Yates."

"It was that Marek fella, that's for sure. He's out of his head, like the papers say." She shuddered and drew her faded wrapper around her more closely.

"You don't get much heat in here, do you?" He reached into his pocket coat, took out a flask and set it on the table. "A sip of brandy will warm you up."

She wiped a soiled glass with a rag, then filled it to the brim, and took a swallow. "This is good stuff." She gave him a smile and drank again. He saw the tension ease out of her body. "I already told the cops all I know."

"I'm sure you cooperated with the police in every way," he said. "But you couldn't have been expected to remember all the details, not so soon after you'd found out about Violet's murder. It must have come as a terrible shock."

"What're you gettin' at?"

"Did you tell them Marek used to work as a bouncer at Ryan's saloon, around the corner?"

"They never asked me. And, like you say, it was a shock

hearin' about Violet that way."

"Do you remember seeing him at Ryan's?"

"Sure—sometimes, when me and some of the other girls went in for a drink after the show. But he was fired months ago, for getting drunk on the job."

He refilled her glass. "You haven't seen him since then?"

"No, I haven't! And I hope I never lay eyes on him again."

"What about Violet? Did she see him, after he left Ryan's? Maybe go out with him?"

"If she did, she never said anything about it. But then, she wouldn't."

"Because he was married?"

"Because she acted like she was better than the rest of us. Said she used to act in plays, in them uptown theaters. She laid it on thick. She said she wouldn't be workin' here much longer, because she had a rich gentleman friend who was going to set her up in a fancy flat."

"Did you ever meet him—this rich friend of hers?"

"Not me! I'll bet, she made him up." She set down the empty glass. "It's gettin' late," she said. "I've got to change now."

"Just one more question," he said. "Did Violet play her part in a wedding gown?"

"Not likely!" Cora shook her head. "She wore spangled tights like the rest of us."

In the days that followed, he spent countless hours climbing rickety stairs in the crumbling tenements of Hell's Kitchen, prowling through the rat-infested squatters' shacks in the settlement north of Central Park, visiting the brothels, saloons, and all-night dance halls in the "Satan's Circus" district on the West Side. Although he carried the locust wood club he'd kept from his days on the force, he hadn't had to use it so far. His powerful build, his brisk stride, and his air of self-assurance, were enough to discourage a random attack.

But no one he questioned knew Marek's whereabouts— or if they did, they weren't saying. He went home long after midnight, tired and frustrated, to snatch a few hours sleep, before he started out again.

On Friday evening, nearly a week after Violet Yates's murder, he was starting out on his rounds when the gangling young delivery boy who worked in Rockford's pharmacy on the corner called out to him.

"Wait a minute, Mr. Buchanan. Somebody left a message for you. A—lady." He noticed the slight pause. "Miss Sally Flavin. She said you should meet her at Billy McGlory's place tonight."

Ross did not have a telephone in his flat, and since the pharmacy was open for business until midnight, seven days a week, he used it as a message center. He tossed the boy a coin, then headed downtown to McGlory's, on Hester Street. It might be another worthless lead, but he would follow it up.

He entered McGlory's concert saloon through a pair of double doors, walked down the long, narrow passage to the bar-room; it was already crowded and blue with smoke. He went on into a dance hall big enough to accommodate five hundred customers, where waiter girls wearing short skirts and high red boots circulated among the tables. For customers with different tastes, McGlory employed a few slender boys. They, too, were decked out in skirts and boots, their faces rouged and powdered. His ears were assaulted by the sounds of the piano, cornet, and violin. A balcony ran around two sides of the hall with small boxes partitioned off by heavy curtains.

Ross climbed the stairs and found Sally seated at a small table in one of the boxes. She looked up from the empty glass before her, greeted him with a smile, then she signaled to the nearest waiter girl, who brought a bottle and another glass for Ross.

It had been less than a year since he'd last seen the flamboyant redhead, but even in that time, her looks had begun to fade. Not that she'd ever had the exceptional beauty or the polished manners that would have gotten her into one of the expensive parlor houses, like Isobel Hewitt's, but her vivacious laugh, her free-and-easy manner, had drawn men to her. Now she looked drained, lethargic. Her face was puffy, and even a thick coating of rice powder could not quite hide the lines around her full-lipped mouth.

As soon as they'd been served, he drew the heavy curtains closed. "Why'd you send for me, Sally?"

"I hear you're looking for Barney Marek," she said.

"That's right. Know where I can find him?"

"Maybe." She leaned across the small table, smelling of gin, cheap perfume, and sweat. "He came in here one night, drunk as a skunk. Brought me up here and talked to me." She gave a harsh laugh. "He was too plastered for anything else."

"When was this?"

She lowered her voice. "The same night he killed his wife. But I didn't know anything about that—not 'til I read about it in the papers, the next day." She refilled her glass, then poured a drink for him. Knowing the quality of McGlory's gin, he left his glass untouched.

"The same night? You're sure about that?"

"I wouldn't've brought you traipsin' down here if I wasn't."

"And you say he talked a lot. What about?"

She shrugged her plump shoulders. "Nothin' that made much sense—not to me. He kept saying he was in big trouble. He sounded real scared."

"Did he say what he was afraid of?"

"He said there was some important fella out to get him. A millionaire, that's what he told me. How the hell would a bum like Marek get to know any millionaire?"

A rising excitement coursed through him. "Did he mention the man's name?"

She shook her head. "Like I said, he must've had a lot to drink before he got here. He started goin' on about his wife—said he'd given her a rough time. I can believe that. But everything would be different from then on—so he said. He was goin' to make it up to her. He'd take her away from New York. They'd go out west—San Francisco, maybe— and live in high style."

"Did he say where the money was going to come from?"

"He said his wife would get it for him. That if she'd do like he told her this time, they'd have plenty of money. Not just a few pieces of jewelry, like before. He said the fence where he'd unloaded them hadn't paid him enough to make the job worthwhile."

A few pieces of jewelry.

Had they belonged to Jessamyn? He was sure Everard hadn't given her money of her own, except for a small allowance. Of course, she might have bought whatever she wanted in any of the fashionable shops on the Ladies Mile, but the purchases would have been charged to her father's account.

"Go on," he prompted.

"He kept sayin' that this time his wife was goin' to get paid off in cash. Then they'd have to leave town real fast.

He just went on babblin' like that, and I let him talk, long as he kept drinkin'."

"Do you remember what time he left?"

"About one in the morning."

"You're sure?"

"I remember, 'cause that's when I asked did he want to stay for the circus downstairs, and he said no." The circus was a late-night performance staged in the basement, where McGlory's girls performed whatever erotic exhibitions the patrons demanded, and were willing to pay for.

"I figured he'd find himself a velvet room and sleep it off. But the next day, I heard about his wife gettin' herself killed, same way as the Spencer girl, and I figured he'd done them both in."

"And you haven't told the cops about it?"

Her face went tight with resentment. "The cops! I don't owe them nothin'. Bunch of no-good bums, pushin' girls like me around."

"I used to be a cop," he reminded her.

"But you were different, Ross. Even when you were on the force, you weren't like them others."

Her smile was warm and genuine, and her words brought back the memory of the first time he had seen her. He had been walking his beat on the South Street waterfront all that night, and at dawn, cold and hungry, he'd stopped at the Fulton Fish Market for a plate of fried oysters and coffee.

Then, as he was leaving, he heard an outraged shout. "Come back here, you sneaky bitch!" He stepped outside. The man who ran the smoked herring stall waved his arms and called to him. "Officer! Go after her! That redhead! She stole a box of herring!"

Although Sally had dodged in and out among the stalls,

she had been burdened with the wooden box, and he had finally caught up with her in an alley, where she was cramming one of the herrings into her mouth. His hand closed on her arm. When she tried to twist free, his grip tightened. She swallowed the last few morsels, nearly choking in her haste, then glared up at him defiantly. "A whole box," he said. "You're the greedy one, aren't you?"

She wiped her mouth on the back of her hand. "I was starvin'."

Her eyes looked enormous in her thin, bony face. "How old are you?" he asked.

"None o' yer damn business!"

"How old?"

"Fourteen. What about it?"

"Where's your family?"

"I got none."

"So where do you live?"

She shrugged. "Wherever I can. I been sleepin' in an old scow."

A fishing scow, by the smell of her. Even her tangled red hair stank of fish. "You'll be sleeping in jail for the next few months," he said.

For the first time, he saw a flicker of fear in her eyes. "Blackwell's Island?"

"That'll be up to the judge. Come on."

But she hung back, planting her bare feet on the wet cobblestones of the alley. "I swear I won't do it again!"

"Sure you will."

He had done the same, when he'd been on the street. But he'd been big for his age, a strong, ruthless street fighter. And it was harder for a girl on her own. She could find work sewing buttons or making paper flowers in a sweatshop for fourteen hours a day, at starvation wages. Or she could sell herself on the street, or in a Greene Street cribhouse.

She must have sensed his hesitation. "Don't take me in—please! I heard about Blackwell's Island. They do awful things to the girls there—the guards an' some of them older women, too." She looked up at him hopefully. "I only ate one of them herrings."

He jerked his head toward the mouth of the alley. "Get moving. And try the West Side piers from now on. Stay off my beat."

He figured he hadn't done her much of a favor that day, since she'd ended up in a dive like McGlory's. But she hadn't forgotten and, now and then, she'd given him a piece of useful information. This time, she'd outdone herself.

"When I found out you were workin' for that Spencer fella, I figured maybe I could help."

He didn't bother to ask how she had found out. Cops from headquarters over on Mulberry Street often dropped in to watch a circus, or one of the illegal bare-knuckled boxing matches downstairs. McGlory paid them off regularly, and he knew better than to serve them the vile liquor he sold the customers. He kept an ample supply of the good stuff, just for them.

"If you find Marek before the cops do, it'll do you some good—right?"

His muscles tightened as he tried to control his rising anticipation. After so many false leads, this could be his lucky night. "Can you tell me where to find him?"

She paused, frowning in an effort to remember. "He said he had a place to hide, while he was waiting for his wife."

"Where was it, Sally? Did he tell you?"

"The ring."

"The ring? That's all?"

"That's it, Ross. It didn't sound like he meant the kind of a ring you wear. It was like—a place where his wife'd know to find him."

He lapsed into silence as he tried to get the pieces to fit together. Gertrude must have told Barney about seeing Jessamyn at Talley's that afternoon back in September. And he had forced his wife into blackmailing the girl. The ring. Had Jessamyn given Gertrude a ring, to keep her from talking about the affair with O'Shea, and its unhappy consequences?

She could have gone to her father, and let him deal with that matter. But she was under a nervous strain, with the approach of her wedding to Howard Thornton. Maybe Gertrude's threats had caused her to panic completely, so that she had acted on impulse.

"Did Marek say anything else about the ring? Did he tell you where it was?"

She shook her head. "He only said Gertrude'd know to meet him there. That's all I know."

Outside McGlory's, the snow was already turning to dirty slush. A fog from the river swirled along the narrow street, making it difficult to see more than a few feet ahead.

The ring. Not a piece of jewelry, but a place. What the devil had Marek been talking about?

Had he fenced a ring, and whatever other jewelry Jessamyn might have given him? Maybe he was planning to meet Gertrude at the fence's shop. But all that talk about cash, what had he meant by that? Where could his wife get her hands on enough cash to make it possible for them to leave the city? Surely not from Everard Spencer.

He was rounding the corner of Hester Street, when a

short, stocky man loomed up in front of him. "That's him. That's Buchanan." Ross turned and saw another man, tall and heavy-set, standing behind him. He caught a glimpse of movement, then something struck him on the side of the face. He was being dragged into the nearest alley.

They pushed him against a wall. The stocky one twisted his arms behind him. The other raised a length of iron pipe, struck him on the forehead. Blood streamed into his eyes. The man kicked him hard in the belly. He doubled up, gagging and fighting for breath. He slammed the heel of his boot backward, raked it down the shin of the stocky one. The man swore, relaxed his grip and Ross twisted free.

The taller man swung at him. He ducked, feinted, then smashed his fist into the man's face, with all his strength behind it. He heard the crunch of bone and hoped he'd broken the man's nose. He saw a movement to his right, and tried to dodge but the iron pipe landed on the back of his skull, and he went down. Although sparks of fire danced before his eyes, he reached inside his coat. His hand closed around the locust wood club. He brought it down on the shorter man's knee. But before he could strike again, the other man kicked him in the elbow with a hobnailed boot. His right arm went numb and he dropped the club.

He closed his eyes, and lay still.

"Finish the bastard," he heard one of them say.

He drew a deep breath, and rolled over twice, away from the men, his fingers groping in the icy slush. Then his left hand closed around the club. He rapped hard against the wet stones in the alley. The sound that echoed off the walls would summon any cop in hearing distance. He took a kick in the ribs, then another, but somehow he kept his grip on the stick and rapped again.

Then he heard heavy, running steps, the piercing sound

of a police whistle. He scrambled to his feet, panting. He caught the taller man off-guard, swung him around and kicked him in the crotch. The man swore as he slumped forward.

Then a bull's-eye lantern sent a beam of light into the alley, and a deep voice shouted: "Hold it there!" But the men were already racing down to the other end of the alley, with the cops after them.

Ross dragged himself to his knees, and tried to cry out for help. He could only make a croaking noise, as he fell face-down, into the slush. Darkness enveloped him.

On Friday morning, Amanda arrived late for work for the first time since she had started working for the *Gazette*. She had gone to Ross's office on her way downtown, but it had been locked. She seated herself at her desk, but she couldn't concentrate on the work before her, an article about Mrs. Astor's cotillion. She tried again to reach him by telephone. And again, there was no answer.

"Amanda, why on earth are you glaring at that telephone, as if you wanted to pull it out of the wall?" Maude stood in her office doorway, the picture of elegance in a velvet walking suit of the new grey-blue shade, called *grande clematite*. "Surely it isn't out of order already?"

"The telephone's working well enough." She motioned Maude to the chair on the opposite side of her desk.

"What is wrong, then? Have you and Clifford had your first quarrel already? Ah, well—the course of true love never did run smooth—"

"Don't be ridiculous, Maude. I'm not in love with Clifford Spencer. Just because he took me to lunch yesterday—" She hesitated for a moment, before she went on. "Do you know of a saloon called Murphy's?"

"Surely you haven't taken to drink?"

But Amanda wasn't able to force a smile. "Please, Maude—it's important."

"There must be at least a dozen Irish saloons by that name in the city."

"But a lot of reporters go to this one. And ward-heelers."

"That sounds like Charles Murphy's place, over on the East Side. Murphy's a Tammany man with big political ambitions."

"Where on the East Side?"

"If it's the place I'm thinking of, it's somewhere around Nineteen and Avenue C. But women don't go there. Not even—prostitutes." Her eyes widened. "Good heavens, Amanda. Surely you aren't thinking of going there?"

She had never been inside a saloon in her life, and she had no desire to go to one now. But if she couldn't get in touch with Ross by phone before the end of the day, she'd have to try to invade Murphy's all-male bastion.

"Sorry," the bartender said. "We don't serve ladies here."

Amanda had gone home after work and fed Leander. Then she had changed into her plainest outfit, a well-cut but simple dark green walking suit and matching bonnet. She was sure she looked the model of respectability. But already, some of the customers were staring at her, ignoring their drinks, and the free lunch spread out on the bar before them—an assortment of pickled oysters, hard-boiled eggs, sauerkraut, and crackers.

"I'm not staying," she said briskly.

"You certainly are not!"

She kept her voice low, but firm. "I'm looking for a friend here."

"Look somewheres else, lady," he said impatiently. "Didn't you see the sign outside? This place is for gents only. So you'd best be on your way."

But having come this far, she was not going to be put off so easily. She raised her chin and stared the man in the eye. "My friend's name is Ross Buchanan. I know he comes in here."

"Buchanan? Sure he does. But he ain't been in here for a couple of weeks. Try his office, why don't you?"

"I already have," she said. "He wasn't in. I need to talk to him. If you can tell me where he lives, I'll go there."

One of the men laughed. "Better not walk in on him, unexpected, Miss. You might find him with another girl." He edged closer. "But if you're lookin' for a friend, I'll be glad to—"

"Shut your big mouth," a deep voice rumbled. "Don't you know a lady when you see one?" A stout, balding man in a checked suit pushed his way through the crowd, bowed and took off his derby. "Costello's the name, Miss," he said. "Jerry Costello, at your service."

The name rang a bell; Ross had spoken of him. "You're a reporter for the *Graphic*, aren't you?" She gave him a warm smile, and held out her gloved hand. "That makes us colleagues, Mr. Costello. My name's Amanda Whitney and I work for the *Ladies Gazette*."

"Do you, now? And what sort of work do you do there?"

"I am the society editor."

"I'll bet you do a real fine job of it, too," he said. "You say you're a friend of Buchanan's?"

"Yes, Mr. Costello. I tried to telephone him at his office, but there was no answer. And when I went over there this morning, I found the door locked. So I will have to speak to him at home."

"Well, now—I don't know about that," Costello said slowly. "Buchanan's a man who likes his privacy."

"It's a matter of business," she said. "I have some important information for him."

"It must be important, for a lady like yourself to come in here looking for him. All right, Miss. He's got a flat in a building down on Sheridan Square. I don't know the number but it's right next-door to Rockford's Pharmacy."

The hansom clattered over the cobbles, heading downtown. When Amanda got out in front of the pharmacist's shop, she saw that the clock in the shop window, between the two large glass bottles filled with red liquid, read twelve-fifteen. "You want me to wait, ma'am?"

"No thank you."

But after the cab went clattering off into the darkness, splashing slush to either side, she wondered if she should have accepted the driver's offer. The square was deserted. When she looked up at the narrow, three-story apartment building she saw no light in any of the front windows.

She let herself into the small outer small lobby, with three steps leading up to the inside door. She tried the inner door, and found it locked. Maybe, if she waited long enough, one of the other tenants would come out and she could ask what floor Ross Buchanan lived on. She rested her back against the wall, until her legs grew tired; then she seated herself on the top step, smoothing her skirt of her woolen walking suit around her ankles.

Better not walk in on him . . . might find him with another girl. She supposed the man at Murphy's saloon had said that to tease her. Still, it was possible that Ross had a girl up there with him. What did she really know about his private life?

The minutes crawled by, and she was starting to shiver a little, in the pre-dawn chill, when she heard the sound of footsteps coming up the walk—heavy and unsteady. She sprang to her feet just as the outside door opened. Ross stood in the doorway, his coat torn and filthy. He wore no hat. His face was livid with bruises and smeared with dried blood.

She cried out and he raised his head. "Amanda! Why are you . . ." His voice was hoarse, and the words were slurred. When she reached out to him, he collapsed against her, his weight almost knocking her off her feet.

CHAPTER SEVENTEEN

Amanda braced herself, lifted his arm, and put it around her waist while she fought down the panic that threatened to overwhelm her. Somehow she managed to support his weight long enough to get him up the three steps to the inner door.

"It's locked," she said. He looked down at her with a dazed expression, and she saw that his right eye was half-shut and circled with an ugly purple bruise. He wore no hat, and his dark hair was matted with blood.

She forced herself to speak firmly. "I need your key, Ross."

He leaned against her more heavily, and made a wordless sound deep in his throat. Didn't he understand what she was saying?

"Your key," she repeated.

He fumbled inside his coat, then held out his key chain. She had to try a few keys before she found the right one. Still supporting his weight, she turned sideways and pushed open the door with her hip. "Where's your flat?" And, when he did not answer: "Which floor?"

"Third."

It would be, she thought grimly. He leaned heavily against her all the way, and gripped the wooden banister with his free hand. By the time they reached the third floor, her camisole was damp with perspiration, her knees were unsteady, and all her muscles ached.

After she unlocked the door of his flat and half-dragged,

half-carried him inside, she stopped for a moment to peer into the darkness. Her skirt brushed against a small table. "Matches," she said. He groped about on the tabletop for a moment, then found a metal match holder, but when he reached up and tried to light the wall jet, she heard him gasp with pain. She took the match holder from his hand. "I'll do it." She struck a match and turned up the gas as far as it would go, so that the parlor was bathed in a soft glow. She scarcely took time to glance at the heavy black walnut furniture, the wine red carpet, and heavy drapes.

He tightened his arm around her waist, and stumbled forward. She helped him across the parlor, then into the bedroom beyond. She sighed with relief as she lowered him into the nearest chair, then took a moment to catch her breath. She lit the lamp on the bedside table, and hurried back to him. She stood staring down at him, and her eyes widened with shock. "Ross—your face! What happened to you? Were you in an accident?"

He shook his head. "No accident," he muttered thickly. "Somebody set me up."

Although she was not familiar with the phrase, she understood. Later, she would find out who had done this to him. Right now, she had to get him out of his wet clothes and into bed. She started to help him off with his coat, then flinched as she heard his cry of pain. "I'm sorry," she said.

After she had got the coat off and dropped it to the floor, she saw that his shirt, too, was torn and bloody. "Where do you keep your nightshirts?" she asked.

"Never wear them."

She searched his closet and found a thick woolen robe; it would have to do for now. When she returned to him, he was fumbling with the buttons of his shirt. She saw that his knuckles were swollen and caked with blood.

"Let me do that." She supported him against her shoulder, while she took off his shirt, then his undershirt. She bit back a cry when she saw the deep lacerations and livid bruises on his chest. His skin was icy-cold to the touch. Quickly she wrapped the robe around him, then knelt, unlaced his shoes and tugged them off. His trousers were soaking wet, and muddy, too, as if he'd rolled about on a slush-covered street.

She hesitated only a moment, then drew a deep breath, and told herself this was no time for delicacy. But her fingers fumbled with his belt buckle, and he pushed her hand away. "I'll do that," he told her.

She busied herself preparing the bed, drawing back the blanket, folding back the top sheet. From behind her, she could hear his heavy breathing. When she turned back, his sodden trousers and undergarments lay in a heap on the carpet. He had pushed his arms into the sleeves of the robe, and was trying to tie the belt. She did it for him, then let him lie back in the chair, while she scooped up his discarded clothes.

Holding the lamp in her free hand, she found her way to the bathroom, which was large and well-equipped, with a walnut enclosed zinc tub, and a set of shelves that held clean towels and washcloths. She dropped the ruined coat into the tub, along with the rest of his garments.

She took off her jacket—it was blood-stained, too—and tucked a large towel around her waist. She returned to the bedroom, where she spread thick towels on the sheet, to keep it clean and dry, then helped Ross to the bed. He lay back, watching her with half-closed eyes.

But when she began to wash the blood from his face, he groaned and pulled away. Her legs were starting to quiver, and she sat down on the side of the bed. She must not lose her hard-held self-control; not while she was the only one here to care for him. After she had sponged away most of the blood, she saw that his face was a greyish color—except where it was purple with bruises. She winced at the sight of the deep, jagged cut on his forehead. "Ross—you look awful."

"You look fine." Then he was reaching up, touching her cheek. "You smell good, too—" A corner of his mouth lifted, as if he were trying to smile; but the movement started the blood trickling from his split lip.

"For heaven sake, be still." She drew the blanket up and tucked it around him. Although she had done all she could to make him comfortable, he needed more expert care than she could offer him. "Who is your doctor?" she asked.

"Get Saul Goldman," he said thickly. "He's at Bellevue."

She glanced around the bedroom. "Do you have a telephone here?"

He shook his head, and his eyes closed again. Had he fallen unconscious? How severe were his injuries? Although the steady rise and fall of breathing reassured her a little, she was still uneasy. But she dared not leave him alone, while she went out to look for a cab to take her across the city to Bellevue. If, indeed, she could find a cab at this hour.

She would have to wait until morning. With a sigh, she pulled the armchair closer to the bed, then felt a wave of weakness pass over her. She sank down, leaned her head back. Although she tried to keep awake, she was overcome by exhaustion. For the next few hours she drifted in and out of a fitful sleep, waking each time Ross cried out, then rising and hurrying to his side. Later, he called for water. She raised his head and held the glass to his lips. Some of it spilled, and she wiped it from his face. Once he grasped her hand and clung to it tightly, while he mumbled words she could not understand. She stroked his hair back from his forehead, careful not to touch the ugly, jagged cut.

The first rays of pale winter sunlight were already slanting through the half-open drapes, when Amanda got to her feet again. She looked over at the bed, where Ross lay sleeping. Quickly, she went into the bathroom, where she washed her face and tidied her hair as best she could.

Next, she prepared a pot of coffee in the small kitchen; like the rest of the flat, it, too, was clean and orderly, the dishes and the few pots neatly arranged. She drank two cups of coffee and the strong, hot brew helped to clear her head.

"Amanda—"

She hurried back to the bedroom.

"You're still here," he said. She thought she saw a brief look of surprise on his battered face.

Had he really thought she would leave him, badly injured as he was? What sort of life had he led, that he expected so little from another?

She brought him pencil and paper, and he scrawled a note to Saul Goldman. "The kid at the chemist's shop will take it over to Bellevue for you," he told her. She hurried downstairs, gave the note to the errand boy, and returned quickly, to find Ross asleep again.

Less than an hour later, Saul Goldman, a thin, red-haired young man, knocked at the door. She looked at him doubtfully, for a moment; her own family doctor was a white-haired gentleman with a small, pointed beard and a tall silk hat. "I only got off duty half an hour ago," he told her, as she took his coat and derby. If he was surprised at finding her in Ross's flat, he did not show it. He followed her into the bedroom, set down his black bag on the table. Ross started to sit up.

"Stay still," the doctor ordered. "You look like you were run down by a brewery wagon." He took Ross's pulse, then opened his black bag. "What happened to you?"

"It was a set-up. A couple of hired toughs jumped me, down on Hester Street."

"And what were you doing there?"

"Sally Flavin sent for me. She's one of McGlory's girls."

"And she set you up?"

"Not Sally. She gave me the first real lead I've had so far. As soon as you get me patched up, I'll go out and get him."

"The hell you will!" Saul said. He turned his head briefly. "Sorry, Miss Whitney." Then he put a firm hand on Ross's shoulder and eased him back against the pillows. "You'll stay right here, until I tell you otherwise."

He felt the back of Ross's head. "What did they use on you? A brick?"

"Their fists and their boots. And an iron pipe."

"Good thing you've got a thick skull. All the same, you'll follow my orders." Before Ross could protest, he added: "Otherwise I'll send for an ambulance and get you into a ward at Bellevue."

"I took worse beatings—plenty of them—when I was a kid. And I got over them, without any doctor to—"

"Be quiet," Saul ordered. "Let's have a look at the rest of you." He started to pull back the blanket, but Ross stopped him.

"Amanda, go and make Saul a fresh pot of coffee, will you?"

Was he trying to spare her modesty? The corners of her lips twitched in a brief smile. Maybe he had no memory of last night, when she'd helped him to undress.

While she rinsed the tall, enamel pot and refilled the basket, she heard the rise and fall of the men's voices, but she couldn't catch the words. She waited impatiently for the coffee to perk, then came back into the bedroom, carrying a tray.

The doctor had bandaged Ross's head, but the bruises around his eyes only looked more livid by contrast. "Don't worry, Miss Whitney." Saul gave her a reassuring smile. "He's got no broken bones, and I don't see any sign of a concussion."

She gave a sigh of relief, as she set down the tray.

"Miss Whitney's one of those 'new women' you hear about," Ross said. "I don't know if she can cook. But her coffee's not bad."

When Saul had finished his coffee, he reached into his bag and handed her a small bottle. "Tincture of laudanum, for the pain. Give him eight drops in a glass of water twice a day. Keep him on a light diet. And plenty of rest. You see to it he follows my orders, Miss Whitney."

"She's not one of your nurses," Ross protested. "She writes the society gossip for the *Ladies Gazette*." He turned to her. "Aren't you already late for work? What will Mrs. Fairlie say?"

"Today is Saturday," she told him, with a touch of satisfaction. "So I have the rest of the weekend free, to stay here and carry out Doctor Goldman's instructions."

He gave her an outraged stare. "You can't spend the night here!"

"I already have. Or perhaps you've forgotten."

Only a few months ago, she could not have imagined

speaking that way. Or finding herself in such an unconventional situation. But then, she had ignored so many of the proprieties since she'd met Ross that one more did not seem to matter.

She stayed with him until early afternoon, then gave him a dose of laudanum, hoping it would help him to sleep, while she made a quick trip back to her own place to change her clothes, and ask Mrs. Morton to feed Leander for the next few days.

"A friend of mine has been taken ill," she told the concierge.

The woman looked at her disapprovingly. "Nothing contagious, I hope."

"No, indeed, he—" She caught herself in time. "My friend's husband, that is. He's away on business. Her baby came early, and there are two other little ones at home."

"And I suppose you know all about taking care of babies?"

"I'm learning," said Amanda.

Before Mrs. Morton had a chance to question her further, she was already on her way downstairs.

Ross heard the front door open and lifted his head, gritting his teeth against the throbbing pain that shot through the back of his skull. Amanda came into the bedroom, her cheeks deep pink with the cold. She paused to set down two large shopping bags, then took off her cloak, and hung it away in his closet. She removed her hat, placed it on the dresser, and stood before the mirror a moment, to smooth her hair.

"If you're planning to move in, you should have brought a trunk."

"I've only brought a few aprons," she said. "And here are two nightshirts for you—Lord & Taylor's best quality flannel. I would have come back sooner, but the store was crowded with holiday shoppers."

"I don't wear nightshirts."

"So you told me last night. But you will wear them while I'm taking care of you. I wasn't sure of the size, so I bought extra-large."

Before he could protest, she went on with calm self-assurance, as if she was accustomed to caring for an injured man. "And I picked up a pound of tea. Coffee may be over-stimulating in your condition. A dozen eggs and some fresh-baked rolls for me. And a jar of Mellin's Food for you."

"Mellin's Food—what's that?"

"It's rather like gruel, I think. The chemist at Rockford's recommended it highly. He said it was suitable for infants and invalids."

He glared at her. "Since I'm neither, you can eat it yourself."

"You're to stay on a light diet. Doctor Goldman said so, and I intend to see that his orders are carried out."

The throbbing pain in his head was getting worse by the minute, and when he tried to draw a deep breath, a stab of pain shot through his ribs. "If you want to fuss over someone, go home and fuss over that fool cat of yours!"

"Leander's no fool," she retorted. "He has more sense than you do. He doesn't go roaming around the slums at all hours, getting himself beaten half-dead—" Then he heard her voice waver and saw the glitter of tears, before she blinked them back. "I'm staying here whether you want me to, or not."

She started to turn her head away, but his hand shot out

and closed around her wrist. "Look at me, Amanda. What are you crying for?"

"I'm not crying." She sniffed, fumbled for a handkerchief, then wiped her cheek.

He felt an unaccustomed pang of guilt. Although he had never found it easy to apologize, he made an attempt at it. "You must have had a rough time of it, last night. I suppose I should thank you for getting me up here and all the rest of it."

"There's no need for thanks," she said, as she started unpacking the shopping bags. "I only did what anyone would have done under the circumstances."

He doubted it, but he didn't bother to contradict her. Instead, he asked: "How did you happen to be here when I got home?"

"I got your address from Mr. Costello."

He raised himself on his uninjured arm and stared at her in disbelief. "Jerry Costello? And where'd you find him?"

"I remembered your telling me about Murphy's Saloon. So I went there and asked if anyone knew where I might find you."

He stared at her in outraged disbelief. "The hell you did! They don't let women inside Murphy's. They never have."

She ignored his profanity. "That's what the bartender told me," she said. "But I wasn't about to leave, until I found out where you lived. I'd been trying to reach you by telephone at your office for days but you weren't there."

What could have been important enough to force a well-bred young woman like Amanda to invade Murphy's saloon and stand her ground against the bartender's protestations? He searched her face, the pain forgotten for the moment.

"I needed to tell you what I found out from Miss Tuttle."

"The woman who used to be Jessamyn's maid? When did you see her?"

"A week ago, when I went to tea at the Spencers' home. I'll tell you all about it later. Now you must lie back and rest."

Her take-charge attitude was becoming infuriating, but he managed to keep his resentment under control. He spoke quietly, but firmly. "You'll tell me right now."

"Don't excite yourself." Her tone was soothing, as if she were speaking to a fractious child. "It's not good for you, in your condition."

His jaw tightened. "Never mind my condition. Just tell me what you found out from Miss Tuttle. You must have thought it was important, otherwise you wouldn't have gone into a saloon to track me down."

"All right then. Ottilie Spencer invited me to tea last week. I must confess I was surprised when I received her invitation, because I never thought she considered me a friend. But I accepted because I thought it might give me an opportunity to find out more about the family."

"And just how were you going to do that? Were you planning to keep your hostess waiting, while you cross-examined Nellie again? Or question the maid who brought in the tea?"

"There is no need to be sarcastic. I wasn't sure exactly how I would go about it. First, I thought I might get some new information by talking with Ottilie over tea."

"And did you?"

"I found out that she had been staying shut up in the house for some time. And I doubt that she has had any callers. Even when Clifford offered to drive her downtown to look at the holiday show windows, she refused."

So Clifford had been there, too. Maybe he had persuaded his mother to invite Amanda to tea.

"I suppose Ottilie was afraid her former friends would avoid her—or even pretend not to see her—because of the scandal. There are times when society can be so ruthless, so unjust," Amanda went on. "Of course, Ottilie blames the newspapers for keeping the Spencer name in their columns. She found fault with the police, too, for what she believes to be their inefficiency. And she was most unfair in speaking about you. She said you were confining your investigation to ogling the housemaids, as she put it. But I told her how wrong she was—I said that you would take any risk to—" She caught her breath, then looked away. "Oh, Ross, I'm sorry. But I couldn't just sit there while she spoke about you that way."

He bit back an oath. "I suppose you told her you were helping me, and had been all along!"

"I did no such thing! I explained we had met, quite by chance, and had shared a hansom."

"And how did you explain how you know so much about me?"

"I only said you had impressed me as a man who would do his job to the best of his ability, that's all."

Maybe Ottilie had believed her. But had Clifford also accepted her improvised explanation?

"So you were able to find out that Ottilie's been ostracized by her friends. That she's concerned about her family's reputation. That's hardly surprising, is it?"

"I suppose not. But I did think you might want to know what I learned from Miss Tuttle."

"How did you make the opportunity to speak to her?"

"It was when I tore my dress—I did it on purpose, of course. Then I made a great fuss about having to go home and change before I went on to the bazaar. Clifford was most solicitous."

"I'm sure he was." His lips tightened. What were Clifford's intentions toward Amanda? He pushed the question aside, and reminded himself that her private life was no concern of his.

"Go on," he urged. "You tore your dress."

"Only the lace on one cuff."

"What happened then?"

"Ottilie offered to have Miss Tuttle sew the lace back on. Of course, I accepted. Poor Miss Tuttle—it's been such a come-down for her. She had been called on to do all sorts of chores for anyone in the house who requires her services."

"She has my sympathy," he said, restraining his impatience with difficulty. "Now, suppose you tell me exactly what you found out from her that you think is so important."

"I was getting to that. It happened on the night Jessamyn was murdered. She told me that the coachman sent in his jacket—badly stained, and with a loose button. She was expected to make the necessary repairs, and of course, she did. But she said she did not think the head coachman had been so careless with his livery. That he was careful about his appearance. She thought that Winfield—he's one of the grooms—had taken the jacket without permission."

"And worn it to impress one of his lady friends."

Amanda looked crestfallen. "You already knew all about it."

"That's right."

"Did you also know that Miss Tuttle found a strand of blonde hair wrapped around one of the buttons on the jacket?"

"No, I didn't. That was something Kendall neglected to mention. Or maybe he hadn't noticed it." After a moment's

280

silence, he went on, "Jessamyn had yellow hair. Maybe she had been going out to meet Winfield."

"Ross! How can you even suggest that she would have done such a thing?"

He caught her look of outrage, and he felt the familiar resentment rising inside him. "Jessamyn was too well-bred, is that what you mean? What about her affair with that riding master, O'Shea?"

"She was only fifteen, then. She must have been in love with him—or thought she was."

"Maybe she thought she was in love with young Winfield, too."

"Miss Tuttle thought that Winfield might have worn the coachman's livery to impress one of the maids from another house on the avenue."

"It's possible," he conceded.

"And she also said he could have been the one who took Jessamyn's jewelry. She has no proof, of course."

"What jewelry?" he interrupted.

"An amethyst ring and a locket. They were of no great value—Everard Spencer keeps all the really valuable jewelry locked in his safe. But they were precious to Jessamyn, because Clifford had given them to her."

"Everard never told me about any missing jewelry."

"Because he didn't know," she said. "No one did. Jessamyn insisted on keeping the theft a secret. She was quite vehement about it, and Miss Tuttle didn't wish to upset her, so she agreed. Ross, what is it?"

"Last night, when I talked to Sally Flavin, she said she'd been with Barney the night Gertrude was murdered. He came to McGlory's, raving drunk." Quickly, he told her what he had learned from Sally. "Most of it made no sense," he finished.

"Are you sure about that?" She leaned forward, her amber eyes wide with excitement. "If he didn't get much money for the locket and the ring, then maybe he went back to the Spencer mansion, and this time he demanded money." She spoke quickly, scarcely pausing for breath. "Don't you see? He threatened Jessamyn, and she started to called out for help. Then he lost his head and strangled her. And he got Winfield to put on the coachman's livery and help him take the body down to the Ladies Mile."

"Slow down, Amanda. Marek used to be the Spencers' head coachman, remember? He could have hitched up the team, put on Kendall's livery, and driven the brougham himself. He could have taken the body down to the Ladies Mile and dumped it in the alley."

"And after Jessamyn's death, he could have planned a different blackmail scheme—one he thought would be more profitable."

"If he hoped to intimidate a man like Everard Spencer with his threats, he really must be a lunatic," Ross said.

She did not contradict him. "Ottilie, then," she said. "Maybe he thought Ottilie would give him money in return for his silence. She would have gone to any lengths to avoid further scandal."

"I don't doubt it," he said. "But if Ottilie was desperate enough to hand over the money to Gertrude, why didn't the Mareks use it to get as far away from New York as possible?"

"Because Gertrude was afraid to go through with his scheme."

"All right, let's suppose he killed his wife, in a fit of drunken rage," he conceded. "What about Violet Yates? Do you think he killed her, too?"

She shook her head slowly. "He didn't even know Violet."

"As it happens, he did," Ross said. "He used to work as a bouncer in a saloon around the corner from the Savoy Theater. The girls used to go in there for drinks, after the performance."

"Then maybe he was attracted to Violet, and she encouraged him."

"Violet was too ambitious to waste her time on a man like Marek."

His words took her by surprise. "How can you possibly know that?"

He told her of his visit to the theater, and his conversation with Cora.

"Then perhaps Violet rebuffed his advances," she said.

"Maybe. But we won't have the answer to that until I find him. Sally gave me a lead, that's all."

"A lead? What kind of a lead?"

"Something to do with the ring. He fenced the ring, along with the locket. Maybe the fence had a backroom or a cellar where a wanted man could hide. Barney might have waited there for Gertrude."

"But he wouldn't still be there after all this time, would he?"

"No, but the fence—whoever he is—may be able to tell me where he went from there."

She went cold inside as she thought of Ross, going out into the streets and alleys of the slums again. "You can't leave here—not as badly hurt as you are. I—I won't let you!" She gripped his arm, as if she meant to restrain him by force, if necessary. "I won't let you."

In spite of himself, he was moved by her fierce determination to protect him. He put his hand over hers. "Calm down, Amanda. I have no intention of going after Marek, until I know I can deal with him."

★ ★ ★ ★ ★

That evening, after he'd insisted he was having none of "that gruel concoction," she compromised by fixing him two boiled eggs, tea, and toast. Later, she carried in a basin of warm water and a cloth, and helped him to wash. Her cheeks looked a little flushed in the soft lamplight. It could not have been easy for a carefully-reared young lady like her to perform such an intimate service for a man. When she handed him one of the new nightshirts, and said, "The flannel is softer than that woolen robe of yours," he decided that he could compromise, too.

But when she had turned down the lamp, and seated herself in the large armchair and covered herself with a blanket, he protested. "You're not going to sleep there."

"Why not? It's comfortable enough."

"You would be much more comfortable in your own bed."

"Probably. But I can't leave you alone, not yet."

There it was again: her unshakeable sense of responsibility. He controlled himself with difficulty, and made one final attempt. "What about Leander? He'll think you've abandoned him."

"So long as Mrs. Morton feeds him, he'll be all right." Her lips curved in a faint smile. "Your concern for my cat is touching. But at the moment, you need me more than he does."

He realized that further discussion would be useless. "Suit yourself," he said. He turned over on his side, his back to her, and shut his eyes. But he was sharply aware of her presence, and it took awhile before he could fall asleep.

The following morning he insisted on getting out of bed, washing himself, and putting on a clean pair of trousers, a shirt, and jacket. Ignoring her protests, he insisted that she prepare a substantial breakfast: four fried eggs, bacon, toast, and coffee.

After breakfast, they sat together on the parlor sofa, with the brilliant sunlight streaming in through the half-open drapes. She was relieved to see that his color was coming back, and that the bruises had started to fade from purple to yellowish-green.

"Ross, you said someone had set you up. You really think someone hired those thugs to do this to you?"

"I'm sure of it. There are plenty of toughs for hire, down there on the east side." His mouth twisted in a mirthless grin. "They have their standard rates—they charge five dollars for a broken arm or leg. Twenty-five for a jacking." Seeing her puzzled look, he explained. "That's knocking out their victim with a black-jack. And a hundred for doing the big job."

"Murder? They would kill someone for a hundred dollars?"

"The rates probably have gone up since I was a street kid."

She looked away, then spoke hesitantly. "Ross! Did you ever—"

"I never killed anybody for money," he told her.

"How long did you live on the streets?"

"From the time I was ten."

"But your parents—where were they?"

He shook his head. "My father was a doctor. He and my mother came over from Scotland, shortly after I was born. He worked among the poor here in the city, until the war broke out. Then he enlisted in the Union Army when the war started. He was killed at Bull Run."

"And your mother?"

"No one would hire a governess or even a housemaid who was burdened with a child. She went to work in a sweatshop. She sewed army uniforms fourteen hours a day. She died of consumption."

"Weren't there any relatives in this country to care for you?"

"I don't think so. If there were, they didn't come looking for me. So I was put in a home for orphans." Even now, those old memories aroused a deep resentment. "I stood it for almost a year, and then I ran off."

"But why? I'm sure it wasn't like a real home—but you had a roof over your head, you were fed and cared for."

"They took care of you all right. The older boys beat you up and stole your food—what there was of it. And the care-takers were worse. If you broke one of their rules they stripped the hide off you with a leather strap. Not that some of them needed a reason."

"But surely there must have been a—a Board of Trustees to oversee them."

"A few well-dressed, well-fed gentlemen in high silk hats came there once. It was on Christmas, I remember. Our food was half-way decent that day, and we got heat in the dormitories."

"And none of you told them how you were treated all the rest of the time? The abuses you suffered?"

"We never got the chance," he said. "The gentlemen didn't stay long, because they wanted to get back to their comfortable homes and their Christmas dinners. And even if they had questioned us, we wouldn't have dared tell them the truth."

Her eyes were filled with pity, and she touched his hand lightly. "Oh, Ross—how awful it must have been for you."

He jerked his hand away. He didn't want her pity. He

286

had told her about his past because he wanted to remind her of the gulf that separated them. And always would. "That's how it was. And that's why I ran away, as soon as I got the chance."

"Maybe it's different now." She spoke hesitantly.

"Maybe—but I doubt it."

"But after you ran away, what happened then?"

"I slept in abandoned shacks, or warehouses like all those other homeless kids. I did everything the other street kids do to keep alive. I rolled drunks and picked pockets. I was big for my age, and I learned how to fight. I joined a gang, and they taught me how to survive. We stole food from the pushcarts and the markets. Or other stuff we could fence for cash."

"Didn't any of you ever get caught?"

"Sure. Not me, though. Even so, I figured it was only a matter of time before I landed in a cell in the Tombs."

She was leaned forward toward him, her lips parted, taking in his every word.

"I started hanging around the saloons, running errands for the ward-heelers. I got to know some of the big shots from Tammany. And when I was old enough, they helped me to get on the force." He broke off. "So now you know all about me."

Her eyes searched his face. "Not all," she said softly.

CHAPTER EIGHTEEN

Amanda dipped her pen in the brass inkwell on her office desk. Two more pages, and her lead article for the society section of next week's *Gazette* would be finished. But before she could resume her work, Maude came sweeping into her office, wearing a dove-grey velvet walking suit, probably the latest creation of Madame Duval or one of the other fashionable dressmakers on the Ladies Mile. The red brocade insets in the skirt matched the wide lapels of the close-fitting jacket and the trimming on the bustle. A grey velvet hat with curling red plumes was perched forward over one eye, at a rakish angle. She seated herself on the edge of the chair opposite Amanda, smoothed her skirt carefully, then drew off her grey suede gloves.

"I do hope your friend has recovered," she said. "And that the new baby is thriving."

Her words caught Amanda off-guard. She gave her friend a blank stare.

"I shouldn't have thought you had much experience in dealing with such emergencies."

Amanda set her pen in its holder, and blotted the top sheet of paper before she remembered the explanation she had given Mrs. Morton, to account for having been out overnight during the weekend. "The baby is doing well. It—she—arrived earlier than expected," she improvised.

"That's what your concierge told me."

"I was only helping out until my friend was able to hire an experienced nursemaid, one with suitable references," she said. Confronted by Maude's searching look, she felt slightly uncomfortable. "How did you happen to speak to Mrs. Morton?"

"I dropped by your house late Saturday afternoon, after finishing my Christmas shopping. I had bought a box of petite fours, and I thought we might have tea together. But Mrs. Morton said you had been out all the night before, that you had returned to pick up a few things and to ask her to feed your cat—and then you had left again, in a great hurry. I must confess, I felt somewhat concerned for you. You've not been living on your own long, and—forgive me, Amanda—but you do tend to act impulsively at times."

Did Maude suspect that there had been no female friend in distress, no newborn infant? Amanda looked away hastily, unable to meet her friend's blue-grey eyes.

She would have liked to confide in Maude, but that, of course, would have been unthinkable. No young lady with the slightest claim to respectability would admit she had spent a night—two nights—in a gentleman's bachelor flat. It was not even acceptable for an unmarried lady to pay an afternoon call on a gentleman, unless she was accompanied by a chaperon. Of course she had behaved impulsively, and now she had no choice but to brazen it out. "I appreciate your concern for my reputation, you have no need to be."

"Reputation, fiddlesticks! It was your safety I was thinking of."

"My—friend lives in a perfectly safe neighborhood," she began.

"For goodness sake, Amanda!" Maude interrupted, with an impatient flick of her hand. "Don't you read anything but society gossip these days? All the newspapers in the city have been warning unescorted ladies to stay off the streets after dark, until this Marek creature has been caught. They say he is a madman, who chooses his victims at random!"

"Those reporters are ignoring the facts—as they often do. They will stop at nothing to titillate their readers, terrify them, if necessary, in order to sell more papers. Stop and think a minute. Haven't they already said that he used to work for Jessamyn's family, as head coachman?"

"Suppose he did?" Maude raised her carefully-arched brows. "Surely you are not suggesting that gave him a perfectly logical reason to come sneaking back into the Spencer mansion after all this time, to strangle their daughter?"

"Perhaps he held some grudge against his former employer, for a real or fancied wrong."

"If every servant who held a grudge against his former master came back and strangled a former employer, or a member of the family—no prosperous home in New York would be safe."

"Perhaps Barney Marek is one of those foreign anarchists who feel an unreasoning hatred for anyone who has amassed a great fortune. Or—maybe he had read about the wedding, and decided it was an opportune time to kidnap Jessamyn. And then release her after he had collected the ransom."

"If that is so, why didn't he carry out his original plan?"

"Maybe she started to call out for help, and he feared one of the servants might hear her. Maybe he only meant to silence her. The killing could have been accidental," she went on quickly. "Marek is a drunken brute, rough and hulking, with an evil temper!" She faltered, then added: "At least, that's what the papers are saying."

"So you believe that Barney Marek might have strangled Jessamyn in the course of a bungled kidnapping. But why would he have killed his wife? Have you also worked out an explanation for that?"

Amanda felt herself getting more rattled by the minute, and she longed for an interruption: the appearance of the copy boy, or a call from Mrs. Fairlie. "He might have confided in his wife when he was intoxicated—or maybe he told her he had murdered Jessamyn, hoping she would provide him with an alibi. But instead, his wife may have refused to become involved in the crime, and threatened to go to the police."

"So he strangled her, too. Yes, I suppose it's possible," she said slowly. "But what about his third victim—this actress, Violet Yates? What possible connection could she have had with the other two? And why were all three wearing wedding gowns? Why had they been strangled with their bridal wreaths? If Marek isn't mad, why did he choose such a bizarre method of destroying his victims?"

"How on earth would you expect me to know?"

"You obviously have given the case considerable thought," Maude said. "So I thought maybe you had already worked out an explanation for the murder of the unfortunate Miss Yates, too."

Amanda took a long breath, then pressed her lips together. She might have told her friend that Barney Marek and the Yates woman had been acquainted; that he had seen the actress often enough, in Ryan's saloon. But how could she possibly have explained where she had come by that piece of information, without telling her the rest? She would have had to reveal that she had been assisting Ross Buchanan, a private detective, since the beginning of the investigation. "I suppose the police will discover the connection between him and Miss Yates—if there is one—when they track him down."

"So you are willing to leave the solution to the authorities." Maude's smile held a touch of irony. "I was beginning to wonder if you had already become bored with your society reporting, and had decided to take up detection on the side."

"Really, Maude! What a ridiculous notion!" But she flushed slightly under her friend's searching look. "I'm perfectly satisfied with my present position."

"You relieve my mind." She glanced at the half-empty sheet on the desk. "I'd best be on my way, and leave you to finish whatever it is you've been working on."

She felt distinctly relieved when Maude departed. Although there was no possible way her friend could have guessed at her involvement in Ross's case, it had been difficult for her to conceal her preoccupation—even for a little while. But after Maude had returned to her own office, Amanda could not force her thoughts back to her current project, a description of Mrs. William Astor's masquerade ball.

It took all her resources to shut the thought of Ross from her mind. She drew a deep, steadying breath, then reached for her pen. She wrote slowly at first, pausing after every phrase. *Ross is strong!—he's a survivor—you have a job to do.*

Her pen moved more quickly now, as she described the guests' costumes: they had been decked out as eighteenth century French courtiers; the ladies in enormous hoop skirts, daringly low-cut bodices, with a dazzling display of their finest jewels; the gentlemen had worn satin knee breeches, long jackets with embroidered cuffs and powdered wigs. Lanoutte, the famous costumer, had created more than one hundred and fifty of the gowns. They had cost more than thirty thousand dollars, and one hundred and forty dressmakers had worked night and day for five weeks in order to complete them in time for the ball. Since such extravagance was far beyond Amanda's limited means,

Maude had provided her with the name of a theatrical costume shop, where she had rented her finery for the evening: a topaz velvet gown, complete with hoops, powdered wig, and plumes.

Howard Thornton had escorted Phoebe Armstead, and had danced with her three times: a positive indication that it would not be long before her parents would make a formal announcement of their daughter's wedding.

Amanda was careful to include the smallest details, for the vicarious enjoyment of her readers: the supper table, with its gold candelabra and a crystal and gold epergne, filled with hot-house flowers: *gloire de Paris* roses and camellias. The guests had dined on terrapin, woodcock, truffled capon, and *bombe de glace*. She was sure her article would meet with Mrs. Fairlie's approval; it would provide vicarious satisfaction to her readers—those who would never have an opportunity to attend such a ball. And in no way would it offend their delicate sensibilities.

But she could feel no such satisfaction, for it was all so remote from the daily life of the denizens in the underside of the city, the side she never would have known about, had it not been for Ross. Her thoughts shifted to the precarious existence of all those abandoned children who lived in the slums, who slept in doorways or abandoned warehouses. She shuddered inwardly, as she remembered what Ross had told her of the orphanage where he had been placed after his mother's death. And Ross had been only one of so many. One of the lucky ones, so he had said.

She remembered the thin, bare-footed children she had seen on her one brief foray down to the Bowery. And the slatternly women, old before their time, defeated by poverty. The rat-infested hallways with their foul-smelling privies. Even now, in the warmth and safety of her office, she felt a chill. She could not blot out the memory of her visit to the Mareks' flat. Of Barney's flushed face close to hers, his brutal grip on her shoulder, the drunken rage in his eyes.

She could well believe a man like that would have turned on Violet Yates in a fit of jealousy, and strangled her. But if he had been in hiding from the police all this time, why would he have risked arrest by leaving his hiding place—wherever it might have been—to take his revenge on a third victim? Or had Violet known where he was hiding, and had she been reckless enough to go to meet him there?

It was not until evening that Ross heard Amanda's quick, light footsteps in the hall, her knock at the door. He opened it, helped her off with her cloak, then led the way into the parlor. He saw the concern in her amber eyes, as she examined his face carefully by the light of the gas jet over the sofa.

Saul Goldman had come by to remove the bandage from his head, and the other from his ribs. "That arm's still stiff, though I suppose there's no use warning you to stay inside and get another week's rest."

"Not while Spencer's paying me to find Marek."

Now he realized that Amanda was looking at the scar on his forehead, with a troubled expression. Then, as if fearing she had embarrassed him with her scrutiny, she dropped her gaze. "I'm sorry I could not come back sooner," she said. "With the holiday season in full swing, I've had more than the usual number of assignments. A musicale, a cotillion, and yet another charity bazaar."

"You go to many of those?" he asked.

"Indeed, I do." She seated herself on the sofa, as if she felt quite at home here. "All those ladies, with nothing better to occupy their time," she went on. "When they are not paying calls on one another, or shopping for clothes, they busy themselves for hours making beadwork tea cozies and bell-pulls, embroidered pen-wipers, and hand-painted pin-boxes to sell to one another."

"Surely you're not expected to contribute such handiwork."

"No, but I do feel obliged to make an occasional purchase. I bought a wickerwork basket for Leander, with a hand-embroidered cushion."

"I'm sure he appreciated it."

She laughed softly. "The ungrateful creature still prefers the sofa, or the foot of my bed. At any rate, my article on Mrs. Astor's masquerade ball has already gone to press, and I have no further assignments for this week's *Gazette*. So if I can be of any help to you—shopping for food, perhaps? Or preparing dinner?"

He considered telling her that he had already gone out more than once; that he had eaten most of his meals in a nearby restaurant, and that there was no further need for her visits. But he realized that he was pleased to see her here; that he even enjoyed hearing her chatter about her assignments. The sound of her soft, low-pitched voice, accompanied by small, feminine gestures, pleased him. Perhaps they were starting to please him more than he would have wished.

"I don't want to keep you from your work," he said. "I suppose it should ease off after the holidays."

"I can handle my assignments well enough," she assured him. "But as for my co-workers, that's not always so easy." She went on to tell him about her conversation with Maude. "She was concerned about me. I'm not sure she believed the excuse I'd given my concierge for staying away two nights in a row."

"Does that worry you?" And before she could reply, he went on: "Why did you have to give Mrs. Morton any excuse at all?" he demanded. "Or Miss Hamilton, either?" His mouth curved in a mocking, half-smile. "You're an independent young lady, with a promising career. You're free to come and go as you please, without accounting to anyone."

"No lady is all that independent—not unless she wants to become the object of salacious gossip."

"As long as you pay your rent on time, you needn't worry about what your neighbors think. Or your concierge."

"That's where you are mistaken. Only ladies of impeccable reputation are permitted to rent flats in my building. Even the fact that I live alone, instead of sharing with another young lady, has caused a few raised eyebrows."

"And what about Maude Hamilton? If she knew where you'd really spent the weekend, would she run and tell Mrs. Fairlie?"

"Certainly not! Maude's my friend. She explained that she was concerned for my safety. She was worried about my going about the city alone at all hours. Don't you realize how many ladies are fearful about going out alone?"

Not only ladies walked in fear, especially as the days grew shorter, and the winter twilight came on so swiftly. How could he have forgotten his encounter with Kathleen, the young prostitute from the Bowery; the terror in her eyes when he had accosted her in the tenement hall, to question her about Marek's whereabouts?

"Miss Hamilton surely didn't think you were in any danger from Marek. He may be a maniac, but he doesn't strike at random."

"That's what I told her. I reminded her that he once had

worked for the Spencers. And that the second victim was his wife. But when Maude said there had been no connection between him and Violet Yates, I couldn't tell her she was mistaken. Not without also telling her that I have been working with you all this time." Her brows drew together in a troubled frown. "As a matter of fact, I find it difficult to believe there ever was more than a casual acquaintance between Violet and Marek."

"But we can't be sure, can we? For all we know, Violet might have been attracted to him, at least for awhile. They could have been seeing each other, meeting somewhere in secret, even after he was fired from his job at Ryan's."

"Are you saying that they were lovers?"

"You don't think that's possible?"

"Hardly! Miss Yates was an actress, so she must have been pretty enough to take her choice of far more acceptable men. She said she had been seeing a wealthy gentleman, didn't she?"

"But the other girls in the show weren't convinced of it. Cora wasn't. The Savoy isn't at all like Wallack's or Booth's. If a girl looks good in tights, if she can sing and dance a bit, that's all she needs to work in a second-rate variety house."

"I can't imagine any woman feeling anything except disgust for a man as crude and violent as Barney Marek."

He could have told her that there were many ladies from the highest social circles, who were aroused by just such primitive qualities. But he doubted that she would believe him.

Instead, he asked: "Why not? Gertrude married him, didn't she? And handed him the money the Spencers gave her so he could set himself up in a business of his own."

"A shooting gallery, with a ring for dog-fights in the

basement." Her face tightened with revulsion. "Dog-fighting is not a sport at all—it is an abomination! If there isn't a law against it, there should be!"

"What did you say?" His hand shot out and he gripped her arm.

Her amber eyes widened. Obviously, she had not anticipated his response. "I said that dog-fighting's an abomination. And I can see you feel strongly about it, as I do."

But he scarcely heard the rest or her indignant diatribe. "That was it! That's what Marek was telling Sally Flavin! His wife was going to get her hands on enough cash so that they could get out of the city and live in style. He'd told Gertrude to meet him at the ring," he said. "Not the pawn-shop where he had fenced Jessamyn's jewelry. The dog-fight ring under his shooting gallery."

She winced, and he eased his grip on her arm. "But he lost his money—and the shooting gallery—years ago," she reminded him. "He had been working as a bouncer in cheap saloons, you told me so yourself. And when his drinking got out of control, he hadn't even been able to keep his job in any of those places."

He brushed aside her protests. "That day you met Nellie in the park, did she tell you where the shooting gallery was?"

After a moment's silence, she shook her head. "I'm sure she didn't. I never thought to ask her."

"Never mind. Did she, or any of the other servants, go to visit Gertrude, after she'd left the Spencers and married Barney?"

"I don't think so. But she did say that Gertrude had come back to the Spencer mansion just once to visit down-stairs, in the servants' hall. Nellie said she acted smug and self-satisfied, because she was no longer in service. And she told them Barney owned his own business now. The shooting gallery, and the dog fight ring down in the basement. I said I hoped she hadn't spoken to Jessamyn about that part of it, because Jessamyn was sensitive, and fond of animals. Nellie said that Gertrude hadn't gone upstairs to speak to Jessamyn at all."

"But what about the shooting gallery? Didn't she tell the servants where it was?"

"Why should that matter now, for goodness sake? Even if Barney did go to the shooting gallery to wait for Gertrude, if she came to meet him there, and he killed her—you surely don't think he'd still be hiding there after all this time."

"Maybe not. But somebody may have seen him there, spoken to him. If he was drunk, he might have bragged to one of his cronies, and said where he was heading next. Are you sure Nellie didn't say anything at all about where the place was?"

"I've already told you so—" He heard the sharp intake of her breath. "I do remember Nellie said it was down on the waterfront."

The waterfront! He felt his muscles tighten with frustration. "Did she say it was on the Hudson? Or the East River? Somewhere around South Street? Corlear's Hook? Mulberry Bend?"

"It was somewhere on the waterfront—that's all I know. And there's no need to shout at me."

"Sorry, Amanda. You've given me a starting point, at least." He stood up, took her hands in his, and drew her to her feet. "I'll take you downstairs and find you a hansom."

"And what then? You're going out to look for Barney, aren't you? But you can't! I won't let you! You must wait until you're stronger. Ross, please!"

Her caring look moved him more deeply than he could have imagined. He took a step toward her, and held her arms carefully. When she did not resist, he drew her against him. He bent his head, felt the softness of her chestnut hair against his face, and inhaled its delicate scent. His lips brushed her cheek.

When he released her, she stepped back and stood looking up at him, her eyes wide with an unspoken plea. He turned away, then went to get her cloak. Carefully, he put it around her, and let his hands rest for a moment on her shoulders.

"Is there nothing I can say to stop you?"

He did not answer. He took his heavy coat from the closet, reached up on the shelf. This time he would go armed, not only with a club, but with a revolver, too.

A bone-chilling wind blew across Chatham Square. The stoop of the tenement where the Mareks had lived was empty now; the slatterns who had sat gossiping and drinking beer only a month before had retreated to their flats, seeking a measure of warmth. The windows rattled in their rotting wooden frames; the cracked panes were stuffed with rags.

Yesterday's slush had frozen into a greyish crust of ice enclosing heaps of congealed garbage. Even dressed as he was, in his heavy coat and wide-brimmed hat, he felt a dull ache in his bruised ribs, a lingering stiffness in his arm. He could only hope his visit to the Bowery on such a frigid night would prove more profitable than the others. He would start on the first floor and work his way up, questioning any of the neighbors who might have known the Mareks. Had Barney still owned the shooting gallery when he and Gertrude had come to live here? Or if not, maybe he had boasted of his former prosperity to anyone who would listen.

When he pushed open the front door, the heavy stench of the tenement enveloped him. He paused for a moment, then started up the stairs, going from one door to the next. Some of the tenants recognized him from his previous visits, when he had passed himself off as a reporter for the *Graphic*.

Ross went on to a one-room flat, where he spoke briefly with Kathleen's mother, a thin, haggard woman who bore a marked resemblance to the frightened young prostitute he had questioned shortly after the second murder. Four children lay huddled together on a mattress in one corner of the room; they watched and listened in wide-eyed silence. "Kathleen won't be home for hours yet," the woman said. "She shouldn't be out at all, not on a freezin' night like this, but there's the rent to be paid, and the kids got to be fed. She's a good girl, my Kathleen is."

Was it possible she did not know how Kathleen earned her money? Or had she guessed, and did she ease her conscience by pretending to herself that the girl sold flowers, hot chestnuts, or boot laces in the streets?

He felt a brief stab of pity, but he tried to ignore it. He asked her if she knew the location of Marek's shooting gallery. "Not me. A mean one, he was. I never had nothing to do with him. Or his wife, either."

He went down the hall and knocked on another door. Conners, a stout, red-faced man with small, pale eyes, looked him over in the dim light from the hall gas jet. "You're that reporter fella—Buchanan. I already told you all I knew about Marek. How come you're pokin' around here again? If you want to find out about that Yates woman—I never seen her an' I don't know nothin' 'cept

301

what's been in the papers."

"That's too bad. I thought you might've seen her with Marek, in one of the neighborhood saloons, maybe."

"You thought wrong."

"So it looks like I came down here for nothing."

"Too bad, mister." The man shrugged and started to close the door.

"Wait a minute," Ross said. "My editor's willing to pay for any kind of information about Marek, as long as we can use it in the *Graphic*." He looked past the man's shoulder, fixing his gaze on the pot-bellied stove in the corner.

"Freezin' outside, ain't it?" Conners said. "You might as well come in and warm up a bit. Maybe I can remember somethin' you might be able t' use in your paper."

Ross followed him inside and took a seat close to the stove. "Marek used to be in business for himself, so I've heard. Did he ever talk about that?"

"He sure did. Once he got started, you couldn't shut him up. He used to brag about his shooting gallery. I guess he figgered it made him somethin' special, havin' his own place an' all. But then he went broke an' after that, he lived off his missus. A no-good bastard, that's all he was. He took his wife's pay, and knocked the bejesus out of her—an' then he went an' killed 'er. And now he's done in another one. He's a loony for sure."

"I don't doubt it," Ross agreed. "But let's get back to this shooting gallery of his. Where was it, do you happen to remember?"

"Somewhere down on the waterfront, that's all I know." Conners shrugged. "Don't see as it makes much difference now." His eyes narrowed slightly. "Say, I thought you came here askin' about the Yates woman."

"I did. But you just said you don't know anything about

her. So I figured, as long as I was here, I might try to dig up something about the shooting gallery. I should be able to get a column out of that, maybe. How Marek'd been his own boss, a big shot. How he lost his business and it drove him to drink."

"He was never no big shot. An' losin' the business ain't what drove him to drink, and drove him out of his head—if that's what you're gettin' at. He was always on the booze."

Restraining his impatience, Ross steered the conversation back. "So he told you the shooting gallery was on the waterfront. That's all?"

"Oughta be worth somethin'," Conners said.

Ross shrugged. "I don't see how. The city waterfront covers a lot of territory. Guess I'd better be on my way." He was about to rise, when the door swung open, and a boy came sidling in. His skinny wrists protruded from the sleeves of his torn jacket, he wore no gloves, and his hands were red with cold; his woolen hat was pulled down to his eyebrows.

"What the hell're you doin' back so early?" Conners demanded.

The boy didn't answer. He looked up at Ross with a grin. "Hey, Mister Buchanan—don't ye remember me?"

"Sure I do, Pete. I've just been having a talk with your father."

"I know—I heard you. Pa don't know nothing about Marek's place. But I do. I can take you down there."

"Shut your face, an' hand over the money. Unless you've gone and spent it." He drew back his arm.

But Pete ducked with a swiftness born of practice, and moved behind Ross. "I'm tellin' the truth, Mr. Buchanan! I know about Marek's place 'cause I was there once."

Ross wasn't sure whether to believe him, but since he

had gotten nowhere with the rest of the tenants, he would take a chance. "Come along," he said. "You can tell me all about it, on the way."

"Hold it." Conners lumbered to his feet. "I don't let my kid go roaming around the streets with strangers at night."

The boy stared at his father, no doubt taken aback by this unfamiliar show of parental concern.

"Pete and I are friends," Ross said, putting a hand on the boy's bony shoulder. "Come on, kid. Let's step outside and you can tell me all about it."

Conners took a step forward, as if to intervene, but Ross's size, his hard stare made the other man think better of it.

He led Pete out of the flat and down the stairs. "What were you doing at the shooting gallery?"

"It was like this. A dog got himself torn to pieces in a fight, the night before, an' some fella stole another an' brought it over here in a wooden crate. He said Marek'd want it right away, and he gave me a quarter to carry it down to Water Street." He looked up hopefully. "I can show you where I took it, Mister Buchanan." No doubt he was remembering the substantial meal Ross had bought him at Havemeyer's. The kid still looked half-starved.

"You don't have to come with me," he said. "Just tell how to find the place."

"I don't mind comin' along. I can't go back in there yet, anyhow. My ol' man'll skin me alive 'cause I can't come across with any money. He says I'm old enough to earn my keep."

"Still rolling drunks for a living?"

Pete shrugged. "There ain't many drunks walkin' around outside on a night like this. Mostly, they do their drinkin' in the saloons or the velvet rooms. I figured maybe if I was to show you where the shooting gallery was, you'd make it worth my while."

"All right, let's go." He would find the shooting gallery on Water Street faster with Pete along as a guide.

The East River was crowded with steamers, barges, and clippers riding at anchor. There were fewer sailing ships than there used to be, but they made a fine sight, with their rigging, masts, and spars glittering in the moonlight; their sharp icicle-hung bow-sprits thrusting out over the length of South Street. A few wind-driven clouds scudded overhead.

Pete trotted along quickly, panting as he tried to match his pace with Ross's. From the saloons and cheap brothels that lined the street, they heard the noise of pianos and fiddles, and the shrill, drunken laughter of the harpies who preyed on the sailors. Here and there, a red glow marked a fire, where tramps or street kids gathered to keep from freezing.

"It oughta be right here—" Pete began. "Jeez! Will you look at that!"

Ross stopped short, and stood staring at the charred shell of a one-story wooden building. The roof had caved in and side walls swayed and rattled in the wind. The front door had been torn from its hinges, and carted off. "Are you sure this is the place?"

"This is it, all right," Pete said. "But I was only here that one time." He shrank back and eyed Ross warily, as if expecting instant retaliation for his blunder. "I didn't know it'd burned down, Mister Buchanan. Honest, I didn't."

"I believe you." Ross stepped over the sagging threshold and peered into the darkness. He caught the rancid smell of rat droppings, and heard the scurrying sound of clawed feet.

"Ye ain't goin' in there, are ye?"

"Not right now." He turned and started down the street, then paused in front of a shabby restaurant. He pushed open the door. The place was lit by oil lamps, and most of the scarred wooden tables were occupied by sailors, long-shoremen, and watchmen from the nearby warehouses, who wolfed down bowls of stew. A few ragged whores, long past their prime, drifted around, looking for customers.

He sat down at the counter on one side of the low-ceilinged room, and turned to Pete. "I suppose your appe-tite's as good as usual."

"You bet." Pete grinned and climbed onto the seat be-side him.

The counterman took the order for oyster stew, fried po-tatoes, two thick slabs of bread and butter, and steaming mugs of coffee. As soon as the bowls had been set down, Pete ignored his surroundings and began stuffing himself. The food was hot and surprisingly tasty, but Ross took only a few bites, then motioned to the counterman.

"I hear there's a place somewhere nearby where they're having a dog-fight tonight."

The man shook his head. "Not that I know of, mister."

"That burned-out shack down on the corner—they used to have a dog-fight ring downstairs, didn't they?"

"I wouldn't know. If it's a dog fight yer lookin' for to-night, ye'll have to go over to Whitehall Street. Delaney's place."

He gestured at Pete. "The kid here told me he brought a dog down to that place on the corner. He says there used to be a shooting gallery on the ground floor, and the fight ring down below."

"That must've been before I came t' work here."

"When was that?"

"Last winter. After I near broke my back, unloadin' the ships. Back then, Gallus Mag was runnin' a saloon in there. Ever hear of her?"

"Who hasn't?" Gallus Mag was a huge woman, over six feet, who had gotten her name because she kept her skirt up with a man's suspenders. "Last I heard, she was working as a bouncer in a waterfront dive," Ross went on. "They say she was more than a match for any sailor that was fool enough to start any trouble."

"And that's the truth! I wouldn't want t' tangle with a female like her. Strong as a dray horse, she was. Went around with a pistol stuck in her belt and a bludgeon strapped to her wrist. But she had bigger plans. She got herself a place of her own, Mag did. She had a good business goin' down there on the corner. For awhile."

"Guess she ran into some bad luck?"

"You might call it that. Only some said it weren't no accident. All I know is, late one night last fall, it burned t' the ground."

"So how do you think the fire started?"

"Well, now, it was like this. Kate Flannery had been runnin' her own place, around the corner, see? And Kate was a hard case, too. She wouldn't take too much competition from Mag. Them two harpies was in the same line of work, if ye know what I mean."

Ross nodded, paid the bill, along with a substantial tip. Pete was gulping down the last morsels of stew. "As soon as you're done, you'd better go on home."

"I'm done now, I guess." He slid off the stool and followed Ross outside.

Ross strode along in silence, his hands jammed into the pockets of his coat, his head bent against the wind. He was heading back toward the sagging ruin on the corner.

"Are you goin' into that dive by yourself?" Pete asked.

Ross did not answer. The counterman had told him there had been competition between Kate Flannery and Gallus Mag. Kate must have been raking in a handsome profit from her sideline: doping sailors' drinks, dropping them through a trapdoor behind the bar, where her hired thugs kept them tied up until they could be dragged through an underground tunnel and turned over to any captain whose unsavory reputation had left him short of men for a full crew. And Mag had practiced the same trade.

He quickened his stride, heading for the ruins of Mag's saloon.

"Wait fer me!" Pete was still following him. "If you're goin' in there, so am I."

"The hell you are!" He reached into his pocket, and gave Pete a handful of coins. "Here, take it. That ought to satisfy your father."

Pete pocketed the money, but remained where he was, his feet planted apart. "Ye goin' to look for Marek. Are you lookin' t' get your neck broke? If you think Marek's hidin' there, why don't you go tell the cops?"

Ross glared down at him. "Go home, Pete. Now." He gave the boy a light shove. "Get moving."

"Why would ye risk yer neck t' get a story fer the *Graphic*?" He stared up at Ross, searching his face. "You ain't no reporter, are you?"

"Mind your own business."

But the boy wasn't put off by his surly answer. "An' ye ain't no cop, neither. So why've ye been out lookin' fer Marek all this time?"

"Because I'm being well paid to find him." Before he could speak again, Ross said: "No more questions. You kept your part of the bargain. You brought me here. And I paid you. So now we're even."

"That's right, we're even." But the boy gave him a re-proachful look, before he turned away and started down Water Street. The loose sole of one of his torn shoes made a flapping sound on the ice-covered cobblestones.

The ground floor of the wrecked building was littered with the charred remains of what once had been Gallus Mag's saloon. And before that, Marek's shooting gallery. Most of the furnishings, however badly damaged, had been hauled away long ago; some of it had been sold to junk-yards, the rest used for kindling.

Ross took a bull's-eye lantern from inside his coat, and looked around. To his right, he saw the remains of the bar. Shards of glass from a smashed mirror sparkled in the lan-tern's beam. Moving cautiously, he tested the floor as he went, to avoid putting his weight on a loose board. A single misstep would send him toppling into the cellar. During his years on the force, he had taken part in raids on enough of these waterfront saloons. It did not take him long to find the open square in the floor, behind the bar. Someone had ripped off the trap door leading to the cellar.

There would be a panel, leading from the cellar into the tunnel where Mag had stowed her drugged and tightly-bound customers, until she could find a buyer for them. Then her thugs would have dragged them to the far end of the tunnel and hoisted them up onto the pier, where small boats were waiting to carry them to their ship.

Broken steps led to the cellar. He climbed down, then stopped to look at the remains of the ring, where the dogs had torn each other to pieces. He had watched such 'sporting events' when he'd been a kid. The first time, he'd been sickened by the yelping of a dying terrier, and the blood that had gushed from the beast's torn throat. But he'd managed to hide his feelings. The slightest sign of pity or revulsion would have lowered his standing with the other kids in the gang.

Gradually, he had come to accept such spectacles, as he had taught himself to accept most of the senseless cruelty that was part of his daily existence. He had seen a single terrier tossed into the ring with a hundred or more rats. The dog had held his own for over an hour, before the rats had mutilated him so badly that his owner had finished him off. Another time, he'd watched with his friends as a half-witted man had bitten the head off a live rat for a quarter.

Earlier tonight, he'd seen Amanda's indignant look, and heard the outrage in her voice when she had called dog-fighting 'an abomination.' If she had not been fortunate enough to have grown up on Stuyvesant Square, the cherished daughter of prosperous, respectable parents, she would have come face to face with plenty of such 'abominations,' at an early age. She might have been working in a sweatshop before she was ten. Or selling flowers on the street. She might have had to sell herself to survive, in a parlor house, or in an alley.

The cold of the deserted cellar began to penetrate his heavy coat, and he moved on.

He had to examine more than a dozen panels in the wall before he found the entrance to the tunnel. He couldn't pull it aside; it had become jammed into place. He put his shoulder to the panel and threw his weight against it. Once, then again. The ache in his arm reminded him that he had not completely recovered from last week's beating. But tonight, he had armed himself with a revolver.

He threw his weight against the panel again and it gave way with a creaking noise, shockingly loud in the silence.

He closed his lantern and stood still, listening. Only the scuttering feet of the rats.

He started moving again, keeping to one side of the tunnel. Then he heard a lapping sound and smelled the damp salt tide of the East River. He had reached the end of the tunnel.

And he stood alone. Another false lead.

But the river smell was stronger now, and he felt a frigid wind against his face. When he raised the lantern's shutter, he saw an overhead door that had been propped up a few inches, with a brick wedged in to hold it open. He lowered the lantern. In its beam he saw the torn, filthy mattress and the litter of decaying food, candle stubs, empty bottles, and crumpled newspapers.

He thrust his gun into his belt, and kept his eyes fixed on the overhead door. He heard the steps behind him, and caught the stench of sweat and whiskey.

He turned around swiftly and lunged at the stocky, broad-chested man who advanced on him.

"Marek."

"Who're you?"

His fist caught Marek on the jaw. The man shook his head, grunted, and came at Ross. He struck again, hitting him in the belly, all his weight behind the blow. Marek staggered, but did not go down. He grabbed Ross around the chest and held him in a crushing grip. Pain shot through Ross's ribs. He fought for air, and black dots danced before his eyes. He tore one hand free, and slammed it into Marek's throat. The man's grip loosened slightly. Ross brought down his head and butted it into Marek's face.

He spun the man around, bent one of his arms behind him and brought it up hard. Marek gave a yell of agony. Ross ran him against the stone wall, head first. Marek groaned and slid to the floor. Ross kicked him in the side of the head. Marek lay on his side, looking up at the revolver Ross was pointing at him.

"I work for Spencer. You killed his daughter. You killed her there in her house, didn't you? You killed your wife, too. And the Yates woman."

"I didn't kill nobody. It's all lies!"

Ross planted a well-aimed kick in Marek's ribs. "So suppose you tell me how it really was," he said. "Start with Jessamyn Spencer."

"I never did nothin' t' her."

"Try again."

"All right, so she gave my wife a couple of pieces of jewelry. None of the good stuff. A locket and a ring. That's all."

"Blackmail's a crime."

"So what? The Spencers weren't no better than us. The girl was no better than any cribhouse slut. Acted prim and ladylike, but Gertrude told me all about little Miss Jessamyn an' the ridin' master, that O'Shea fella."

"And you figured that, with the girl about to get married, she'd pay you off to keep her secret from her future husband. So you got inside the house late that night, when the rest of the family were out, and the servants had gone to bed. You tried to blackmail her, but she got hysterical, she screamed. Or tried to. And you strangled her."

"That ain't true! I never went near the girl! I sent Gertrude."

"I'm supposed to believe your wife strangled Jessamyn Spencer and carried her out of the house? That she put on the coachman's livery, hitched up the team, and drove down to the Ladies Mile with the body inside the brougham?"

"I never said that. My wife got together with the Spencer girl in one of them big department stores. But she didn't bring no money. Only the jewelry."

"And you wanted more. So you went to visit her, late at night."

"It ain't true—it didn't happen like that—"

Ross ignored the interruption. "The girl was dead, and you were still broke. So you beat the hell out of your wife, until she said she'd go get money from Ottilie Spencer. Or maybe the girl's brother. But at the last minute, she was afraid to go through with it. She showed up here, empty-handed, and you killed her, too."

"I didn't kill her. I didn't kill any of 'em," Marek insisted. "An' I ain't no loony, like the papers say."

"You've been down here all this time. Except when you went out through that trap door up there. You stole food or found it in the garbage cans, and came back here. Or did the Yates girl come here to visit you, so you wouldn't get lonesome?"

"I never knew Violet Yates!"

"She and her friends used to come in to Ryan's from the Savoy."

"Okay, so I used t' see her, along with the others. But it wasn't like you're makin' it out to be."

"Stand up and start climbing that ladder." Marek got to his feet, but he didn't move. His eyes went to the gun. "If I put a bullet in you, here and now, Superintendent Walling will probably give me a medal. But if you do as you're told, maybe you'll get to meet him yourself. Then you can tell him how it really was."

Marek turned and started up the ladder. He reached the top and pushed the trap door open. Ross started up after him. Marek climbed out, kicked away the brick. The door struck Ross's injured arm as it slammed shut. Pain spiraled through the arm into his shoulder.

He swore, and shoved the gun into his belt. He pushed upward with all his strength but the door did not budge. He thrust at the door again, using both hands, while the ladder swayed under him. It wouldn't take more than a minute before Marek disappeared into the maze of alleys that crisscrossed the waterfront.

"Mr. Buchanan—you down there?"

"Pete!"

"Right here!" He heard the boy grunt with the strain of his effort. The door started to creak open. Ross pushed it from his side. A blast of icy wind struck him, but he scarcely felt it.

The boy was panting so that he could not speak, but he pointed in the direction of the pier. Ross saw the dark figure running down the pier, toward the jutting bowsprit of a schooner. "Marek!"

Marek did not turn his head. He grabbed for an ice-sheathed rope, started to climb, slid back, then tried again. Ross fired into the air; the shot echoed through the darkness.

He ran forward, closing the space between him and Marek. Sailors came clambering over the sides of the nearest ships, while others came running out of the nearby saloons. "Hold it, Marek!" he called out again. But over his warning cry, came a rising chorus of angry voices: "It's him! The maniac! There he is. Let's go get him."

A huge longshoreman, brandishing a baling hook, led the mob. Armed as he was, Ross could not hold off so many men. He positioned himself between Marek and the mob. "Come on. Move!"

The mob was growing, their angry shouts echoing down

the length of South Street. Marek raised his hands. Ross positioned himself between the mob and their quarry. "Pete! Go get the cops! Run!"

But even as he spoke, he heard the clop of a horse's hooves, the clatter of wheels on the icy cobbles. A paddy wagon turned onto the street, pulled to a halt. "I already been t' the station house," Pete said, with a grin. "Don't know what took 'em so long."

CHAPTER NINETEEN

On the day before Christmas, the freezing cold had abated, but the grey, low-lying clouds promised another snowfall, and, by the time Amanda got out of the hansom, the first few flakes were drifting down.

When she had spoken with Ross on her office telephone earlier that morning, he had assured her he had not been injured; she had not entirely believed him. And although she, along with countless others, had read the lurid newspaper accounts of Marek's capture, she wanted to hear all he had to tell her about it.

She hurried up the steps to his office, and as soon as he opened the door, she searched his face. She saw no fresh cuts or bruises. As for the scar on his forehead, it was healing, but she doubted it would ever disappear completely. He stood aside and motioned her to come in.

"Mrs. Fairlie closed the *Gazette* office at noon," she said, brushing the snowflakes from the velvet collar of her russet coat. "I would have arrived here sooner but the streets are crowded with shoppers."

He helped her off with the coat, then led her to the leather sofa. When they were seated, she turned to him and said: "It was thoughtful of you to send that boy to tell me that you'd found Marek and turned him over to the police. And that you were safe."

"The boy's Pete Conners. He comes from a flat in the tenement where the Mareks used to live. He knew where the shooting gallery was. He took me down there."

"And that's where Marek had been hiding all this time?"

"The gallery was closed a few years back, and the building, itself, burned down months ago. Marek been living in a tunnel underneath." Quickly he told her the rest.

"I read about the arrest in the newspapers." She gave him a small, rueful smile. "The police took most of the credit."

"They deserved their share," he told her. "And so did Pete."

"But it was you who went down into the tunnel alone. You found Marek, and you held off the mob, until the police got there."

"I'm not sure how much longer I could have kept them from tearing him to pieces. One minute the pier was empty. The next, it was swarming with sailors and longshoremen, armed with clubs and knives and baling hooks. At least, he's safely locked away in the Tombs now. He'll stay there until he stands trial."

"And what do you think will happen to him then?"

He shrugged. "We don't have public hangings, not any more. It'll be over soon enough."

She stiffened at his matter-of-fact dismissal. "You sound as if you are sure he'll be convicted."

"Certainly, I am."

She put a hand on his arm. "You're so sure he is guilty?"

"I found him and I handed him over to the police. They'll take over from here."

"Surely you are not yet able to put the whole case from your mind?"

"Not before I go to the Spencer mansion to pick up my check." How could he speak in such a detached way? "Everard phoned me this morning," he went on. "It seems he has a group of business associates, Pennsylvania steel mill owners, who may have a really big job for me."

She heard the open satisfaction in his voice, but she could not bring herself to congratulate him on his new, and probably lucrative, assignment. "Then perhaps I'd best be going. I don't wish to delay your meeting with Mr. Spencer."

"It shouldn't take too long." He gave her a warm smile. "Why don't you go home and put on your most fashionable outfit. Then, after I've finished with Spencer, we'll go out and celebrate. We'll have dinner at the Brunswick Hotel. And after that, an evening at the theater, if you like."

She was taken aback, but she spoke evenly. "You think a celebration is in order. And you want me to share it with you."

"Of course I do. I'll admit when you walked in here and offered to help me with the case, I wanted to toss you out. But you did help, every step of the way. You did more than I could have expected. I guess I should have told you that before. You're a remarkable lady, Amanda Whitney."

When she did not reply, he searched her face. "Something's worrying you. Do you want to tell me what it is?"

"I'm not sure you would understand."

"Maybe I do. Marek will be convicted. He'll go to the gallows. It's an ugly business, isn't it? But there's no need for you to make yourself miserable, brooding over it. So put it out of your mind."

"I'm afraid I can't do that, not yet. If there is even the slightest chance he isn't the one who killed those women—"

"Let it go, Amanda."

Although she heard the rising anger in his voice, she could not remain silent. "And what about you? Can you let it go so easily? I don't believe you are sure he's guilty, either."

"Believe what you like. I won't lose any sleep over the outcome of Marek's trial. He's a worthless bastard." She half-expected Ross to apologize, but he went on. "He would have shoved you down that flight of stairs and maybe broken your neck, if you hadn't gotten away. He used to beat the hell out of his wife, whenever he came home drunk. He forced her to blackmail Jessamyn for him."

"That makes no difference. He is not going to be tried for any of that. He will be charged with three murders. He will be found guilty. And he will hang."

"That's up to a judge and jury. Not to us."

"But what if he is innocent? No one has found any positive proof that he was inside the Spencer mansion, the night Jessamyn was killed."

"Leave that to the police. After a few hours of questioning, he'll tell them how he got inside the house. And strangled the life out of Jessamyn."

She flinched at the deliberate brutality of his words, but she went on: "It must have been late, because Clifford and his mother had already gone to the theater. Everard had left to spend the night with his mistress. The servants were asleep. But what about Jessamyn? Did she go to bed for the night, still wearing her wedding gown?"

"Maybe she did, if she was completely exhausted. Or maybe she undressed herself."

"That is not likely. The gown buttoned up the back. And there were her corset laces—and Miss Tuttle didn't help her to disrobe—she told me so."

"You don't have a lady's maid. How do you manage to undress yourself?"

She ignored the interruption. "So you think Marek came in and found her wearing her wedding gown. He woke her, he had to find the veil, the bridal wreath. She didn't run out

319

the bedroom door—didn't even scream for help?"

"Maybe she was too frightened to move or even scream. It wouldn't have been the first time she panicked. Remember how she acted when she saw Gertrude that day at Talley's."

"She was terrified, yes—but she didn't freeze. She got to her feet and ran so fast I scarcely could keep up with her."

"Panic takes different forms. Seeing Gertrude in Talley's, she ran. Maybe, facing Marek alone in her bedroom, she couldn't make a sound."

"Then why did he have to kill her?" Amanda asked. "Why not just take her jewelry and get out of there? Why did he put her whole bridal outfit back on her, and carry her out to the stables? And drive her downtown to the Ladies Mile—"

"I don't have all the answers. Neither do you."

"Not yet. But consider what we do know. Gertrude's wedding gown had not been made for her. And what about Violet Yates? Marek told you he only knew her by sight. What possible reason would he have for killing her, too?"

"Because he's a damn lunatic. That's what the papers have been saying all this time. That's what everyone believes. A lunatic doesn't need a reason to kill. Not a reason we'd understand, anyway."

"Do you believe he is insane?"

"I don't know and I don't care." She saw his heavy shoulder muscles tighten; saw his lips clamp together hard. Then he was on his feet.

"What do you care about?" she demanded. "Collecting your fee from Mr. Spencer and getting on with your next case, in the Pennsylvania steel mills?"

"That's right. Do you find that hard to understand? You call yourself a professional journalist. You have a job to do, and you do it. You write the article about Mrs. Astor's ball, you hand it in, and then you go right on to your next one."

She stood up to confront him. "That's not the same!" Her voice shook with indignation. "We are talking about the possibility that an innocent man may hang."

"You are. As far as I'm concerned, this particular discussion's finished."

"Very well." She spoke with quiet determination. "You're willing to let the Marek case go. To forget all about it. But I am not."

"I see. Then what will you do? Maybe you'll turn in an article to the *Gazette*. Your own version of the case, closing with a spirited defense of Barney Marek."

"Mrs. Fairlie would never allow me to do that."

"I don't think she would. So what are you going to do?"

"Since you won't help me, I will continue the investigation on my own."

"That's fine. Go to it, Amanda. I'll give you a list of my informants, if you want it—prostitutes, pimps, bartenders, fences."

"Don't take that tone with me, Ross! If there's the slightest chance that Marek didn't kill Jessamyn and the other two women then I will—"

"You'll go out and track down the real killer."

"If I have to."

"And you'll bring him in, single-handed, I suppose. Or will you ask him to wait while you run and get the police? Or maybe you haven't thought about that. But then, you never do think ahead. Not once, since I've known you." He cupped her face in his hands and looked down at her. His touch was warm and light against her cheeks. And when he spoke again, there was no sarcasm in his tone. "Even after all you've seen and heard, you haven't changed, not really. I doubt you ever will."

"I haven't asked for your opinion of my character."

"Then I'll spare you the rest, for now. I'll take you home. Then, after I've talked to Spencer, I'll come back. We'll have dinner in front of your fireplace, if you prefer."

"As it happens, I already have an engagement for this evening. I've been invited to Mrs. Fairlie's Christmas Eve party."

"Then I suggest you leave early and go straight to bed."

"Do you have any more sensible advice for me?" Although there was an edge to her voice, she was touched by his concern.

"As a matter of fact, I do. Go back to the *Gazette* where you belong. And when you've finished work, go home to your flat, and take good care of Leander. Make the most of your independence."

"Is that all?"

"Not quite. After the novelty of your career wears off, why not do what most women do? Find yourself a husband who will make sure you stay out of trouble."

"You think that's what every woman needs, don't you? A man who will provide her with a home and take care of her. Who will tell her what she may or may not do. What she should think and feel—"

"Be still, Amanda." He reached out and his hands closed around her arms. "I suppose there are women who find all the satisfaction they need in their work," he said. "But not you. You need a man. A husband."

His dark grey eyes held her gaze. She felt the warm, stroking movement of his hands. For one moment, she wanted to lean closer, to rest her face against his chest. But she pushed aside the impulse, and drew away.

"Do you really suppose I could marry you? A ruthless

opportunist who is ready to take Spencer's money, his patronage, to further your career? I doubt any woman would want you for her husband. Certainly, I would not."

His dark brows shot up. "I'm afraid I haven't made myself clear. Because I've never thought of marrying you, or any woman. I was only offering you some well-meant advice. You should marry, and soon."

Shaken and deeply humiliated, she did not allow herself to look away. "I appreciate your concern," she said. "And who knows, you may be right. Maybe I will marry, one day. If I should find a suitable gentleman."

"One of your own class."

"Certainly."

His face darkened. "Not Howard Thornton."

She smiled. "Mr. Thornton is going to marry Phoebe Armstead. Her parents are going to announce the engagement at a dinner, shortly after the beginning of the New Year."

"If I moved in your social sphere, I would already have known that. Who do you have in mind, then? Clifford Spencer?"

"That is surely no concern of yours."

But he ignored her rebuke. "You might at least consider him. He's handsome, eligible. It's true his family pedigree leaves something to be desired. But, with his father's fortune, and your background, it could be an excellent match."

"I'll consider it."

"Don't wait too long. He's an excellent catch, as I'm sure you know. But the season's still in full swing, and I'm sure you'll be seeing him often."

"As a matter of fact, Clifford and I are going on a sleighing party in Central Park, the day after tomorrow."

"Not unchaperoned, I hope. Perhaps your friend, Miss Hamilton might be persuaded to go along."

"We are to join Clifford's friends in Central Park, at the Bethesda Fountain, and later, we are to dine at Delmonico's. He has reserved a private dining room for twenty."

"A sleigh ride in the moonlight. A brand new sleigh with bells on the horses' harnesses. Yes, the coachman showed me the sleigh and told me all about it. A fur robe to keep you warm, and the horses with plumes on their heads. The perfect opportunity. Make the most of it."

He glanced at the wall clock. "I don't want to hurry you, but Everard doesn't like to be kept waiting." He helped her on with her coat. "Let me take you downstairs and find you a hansom. And since we're both heading uptown, we can share it."

She could not trust herself to speak. Was he remembering their first meeting outside the Spencer mansion, back in September? She had defied convention to share a cab with a stranger that day.

"There's no need," she said. And before he could stop her, she was out the door.

He stayed at the window, watching her as she stood at the curb, a figure in russet, with the snowflakes falling around her. At her signal, a hansom drew to a halt; she climbed inside, and the vehicle moved briskly down the street, then turned onto Broadway. It was time for him to leave, too; it would take longer than usual to get uptown with so many Christmas shoppers out on the streets. But he waited a moment longer, staring moodily down at the street.

Was it possible Amanda would take his advice, and exchange her position on the *Gazette* for a proper marriage? It would be best if she did. With a husband and a home of her own, she would live the life she'd been trained for.

He turned from the window, took his overcoat from the closet, then locked up and went downstairs. But during his ride uptown, through the noisy, crowded streets, he couldn't forget his talk with Amanda. She hadn't been serious about carrying on the investigation alone. She had been angry with him, because he had refused to consider the possibility of Marek's innocence.

But what about her reluctant admission that, if Clifford were to propose marriage, she might accept? Even if she did not love Clifford, his attentions during the past months had not been unwelcome. After that chance meeting at the opera, he had taken her to a museum reception; most likely he'd persuaded Ottilie to invite her to tea. How often had they been together after that? Ross had never questioned her about her social life, unless he'd thought it might have some bearing on the Marek case.

No doubt Amanda's mother would approve of such an advantageous marriage; she would come hurrying home from Europe, to help with the arrangements for a spring wedding.

Clifford might be an indulgent husband; but he certainly would draw the line at allowing his bride to involve herself in any further investigations. Surely, she would never tell him about the part she had already played in the Marek case.

Everard rose from his armchair and accompanied Ross to the library door. "You'll have to stay in New York long enough to testify at Marek's trial. But when that's over, you'll leave for Pittsburgh right away. The mill owners need to get the names of those damn agitators. I gave you a good recommendation. You had better live up to it." He shook Ross's hand.

The heavy oak doors closed and Ross stood in the over-decorated entrance hall.

Marek would come to trial soon enough, and after that, he would get away from New York. Everard's Pittsburgh associates would put him to work in one of their mills, where he would mingle with the workers, and gain their trust. It wouldn't be easy. He knew how the mill workers would deal with a company spy.

He didn't have to wonder how Amanda would feel about his next assignment; he knew well enough. It didn't concern him. It wasn't likely he would see her again. But he would not forget her.

Even now, a vivid image rose in his mind. Amanda in coral silk, her shoulders bared, her hair piled high on her head. The amber necklace that had encircled her throat. If she married Clifford Spencer, she would have no need to wear that necklace again. Clifford would deck her in diamonds. He would provide a carriage, a personal maid, a staff to take care of the house he would build for her. She would be where she belonged, safe and pampered.

These last few months would be forgotten. Not right away, of course. She would feel uneasy as she followed the newspaper accounts of Marek's trial, and the inevitable sentence. And probably she would have a few bad dreams, one the night before he went to the gallows.

"Were you wishing to speak with Mrs. Spencer, sir?" Nellie stood beside him, in her starched cap and apron. "I'm sure she would want to thank you herself for all you've done."

He didn't doubt it. With Marek out of the way, the scandal soon would be laid to rest, and Ottilie Spencer could take her place in society, again.

"Mrs. Spencer is in the drawing room, sir. I'll tell her you're here."

"That won't be necessary," he said. "I've got to be on my way."

"Certainly, Mr. Buchanan. I'm sure you've plenty to do, what with the holidays and all."

Tonight there would be a bigger crowd than usual at Murphy's saloon. The minute he walked in, he'd be surrounded by newspapermen, trying to get all the details about Marek's capture. He'd have a few drinks with Jerry Costello. Maybe more than a few.

He turned to the parlor maid and smiled. "I'm sure you have plans of your own. Have a happy Christmas, Nellie."

"Thank you, sir. That I will. But I can't say as much for poor Miss Tuttle, though."

He could see that Nellie was eager to share a bit of gossip, and he would not deprive her of that pleasure. "Is she a particular friend of yours?"

"I wouldn't say that, sir. She's not been easy to get along with. But even so, if you ask me, it's not right to let her go, not today. Mrs. Spencer might have waited until after the holidays."

"Miss Tuttle's been fired?"

"Just this morning. She only had time to pack her things. She's got no family. Cook gave her the address of a boardinghouse for single ladies. But what kind of a Christmas will she have there?"

He tried to recall what Amanda had told him. Miss Tuttle had been Jessamyn's personal maid. But now she did whatever chores came her way. She had cleaned Kendall's soiled coat, and had repaired the torn lace on Amanda's gown. She must have resented her loss of status among the other servants. But he did not suppose she had dared complain to Ottilie Spencer. So why had she been let go, apparently without warning?

"Where is Miss Tuttle now?"

"Downstairs in the butler's sitting room. Mr. Harland offered to let her wait there, until she's ready to leave. Better than having the rest of the staff gawking at her."

"I'd like to speak with her."

Nellie gave him a puzzled frown. "I'm sure you mean well, sir. But I'm not sure as Miss Tuttle's lookin' for anybody's sympathy. She's got her pride."

"I can understand that. But perhaps I may be able to help her in a more tangible way."

"Pardon?"

"It's possible I may be able to help her find another position as a lady's maid."

"That is kind of you, sir."

But he had not spoken out of kindness. And at the moment, he did not know any lady who needed a personal maid.

The butler's parlor was a pleasant room, with a small iron stove, a flowered carpet, and good walnut furniture. But Miss Tuttle, who was seated in a red plush armchair, with her trunk beside her, seemed indifferent to her surroundings. When he asked if he might speak with her, she agreed, without a trace of interest; probably she was still dazed, unable to cope with the realization that she was unemployed.

"What is it you wish to speak to me about, Mr. Buchanan?"

He could not tell her his real reason for intruding on her at such a time. In fact, he wasn't sure why he wanted to pursue the matter. Except that her abrupt dismissal had aroused his curiosity. He found himself thinking of Gertrude; she, too, had been Jessamyn's maid. And she had been let go, right after she had brought Jessamyn back from upstate, leaving the unwanted infant at a baby farm. The Spencers had lost no time in ridding their home of a servant who knew too much about their private affairs.

Only a few hours ago, he had told Amanda that, as far as he was concerned, the Marek case was closed. But now he knew it wasn't that simple.

Miss Tuttle's faded eyes searched his face with the first hint of curiosity. She was waiting for him to explain why he had come to seek her out.

"Nellie told me that you were leaving. No doubt you wish to find a position more suitable to a lady of your experience and ability."

"And why should that concern you?"

"Because I know someone who might be of assistance to you. Miss Amanda Whitney. She is an acquaintance of mine. You remember having met her, perhaps?"

"Yes indeed, Mr. Buchanan."

"She happened to mention to me how she had torn her dress, that day she took tea with Mrs. Spencer and her son. She told me how helpful you had been."

For the first time, he saw a flicker of hope in the woman's thin, lined face. "I only did a bit of mending for her. And I offered her a few suggestions as to how she might care for her wardrobe."

"So she said. She was highly impressed with your skill and experience."

Miss Tuttle's faded eyes brightened. "Is she looking for a maid?"

"I don't believe so," Ross said. "But if I were to tell her

that you are seeking a change of employer—with your permission, of course—maybe she'd know of someone who would might offer you employment."

The woman's narrow shoulders stiffened. "That is most kind, Mr. Buchanan. However, I am not in need of charity."

"I meant no offence," he said quickly. "I'm sure Mrs. Spencer has provided you with the highest references, and suitable compensation, as well. But, if I may speak frankly—" He paused for a moment.

"Please do."

"Miss Whitney told me about the rest of your conversation with her. She understood how difficult it must have been for you, working here these past months. Doing whatever menial chores came your way. Had it not been for Miss Spencer's untimely death—"

She flinched at the mention of Jessamyn's death. He disliked having to inflict further distress on Miss Tuttle, but he could think of no other means of getting the information he wanted.

"You devoted yourself to Jessamyn Spencer's comfort and well-being. Miss Whitney told me that. She said that you did your best to carry out your duties. That last afternoon, when the dressmaker had kept her standing too long, doing all those alterations on her wedding gown, you brought up her tea tray. But, as I understand it, Mrs. Spencer sent you away."

"Miss Whitney remembered my telling her that?" Her expression softened. "I would not have expected her to."

"Miss Whitney has an excellent memory for details," he said. "She said you were troubled because you had not been allowed to offer Miss Spencer even that small service."

"But I did come back later, Mr. Buchanan. I thought

Miss Jessamyn might need me to help her prepare for bed, as I always did. I would have helped her off with her gown and brushed her hair. But before I could go into her bedroom, the door swung open, and there was Mr. Clifford. He stood, blocking my way. He said Miss Jessamyn had fallen asleep and that I was not to enter her room again that night. Not under any circumstances." Her brows drew together in a puzzled frown. "I must admit, I was taken aback."

"He must have realized that she was exhausted. I suppose he wanted her to get a good night's rest," he said.

"I suppose you are right," she said slowly. "But I was surprised by the way Mr. Clifford spoke to me. He'd always had a smile for me, and a pleasant remark. But that evening—he was different."

He kept his voice casual. "In what way?"

"I was disturbed by the look he gave me—and his tone of voice."

"He was rude to you?"

"No, not downright rude," she said. "But not at all like his usual self, either."

She was interrupted by a knock on the door of the butler's sitting room. One of the maids put her head in and said: "Your cab's here, Miss Tuttle." She turned and went away with a swish of her starched skirt.

Ross waited a moment, expecting a footman to appear, but no such help was offered. He bent and picked up her worn, horsehair trunk. "Let me carry this out to the cab for you."

"You are most kind, Mr. Buchanan."

Before he assisted her into the waiting hansom, he asked her for the address of the boardinghouse where she would be staying. "I will speak to Miss Whitney about a new position for you," he said. "I know she'll do her best to help you find one."

He felt a growing uneasiness, as he watched the cab drive down Fifth Avenue and disappear into the grey twilight.

CHAPTER TWENTY

Union Square, once an exclusive residential neighborhood, had changed to a lively business district. Even now, on the day after Christmas, the sidewalks were crowded with shoppers. Ladies in velvet and fur bustled in and out of Tiffany's jewelry store, and Brentano's Literary Emporium, their arms laden with packages. Carriages, hansoms, streetcars, and delivery wagons rattled over the square. In a few hours, the blaze of the new electric lights would illuminate a different crowd, bent on an evening's entertainment at Tony Pastor's variety house, followed by a lavish dinner at Luchow's or one of the nearby hotels.

Ross paused to read the lettering on the small, plate glass window: GARTNER'S THEATRICAL COSTUMERS. And, in smaller script: Mrs. Elsa Gartner, Prop. Earlier that day, he had visited the Savoy Theater before today's matinee performance. There, he had persuaded Cora to give him a list of every costume shop she could think of.

He already had gone to four of them, had questioned clerks and managers.

And had drawn a blank every time.

Although it was nearly five o'clock, he decided to give this shop a try.

"I'm just closing, sir," said the stout, grey-haired woman in fine quality black bombazine with white collar and cuffs. She placed a feather boa in a tissue-lined cardboard box, then put on the lid. "Please come back tomorrow."

But Ross came and planted himself in front of the

counter. "My business won't wait, Ma'am."

She looked him up and down, then shook her head. "You're not one of our regular customers. What theater do you work for?"

"I've come here from the Savoy." Although his reply was ambiguous, he hoped his mention of the name might give him a certain credibility.

The woman did not seem to be at all impressed. "Try Blumenfeld's—they're down on Delancey. We cater only to the better class of theater."

"That's what I was told. But I'm not here to look for costumes. It's information I need. Are you Mrs. Gartner?"

"I am."

"Then perhaps you may be able to help me. One of the performers at the Savoy gave me the name of your shop. She shared a dressing room with Miss Violet Yates."

Mrs. Gartner caught her breath and drew back, as if he had dropped a live snake on the counter. "I don't know anything about that unfortunate girl. I read about her in the papers, that's all." But she spoke with more vehemence than was called for, and he saw a hint of fear in her eyes.

"When her body was found in the theater, she was wearing a wedding gown and veil. But I suppose you remember reading about that, too."

She looked down at the cardboard box before her. Her finger traced the raised lettering that spelled out the name of her shop.

"Miss Yates didn't wear such an outfit for any of her performances," he went on. "None of the performers did. As a matter of fact, there are no bridal outfits in the Savoy's wardrobe department."

"I wouldn't know anything about that," she said. "I do

business with Wallack's, with Booth's. Not with a cheap variety house like—"

"Did Violet Yates rent a bridal outfit from you?"

"What makes you think she rented it at all?"

"You think Marek carried it with him?"

"I never thought about it at all. Why should I?"

"Because it might have come from your shop. Perhaps one of your clerks rented it to Miss Yates, and never mentioned it to you."

"We keep a record of every costume we rent out, with the name of the customer and the date—"

"That makes my job easier," he said with a smile. "Perhaps you would do me the favor of looking back over your records."

"Violet Yates was never here." But the light from the gas lamp overhead revealed the sheen of perspiration on her forehead.

He took out one of his business cards and handed it to her. She glanced at it, then dropped it on the counter with a look of distaste. "So you are a private investigator. That doesn't give you the right to come into my shop and—"

"I work for Everard Spencer. He hired me to find his daughter's killer."

The Spencer name had the effect he'd expected. The woman's fingers tightened on the box in front of her. Then she rallied. "So you found him. And now he's locked up in jail."

"That's right. But there are still a few questions that need to be answered. Before the case comes up for trial."

"I can't help you—I don't know anything."

He went on as though he had not heard her. "You don't want to get mixed up in the case. You don't want to be dragged into court, to have your name spread all over the papers. But that's what will happen, unless you tell me what I need to know."

"I make a decent living, no more. Since my husband passed away—that was fifteen years ago—I've worked hard. I've built up a respectable business, all on my own. Do you blame me for wanting to keep what I have?"

"Of course not. It's hard for a decent woman to make her way alone. I understand that. Tell me the truth, and I'll do all I can to keep your name out of this. If you don't co-operate, I'll have to go to the police. They may not be so understanding."

Her eyes were bleak now, and she spoke with dull resignation. "What do you want to know?"

"Violet Yates was wearing a wedding outfit when she was killed, but so was Gertrude Marek. And Mrs. Marek's outfit wasn't made for her. It was too small for her, and too short." He searched his mind for Amanda's exact words. "It hadn't been properly finished. The seams were only basted."

"That was so we could alter it to fit the girl who was going to wear it. It's part of our service. But the Yates girl didn't want the dress for herself, that's what she said. She was renting it for somebody else."

He felt a brief surge of triumph. "When did she rent the outfit? Suppose you look it up in your records."

"I don't have to," Mrs. Gartner said. "It was the first week in October."

A week before Gertrude Marek's murder.

"And that outfit was never returned, was it?"

"That happens sometimes. I kept the deposit."

"But you made no connection between that missing bridal outfit and the one Gertrude Marek was wearing when they found her body?"

"I never thought about it."

She was lying, but he didn't press it. "So who rented the second bridal outfit? The one Violet was wearing when they found her?"

"It might have come from another shop. But it didn't come from here. We haven't had any call for another bridal gown, not since they found the Marek woman's body. Check my records if you want to. Come back first thing tomorrow and question my clerks. I haven't had another one in stock since October. I'm telling you the truth, I swear it."

"All right, Mrs. Gartner. I believe you."

"And you'll keep my name out of this, like you promised?"

"I'll do everything I can. I give you my word."

He turned and left her there, leaning on the counter, her face still drained of color.

As he closed the shop door behind him, he saw the electric lights go on. Most of the passersby paused, impressed by the dazzling glow. But Ross kept going, indifferent to this nightly spectacle.

I don't have all the answers. Neither do you.

He'd been unwilling to pursue those answers. So why had he spent the day walking the snowy streets, asking questions?

Because of Amanda.

Impulsive, vulnerable, she would not stop until she had done all in her power to find those answers. And now, as he crossed Union Square jostled by the crowd, the wind stinging his face, he knew he could not leave her to pursue her search alone.

A few weeks ago, Amanda had come to Central Park to watch a sleighing party from a distance. Standing on a narrow path, she had taken down her notes. Later, back in her office at the *Gazette*, she had written her article, describing Mrs. Cornelius Vanderbilt's red sleigh with its gold bells, and her fine horses, decked in crimson plumes, the Townsend Burdens' turn-out, in tones of blue from turquoise to deep sapphire. And the Horace Hamersley troika, imported from Russia, along with the coachman and footman.

Every winter these splendid equipages become more dazzling to the eye . . .

Now, on this afternoon after Christmas, she was no longer an onlooker; she was a part of it. Wrapped in a cinnamon wool cloak, with a velvet-trimmed hood, she sat beside Clifford on the high leather seat. Pedestrians turned to admire the yellow and black sleigh, as it sped along the south end of the park, then turned in through the Scholar's Gate.

The ball was up at the lake, to signal the public that the ice was frozen solid. "Shall we stop here for awhile, and watch the skaters?" Clifford asked.

"I'd like that." He reined in the team, then motioned to a chestnut seller, who came hurrying over. Amanda smiled as she inhaled the fragrance, then shared with him a paper bag of the hot, tasty morsels. Mothers and nursemaids had begun to lead the children from the lake; but courting couples, oblivious to the lengthening shadows, still skated hand in hand. The high clouds in the west were streaked with crimson and gold.

Clifford gave her a small, metal hand warmer with charcoal inside. "Put it inside your muff." Then, as he tucked the sable rug more closely around her, he asked: "Did you have a pleasant Christmas?"

"I dined with Maude Hamilton and her two maiden aunts."

His lips curved in a smile. "I don't suppose an afternoon with Miss Hamilton and her aunts was particularly stimulating. But I'm glad you weren't alone. I kept thinking of you all day, wondering if you were spending the afternoon in your flat, with only your cat for company."

She was moved by his concern. "Miss Hamilton and I are good friends," she assured him. "And her aunts are a lively pair, who feel it their duty never to allow the conversation to lag for a moment."

He flicked the reins, and the sleigh moved on past the lake. The shouts and the laughter of the skaters were lost in the distance. The light was starting to fade when they reached the Bethesda Fountain. Frost crystals glittered in the cold, still air, and purple pools of shadows lay in the hollows of snow. The bronze angel brooded above the fountain, wings outstretched. The water had been turned off for the winter, and she missed its rippling sound. A sudden gust of wind rattled the leafless branches overhead.

She closed her fingers around the little hand warmer, and moved closer to Clifford. "We seem to have arrived before any of the others," she said. "I hope we won't have too long to wait."

But he said nothing, nor did he draw the team to a halt. "We were to meet your friends here, weren't we?" she asked.

He kept his gaze fixed straight ahead, as the sleigh sped past the fountain. Amanda turned her head, but the bronze angel with its outstretched wings was already lost to view.

She remembered something Ross had said, the last time she had seen him. *A moonlight sleigh ride . . . the perfect opportunity. Make the most of it . . .*

Perhaps Clifford wanted to drive her a short distance from the fountain before the others arrived, then stop in the shelter of the trees by the Ramble, so that he could speak to her alone. Yes, that must be it.

But now they were passing the Ramble, the horses moving at a steady trot, the snow flung upward in a glittering spray on either side of the sleigh, and still he did not slow down. He cracked his whip over the backs of the team, and guided them onto a narrow path that ran between high, jagged rocks.

Had Clifford been about to ask her to marry him? Had he been seized by anxiety, at the last moment, fearing that she would refuse? No, not Clifford. From their first meeting, he had behaved with the easy self-assurance natural to a young man born to wealth and power, and gifted with such striking good looks.

The silence stretched between them, until her growing bewilderment moved her to speak. "Perhaps we ought not to drive too far from the fountain. Your friends will be arriving any moment now. Maybe some of them are already there. They'll wonder what's become of us."

"My friends are not coming." He leaned forward to light the lamp that hung from his side of the sleigh. The yellow light flared up, gilding the contours of his face.

She tried to remember exactly what he had said, when he had invited her on the sleigh ride. "I thought we were to join them at the fountain." He did not answer, and she tensed with the first stirrings of uneasiness. "Are we meeting them at Delmonico's?"

"We are not meeting anyone this evening. Not here. And not at Delmonico's."

She distinctly remembered that he had mentioned the name of that popular, highly-regarded restaurant.

"Delmonico's only has private rooms for large parties," he said.

"Yes, but—you said we would be a party of twenty."

"I changed my plans. Hotel Brunswick has several charming private supper rooms for two. I have already made our reservations there. I want you to myself tonight."

She went hot at his words and the look that accompanied them.

"Surely you are not offended." Although he spoke softly, she caught the irony in his tone. "Not you. A free-spirited lady who pursues a career, who lives alone. You don't share your flat with another young lady, do you? Or a maiden aunt. You come and go as you choose."

She raised her chin, and spoke in a clipped tone. "That's right. And I choose to go back to my flat. So you will please turn the sleigh around at once, and drive me home."

He thrust the handle of the whip into its brass holder, then reached out and drew her against him. She tried to push him away, but his grip tightened. Always, until now, his touch had been gentle, respectful. She had not been conscious of the hard strength in that lean, graceful body of his. "There is no need to play the outraged innocent, Amanda. Not with me." He pushed her down across the seat, his face hovered above hers.

His lips brushed hers, but although the touch was light, almost tentative, she stiffened. "Let me go, Clifford."

He released her and she drew herself upright.

"I could take you here and now," he said softly. "I don't believe you would mind that too much. But you are used to more civilized surroundings. That room at the Brunswick is furnished in excellent taste, with a fire to warm you. So let us not be impatient. It's still early. We have the whole evening ahead."

She forced down her anger. "Then you will have time to drive me home," she said. "And to find yourself a girl who

341

will appreciate such arrangements."

"You disappoint me. I thought you would be different." He sighed and shook his head. "But you are a hypocrite, who makes a display of outraged virtue. As Jessamyn used to do."

She stared at him in disbelief, unable to speak. She could only stare at him. At those eyes, the color of sapphires. And as hard.

"Jessamyn. My delicate, ladylike sister. She would have walked down the aisle of Grace Church, decked out in that white gown and veil. White for virginity. But Jessamyn was no virgin."

She began to tremble with anger. "You are contemptible."

"Jessamyn was a whore."

"That's not true!"

He ignored her protest. "A whore, who came to a fitting end. Lying there in that alley, next to Isobel Hewitt's brothel."

"Jessamyn was shy and lonely. And only fifteen, when Devin O'Shea seduced her. It must have been easy for him to convince her that he loved her—"

"Devin O'Shea was her riding master—a servant—but nothing more. She was a virgin the first time I took her. And even after that—every time I had her—she struggled and cried and pleaded with me to leave her alone. But that was all a sham. She wanted it."

Clifford had been Jessamyn's only lover. The father of her child.

She wanted to shout at him, to revile him with every insult at her command. But instead, she heard herself saying, "So that's why you hated Thornton so."

"Thornton." He repeated the name with contempt. "Do

you suppose that their marriage would have changed what I shared with her? He only wanted her fortune. He would not have interfered with me. I meant to reassure her about that, to tell her my plans, when the time was right. But I never had the chance."

Clifford had already defied the laws of God and man, when he had committed incest with his sister. Why should Jessamyn's marriage have proved a barrier to his unnatural lust? Amanda sat and listened in dazed silence, as he went on.

"Early that evening last September—that was when it all began to go wrong. Mother and I were going to the theater that night. I was on my way to my room to dress for the evening. As I passed Jessamyn's door, she called to me to come in. I could see that she was deeply agitated. She hadn't even called her maid to take off her wedding gown. I don't suppose she realized she still was wearing it.

"I went inside. She locked the door, and then she told me about Gertrude Marek. That greedy fool was blackmailing her. She'd already given Gertrude a few pieces of jewelry. But the woman wanted more. Or her husband did. I told her she had nothing to fear, that I would deal with the Mareks. I said I would always care for her and protect her. I took her in my arms to soothe her, to reassure her, nothing more."

"And then?" Amanda heard herself ask. Her voice sounded faint and unfamiliar.

"I had planned to wait until after the honeymoon to take her again. But the sight of her in her bridal gown and veil—it aroused me. I had to have her, there and then. I kissed her, then started to remove her veil. She protested."

"The same as always," Amanda said.

"No! Not the same at all. Always before she only cried

and pleaded with me to let her go. But I knew—we both knew—she was only pretending. This time she was—different."

"How was it different?"

"She swore she'd break off the marriage. She said no one would stop her. If they locked her in her room until the wedding day, she would cry out the truth right there in church."

"You believed her?"

"Not at first. But as she went on, I began to think she might carry out her threat."

"And then?"

"I said the marriage would change nothing. She would be mine, as she always had been. I led her toward the bed, but she broke away and ran for the door. She fumbled with the lock and then she screamed. I caught her. She struggled like a mad woman. The wreath came loose. I held it in my two hands. Then it was around her throat. I was only going to keep her quiet. She went limp and her head fell back. I caught her in my arms. I held her against me. Then I knew."

Amanda was racked with pity for Jessamyn. And revulsion for her brother.

Then another, more primitive emotion seized her. Fear for her own life.

She saw his hard, set face in the lamp light and she knew he would not let her leave here alive. Every instinct told her to get away, to run from him into the darkness. But she forced herself to remain motionless as he picked up the reins and drove on. Over to the east, she saw the museum. And the obelisk—the great granite shaft they called Cleopatra's Needle—stood out against the sky. It had taken on a silver sheen from the light of the rising moon. A brilliant star glittered directly above its sharp peak. A star—or was it the planet Venus?

They were moving north, where the leafless trees grew close together. This stretch of the park might have been a woodland, far away from the city. A place of towering rocks and ancient trees, of tangled vines where small animals sought refuge from the raptors: the owls and hawks that wheeled overhead on silent wings.

The moon was higher now. She felt a bone-deep chill. And still Clifford drove north. She forced herself to focus her whirling thoughts. She could not give way to panic. Because if she did, she knew how it would be. She went rigid at the vivid picture of what was to come. Her body lying outstretched, white in the moonlight. There would be no bridal gown for her, no veil. He did not need them, because Barney Marek, locked up in the Tombs, could not be blamed for this crime. But that did not matter. Beyond the north end of the park lay the squatters' shantytown. If her body was discovered near their settlement, one of them surely would be blamed.

Clifford's hands, those hands that now held the reins with such ease, guiding the team, would close about her throat, and strangle the life from her. And then? Would he strip her naked to make it more difficult to identify the body? Would he rape her before he killed her? If she pleaded with him, if she tried to fight him off, her struggles might arouse him, as Jessamyn's had. She had no weapon, and her own strength was no match for his. Would it not be better to submit, to give herself up to the darkness?

No, never! She was alive and she would fight to stay alive. She felt the blood surge through her, felt the beating of her heart, the bite of the wind against her face. She would not surrender without a struggle. Not as long as there was still the slightest chance of escape.

Even here, in this silent, moonwashed desolation, it was possible that another sleigh, a whole party of them, would drive by. She held on to that slender hope, and found the strength to speak.

"You didn't mean to kill Jessamyn. You told me so. Her death was an accident." Her tone was gentle, as if she were comforting a confused child. "You didn't mean to kill her. You loved her." She spoke without a trace of reproach. "You were the only one who ever really loved her."

"Who would have believed that? Who would have accepted our right to such a love? You don't, do you, Amanda?"

"I'm not sure. How can I be sure? If only you had confided in me sooner. If you had given me time to know you better—then perhaps—" She put a hand on his arm.

"You'd have listened to me, as you are listening now. Wide-eyed and trusting." He turned on her, his voice harsh with anger. "And then you'd have gone running to Buchanan. To tell him all about it."

The mention of Ross's name caught her by surprise, but she recovered quickly. "Mr. Buchanan? Why, I scarcely know him."

"Lying bitch! You've been working with him from the beginning. Because you wanted a share of his fee, I suppose. Or maybe that wasn't the only reason. Maybe you wanted him in your bed."

"That's not true!"

"It doesn't matter now. No man will ever have you again. And that's too bad, Amanda. Because you really are desirable. I would have enjoyed making love with you." He thrust his hand under her cloak and cupped her breast. "Maybe, even now . . ."

She let herself go limp, to stretch herself across the fur robe that covered his knees. With his other hand, he stroked her throat, then began to undo the buttons of her dress.

She flung back her arm, and made a soft, moaning sound deep in her throat. Her fingers found the handle of the whip, and closed around it. His hand slid under her dress, and he took her nipple between his fingers.

She swung the whip at his face. But she was off balance and the whip had only grazed his cheek. He swore and his fingers pinched on her nipple. She cried out with pain.

She pulled herself up, and threw herself over the side of the sleigh. And landed on her knees in the snow. She was still clutching the whip.

Gasping, she struggled to her feet. Her first impulse was to run. But he already was standing up in the sleigh. He would overtake her easily.

She drew her breath and slashed the whip down on the flank of the nearer horse. The terrified beast neighed loudly in protest, then reared up. Clifford was thrown back on the seat. The team was out of control, galloping away with the sleigh jouncing behind them.

She turned and started to run in the opposite direction, her boots sinking into the snow.

From somewhere behind her, she heard the crash of wood and metal. The sleigh had overturned. Clifford lay in the snow, a dark shape against the moon-silvered whiteness.

Amanda hesitated only a moment, then began running again. She stumbled, fell, then clutched at the nearest tree trunk and regained her footing. She searched the sky, until she caught sight of the obelisk and the brilliant star above it. The obelisk, the fountain, and beyond it, the skating pond. How far away were the familiar landmarks? The icy wind tore at her cloak and seared her lungs. Branches of the leafless shrubs caught at her skirt. Panting, she tore herself free, then turned her face to the south and kept on going.

CHAPTER TWENTY-ONE

Ross found Cora at one of the tables in Ryan's saloon, around the corner from the Savoy Theater. She greeted him with a smile, and waved him to a chair opposite her. "Did you find what you were looking for on that list I gave you?"

"It was a real help to me," Ross assured her. He signaled to the waiter, and ordered a bottle of brandy. "You prefer this brand, don't you?"

Her smile deepened. "Imagine you remembering that." She leaned across the table, and he caught the musky scent of her patchouli perfume. "Say, Mr. Buchanan, you must be done in from running around to all them shops. What you need is bit of fun. How about coming to the Savoy for tonight's performance?"

"There's nothing I'd like better," he assured her. "But I haven't finished my investigation yet."

Her face fell. "I thought you already found out whatever it was you need to."

"Not quite everything," he said. "I know where Gertrude Marek's gown came from, but not Violet's. Maybe you can think of another costume shop where she might have rented her outfit."

"What makes you think she rented it?"

He looked up at a full-figured, olive-skinned brunette in tangerine velvet, who had stopped beside their table. "My friend, Leatrice Joyce," said Cora. "She's in the chorus at the Savoy, too. Leatrice, this is Mr. Buchanan."

"That detective you been telling me about?" She gave

Ross a flirtatious glance and without waiting for an invitation, she sat down beside him.

Damn! He needed to talk to Cora alone. But he acknowledged the introduction with a warm smile, and signaled the waiter for another glass.

"Violet didn't need to go to a costume shop—she could have gone to the fanciest dressmaker on the Ladies Mile, and had her bridal gown made to order for her," the brunette said.

Cora's rouged lips twisted in a mirthless grin. "Not on her salary, she couldn't."

Leatrice turned to Ross, and put a hand on his arm. She spoke softly, as if sharing a confidence. "She didn't have to pay for it herself. Her gentleman friend gave her the money."

"Are you sure about that?" Ross asked.

"Violet told me all about it. We lived in the same rooming house. She was a dear friend of mine, poor thing."

"Violet Yates was a snob and a liar," Cora said.

"Speak no evil of the departed," Leatrice reproached her.

Cora shrugged. "All right, so maybe she wasn't a liar. Maybe all that time she toured with that two-bit stock company, acting in them melodramas—*Under the Gaslight* and *Barriers Burned Away*, she got to believin' all that twaddle was true."

"She was tellin' the truth about her rich gentleman friend," Leatrice said smugly. "I know, because I saw him pick her up on the corner, in a cab."

"A real gentleman would have driven up to the door," said Cora.

"Her gentleman friend was real enough, all right," Leatrice insisted. "He wore a fine black cassimere coat and a cravat with a pearl stickpin. Soon as he saw her, he got out, took off his high silk hat, and bowed to her." She put a plump hand to her ample bosom, and gave an envious sigh. "He was handsome, too—even better looking than Edwin Booth, and a lot younger. And his hair was blond."

"How come he didn't call for her in his own carriage?" Cora persisted.

"Because he didn't want anybody to recognize it, and then they'd know who he was. He made her promise not to tell anybody his name, not even me. But she said he came from a real important family."

Ross set down his glass carefully. His muscles had gone tight. Fear touched a corner of his mind. "This gentleman gave Violet the money for a bridal gown?"

"Yes, he did," said Leatrice. "They were going to run off together and elope. And she wanted to get married all in white."

Cora gave a derisive laugh. "Oh, sure. And then I suppose he was going to take her home and introduce her to that high-toned family of his. His little bride from the chorus at the Savoy."

But his attention was fixed on Leatrice now. "What else did Violet tell you?" he prompted.

Flattered by his interest, she went on. "She and her young man were going to keep it a secret until the right moment. Then he was going to take her to his house and—"

"And his folks were going to throw a big party to welcome her into the family," Cora interrupted. "With the Astors and the Vanderbilts and all that bunch. Bushwah! She was handing you a lot of bushwah and you fell for it!"

"She was telling the truth!" Leatrice insisted. "Violet had a rich gentleman friend, and he was going to marry her. What do you think, Mr. Buchanan?"

He made an effort to keep his tone light. "I think I owe both you lovely ladies a good dinner." He gave them an affable smile, then set a couple of bills down on the table.

"We performers don't dine until after the show," Leatrice began. "Oh, my!" She was staring down at the bills, her rouged lips parted. "You're a fine gent yourself, Mr. Buchanan. Why don't you come and join us for supper?"

But he already was on his feet, heading for the door. Outside the saloon, the yellow gaslights glowed through the evening mist like dim, floating moons. Sweat sprang out on his body, plastering his shirt to his skin. Even though he wore a heavy overcoat, he was gripped by a chill. His insides tightened.

He hadn't felt this kind of fear since he'd been a kid back in the shelter, bending over a bench and bracing himself for the first cut of the overseer's leather strap.

But for the first time he could remember, he wasn't afraid for himself.

The thin soles of Amanda's kidskin shoes were soaked through. She stumbled over a fallen log and struck her knee. She cried out as pain shot up her leg. She tried to draw a deep breath but the whalebone stays of her corset bit into her flesh.

Low-hanging branches lashed her face, opening the skin. Blood trickled into her eyes, and she wiped it away. And went on.

Somewhere behind her, Clifford lay in the snow, a dark, motionless shape. Maybe he was dead. If so, she had killed him. She had struck the blow that had sent the panic-crazed horses racing off. She could still hear their shrill neighing, the splintering wood, the crumpling metal runners.

I had to do it. He would have killed me, otherwise. As he had strangled Jessamyn.

Maybe he was only unconscious. Even so, he might freeze to death. How long would it be before someone found him in that deserted place? She should have stopped to find out if he was still alive. Even now, it wasn't too late. She could turn around and find her way back to where she had left him.

Keep moving, Amanda. Don't stop, don't think. Keep going.

She gave a start as a small animal ran across her path. A squirrel? A fox? Were there still foxes here in the park?

She struggled on through the deep gorges of the Ramble, pushing her way through the tangle of shrubs. The barren rhododendrons and azaleas were heavy with snow. Her thin-soled slippers had not been intended for walking over such terrain, and she flinched each time she stepped on a sharp stone underfoot.

Now the Ramble stretched behind her, and she felt the first faint stir of hope. Somewhere up ahead lay the fountain. If she could keep going on, only a little longer, she would catch sight of the circular balustrade and the broad steps leading to the brick terrace. And in the center, the bronze angel with its wings outspread. She tried to move faster, but she couldn't; her legs were numb, her lungs ached, and a sharp pain stabbed her side with every breath. Doggedly she plodded on, her feet sinking deep into the snow.

The snow was her enemy, pulling her down, forcing her to call on every ounce of her strength to wrench herself free with every step.

Not much longer now. Keep going.

Her foot caught in one of the upraised roots of a tree. She fell forward, and landed face down, striking her fore-

353

head on a jagged rock. Pain tore through her head, and blood gushed down her face, blinding her. She tried to wipe it away with her hand, but it kept flowing.

She tasted blood and snow on her lips. When she tried to raise her head, the pain was unbearable. She tried again, then gave up the effort and dropped forward.

The strength that had sustained her so far was draining away. She could not get up and go on.

But there was no need for her to go on . . . so much easier to lie here . . . until someone came along to help her . . . she closed her eyes . . . and waited . . .

"Amanda." Had she heard a voice call her name? "Amanda." Was it possible that rescue was already at hand? Or was she deceived by the sighing of the night wind?

From somewhere in the distance, she heard the crunching of footsteps in the snow. "Amanda. Where are you?" Not the wind, but a voice, soft, caressing. "You know you can't hide from me."

Terror shot through her, sweeping aside her lethargy.

"Amanda . . ."

Clifford's voice. The sound of his steps coming closer now. She balled her hands into fists and tried to lever herself upward. Pain in her head. And in her wrist. Had she sprained her wrist? Broken it?

She couldn't raise all her weight on one arm. She couldn't. It would be impossible.

But somehow she could. And she did. She wiped away the blood and tried to see clearly, to find her direction again. Snow-covered trees, glittering rocks seemed to dance before her eyes, tilting, swaying.

And the angel. The bronze angel, up ahead. Waiting for her. Waiting to enfold her, to protect her . . .

She took a step forward, another. And then an arm seized her from behind. Clifford's arm, hard and muscular, closed on her waist, crushing the breath from her lungs. He jerked her around. She fought to break free, twisting her body, kicking at his legs. He pulled her against him. She felt the warmth of his breath against her lips. "You tried to kill me . . . you shouldn't have . . . you must be punished . . ."

She turned her head away and felt the cold of his cheek. And sank her teeth deep into his flesh.

He yelled and struck at her with the back of his hand. And still she kept her jaws shut. She saw him raise his arm to strike again. She let go then, threw back her head, and screamed. And kept on screaming. His hands closed around her throat.

A cracking sound split the night, echoing off the surrounding rocks.

"Spencer! Let her go," Ross shouted a warning.

Clifford swore, and she felt his grip loosen. She broke free, staggered forward, and fell again.

"Stay down, Amanda."

It was Ross's voice, again. She heard other voices, too. His was the only one that mattered.

But Clifford was bending over her. He was going to lift her, to use her as a shield. Summoning up her strength, she rolled away from him. She set her teeth against the pain that seemed to radiate to every part of her body, and rolled over again and again, down a slight incline.

She heard a second shot, much closer this time. Clifford gave a hoarse, wordless cry and toppled forward, a dark shape against the snow.

She raised her head and blinked at the yellow lights that danced before her eyes. She heard more footsteps, breaking through the crusted snow. The piercing sound of a police whistle. Then a man's deep voice, unfamiliar, authoritative. "Get back, all of you."

The light of the bull's eye lanterns moved closer, and she was encircled by the men who carried them. Someone raised a lantern high above her face, and she narrowed her eyes. And the same deep voice. "Is that her, Buchanan? Is she the Whitney girl?"

"That's her." As Ross spoke, he dropped down and held her against him. She tried to reach out to him, her arms fell back.

"Ross," she said. Her own voice sounded strange to her. He cradled her closer.

"I'm here," he said, stroking her hair back from her face. She felt comforted by the rough feel of his coat against her cheek.

"Did you—is he dead?"

"I hope so," Ross said.

"You only got him in the shoulder," said another man's voice.

She forced herself to speak again, her voice muffled against Ross's chest. "Barney didn't kill Jessamyn. It was Clifford."

"Be still, Amanda."

CHAPTER TWENTY-TWO

"She was asleep, the last time I looked in on her."

Amanda opened her eyes and tried to raise her head. A sharp pain shot through her temples, and for a moment, she was completely disoriented. Then she saw Leander curled up in the bottle-green velvet chair beside the bed. Her bed. And her bedside table, with its ecru lace covering.

She heard Maude's voice. ". . . a sprained wrist. Dr. Goldman thinks she must have had a bad fall, and struck her head against a rock. But he found no symptoms of concussion. As for those bruises on her throat—if it had not been for you, that creature might have strangled her, as he did those others."

"Miss Hamilton," Ross interrupted, his voice harsh and unsteady. "Did Clifford harm her in any other way?"

"I've already told you—" Then, after a brief, charged silence: "He didn't rape her."

Amanda, startled by her friend's blunt reply, sat up too quickly. The room swayed before her eyes. Leander raised his head, stared at her a moment, then settled himself into a furry black and white ball again.

"May I see her, just for a little while? I promise not to wake her."

"Come in, Ross," she called to him.

He paused in the doorway then crossed the room and stood beside the bed. Carefully he lifted Leander out of the velvet chair, set him on the floor, and sat down. The cat jumped up onto the quilt, pressed himself against the curve of her hip, and resumed his nap.

"I would have come sooner," Ross said. "But I needed to be at Bellevue while the police questioned Clifford. I had a few questions of my own."

"The police allowed you to take part in an official interrogation?"

"Fallon owed me that much." He spoke grimly. "I had hell's own time convincing him to send a squad of his men to help me search the park."

"And Clifford—is he badly injured?"

"My bullet caught him in the shoulder. He'll live to stand trial."

She stared at him, bewildered. "But why did you come to the park last night? What made you think Clifford might try to harm me?"

Quickly, he told her about his talk with Miss Tuttle at the Spencer mansion, his visits to the costume shops, and his encounter with Leatrice Joyce at Ryan's saloon.

"So you see I was right. Marek didn't kill any of those women, not even his wife," she said.

"No, but he beat the living daylights out of her. He figured if he could force her to blackmail Clifford, he'd get enough money to leave New York and start over. And Clifford pretended to play along. He set up a meeting with Gertrude in the garden behind the empty house on Fifth Avenue. The one that used to belong to Madame Restell."

"But why did he choose that particular house?"

"I think Clifford was playing a bizarre kind of game with me and with the police, too. He left a series of clues he was sure we'd be too stupid to figure out." Seeing her bewildered look, he went on: "Madame Restell had been an abortionist, but she also offered her services as a midwife. If a girl wanted to bear her baby, Madame Restell kept her there throughout the pregnancy, and then assisted at the delivery. Clifford must have seen a certain similarity between the Restell woman and Gertrude."

"And the bridal gown Gertrude was wearing when she was murdered?"

"He wanted to rid himself of Gertrude and her threats of blackmail, once and for all. But he used her murder for another purpose, as well. After he'd killed her, he dressed her in the bridal gown and twisted the wreath around her throat to create the myth of a madman, running loose in the city. The Ladies Mile Maniac."

"But wasn't he afraid that Mrs. Gartner would come forward to identify him?"

"He never went near the costume shop," he said. "Violet rented the gown. He told her it was for a friend to wear to a masquerade ball."

She forced herself to go on. "What about the gown Violet, herself, was wearing when they found her body?"

"Violet bought that gown from an expensive dressmaker with money he'd given her. He'd been courting her and he'd promised to marry her—secretly, of course. Later, he said, he would introduce her to his family."

"And Violet believed him?"

Ross shrugged. "Clifford has a way with women. He can be most convincing, when he chooses."

As he was with me. Amanda's face went hot, and she looked away quickly.

"He was using Violet, as he had always used any woman who served his needs," Ross went on. "Even his own sister."

Revulsion stirred inside her. "He told me about that," she said. "When he went into her room early that evening, she still was wearing her bridal outfit. He was—aroused at the sight of her, dressed that way."

Ross nodded.

"But wasn't he afraid that Miss Tuttle might have gone into Jessamyn's room later to help her get ready for bed?"

"She nearly did, but he stopped her. He said his sister had retired for the night, that she was exhausted, and must not be disturbed. Miss Tuttle was taken aback by his high-handed manner. He usually went out of his way to be pleasant to her, and the rest of the staff."

"But he still was taking a risk," she said. "After he'd left for the theater with his mother, and Everard had gone off to spend the night with his mistress, one of the other servants might have entered Jessamyn's room."

"I suppose that sort of risk gave him a perverse thrill."

"Maybe he also took some kind of twisted pleasure in spreading fear among those women who were forced to be out on the streets alone, after dark."

Ross nodded. "I'm sure he did. And the discovery of Violet's body, dressed in a bridal gown, was calculated to add to that fear. He was so sure of himself." His grey eyes darkened with anger. "It fed his vanity, standing back and watching me trying to track down Marek. He felt safe enough until that afternoon his mother invited you to tea. When you let it slip that you and I knew one another, it put him on his guard."

"I told him we'd only met that one time, when we shared the cab," she said defensively.

"But he couldn't be sure you were telling the truth. You'd been in and out of his home so often. He thought it possible that you'd been working with me all along. And he was afraid I might start wondering if Marek really was the killer. He wasn't willing to risk that. So he had me set up for one hell of a beating."

She flinched at the memory. "Ross! Those men might have killed you. If they had—"

"No doubt you never would have forgiven yourself." He smiled wryly, then placed his hands on her shoulders and eased her back against the pillows. "Now suppose you give your iron-bound conscience a rest, and let me finish, will you?"

"As you wish."

"After I'd finally tracked Marek down, Clifford felt safe again. He was sure the drunken sot would be tried and hanged for all three killings."

"And Marek would have been, if not for you." She looked up at him with a puzzled frown. "But you told me that, as far as you were concerned, the case was closed. So why did you go on with it? Why did you question Miss Tuttle? What made you go chasing around to all those costume shops?"

"No more questions," he interrupted. "Not now." He glanced at the bedside clock. "I didn't mean to stay so long. I wouldn't blame Maude if she threw me out." He got to his feet, but she reached out for his hand and held it.

"You couldn't let Marek hang for a crime he hadn't committed."

"That had nothing to do with it. I'd already lined up my next job, a good one. I didn't want to go off to Pennsylvania and get started on a new case, with any unanswered questions about the old one to distract me."

"So you were simply following established professional methods." Her lips curved in a brief smile. "I don't believe you."

He shrugged. "Believe what you like." He started to draw his hand from hers, but her grip tightened.

"You're not going anywhere, not yet." She gave a quick,

hard tug, catching him off-balance and he found himself sitting beside her on the bed. "Not until you've told me the truth."

"All right, then. I didn't want you running around, poking into every hellhole in the city, risking your neck." With his fingertips, he touched the livid bruises on her throat.

"I didn't get those marks in any 'hellhole,' " she reminded him. "I was just following your advice. 'Take a romantic moonlight sleigh ride. The perfect opportunity to find a suitable husband.' "

"I suppose you'll never let me forget that."

"I won't have the chance to remind you, since you'll be away in Pennsylvania."

"You think Everard Spencer will recommend me to those business associates of his, after what's happened?"

"I suppose not," she conceded. "But once the newspapers tell how you solved this case, you'll get plenty of other opportunities. Probably more than you can handle—alone."

He looked at her warily. "Amanda! Stop right there!"

"But that won't be a problem," she went on quickly. "Because I'll be here to help."

He took her by the shoulders and shook her gently, his eyes searching her face. "What am I going to do with you, Amanda?"

"Take me on as a partner, of course."

"Not a chance."

"You said I'd been of help to you. You know I can help you even more now, because of all you've taught me. You won't have to pay me a salary, because I'll go on working at the *Gazette*."

"Don't even think of it."

He drew her close, and stroked her hair. "I'll never let

you take such risks again. Never."

She pressed her face against his chest, so that her reply was muffled. "We'll see about that."

About the Author

Diana Haviland is the author of fifteen best-selling historical sagas. She lives in New York City with her husband, who is also a writer, and two cats.

In addition to writing historical sagas, Ms. Haviland has also been an editor, has lectured to aspiring authors and has taught extension courses in fiction writing at New York University. She has also written science fiction, non-fiction occult and magazine articles.

Among the awards Ms. Haviland has received are: *Romantic Times* "Best Historical Saga" and the *West Coast Review of Books* "Porgie."